"*Faith's Reckoning* is a moral, educational, and thoroughly enjoyable novel about men and women courageous enough to face our country's history of slavery and racism. Deeply felt and engrossing, it moves deftly back and forth in time to build the story of hard lives in the Depression-era south, the generations that follow, and how one woman measures up to the difficult challenge of making reparations for the wrongs of others and a society. An uplifting celebration of human goodness and possibility."

Tad Crawford, author of *A Floating Life* and *On Wine-Dark Seas*, Arcade Publishing.

I0700892

Praise for *Faith's Reckoning*

"A warm sense of humanity pervades this novel. *Faith's Reckoning* is a tender story of redemption and atonement infused with the author's love of her characters. Immersed in the culture of the South this multigenerational story is both a tale of the awakening of individual conscience and reparation, as well as a genuine introduction to the early struggles of the civil rights movement. The influence of the Blues is beautifully woven through the storyline proving the reconciling and healing power of music."

Joe Kulin, Former Publisher of *Parabola Magazine*

"*Faith's Reckoning* is a courageous gem of historical fiction, revealing little known but important aspects of the history of racism and social injustice in the Deep South, spanning the time of the 1930's to the 1990's. I am grateful to learn about the vital role that Black Pullman Porters played in the early days of the civil rights movement, something my education never taught me. As a writer and Southerner myself, I appreciate the author's authentic Southern voice, and the gift of her storytelling ways. I relish her vivid descriptions of trains and rails, Mississippi back roads, sweltering summer nights, grits and tamales, and the powerful presence of Delta Blues music dancing through the pages. Most of all, I love her characters, and how they set up house in one's heart, and linger in one's mind, long after their stories end. Reading *Faith's Reckoning* now, when issues of racism and social injustice need our full attention and care, can become an act of faith in itself, part of the greater recognition and awareness so needed for our time."

Lucinda Herring, author of *Reimagining Death: Stories and Practical Wisdom for Home Funerals and Green Burials*, North Atlantic Books

"Soulful and evocative, the story of *Faith's Reckoning* is told with a Southern voice that rings with authenticity and compassion for the characters who must survive in the Jim Crow landscape. We see how vastly different these worlds are from the perspectives of a Black family and a White family whose lives are intricately intertwined. Beautifully researched, this novel takes us on a momentous, transformative journey in its quest for justice and healing."

Susan S. Scott, author of *Healing With Nature*,
Skyhorse Publishing

"BREAKING NEWS. SCREAMING HEADLINES. Urgent commentaries. The daily shock of racial violence, institutional racism, ubiquitous inequities floods our awareness, immerses us. Yet, the intensity of affect has a strange distancing effect, inuring us to the horror. The very "nowness," the standstill of time, freezes out the real story, like a photograph. The power of the novel form is that, when well written, the depth of story emerges. *Faith's Reckoning* is such a novel. It frees time from the now by alternating the telling from the 1930s and the 1990s. It takes time to allow us to get to know and to feel the full fabric of the characters against the backdrop of genuine history. We are drawn into the intimacy of White and Black families and the entanglements that kindle the violence of events rending this intimacy, forcing us to feel deeply. There is no distance. And in this way, we can begin to understand our deep complicity in realities that continue to haunt us. Is there an answer? Barbara Small's deeply moving story makes a persuasive case for the much-needed healing medicine: the power of truth, the power of music, and most of all, the power of love."

Russell A. Lockhart, PhD, author of *Words As Eggs*
and *Psyche Speaks*, The Lockhart Press

FAITH'S RECKONING

Barbara Small

Coyote Moon Paperbacks ™

Langley, WA

Coyote Moon Paperbacks ™
An imprint of Babs Small Publications, LLC

Library of Congress Control Number: 2023902624

ISBN: 979-8-9877834-0-5 (paperback)
ISBN: 979-8-9877834-1-2 (eBook)

First paperback edition March 2023

Cover illustration Gary Kelley
Book Design Jeanne Juneau
Photograph Susan S. Scott

Printed by IngramSpark in the USA for
Coyote Moon Paperbacks ™
Langley, WA

Babsmallpublications.com

This is a work of fiction. All characters are fictional except those who depict historical figures.

To the enslaved African people, on whose backs this country was built, and to all their descendants.

Preface

The challenge of historical fiction is to create characters who animate the lives of actual public figures. I tried to portray these public figures as accurately as possible and to imagine their conversations based on my sense of the intentions underlying their actions. The conversations in this book are imaginary and do not represent known quotations. Creative license was used to present historic events that are factual in essence though imaginary in detail.

Another difficult navigation is the appropriate use of language regarding racial identification. Because language has been weaponized to denigrate people of color, a heightened sensitivity is needed to prevent repeating the injury. African Americans or Black Americans have been addressed by a variety of terms specific to historic period, geography, and whether the term was self-imposed or intended to insult. The word Black was introduced in the early 1900s but was primarily used in activist political circles. Not until the 1960s did the civil rights movement bring it into wider cultural use. Negro was the governmental/institutional term. Census forms used Negro as a racial identifier through the 1960s, transitioning to Black in the 1970s. Colored was a term prevalent in the segregated South and was used to identify, as well as insult. More recently, journalistic publications have chosen to capitalize all racial identifiers.

I have used the racial identifiers that were common to the time, places, and people speaking in the book, evolving to the use of Black as the characters themselves change. I have taken care not to use the most offensive terms even when the speaker intended to malign. Those words are not mine to use. I have opted to capitalize all racial identifiers.

Barbara Small

LOUISIANA 1998

Shawls of Spanish moss draped the trees lining old Highway 12. Sylvia turned on the car radio for company as the black Louisiana night closed in around her. She washed down a bite of fried catfish and hushpuppy with thick chicory flavored coffee and scanned for a station through the crackling oblivion of radio static. Pitch black is a state of utter darkness, devoid of all light and color. And the swamps of Louisiana on a moonless night are just that. Pitch black and full of ghost stories.

Sylvia remembered crossing this same terrain in the back seat of a Chevy coupe as a child, huddled beneath a blanket with her sister and brother. She felt transported back to that time, the specter of Clarence Boudreaux shimmering across her memory. Her father Phil, master of the tall tale, was conjuring the story of the Boudreaux brothers' recent prison break. Clarence was the eldest of the dim-witted clan, and the biggest, which made him the most dangerous. At six foot five inches and two hundred and fifty pounds, he could squeeze the life out of a child with one arm. And his hands could crush your skull like an overripe melon. With a chest length beard, coal black eyes and tobacco-stained teeth, it might have killed you just to look at him.

Phil eased the bench seat back a notch, and let the story unwind slowly. His long arms draped over the steering wheel in full extension; dark hairs curled from beneath his cuffs. He turned on the radio and let it play for a while, then turned the volume down and dialed it between stations, disguising his voice amidst the scratchy reception to simulate a public service announcement.

"Clarence and Pierre Boudreaux have escaped into the bayou near the Southwest Louisiana State prison. They were last seen around six p.m. near the town of Basile."

From the rearview mirror Phil watched his three children wiggle closer, clutching the blanket under their chins. His wife Grace sat contentedly by his side, listening with rapt attention to the story he told. She longed for more of these moments when they were all together, happy and unhurried, and she dared not flinch for fear she might break the spell.

"Anyone back there hungry?" he asked. "There's a town just down the road where we can stop for burgers and shakes."

He pointed to the highway sign as they passed it: Baton Rouge, ninety-five miles; Basile, ten miles. Empty stomachs and the promise of a chocolate milk shake were too powerful to resist. Without even pausing, three little voices chirped, "Yes!" in unison.

Only moments later did the children register that they were headed to the very place where Clarence and Pierre had just vanished.

Sylvia was snatched back to reality by the thump thump of her right rear tire going flat. She groaned and tried to remember the last time she had checked the air pressure in the spare. She had made up her mind to take this trip at the last minute, after pondering the news about her Aunt Faith. She had barely managed to arrange coverage for her workshops back in Austin, much less get the car in for maintenance.

Sylvia Barbarino worked as a juvenile justice attorney for the great state of Texas, as it liked to call itself. She was General Counsel at the Texas Juvenile Probation Commission (TJPC) and served as a bridge between legislators, prosecutors, social workers, public defenders, and the marked child. Her job was to provide a voice for youthful offenders, to make the case for their redemption in a less than perfect justice system. Her boss was none too happy about covering two weeks of meetings and training workshops while Sylvia was in Mississippi.

Fortunately, the site visit at Last Chance House in Austin had gone well and Sylvia had reassured her boss she would be back before the new facility opened in October. 'Chance House' was her baby, a joint project of TJPC and the Texas Youth Commission. The new secure detention center was controversial, taking select students from the Giddings State School and placing them in a neighborhood community. Dozens of people had invested heart and soul in making this happen and she made it clear she was available for any questions while she was away. Her cell phone buzzed again, relentlessly reminding her of the three messages awaiting her.

Sylvia eased her blue Miata onto the shoulder of the highway and groped beneath the seat with her left hand until she located the flashlight. She flipped the switch on the handle and a bright light dispelled a narrow shaft of the darkness. She opened the door and stepped out into the thick warmth of the August night. She swung the flashlight back and forth like a blind man's cane guiding her to the trunk of the car. Sylvia easily accessed the spare from beneath her single suitcase. It bounced briskly when she dropped it to the ground. "Thank you," she sighed.

The jack and lug wrench were where she expected, and she could feel her heart rate slow to a normal rhythm again. She estimated this should be a fifteen-minute job. The lights from a passing car helped illuminate her task. Her white cotton blouse and expensive jeans would be sullied by the grease and tar of the road, but emergencies seldom allowed for a change of clothes. She propped the flashlight beneath the car, stretched the long lank of her five-foot eleven-inch frame on the uninviting gravel, placed the jack under the right rear axle and became an efficient machine. Jack placed, raised to a snug fit, lug nuts loosened, axle lifted, and wheel removed in less than ten minutes. She popped the spare tire onto the hub and was tightening the last nut when a semi rattled by, dangerously close. Sylvia jumped up and back, away from the road, and found herself lost in the darkness. Something ensnared her right ankle, and she jerked her leg forward instinctively. A ripping sound met her ears as the densely tangled kudzu vine released its hold on her. She quickly lowered the jack, tightened the lug nuts one last time, and dumped the tools into the trunk. Safe within the car, she stopped to catch her breath.

She turned the key in the ignition. The engine turned over and she felt the reassuring clunk as she pressed the driver's door lock, relieved she had secured the convertible top of the Miata after dinner at the Pappadeaux in Beaumont. She reached into the front pocket of her leather satchel and retrieved a piece of gum. The sweet taste and her ferocious chewing calmed her as she pulled back onto the highway. She glided down the road on four secure tires and a well-oiled faith in her ability to meet whatever awaited her. She would try to make Baton Rouge tonight, giving her plenty of time to get to Jackson by Friday, still two days away. She thought about driving down to New Orleans in the morning. Maybe strong coffee and sweet beignets would make her task more palatable, make it easier to read over the Will again.

Sylvia had not spent any real time with her Aunt Faith in six years although they still exchanged letters. Faith had always been so vibrant that Sylvia could not believe she was sick. But worse than that, Faith had known for months and had not called Sylvia until now. Time was running out and Sylvia had nothing to say about it. The forever-adventuring Faith was living this time as she had always lived, savoring it with fierce independence. She had called Sylvia the week before to ask her to be the executor of her Will. Sylvia remembered the conversation on that Sunday morning.

"Sylvia?" searched the voice on the phone.

"Aunt Faith?" Sylvia replied after a faint pause.

"Hello hon, I'm so glad to catch you at home. Good to know the Probation Commission gives you Sunday mornings off to go to church."

"You know I don't go to church, Aunt Faith, and it is wonderful to hear your voice. Speaking of which, why aren't you nestled into the pew at Emanuel this morning?" Sylvia remembered attending the service with the small neighborhood congregation the last time she had visited Faith.

"Well, Sylvia, that's why I'm calling."

Sylvia's stomach clutched, that momentary paralysis

that occurs when you hear the freight train of wind before a tornado hits.

"I don't have as much get up and go these days, so I just have church at home. That's the nice thing about the Lord. He's everywhere. And..."

"What's wrong?" Sylvia asked, cutting her off.

"Oh, Honey, I'll just say it. I have leukemia. But listen to me now. It is chronic myelogenous leukemia, and the doctor says I probably have plenty of living left."

"What's that mean?" Sylvia said. A faint flush spread over her creamy complexion and the fading freckles of childhood reemerged, awakening the fleeting apparition of her Irish grandmother. She shuddered as a chill of perspiration followed.

"It's OK, Sylvia. Nothing is imminent. But you know me, I don't like to leave things to the last minute. This leukemia has been smoldering inside of me for months, maybe years, and it could go on that way for a long time. In fact, there is a new medication, a daily oral chemotherapy with very few side effects that might keep me in remission indefinitely....."

"But what did the doctor say?" Sylvia interrupted. She swept a lock of auburn hair behind her right ear where it rested in a soft curl at the angle of her jaw. The brown flecks in her hazel eyes darkened.

"Sylvia, look, he said just what I'm telling you. And remember, I am a nurse. Almost became a doctor myself. Anyway, I may be fine for a long time but at seventy-five, there are no guarantees. So I am getting my affairs in order, and I am asking you to be the executor of my Last Will and Testament. Can you do that?"

Sylvia detected a hint of impatience in Faith's voice.

"Of course, of course, but...." she replied, trying to relax.

"…. isn't there more I can do?"

Faith paused, gathering herself. Even with her own flagging energy, Faith knew Sylvia still needed the sturdy container of her steadfast love. Actually, Sylvia needed the abiding embrace that only God could provide, but Faith and Sylvia had had that conversation too many times and Faith had finally given up and just assented to be His stand in.

"Sure, Sylvia. You can come see me and make me a big pot of Creole gumbo with white rice. And you had better take your time with the roux, like I showed you. A half-hour at least."

They made plans for Sylvia to come to Mississippi over Labor Day weekend. They would talk and eat and putter in Faith's garden. Faith told her to stay as long as she wanted. Sylvia had felt a little better after they hung up the phone.

As the days passed, however, the urgency inside her grew. She was distracted at work. The large number of cases awaiting her legal opinion, something she had always handled efficiently, suddenly felt unmanageable. Her instincts told her to spend more than just a weekend with Faith and visit her sooner. When she called with the change of plan, Faith was thrilled.

Sylvia now stared down the endless dark tunnel of the road, the bayou encroaching all around her. She thought about Faith's life. She understood why Faith had never married, had deliberately chosen a life without children so she could give all of herself to her career. As a nurse, Faith had traveled the globe, exploring other cultures as she worked in orphanages and refugee camps. She had served as surrogate mother to a multitude of children through her work. She had also taken that role with Sylvia at times. Faith had granted Sylvia the singular honor of being her traveling companion in Italy six years ago when Sylvia's life had been at its bleakest.

The lights at the outskirts of the city roused Sylvia from her reverie. Baton Rouge rests on the bluffs overlooking the Mississippi River at the head of the deltaic plain, where the mighty river branches into channels carrying the silt of a country back to the sea. It was known as a blues town although everyone knew that the real home of the Delta blues lay upstream, some seventy miles south of Memphis.

By taking the back road, Sylvia avoided the neon purgatory of endlessly blinking casino signs. She was tired, ready for a drink and bed. Uncharacteristically, she hadn't booked a reservation for the night. Usually, she would have found the best deal on a four-star hotel at her expected destination after reviewing lodging options on the top three Internet sites. But the news about Faith had derailed any notion of planning and she had sought the refuge of the road, not knowing where she would land at any point in time.

A cluster of buildings crouched beside the road up ahead. As she approached, she could see a flock of pickup trucks and well-worn cars parked at Swamp Daddy's Blues Bar. The adjacent ten-room motel seemed more likely to rent rooms by the hour than by the night. Not the kind of place Sylvia was likely to stay. The gas station across the street was just closing for the night. Sylvia pulled into the parking lot, feeling a little reckless. She was too edgy to sleep yet. She needed some soothing, maybe some bourbon and the slow sweet wail of a slide guitar. She parked off to the side with the other cars, locked the Miata and headed toward the bar.

~

Back in Austin, Joe Lambert stood at the kitchen sink wondering how far Sylvia had driven before stopping for the night. He rinsed the last of the bloody steak juice from his dinner plate and placed it in the stainless-steel dish rack. Joe liked his rib eye rare on the infrequent occasion he allowed himself one, being determined to dodge the bullet of early death conferred by a family legacy of heart disease. He lifted the wine glass from the counter and swirled the deep ruby Barbera a couple of times before decanting it through his parted lips. He let it languish on his tongue before swallowing. The porch lights illuminated the limestone cliffs of the Texas hill country surrounding his caretaker's cabin as the cicadas started winding down from their hot summer serenade. Joe walked to the front door and opened it to let the night breeze blow through the screen, then turned toward the second-hand piano that stood in the corner of the room.

This cabin was all the home he needed. Other than an attached bath, the cabin consisted of a single large room. A table sat in one corner, along the back wall. The bed rested in the middle under an enormous window that allowed a perfect crosswind when the door was open. An upright piano snuggled at a diagonal into the other back corner. The kitchen occupied most of the front wall, leaving just enough room in one corner for a dresser and wardrobe.

Joe deliberately chose this simple life, his desires rendered to a few after he sifted through the ashes of his brief academic career. He had been a rising star in the Philosophy department at the University, expected to be the youngest Chair in its history. He left a year after receiving tenure. The study of Philosophy carries a risk. The scaffolding of the mind can buckle under its labyrinthine thought. But Joe was blessed with a mental sturdiness, a capacity to understand conflicting principles and discriminate a higher truth. He discovered the teachings of Plato and Aristotle when he was a senior in high school and undertook a slow and deliberate study of classical philosophy. Joe believed Nature held the key to some absolute truth if only the inquiry were keen enough.

The conflict between this foundational view and the academic pressure to slant his writings in another direction weighed on him as a young professor. Cultural relativism, a stance that the beliefs of all societies are equally valid, was the new dogma. The tenure committee had granted him its prize based on the exceptional quality of his scholastic writings in classical philosophy. At the same time, the committee warned him that to make full professor he needed a more contemporary perspective on morality.

The University would not support the concept of an absolute truth that ignored cultural context. Joe's 'intolerance' would not be tolerated. The irony proved too much, and like a top at the end of its spin, he felt his mind begin to topple. With an impulse toward sanity, he chose Nature and a life grounded in the body. He took a job as a ranch foreman, having learned the business from his father. Physical labor and music saved him. He now wanted only three things: to steward the land he inhabited, to cultivate an uncluttered mind through music and meditation and to have a family. He had the first two. Sylvia wouldn't agree to the last.

Joe walked over to the piano and set the wine glass on top. He slid onto the bench. His long, well-articulated fingers lightly traced the tops of the keys reading, like Braille, the melody hidden there. Eyes closed, his body leaned into the music as the first jazz strains of Joe Sample's "A Long Way from Home" lifted into the humid darkness. An oil lamp flickered on top of the piano. As his hands recalled this familiar excursion, he let his senses drift back to the memory of Sylvia's scent at sunrise. He had coaxed her to stay a little longer before leaving for Mississippi, stroking the small of her back as they lingered in bed. Joe had fallen in love with Sylvia in the first months of their courtship. It certainly helped that their lovemaking was unrivaled in his experience. But her complexity was the attraction. She was hard working, as tough an advocate for children as anyone he knew. Yet she could be suddenly open and vulnerable only with him. He knew this would be a hard trip for Sylvia even though she had insisted she was fine. When he tried to pull her closer that morning, pressing himself against her, she pushed away. 'I'm late already,' she said, her tone clipped.

'So go,' he'd replied, jumping out of bed, and dressing quickly. He headed out of the cabin toward the stables before she finished her shower. The sting of their parting lingered. He doubted that she would call tonight, and he missed her. But Sylvia was Sylvia, and she would not be corralled. He felt the smoothness of the keys beneath his fingers and let the music take him.

MISSISSIPPI 1930

Fletcher Moody stood on the threshold to the front porch, his right shoulder pressed against the doorframe. An unseasonably warm winter breeze stirred the air. He eyed the house across the street, on the corner of Sixth and Main. It had sold the week before and Fletcher was curious as to who was moving in. The house had stood empty, quietly forlorn for almost a year now, its L shaped structure and wrap around screened in porch designed for the beehive business of a large family. A newer model Cadillac La Salle pulled up to the curb in front of the house, paused a moment then killed its engine. Before the occupants could even emerge, the round box of a 1926 Nash Ajax pulled up behind it.

Fletcher watched with disbelief as an endless stream of tow-headed youngsters, pent up way too long, tumbled out of the cars. One, two, three, four.... he could not count fast enough to keep up with them. Like dandelions in the wind, they dispersed onto the lawn, sweeping around the house, and peeking into its sprawling crawlspace. Only when they stopped moving and settled onto the front lawn, could he see that their ages spanned a decade and a half, from the smallest wobbling toddler to the muscular and rangy young man.

Presently, a man of middle years stepped out of the Nash. He was medium height with strong shoulders and a square jaw, his hair noticeably gray at the temples. He circled around the front of the car with a deliberate step, opened the front passenger door and helped his wife down from the running board, her four-foot ten-inch height and babe in arms hampering an easy dismount. They stood there for a moment by the car, looking up at the house and the yard. Fletcher watched as the man took a deep breath and stretched his back slightly. A young couple emerged from the Cadillac, the woman visibly pregnant. The adults met halfway up the sidewalk and the children, Fletcher finally counted seven of them including the baby, coalesced around the grownups in a tight white-headed mass.

"Looks like they brought the cotton patch with 'em," Fletcher hollered to his wife in the kitchen, who was capping off the last jar of apricot pepper jelly.

He eased himself into the sinking cushions of a worn wingback chair that had been relegated to the porch, lit the stub of a cigar, and rustled the daily newspaper open. Fletcher peered over the top of the paper as the late afternoon sun made its lazy crawl toward twilight, keeping a keen eye as his new neighbors entered the house. He was taking stock, as he did with anything new.

The news was primarily local miseries. Almost a third of the city's businesses had closed in the last six months and although President Hoover was cutting taxes and increasing public works projects, his interventions were not helping much in Mississippi. People here had been left to their own devices since that black Tuesday over a year ago. A good vegetable garden and a few fruit trees were essential, and liquor was a regular homemade enterprise, as Prohibition was still the rule of the land.

Sweet smells drifted from the kitchen where Ruth was cobbling together some supper. There was a little leftover rabbit stew, to which she added some new potatoes and green beans, boiled with a little fatback until they were limp as noodles. Ruth could squeeze a meal from an empty can and the dry dust of the pantry, and she never complained. She was raised to emphasize gratitude and she thanked God every day for her life with Fletcher. He had never blamed her for the death of their stillborn son. He just bore the lament with her. She smiled at the sound of his footsteps coming down the hallway. Her shoulders softened when she felt his arms around her waist, reaching from behind to draw her close.

"They've got kids to spare over there, Baby," Fletcher whispered in her ear. "Maybe we can adopt one or two."

They sat down to eat in the dining room. The rectangular table, covered by a green linen tablecloth that was worn but clean, filled the room. As they bowed their heads to say grace, they heard a knock at the front door. Fletcher squeezed Ruth's hand, then rose to answer. He could tell by the silhouette that it was his new neighbor.

Hardee paused, squaring his shoulders before speaking.

"Hello, I'm Hardee Wiggins, and I just wanted to introduce myself. My family and I are moving in across the street and I want you to know that even though we are a large clan, we are a respectable lot. If there is anything we can do to help during these hard times just speak up."

Fletcher shook his hand and asked if Hardee wanted a bite of supper.

"Oh, no. Just a quick hello this evening," he replied. "But we'll share a meal sometime soon and I hope to get better acquainted."

Fletcher nodded in agreement. "I'll be glad to show you around once you get settled. And feel free to drop by if you need anything. Neighbors got to stick together these days."

Hardee turned and walked back across the street, trying to shake the road weariness from his bones.

Hardee Wiggins felt tired but confident. The move from Alabama here to Hattiesburg, Mississippi would surely turn things around or at least give him a fighting chance to feed his family. He had been lucky in the economic boom running up to the big crash. Almost twenty years ago, he had opened a grocery and dry goods store back in Cobb's Ford, just downstream from the confluence of the Tallapoosa and Coosa rivers. And that is where he had married Maureen (Maudie) Cunningham, on the banks of the Alabama River, formed from that joining of waters. She was round hipped and full bosomed and disadvantaged in height. But Maudie had enough fire of the Irish in her to more than compensate. And that fire could be fetching or fierce. It had been on one of those fetching nights, a month before their marriage, that she and Hardee were unable to resist the temptation of their passions. Whether it was his marksmanship or her fertility, she was instantly with child.

Although he had never gotten further than the third grade, Hardee was sharp and had a quick reflex for seizing opportunity. He had seen how rapidly automobile technology was advancing and watched as prices dropped, making cars accessible to the working public. As he and Maudie kept popping little Wiggins into a world that was just recovering from its first Great War, he opened a Cadillac dealership in Montgomery, Alabama. This was in addition to the Cobb's Ford store. It made it possible for him to set aside some cash to buy a house for his growing family.

Initially it looked like they would have a good round mix of girls and boys. Ava appeared first, as though chivalry demanded the lady's rightful place. She was given a baby brother, Brett, for her second birthday and when Claire was born three years later, it seemed the sexes were taking turns, respecting God's great design with sweet statistical symmetry. Turns out the Creator wasn't much of a mathematician after all. Every couple of years for the next thirteen years, Hardee and Maudie had another child, and all the rest were girls: Delta, Emma, Faith, Grace, and Hanna. Brett earned the indisputable name Brother and that is what his sisters called him for the rest of his life.

Amidst this bounty of children to feed and clothe, Hardee prospered in Alabama, largely through his own industry. He was frugal beyond measure. He offered a trade day at his store on Saturdays, where people could come and swap whatever goods they no longer needed. His only profit from the affair was that he got first dibs on any textbooks or school supplies brought there. He insisted that his children attend to their education, and it was the one cause for which he would part with some of his savings.

Maudie supported the family economy by culling through the picked over fruit and produce at the store before it went bad, cooking and canning it. She made the children's clothes or worked a trade with a local dressmaker, getting a new outfit in exchange for doing alterations. She and Hardee were busy from dawn to dusk but she was happy and began to find herself on her knees on a regular basis, in prayers of gratitude. Despite their sinful beginning, the Lord had blessed them, and she began to feel a new devotion to love Him as much as she loved Hardee.

While Maudie was tending their everlasting life, Hardee secured their life on earth. He did not trust the equities markets or even bonds for that matter. He relied on the tangible, putting their savings into what he thought were solid assets. Gold coins or hard cash wrapped in butcher paper and buried in a box in the back yard. Or the sturdy frame of a new car. Even though he owned a Cadillac dealership, he had taken a train all the way to St. Louis, Missouri to buy a Nash Ajax, since that was the closest dealership for the Wisconsin made automobile. 'Give the customer more than they paid for' was their motto. 'Get your money's worth' was his. Maudie didn't even try to talk him out of that Nash.

The years tumbled by with all the flow and backwash of a good full life. He and Maudie gradually found a deeper love amidst the squabbles of getting to know each other. Raising the children became their common passion and they learned to make allowance for their differences. Where she was more likely to get drunk on God, he would seek a little spiritual sustenance of the bottled variety in the evening. Weeks became months, which accumulated into years of a mostly happy life together.

By the summer of 1929, Hardee had managed to set aside almost five thousand dollars, and when the stock market crashed in October he wasn't affected. Like most people, he had no personal stake in Wall Street and its gyrations were not being felt by the local economy. President Hoover had just created the Federal Farm Board and the initial promise of stable crop prices had, in fact, lifted the spirits of most folks around Montgomery. But by the following spring, business was drying up. Car sales had slowed to a trickle by May and many factories stopped production altogether that summer. Sketchy reports of rising unemployment began to appear in the newspaper. Then the price of cotton plummeted, and the people of Montgomery could no longer afford such luxuries as a new automobile. In the summer of 1930, Hardee sat in the office of his Cadillac dealership staring at the dust-covered cars on his lot. The unrelenting sun and hushed air suspended time.

Friends would drop by for a cup of coffee and a bit of talk, anything to punctuate the blank uncertainty of those times. When the first run on the banks began in November of 1930, Hardee knew he would have to close up shop and make a new start somewhere else. It would mean uprooting his family. And where would they go if this Depression were to afflict the whole country?

Hardee thought it through carefully. Housing prices in Mississippi had dropped so low, he would be able to buy a house there outright. Ava was grown and married now. She and her husband Cecil would be able to help him open a trading post and salvage store in Hattiesburg. There was money to be made in junk, meager as it might be. The need was coming for cheap goods, recycled from the excesses of the old Southern aristocracy. Hardee would make a living as a laissez faire Robin Hood.

He kept the best Cadillac on the lot and sold the rest at cost. Then he packed up what was left of his inventory at the Cobb's Ford store. He closed its doors shortly before Thanksgiving. Fortunately, he persuaded his most trusted employee, Delsey Clemons, to move to Hattiesburg with the family. She had been the bookkeeper at the Cobb's Ford store for six years.

Delsey had been forced to grow up too early. She was ten years old when her mother, Lucy, died in the 1918 influenza epidemic. It whiplashed her into surrogate motherhood with a violent force. Her father Tobias, a sharecropper in Macon County, depended on Delsey to assume the work of cooking and cleaning for her siblings. The shock of having her life veer off at a right angle from her dreams was matched only by her determination to complete her education. She had flourished in the Montgomery Industrial School for Girls, which taught academics as well as vocational skills. Lucy had fought hard for her daughter to attend school. Delsey and her father wrestled over his needs and her dreams, but they had finally struck a deal. She would get up as early as needed and work as long as it took to tend the house and kids if he would pay the dollar fifty a month tuition and buy her school supplies. It meant her sisters and brothers would stay home and help him in the fields. This negotiation seemed somehow just shy of a miracle to her. Her father did not believe in education. He believed in land. But there was something indomitable about Delsey and she finally just plain wore him out.

Delsey came to work for Hardee Wiggins not out of any kindness on his part but because he was cheap. Cheap as a Sunday minister with communion wine. He had managed to save his thousands through a combination of his horse trader's wit and parsimonious nature. He would often buy his produce for the store from Negro sharecroppers because he could wrangle a better price. That was how he met Delsey. She had come to the store with her father one day back in 1924, when he was making the rounds in his vegetable truck. As Toby was unloading the crates of corn and sweet potatoes, he could not help but brag to

Hardee about his daughter's arithmetic genius. Because of her perseverance, Delsey had managed to obtain more schooling and was better at figures than many people in the South, including Hardee. The Cobb's Ford store was thriving, and Hardee needed help with the bookkeeping, someone with an organized mind who could account for all the inventory and expenses. Delsey was sixteen years old and had begun courses in the teaching program at the Tuskegee Institute. Hardee knew he could hire her for a quarter of what he would have paid a White accountant. He agreed to take over the cost of her tuition at Tuskegee and pay her two dollars a day.

For the next year, she continued to live on the farm, traveling to Cobb's Ford on Saturdays to work. She gradually prepared her siblings to cook and clean for themselves. Sundays, after church, she would teach them as much as they would tolerate. But when farm prices started falling Toby could barely make the lease on the land. She left school to work full time, the only way for her family to survive. She finally moved into Montgomery, and Hardee kept her on at the store even after times turned lean for him in the summer of 1930. She had convinced him of her worth though she couldn't manage to squeeze anymore change from his tight fist.

The Jim Crow system made it impossible for Delsey to work in the front of the store, so Hardee made a small office for her in the back where the goods were stocked. She entered through the back alley in the morning to keep the financial wheels of the dry goods store rolling. Hardee understood how integral Delsey was to him and his family, but it was hard for him to admit it, to know she was more educated than he.

The Wiggins kids knew Delsey by their senses. They would gather around her in the back of the shop as she went over invoices and inventory, receipts, and accounts payable. One at a time the younger ones would climb into her lap, nesting into her warmth, the smell of Glossine hair oil sweetening the air around them. She treated each of them as a one-of-a-kind special deal. Delsey taught them arithmetic and also how to laugh when Brother or a sister taunted them. It was this last point, especially, this skill at averting conflict by turning insult into laughter that drew the Wiggins girls closer.

When the Wiggins decided to move to Mississippi, Delsey had to determine whether to stay with her family or follow her prospects. She was twenty-two years old and at that juncture where the course of a life turns one way or the other; the way a river flows is never right or wrong. She finally told Hardee and Maudie she would join them in Hattiesburg in a couple of weeks and agreed to live at the Wiggins' Trading Post until she found a room to rent in Hattiesburg. Delsey talked her twenty-year-old brother, Jesse, into loading the Wiggins' truck and trailer with their household goods and store surplus and driving it to Hattiesburg. Hardee promised to pay Jesse fifty dollars if he safely delivered the goods and Delsey to the house on Main Street.

It was an uncharacteristically warm December morning as they got ready to leave Montgomery, the last winter leaves loosening their hold on the branches overhead. The sun was rising, and the day promised clear passage. With the last of the furniture securely covered and lashed, Jesse opened the passenger door of the truck for his sister, then paused a moment before she got in. He was a good six inches taller than Delsey, and ever since he had shot past her at puberty, he had teased her with his height advantage. She might be older, but he was bigger.

"You're doing the right thing, little sister," he said.

"Thank you, Jess," she said as she hugged him so he would not see the tears in her eyes. "I might not let you come back after we get there."

"Whatever you want," he said softly.

He walked around the back of the truck and yanked the ropes one more time, securing the knots for the journey ahead. He opened the driver's door and slid onto the bench next to Delsey. The truck rumbled awake as he turned the key.

"Ready, set?" he smiled to her, his hand poised over the gearshift.

"Go," she laughed, grateful for his company as she set out from the only place she had ever known as home.

LOUISIANA & MISSISSIPPI 1998

Sylvia awoke with a thick-tongued numbness. The remnants of a dream surfaced, the images coalescing. She was in a station of some sort. People transiting. The distinct rumble of a train arriving. The screech of steel on steel as it braked. She didn't know this place or the people coming and going. She looked up at a board announcing arrivals and departures; a blackboard with times and locations chalked over recent erasures. She didn't see him at first, just felt the gentle squeeze of his hand, so much smaller compared to hers. She looked down upon the upturned face of a young boy. Five, maybe six, years old. His eyes were mournful, a long-term sadness, but his face was relaxed, tight brown curls framing it.

"Hi," she said, the lilt in her voice suggesting a question.

"Hello," he replied, his eyes searching her face.

"Are you okay?" she asked.

"Yes, but my mother is gone. I'm waiting for her."

"Oh goodness," Sylvia replied, "Where did you last see her?"

"She's been gone a long time. She left me with the conductor and I don't know where she went."

The whistle of a train announced its departure.

"Last call! Train to Jackson now boarding."

Sylvia caught her breath as she sat up in the bed. She sat silently, adjusting to the steady buzzing in her brain. Her hazel eyes were dulled with the aftereffects of last night's Wild Turkey. Smoke from the bar still clung to her hair. She steadied herself on the side of the bed. The dreams were coming more frequently lately, demanding her attention. She had considered seeing a therapist to decipher them. Was this PTSD from years of seeing children lost in the judicial system? But there was something about this dream that was different. The way the boy looked at her, some recognition they shared. She knew he had to be her child but why did he talk to her like a stranger? A shiver ran up her spine. She stretched, trying to shake it off.

Last night, Sylvia had changed her mind after getting out of the car, choosing to check into the motel before going to Swamp Daddy's Blues Bar. She had deposited her suitcase in the room, a bit shabby but clean enough, and walked outside to return the missed calls on her cell phone. One was to her boss at TJPC and the other to the director of Last Chance House. Neither was urgent. The last call had been from Joe.

"Hey Babe, just checking in. Miss you already. Call me when you can."

She hadn't returned Joe's call, not quite sure why; maybe she was too tired to reassure him, again. Instead, she had followed the music drifting from Swamp Daddy's and taken a seat in the corner booth. She took refuge in the blues and her anonymity. She wanted one night with no souls to tend, no hearts to mend. She had warmed herself with bourbon a little too much. The bartender took a shine to her, and she had granted him a wink, a small crack in her cocoon. When she went to leave, he had put his arm around her waist, steadying her out the door. It had felt good, and they had paused for a minute at the threshold, silently considering the possibilities before he said goodnight to her. This morning she tried to recall his name as the sun filtered through the lace curtains, falling across her face. Jack? No, Jake, that was it. Turns out he had good manners as well as looks. After a few minutes she stood up and went into the bathroom. The pulsing at her temples subsided after a minute.

"Coffee," she croaked to herself, "and a quart of water before breakfast."

Whatever Sylvia had tried to outrun by drinking the night before had managed to catch up with her this morning; the secret she tucked away, which kept her one foot out of the relationship with Joe. Just last week he had nudged her again about having a baby, smiling and nodding at the radio when Bonnie Raitt's "Nick of Time" came on. They had parted roughly yesterday, but that was nothing new. Maybe this trip to her ancestral home was stirring up her feelings. She couldn't remember the last time she had nursed a hangover, years anyway. The warm spray of the shower and the sandalwood scented shampoo refreshed her. She toweled off and carefully combed her hair back, leaving it to dry naturally. She brushed her teeth, then stepped into a fresh pair of jeans, slipped a silk shirt around her shoulders and buttoned it.

After packing up she drove over to the gas station. She bought two liters of spring water and a carton of orange juice and filled up the Miata with premium before returning to check out of the motel.

"Morning Ms. Barbarino, checking out?" the desk clerk inquired.

"Yes, thank you," Sylvia replied, clearing her throat.

"I can put your bar tab on your credit card here if you like, but Jake asked you to stop by the bar before you leave," the bottle blonde declared, then paused.

"I think he wants to get your phone number," she whispered across the counter.

Sylvia winced. She detected a hint of jealousy in the clerk's attempt at sudden friendship. Sylvia remembered that moment at the door the night before and felt the prickly heat of shame.

She thought again about the fight with Joe. She had spent the night with him before leaving for Mississippi, and they had made love with a fresh passion. As she was leaving the next morning, he had wanted her to linger in bed and she had barked at him that she was already late. How could she be so hot and cold with him? She knew he deserved better from her.

"So you gonna pay the bar bill here or go see Jake?" the clerk asked.

"I'll just settle up here," Sylvia answered hastily, looking up from her wallet. She handed her credit card to the woman who smiled and seemed relieved to close the account on Ms. Barbarino. Sylvia didn't need to linger with thoughts of last night's temptations. Whatever flirtations had transpired were booze-induced and better left to evaporate in the bright light of day. She had only slept in this low rent motel because she had enough sense to know she shouldn't drive if she was going to drink. She took a newspaper from the stack on the counter, pushed a quarter across its warped Formica surface and thanked the desk clerk as she left.

"Take care now, hon," the woman said.

Sylvia drove a couple of miles down Highway 12 and

stopped at Sissy's Biscuit Basket for breakfast. The six-table cafe sat at a junction. Highway 12 continued east. She could take Highway 61 north or the Interstate 10 spur south. Over a red plastic gingham tablecloth, she sifted through her options; variations of meats, eggs, and sides with Fresh, Never Frozen, hand-made Southern biscuits. She settled on ham, grits, and scrambled eggs with her biscuits. After the waitress left with her order, Sylvia picked up her cell phone. She flipped it open and started to dial Joe's number, then clicked it closed again. She should call him. She wanted to call him, missed his steadiness, his patience with her complicated ways. But she had been curt with him, dismissive of his invitation to make love, consumed by her own agitation. She held the phone in her hand for a minute, the small muscles of her jaws tensing. She could almost hear the pained silence that would dangle in the distance between them. She put the phone back in her briefcase and finished her cup of coffee. Maybe he would call her later or she could call him tonight.

The waitress returned with a heaping plate of food. Sylvia ate a few of bites of eggs and grits then smothered a biscuit in butter and honey. She downed another glass of water and left a twenty-dollar bill on the table. As she stood to leave, the chair scraped against the hard linoleum floor. She walked the short stretch across the parking lot to the Miata, squinting against glaring sun.

New Orleans was a quick hour south on Interstate 10. Highway 61 north was a slow lazy crawl through unfamiliar territory. Except for a few stretches of freshly paved highway built to accommodate the casinos, it was a small black ribbon of cracked and patched road through some of the poorest towns in America. Eventually it dumped its travelers on the streets of Memphis. On the way, though, about three hundred miles from Sissy's was the Delta Blues Museum in Clarksdale, Mississippi. Sylvia, in her designer jeans and silk blouse, had intended to head south to the city. But when she got behind the wheel of the Miata her impulse said, 'Go north'. She did not understand why, and she was too tired to figure it out. She turned left onto the entrance ramp to Highway 61 and, like a blind old coonhound, sniffed her way toward some instinct of home.

A nagging sick headache dogged her all the way to Natchez. She pushed through the weariness plaguing her body. When she came to a small town she wound her way toward Old Man River. On the radio, the strains of John Lee Hooker's "Wandering Blues" faded away into the sticky morning heat. Her silk shirt wicked the sweat from her skin, and she relaxed into the medicine of his music. She stopped at a small Mexican cafe along the levee near the bridge crossing the Mississippi river and bought a Coke. She sat in the car and looked out over the roiling currents.

She listened to the news at the top of the hour. It was the latest dirt on the president, who could not seem to keep his private business out of the Oval Office. The ongoing Paula Jones lawsuit had been a distraction from Bill Clinton's accomplishments in his first term as president, and now Monica Lewinsky threatened to sink his second term completely. Rumors of impeachment were gathering like storm clouds. Sylvia was disappointed in the man, having been taken in by his true brilliance, his dazzle and jazzy saxophone-playing ways. She was hoping for someone less human to lead this country into the next century. God knows salvation was not to be found in the church, and Sylvia had hoped that the Clintons would bring some measure of justice to the ever-widening divide of rich and poor, Black and White. She knew they had worked hard to find common ground with an oppositional Congress, but she was impatient at the incremental progress. She had witnessed firsthand some of the collateral effects of the 1994 federal Violent Crime Control and Law Enforcement Act, as the 'get tough' approach was expanded by state governments.

She took her time drinking her Coke, mesmerized by the flow of the mighty river. Perhaps she expected too much of the president, hoped he could relieve her of a more personal burden. Sylvia had been a lawyer for almost twenty years. She had started out in Austin working for the County Office of Child Representation, providing legal services for children involved in Child Protective Services cases. She had seen how the consequences of economic and racial inequality robbed children of the chance to succeed, especially when it came to the classroom. The generational cycle was a downward spiral, the frustration all too often playing out on the battered bodies of babies. She had spent untold hours working with social workers making sure these children had food and shelter, trying to preserve families when possible. But the learning disabilities and mental health problems they faced were often insurmountable, given the lack of resources to address them.

Sylvia had moved to the County Juvenile Public Defender's office in 1985 and ended up defending many of the children she had previously represented for CPS. At first, she was able to see the path that had led them to acts of delinquency. Her heart still broke for those kids acting out through vandalism and shoplifting. But something in her began to calcify as she watched them escalate to acts of senseless violence. She started to question what she was doing, whether she was serving the best interest of these kids once they passed a certain, ill-defined threshold. After five years, she had given up and decided to follow her boyfriend, Jack, to New York City. She had been offered a job with a Wall Street firm and it had sounded so unambiguous, almost clean compared to juvenile justice. But Sylvia learned that there was nothing tidy about corporate law and, besides, she loathed it. More importantly she felt she had abandoned a duty by leaving juvenile justice, a duty that felt personal.

She had returned to Texas in 1992 and gone to work for the Texas Juvenile Probation Commission. Sylvia enjoyed her work at the TJPC. She quickly rose in the ranks after taking a job in the general counsel's office. Having learned her lesson with Jack, she committed to never again sacrifice her career for the sake of a man. She had been honest when she met Joe a few months after returning to Texas. From the beginning she was clear about letting her biologic clock expire without having his child. He feigned acceptance, scarcely hiding his anticipation that she would change her mind. But she was certain of her decision.

Her promotion to Deputy Executive Director of Operations at TJPC had rekindled her passion for juvenile justice reform and a faith that even violent offenders weren't lost. It provided her with new opportunities, as the supervisor of special projects. Unfortunately, the explosion of juvenile violent crime in the late 1980s, fueled by crack cocaine, had been exploited politically. More and more states passed legislation mirroring the federal crime bill, allowing tougher sentencing and more restrictive parole for kids. In Texas, the 1995 revision of the juvenile justice code allowed children as young as fourteen years of age to be tried as adults. Once in the adult system, they were lost. But the legislation also increased funding for juvenile facilities and intervention programs. And in a country where most kids graduated from juvenile detention only to become adult offenders, Texas had an island of hope – the Giddings State School.

Chance House, her latest project, was a model that preserved a rehabilitative approach to juvenile offenders. Sylvia had worked with her colleagues in the legal and legislative affairs division at TJPC to lobby for funding for special programs like Chance House. Based on the treatment program at the Giddings School, it was a bridge to reintroduce the best of the 'students' who graduated from the Capital Offenders program into a neighborhood community in east Austin. Sylvia was excited but also anxious. She had spent months meeting with neighborhood businesses and residents. Most people were ambivalent, wanting to give these kids a second chance but worried about their own safety. The outreach proved fruitful because Sylvia listened to their concerns without offering false assurances. She secured funding for increased community policing and delayed the program until she found a campus along the river, offering a naturally secure perimeter. But the truth was she couldn't be certain that boys like Dylan were a low risk to the community.

Dylan was sixteen years old when he shot the cashier at a local 7-11 in the commission of a robbery. He hadn't aimed to kill. In fact, he hadn't aimed at all when he saw the cashier reach for something beneath the counter. He left the cashier paralyzed from the waist down and bought himself a spot in the Capital Offenders program at the Giddings State School.

He had fully committed to the resocialization program, founded on the understanding that humans are profoundly social beings. He memorized the nine thinking errors, like making excuses and overreacting, and learned to catch himself using them. When he told his life story to the group, most of whom had committed violent crimes, he was honest, vulnerable. No faking it. The culture of the school, staff, and students fostered a close-knit community based on empathy and accountability. When his turn came to role play his victim in a group therapy session, he broke down in sobs when he imagined the shopkeeper's lifeless legs.

Sylvia believed in accountability for juvenile offenders but knew from her experience that punishment was insufficient to prevent a trajectory toward a life of crime because it failed to address the hopelessness of racial and economic injustice. True rehabilitation required empathy for others, which first required the offender to experience empathy. She had studied the process used at Giddings, as well as that of the Truth and Reconciliation Commission in South Africa. Chance House wedded accountability and empathy by pairing each boy with a mentor in the community; a guardian angel to guide these young men in giving back to the world. Besides school, each resident of Chance House spent twenty hours a week in community service.

Sylvia had spent time with each of the boys coming to Chance House, working with the director at the Giddings School to ensure the success of the new program. She felt she knew Dylan and trusted he would thrive in the new setting. And now she was about to find out.

Sylvia finished her Coke and got out of the car. She went back to the cafe and ordered two red chili pork tamales to go. The cotton fields had drawn Mexico's migrant farm workers to the Delta to break their backs clearing cypress swamps and planting cotton alongside the descendants of African slaves, who had made the South a thriving economy in the early nineteenth century. The remnants of those cultures could be seen, heard and tasted up and down the whole length of the Blues Highway. Sylvia stopped in the bathroom, relieving herself of the quart of water she had consumed from Baton Rouge to Natchez. She washed her hands and returned to the car.

Sylvia chose to drive the Natchez Trace as far as Port Gibson where it rejoined Highway 61. The ample trees and grassy shoulders welcomed her. Highway signs beckoned from the side of the road, inviting her to visit the historic mansions that once housed the masters of sprawling plantations, over a century ago when cotton was king. A slow laziness began to settle into her body, some revenant from her antebellum heritage taking possession of her senses. For better or worse, this land with its history and grisly injustices was a part of her.

She decided to go to Clarksdale on her way to Jackson, which wasn't really on the way to Jackson but some three hundred miles out of the way. Maybe the spirit of Muddy Waters or W.C. Handy could soothe her. Who knows? She might bump into the haint of old Robert Johnson. She did not believe the legend about him selling his soul to the devil in exchange for his musical talent. Sylvia had never been convinced of the existence of God nor, by extension, his fallen angel. The radio continued to play. Music was redemption enough for her today.

Her cell phone rang. She pulled over to the side of the road and retrieved it from her briefcase. No doubt her boss would ensure this was a working vacation. Or maybe it was Joe, she hoped. The caller had a 601 area code. It took a minute before she recognized Faith's phone number.

"Faith?" Sylvia said her voice lifting.

"Where are you, Honey?" Faith replied.

"Just north of Natchez. Thought I'd head up to the Delta Blues Museum in Clarksdale, follow the old freedom highway for a while," she replied.

"Nothing better than a slow meander, is there?" Faith offered dreamily, "I always loved setting my compass, then letting the wind take me where it would."

"How are you?" Sylvia asked.

"Well, truth is, I'd like you here sooner than later. Hate to change your plans, but a friend is taking me to the hospital for a transfusion," Faith said, switching to her immediate reality. "I feel OK, and with this transfusion I ought to have plenty of energy while you're here. But I sure would love to get this business stuff out of the way so we can just visit."

"A transfusion? What hospital?" Sylvia said, the hairs on her arms suddenly erect. "I'll be in Vicksburg in an hour and can make it to Jackson in another thirty minutes on the interstate. I'll come straight to the hospital."

"Now slow down, girl, before you kill a'fella," Faith chuckled. "Take your time. There's nothing exciting happening. I will be at St. Catherine's, near the fairgrounds. It will take four hours at least to get the transfusion, so there is no need to hurry. You can pick me up and bring me home."

"OK," Sylvia said. "Do you want me to get some dinner?"

"That would be wonderful. I've had a hankering for some red chili pork tamales lately. Do you think you could find some?"

Sylvia smiled to herself. "I think I can do that. And Faith, I promise to slow down. I'll see you about four o'clock."

"OK, Honey, I'll see you then," Faith replied. The phone clicked to a sudden silence.

Sylvia checked the road ahead, looked into the rear-view mirror, then whipped the Miata into a U-turn and raced back to the cafe. She wondered if two dozen tamales would be enough.

MISSISSIPPI 1930

Delsey tucked the wool blanket around Jesse's shoulders, then turned up the collar of her coat. It had taken all day to drive the Ford Model TT truck, a slower but sturdier version of the model T, the two hundred forty miles from Montgomery to Hattiesburg. A cold front had moved through in the afternoon and the open cab of the truck offered little protection from the chill. Jesse drove the back roads through sharecropper country, refilling the tank from gas cans lashed to the side of the truck. Safer not to stop along the way. They breathed a sigh of relief once within the city limits of Hattiesburg. At Sixth Street they turned left, the trailer rattling behind them as twilight descended. Delsey was abuzz inside, straddling that line between excitement and fear. Before today, she had always known what tomorrow's landscape would look like. Tonight she didn't even know where she would be sleeping.

When they reached Main Street, Delsey recognized Hardee's Nash Ajax.

"There's the house," she said, pointing to their right.

Jesse eased the truck into the driveway of the Wiggins' house, squeezed the horn twice to announce their arrival and left the motor running. He wasn't sure if Mr. Wiggins wanted it parked somewhere in particular.

Hardee waved from the back porch and walked down the steps to greet them.

"You gotta back her in, Jess, to unload her," he said.

"All right, Mr. Wiggins. Where do you want her?"

"Back her up so's the trailer's all the way under the carport. There'll be enough headroom to get everything out. We can unload her tomorrow after you've had a good night's sleep." Hardee was glad to have the old store's truck back in his possession.

Maudie appeared at the screen door to the back porch, wiping her hands on the apron that billowed around her waist. Wisps of black hair, already amply streaked with gray, fluttered around her face and at the nape of her neck, having escaped the braided bun pinned to her crown.

"Y'all come get some supper," she said. "What would you like to drink? I've got milk or water or a little sassafras tea."

"Tea for me, Miss Maudie," Jesse replied.

"I'll take some milk, please," Delsey said.

They were invited to sit at a table on the screened in back porch. Maudie had pulled out a clean tablecloth for their arrival. Their places were set with fresh napkins and silverware. Plates filled with cold fried chicken, buttered corn on the cob and boiled cabbage awaited them. Maudie's everyday ministry included emulating her favorite New Testament story, the miracle of the loaves and fishes. Maudie returned to the kitchen to clean up while they ate.

"I've fixed up a little room down at the Trading Post for you, Delsey," Hardee said as the weary travelers sat down to eat. "You two can sleep there tonight. It's just a desk and a bed next to the sink in the back office. There's a small stove and a half-cord of firewood, so you ought to be warm enough. I put an extra cot in there for you, Jesse."

"Thank you, Mr. Wiggins," he replied.

Hardee opened the door from the back porch to the adjoining kitchen. Just beyond the door, Delsey spied the nightgown clad figures of Faith and Grace tiptoeing through the dining room. Maudie stood at the kitchen sink washing the dishes. She pretended not to see the girls because she knew how much they had anticipated Delsey's arrival. Even though it was past their bedtime, they could not wait until morning to say hello. With blinding speed, they swept past their father and jumped into Delsey's lap, each vying for her embrace. Their squabbling sounds made Jesse smile, reminding him of little piglets racing to their mother's side. Delsey settled each on to a leg, which was a bit of a balancing act now that Faith was six and Grace four years old. But they were petite enough and Delsey strong enough to hold them both. They nodded shyly to Jesse.

"We've missed you Miss Delsey," said Faith, a soft blonde curl caressing her forehead, "but we knew God would bring you back to us."

"Actually, I brought her back to you," Jesse quipped.

"Well, Pwaise the Lord, Pwaise the Lord!" Grace piped up, like a little parrot echoing her mother's words.

Their laughter filled the back porch and floated out into the Mississippi night.

"Well I can see you're going to be at home here, little sister," Jesse smiled at Delsey. "No use worrying another hair about it."

Delsey gave each of the girls a hug, then gently shooed them off to bed.

"Will you give me a tour of your new house tomorrow?" Delsey asked.

"Absolutely toot toot," Grace said, unable to master her

brother's favorite affirmation 'Abso tootin' lutely'.

After they had finished eating, Hardee drove Delsey and Jesse the short distance to the Wiggins' Trading Post, an empty warehouse on Front Street next to the red brick Southern Railway depot. The moon was almost directly overhead, reaching towards midnight as Delsey and Jesse arrived at their sleeping quarters for the night. Hardee unlocked the back door and let them in, then bid them goodnight. Jesse started a fire in the woodstove that sat in the corner of the office, while Delsey surveyed her new residence.

"There are a lot of down and outs around here, Delsey," Jesse said. The flames began to catch the kindling he was stoking. The light from the open door of the potbelly stove illuminated his face. Delsey could see his concern, the furrow forming between his eyebrows, the corners of his eyes turning up slightly.

They had passed four bands of hobos gathered around campfires along the rail lines after Hardee had turned from Main Street onto Front. He assured them that these were good folks, just fallen on hard times. Nothing to worry about. But Jesse was starting to waver about leaving his sister here in a new town, without family or friends.

"Stop your worrying Jess," she insisted, speaking with the comforting authority of a big sister. "You know I've fished you out of more trouble than I could ever get myself into. I'll be fine. And you know Maudie has always treated me like an adopted daughter. What you should worry about is who is going to keep you out of mischief if I'm not around. You gotta promise me..."

"OK, OK," he murmured. "But you know I can hop a train back here from Montgomery fast as a fox's tail."

He sat on the cot and untied his shoes. The room had warmed, and they both felt exhausted from the trip. Delsey lay on her bed and sleep descended upon her within minutes. Delsey dreamed that night of riding in a railroad car past snow-covered fields, a small child seated next to her. They came to a large river and crossed over it. She was smiling as the child pointed excitedly out the window to the gleaming white obelisk that came into view.

In the morning, Delsey and Jesse were already awake when Hardee showed up to collect them. It was a Friday, Halloween 1930, and pumpkins populated porches all along Main Street, each awaiting its new face. There was a frisky feeling in the air. Perhaps it was the cold front or maybe the anticipation of children ready to carve pumpkins with their mothers, looking forward to something sweet in their basket that night. For Delsey, it was the feeling that everything was new as they bumped along the road toward the Wiggins house.

Brett was waiting under the carport when they arrived at the house. He had removed the ropes and tarps covering the furniture and boxes in the trailer. At seventeen, his long arms had the young muscularity of a late bloomer, his red beard beginning to assert itself with some seriousness. Hardee waved to him as they drove up. He parked the car in the driveway and got out.

"Did you sweep the shed out too, son?"

"Yep, Dad. Ready to go."

Hardee ached with love for his son. He was a little surprised and disturbed to have such strong feelings. Hardee knew Brett would need to leave home before long, find his own place, but he could not bear to think about it now. Hardee would be left in a sea of women, and though they dazzled him, and he loved them deeply, he would miss the solidness of his son, the fierce understanding they shared.

Brett leaned his head inside the car.

"Mama said to come on in the house. She can get you some water, Jesse, before we start unloading the truck. And I'm sure she'll put you to work, Delsey, if you've got the energy."

Jesse and Delsey climbed out of the back seat of the Nash. Delsey proceeded into the house through the back porch to help Maudie sweep the corners where the furniture would go. The schools had made this Halloween a holiday, a day for teachers to catch up on their work and for children to play in the piles of fallen leaves. The Wiggins girls had been encouraged to stay outside today while the men unloaded the truck and trailer. Faith and Grace were playing with their Raggedy Ann dolls in the back yard. Hanna was asleep in her crib in her parents' bedroom.

Claire and Delta lounged on the front porch, which extended the full length of the house. A pot of tea rested on the table between them. They leafed through old copies of Vogue and Harper's Bazaar. Claire was almost fifteen years old and fully blossomed into womanhood. She was stunningly beautiful, with a face like Joan Bennett and the sultriness of Marlene Dietrich. She was definitely Maudie's biggest concern because Maudie knew the world of men would be wide open to her. Although the Depression had dampened the excesses of the 1920s, it had not made a dent in the aspirations of this wildest of the Wiggins. Claire was full of the roar of those times and dreams of an unbridled life.

Her younger sister, Delta, was perched on the near edge of puberty and emulated Claire in form and fashion, but she lacked the quickness of wit and deep brooding passion. Delta was more the carefree butterfly, possessed of her own fair share of beauty. Maybe it was her docile nature or that she, of all the girls, most resembled Maudie. For whatever reason, she had won favored status in her father's heart and she would sometimes use it to her advantage.

Claire and Delta sat with chenille shawls around their shoulders, the reinvented remnants of an old bedspread that Maudie had fashioned on her Singer, using a pattern from the Illustrated Milliner magazine. They drank their tea with little fingers extended and talked about how they would dine on fine French food and buy this dress or that when they vacationed with their husbands-to-be in Paris.

On the other side of the house, under the carport, Jesse finished the glass of water that Delsey had brought him. He pulled the gloves out of his back pocket where he had tucked them. Brett had already lowered the gate to the trailer.

"Hey there, Jesse. Looks like it's you and me again, doing the lifting," said Brett.

"Guess you're right about that," Jesse replied.

Every Saturday for years, back in Alabama, these two had met at the Cobb's Ford store and unloaded Toby's vegetable truck of produce, or the occasional load of firewood, while their fathers settled the bill. In some ways Jesse was the closest thing to a brother that Brett had, but for the color of their skin. And that difference seemed to be everything.

Brett remembered that Hardee was gone rabbit hunting when word came that Lucy Clemons had died. Jesse had lost his mother at the age of eight. Brett recalled the trip he had made with Maudie to the Clemons home, a sharecropper's cabin nestled in the fertile farmland east of Montgomery. Tobias Clemons had been supplying the Cobb's Ford store with produce for seven years. Maudie went with a smoked ham and a crate of her home canned vegetables, yams, green beans, beets, and okra. She had braved the roads and the risk of contracting influenza from Mrs. Clemons' deathbed to come and pray with Toby and the kids and to prepare the house for the funeral. Maudie left Ava and Claire with a neighbor, but she brought her son with her, even though he was only five years old. She was pregnant with Delta at the time, and it had comforted her to have him by her side.

After they arrived and unpacked the food, Toby suggested that Jesse and Brett go catch a fish to add to the feast. Brett remembered how quiet and sad Jesse was as they walked down the road to the fishing pond, the dirt on his cheeks smeared by the tears he had wiped dry.

"I'm sorry 'bout your Mama," Brett said with a grown-up effort. Maudie had helped him consider what to say when he first arrived.

Jesse just nodded and wiped his face again.

"We brought you a chocolate cake," he added, hoping to make things better.

"Thanks."

When they reached the pond, Jesse pulled a couple of cane poles from under the shrubs next to the bank and dug up some night crawlers from the rich black dirt. He didn't say much. He just showed Brett how to put the worm on the hook then how to fling the line into the water. He explained how you catch a fish, told him 'You gotta stay still and quiet so's not to spook 'em.' Pretty soon Brett's bobber vanished in a sudden jerk beneath the water. Jesse grabbed the pole and quickly set the hook. Then he gave the pole back to Brett and told him what to do, gently and with plenty of encouragement. Brett landed a two-pound catfish with little help, and Jesse knew how excited he was to catch his first fish. He did feel a bit like a big brother as they walked back up the road, toting the prize, Jesse doing most of the toting.

"I can't believe I got a fish. I got a fish!" Brett squealed.

"And you landed him yourself," Jesse said.

"But you helped me."

"I just set the hook. You landed him so he's yours,"

"I got a fish!" he said again and started running toward the house.

When they arrived, Jesse let Brett do all the bragging.

Toby congratulated them. "Well, Jesse, now you gotta teach him how to clean and gut it."

Maudie and Brett had stayed for a bite of pan-fried catfish along with some ham and sweet potatoes. As they were driving home that afternoon, Brett turned to his mother. The breeze from the car's windows was a welcome relief from the sweltering summer heat. Cicada's song swelled then quieted.

"Mama?" he asked, "Am I ever gonna have a brother?"

"Well, I don't know, darlin'. Maybe the Lord's baking up a little brother for you inside me right now," she said. "But then it could be another sister, too."

"Could Jesse be my brother?" he asked, hopefully.

"Well, Sweetie," she paused, searching for the words, "not your blood brother. But that doesn't mean you can't care for him like a brother."

She wondered how to explain it to him. "Some people won't like it though. They don't take to the races mixing."

"Mama?" he said with a puzzled look. "What do you mean a race? A foot race or a horse race?"

"Never mind, Sweetie," she sighed. "You let Jesus tell you how to feel about Jesse."

"OK, good, 'cause Jesus says he's my brother."

That memory seemed like a distant dream to Brett now as the two young men unloaded the trailer. They hauled furniture into the house, stacked tools and boxes in the shed. Sweat soaked the collars of their shirts and glistened on their arms. They were just sitting down to rest and have some tea by the truck when Brett spied his little sister Emma flying across the street from behind the Moody's house with a bag in her arms.

Maudie had sent Emma out to gather pecans from the trees in the park next to Fletcher and Ruth's house. Emma left the house in a plain gingham dress, which was the proper attire for a good Southern God-fearing girl. But Emma was headed back across the street in a new pair of overalls and Brett knew she would have hell to pay if Maudie caught her before he did.

"Scuse me, Jesse," he said as he jumped up and ran towards Emma.

Brett caught her before she got to the house and scooped her up in his arms. She was nine years old and gangly and he could hardly contain the arms and legs flailing about as she protested her capture. Pecans flew in all directions when the bag she was carrying dropped to the ground.

"Let me go, Brother," she hollered.

"You better hush up or you're going to be in a lot more trouble than wrestling with me," he said. "Now, where's your dress?"

"Over there," she said pointing to the Moody's house.

"And where did you get those overalls?" he smiled, trying unsuccessfully to scowl.

"Miss Ruth!" she replied triumphantly.

"Oh, Lord," said Brett, "this could be real neighbor troubles."

"Miss Ruth and Mr. Fletcher aren't any kind of trouble, and they are real nice to me. Even give me a nickel for an ice cream cone."

"OK, then, let's go see Miss Ruth. An ice cream cone is fine, but Mama isn't gonna tolerate those overalls."

"I ain't puttin' that dress back on," she said, with absolute certitude.

"We'll see about that," he said, putting her back down on the ground, but keeping a firm grip on the back of her overalls as they marched back across the street to the Moody's house.

"You're not the boss of me," she said with a half-hearted struggle to escape his hold.

"You'll wish I was, if Mama finds you in these overalls."

Emma considered that he might be right.

"If I put my dress back on, can I hide my britches and you won't tell Mama?"

"If you put your dress on, I won't tell," he said.

"Cross your heart and hope to die?"

"Cross my heart," he said, making the motion over his heart as they stepped up onto the Moody's porch and knocked on the door.

From inside the Wiggins' house, Delsey watched the hubbub in the yard between Brett and Emma. She made sure Maudie was nowhere near the window to see the commotion outside. With the Wiggins family, there was always some kind of a ruckus going on. She shook her head at the thought of how her life was all tangled up with theirs. As she watched Brett walk Emma across the street, she realized that she was beginning to glimpse the landscape of her new life.

MISSISSIPPI 1998

St. Catherine's stood on a grassy rise, a small patch of what had once been pastoral parkland south of Jackson before it was dissected into city blocks in the late 1970s. The Mississippi state fairgrounds lay just to the north. A plush grove of pecan trees skirted the perimeter of the property along its back and sides. The three-story russet brick building had been built in 1940, just before the war when quality of construction was still a thing of pride. It welcomed its visitors through a white portico leading to paneled mahogany doors that were framed by a transom and side windows. With only sixty beds, it was a relatively small hospital compared to the corporate conglomerates that now housed America's ill. Sylvia relaxed as she stepped into the air-conditioned lobby and made her way to the information desk.

"I'm here to meet my aunt, Faith Wiggins," Sylvia said to the young woman at the desk. "She's in the emergency room getting a transfusion."

The receptionist appeared to be in her early twenties and wore a smart navy-blue dress with a modest V-neckline. A single white pearl, suspended in perfect elegance against mocha skin, sat just below the small valley where her collarbones met.

"Let me find her for you," she said, greeting Sylvia with a friendly smile. She looked for Faith's name in the patient register. "Yes, she checked into the emergency room about three hours ago. May I help you find your way?" She started to rise from her chair.

"Thank you," Sylvia said. "You can just point me in the right direction, and I'll find it."

"OK. Go down this hall to your right then take a left and another right," she motioned, her hand taking the appropriate turns. "I hope your aunt feels better after her transfusion."

"Thanks, again," Sylvia nodded.

She found Faith reading a book in a large leather recliner in the back of the emergency room. The chair made her seem more diminutive than she already was. A lap quilt was tucked around her legs. Eight partitioned cubicles lined the back wall of the infusion area, each with a small window that opened to the slightly acrid smell of fresh green pecan husks.

"Well you are as radiant as ever," Sylvia pronounced as she paused at the threshold to the tiny room.

Faith looked up from her book. Her sapphire blue eyes smiled over the top of the reading glasses perched on the rounded tip of her nose. She patted the arm of the recliner.

"And how is my favorite niece, who would never tell any of her cousins that I said that?"

Sylvia came and sat next to her. The bag of thick red blood had almost emptied into Faith's left arm and another bag of saline was diluting the dregs as it dripped in.

"I must say my countenance is improved with a little color in my cheeks," Faith said, fanning her face with the pages of the open book, before dropping the belle persona. "And now I'm as hungry as a bear out of winter. Did you find me any tamales?"

"They're in the car. I'll go get them. Think two dozen is enough?" Sylvia replied, jumping up and turning to go.

Faith reached up, pulled Sylvia back down next to her, and paused. "Probably," she said with a wink.

They leaned into each other and hugged, lingering a moment. A nurse with ample hips filling pink scrubs bustled into the room and headed straight toward Faith. Sylvia barely had time to get out of the way.

"Looks like you're done Miss Wiggins," she said, patting Faith's shoulder. "How 'bout I flush the line and remove your IV. You feel OK?" She wrapped a blood pressure cuff around Faith's right arm, checked her vital signs and recorded the figures.

"I'm fine, Viv," Faith replied to her nurse. Vivien squirted saline through the IV, removed it and placed a bandage on Faith's arm, all in one fluid motion.

"You didn't spill a drop. Perfection, as usual," Faith said.

Vivien gathered the spent IV bags and laughed. "Well we don't put it in to have it come back out, Miss Faith. Who's this with you today?" She nodded toward Sylvia.

"I'm her..."

"She's my..."

"Niece," Faith and Sylvia said in unison.

"OK. Well, you two are good to go," Viv said.

Sylvia located a wheelchair in the adjacent alcove and started to wheel it toward her aunt, but Faith waved her off.

"No need for that," she said.

They walked arm and arm back to the front of the hospital where Sylvia insisted that Faith wait while she got the car. Outside, the sun was making its retreat. At Faith's request, Sylvia lowered the convertible top of the Miata. They nestled into the deep bucket seats for the short ride south on Highway 49. Faith lived in a farmhouse outside Florence, Mississippi. She had let most of the twenty-acre farm go to pasture and leased grazing rights for a nominal fee to her dairy-farming neighbors. She liked the sight of Holsteins meandering at their hebetudinous pace across her swath of land.

Once past the outskirts of Jackson, they were greeted by fields of fescue, the tall feathery seed heads rippling in the wind, bowing to the broad-leafed Bermudas below. Sylvia and Faith rode in comfortable silence, enjoying the brisk wind of the open car ride. After fifteen minutes they turned right, onto the last stretch of road leading up to the house. The crunch of the gravel drive took Sylvia back to the time of her respite here some six years before.

She had just returned from New York City after ending her four-year relationship with Jack. They had been together for a couple of years when he had been hired at a Wall Street firm in 1989. By then she was burning out as a juvenile public defender, ready for change. His firm was hiring junior members in early 1990 and she took a job. She saw it as a chance to be close to family again. Her parents, and younger brother, had moved to New York City in 1972, just after she graduated from high school. Phil had taken over the family import export business when his father retired. She especially wanted time with her brother John who had come out as gay a year earlier.

She had loved New York at first, the intellectual vibrancy, the wealth of art and theater. Days with John and his friends were a welcome escape from the straight jacket of her Bible belt upbringing. But the work left her feeling empty, and no amount of entertainment could fill the void. It was not her right life and she left it all behind – job, boyfriend, and home. She had landed, shell-shocked, in Florence, Mississippi and Faith had given her the room to flounder until Sylvia could find a rudder. Faith had suggested a trip to the "real" Florence and Rome, suspecting those places might top Manhattan, and praying that Sylvia might find Jesus more palatable as rendered by Michelangelo or Ghiberti or Bernini. The adventure they took together had forged a bond that remained to this day.

The Miata approached the end of the drive. A small lavender shiplap house squatted at the back of Faith's farm. Piney woods bordered the house on the west and rolling pastureland stretched for miles in all other directions. A curtain of oaks shaded the house on the north, just past the drive, and a lone magnolia wafted its welcome from the front yard. Sylvia pulled under the porte cochere and parked the car.

"You've got to see the garden," Faith said, indicating the large, tilled plot on the south side of the house. "But let's have some sweet tea first. Would you pour me a glass? The door is unlocked and there are lemons right inside on the counter."

Faith unfolded herself slowly from the low-lying passenger seat.

"Sounds good to me," Sylvia replied. "How about we eat those tamales with our tea, and you can tell me a little about this fellow, McLeod Walker."

Sylvia imagined that the heir to Faith's will was some mysterious suitor who had once lit a flame in her heart. Faith's devotion to God would not have precluded a discreet and considered love affair. She felt honored that

Faith could trust her with such a private matter. She retrieved the tamales tucked beneath her seat and went into the house. Sylvia opened the knotty pine cabinets and put two pale blue porcelain plates on the kitchen table. She gathered napkins and silverware and poured sweet tea into recycled jelly jars placing a wedge of lemon on each rim. Faith had gone straight to her bedroom, and now returned, having shed her stocking and shoes. The smell of tamales, just warm from the oven filled the kitchen. They sat at the kitchen table, the faint ping of forks on plates punctuating the silence as they ate.

"Thank you, Sylvia, for coming to see me on such short notice. And for accepting the responsibility of being my executor. I trust only you to see my wishes through, to refute whatever objections may be raised by my sisters. I want to ensure that the estate is left to the right person." Her determined voice cracked slightly.

"Faith, I can't think of you...." Sylvia shrugged off a fleeting chill.

"It's OK. I'm not dead, yet."

"Well, it's a privilege to be asked, and the least I can do. I hope you know you can trust me to carry out your directives and to be respectful of your privacy regarding this man who must have been a great love."

"What?" Faith laughed. The twilight caught her deep affection for Sylvia's misapprehension.

"Oh, Honey, I never fell for a man who would have any use for my money. Can you imagine me with any man less independent than me?"

"Well, no, but I thought...." Sylvia was mortified. "I didn't mean to imply..."

"Oh, stop worrying. You just made my day, and your

assumptions are not offensive or that far off base. But McLeod Walker is someone else entirely and deserves my money for a completely different reason," Faith said.

"OK, but.... I mean who...?"

"McLeod Walker is Delsey Clemons' son, her only child. I haven't seen him since he was about eight years old, when Delsey brought him down to the farm at Plum Nelly. It must have been in 1942. I was in my first year of nursing school in New Orleans and had come to see Mama and Daddy for a few days. Delsey had heard about Brett while she was visiting her brother, Jesse, in Alabama. She decided to pay Mama a visit and she brought McLeod with her. Last I heard McLeod was living near Clarksdale."

"What? Wait. Delsey who?" Sylvia was lost.

"Delsey Clemons. I doubt you ever met her. McLeod must be twenty years older than you. Delsey is at least half the reason your Grandpa Hardee made a success of the Trading Post, which afforded me the opportunity to go to nursing school. She worked for your grandfather and was one of the best souls the good Lord ever graced me to know. It is actually a long story Sylvia, and not a very pretty one. Suffice it to say that our family has the blood of Delsey's family on our conscience, if not on our hands." Faith hesitated, shifting in her chair.

"I have no idea what you're talking about. But whatever it is, I promise I will honor your wishes to the letter," Sylvia offered, leaning forward now.

Faith looked at her with a weary smile, drew in a slow deep breath and leaned back in her chair. She took a drink of tea and held the glass in both hands, looking into it, figuring how to proceed.

Sylvia caught herself wanting to speak and eased into

the silence instead.

"You are as close to a daughter as I could have, Sylvia, and I don't want to burden you. But I must say it is such a relief to have you here." She paused and emitted a deep sigh, as though laying down a heavy pack after a long hike.

"There will never be sufficient justice on this earth for the unspeakable acts we have committed against our Black brothers and sisters here in the South. I know that and it makes my skin crawl. And I know I could have done more. I spoke up plenty of times when I witnessed the cruelty. I even marched, but I also bit my lip to keep the family peace. Somehow, there must be a reckoning of things. I will not live long enough to see society change so I have decided to begin the Reparation as best I can. One family at a time, from me to McLeod. Guilt is part of it, for sure, but it still feels like the right thing to do."

Sylvia felt a flood of affection for Faith. She rose and walked over to Faith's chair and began to gently massage her shoulders.

"How about I draw you a bath and turn down the bed. And tomorrow you can tell me the rest of the story. I want to hear it all, as long as it takes."

"Sounds great. I'm beat and a true story can't be rushed. It is best told with a long breath after a good night's sleep. I'll even make you breakfast in the morning."

Sylvia drew a bath while Faith changed into her robe.

"I'm going to water the garden for a bit," she called to Faith as she headed out to the yard.

"Oh, thanks. Give it a good soaking. Towels are in the hall closet and the sheets on the guest bed are clean."

"OK, see you in the morning," Sylvia replied.

"Yeah, I'll wake you when the sun's up, if that old rooster

doesn't beat me to it."

"I love you, Faith."

"A bushel and a peck."

"And a hug around the neck."

Sylvia walked out the front door into the fading twilight. She watered the garden, then made her way back to the house. She took a shower, rinsing off the sticky film of sweat and road dust that had accumulated since she left Baton Rouge that morning, lingering beneath the cool mist for an extra minute. She walked down the hall from the bathroom to the guest bedroom and put on a tank top and silk shorts to sleep in. She searched through her briefcase until she found her book. Reading a couple of chapters ought to soothe her to sleep. Her cell phone vibrated briefly, signaling a missed call. It must have rung while she was outside. She opened the phone and recognized Joe's number. She sat down on the bed and paused before dialing, aware of the slight pressure in her chest.

"Hello," crooned the deep voice on the other end.

Sylvia's body immediately softened, pure physiology possessing her.

"Hey there," she said. "I must have been outside when you phoned."

"Or didn't want to take the call," Joe replied.

The cold pained silence she had anticipated rose between them once again.

"I don't know what to say, Joe," she ventured. "It's been a long day and I had to pick up Faith at the hospital. And the office won't leave me alone."

"I know. You're busy."

"Yes. I am. But it doesn't mean I haven't been thinking about you." She tried to suppress a sigh.

"How's Faith?" he asked, regretting that he had nursed his hurt feelings. Joe knew that Sylvia was struggling with the news about Faith's illness.

"She's better after the transfusion. For now, anyway."

"That's good." He paused, not knowing what else to say.

"Joe, I'm sorry about the way I left yesterday. It's just. I was just..."

"Oh Sylvia, I should be the one apologizing, storming out of the house while you were in the shower. Sometimes I can be a petulant brat."

"It's OK, I knew you were hurt. It's not that I didn't want to make love to you. You must know how much I love you, how much I trust you. But I was just so agitated that morning, maybe about Faith. I'm not sure why. You know me, I can be a little..."

"Moody?" he laughed softly.

"Yeah," she replied.

"I have noticed that you seem irritated with me lately. Any reason?"

"Oh, I really don't want to get into it," she said.

Joe waited a few seconds before responding.

"Might as well."

"It's the little hints you drop about having a baby, like the other day when "Nick of Time" came on the radio. We've been over this so many times."

"I was just kidding."

"No. You weren't."

They were silent.

"Joe let's not do this tonight. We can talk about it later. I love you, I miss you. I want to be with you. That's what I wanted to say."

"I love you, too, Sylvia. Forgive my thoughtlessness. I

know your plate is full right now. I'm here whenever you need to call. OK?"

"Thank you."

"See you in a couple of weeks."

"OK, love you. Bye."

"Love you, too."

She stared at the phone as the light dimmed and went out. She set it on the bedside table and picked up her novel. As she slumped against the pillows, the tears within her welled and spilled silently onto her cheeks. Maybe she needed to give up on having a successful relationship with a man. After all, if she could not make it with Joe, it was clear that no man would do. The realms of thought she explored with him fascinated her. But what had stolen her heart was the way he played the piano from the depths of his soul, the same place he took her when they made love. And for all his imperfections, he was a good man. Good to the bone.

She opened the book to its dog-eared page and settled into the salve of a world removed from here and now. Within two pages, her eyelids began to droop, and she slipped into the refuge of sleep.

~

The smell of coffee and bacon roused Sylvia the next morning. She pulled on yesterday's jeans and a fresh blouse and wandered into the kitchen. The electric percolator was just winding down to a slow gurgle and the strips of bacon lay draining on a stack of paper towels.

"Faith?" she called as she stretched, extending her arms over her head, then bending to touch her toes.

"Faith?" she called again and stepped out onto the front porch. The sun was a short stretch above the horizon, and already it was a balmy seventy degrees before the day had even begun.

"I decided to let you sleep in, old girl," Faith replied as she rounded the corner of the house, returning from the garden with an apron full of ripe tomatoes. She held one up, wiped it on her blouse and took a bite. Juice flew.

"To go with the grits."

"Who's calling who an old girl?" Sylvia jousted. "And since when is seven a.m. sleeping in?" She took some of the tomatoes from Faith as they walked to the kitchen.

Sylvia poured their coffee and set the table while Faith scrambled some eggs. They sat across from each other, their plates hosting thick slices of tomatoes on a bed of white grits alongside the bacon and eggs. Faith stirred a spoonful of sugar slowly in her cup, gathering her recollections to continue the story.

Sylvia looked up from her plate. "I'm awake and so curious about McLeod and, who did you say, Delsey?"

"Yes, well let me go back a bit. Let's see.... we moved from Cobb's Ford, Alabama in 1930. The Depression had dried up Daddy's auto business and he somehow figured he could make a go of it in Hattiesburg by starting the Trading Post. Now you must know, he was a genius at wheeling and dealing but he did not know the first thing about keeping books. And Mama, though she had the smarts for it, was way too busy with all us kids to be working his business. So early on in Alabama, he hired a young woman, a girl really, named Delsey Clemons to handle the details of the office work for the grocery store and later the Cadillac dealership he owned. She was the daughter of Toby Clemons, a Negro sharecropper, who sold his goods to Daddy's store. She was bright and well-schooled, and your Grandpa Hardee got her on the cheap. She became an indispensable part of his business. Even helped him with his income taxes so he never had to fork out accountant fees."

"So she worked for him in Alabama?"

"Yes and came with our family to Hattiesburg. At great cost, personally, I would add. Mama loved her like a daughter but couldn't really keep her like one. I think Delsey was lonely, living down at the Trading Post. And she had dreams of her own, dreams that did not get realized working for Daddy. She wanted to be a teacher, to raise her own children, not just help Mama with all of us when she was not working for Daddy. But to her advantage, the move allowed her to send some money back home to her family in Alabama and eventually..." Faith paused to take a bite of her grits.

"And eventually, what?" Sylvia prodded.

"Mouf ful," Faith pointed to her face with her fork then smiled.

She rinsed the grits down with some coffee and unwound the story slowly, refusing to rush it.

"Eventually she met someone, a Pullman porter named Plessy Walker. On her way back to Montgomery, I think. He was a handsome man and full of fire."

"Did you know him?"

"A little bit. I met him on a few occasions when he stopped by to see Delsey at work. In the summertime, Daddy would pay me a dime a day to help him at the store. But mostly, I knew Plessy from Delsey's stories. According to her, he was a year older than she was and he had finished high school at the top of his class. Somewhere up north, can't remember where. I think he got a scholarship to Howard

University in Washington D.C. Got his degree in, hmm....
history and political science as I faintly recall. He had just
begun law school when the market crashed."

"So you and mom and everybody were still in Alabama
when the market crashed, right? You would have been
how old?"

"Let's see. It was the year before we moved so I must have
been five. And Grace was only three. Delsey would have
been twenty-one or so. She and Plessy weren't destined to
meet for a couple more years."

"And how did Plessy end up in Mississippi, after living
in D.C.?

"Well he needed money, is what Delsey told me. And
because he was educated, with the refinement that came
with that, he got a job on the Crescent Limited that
ran between New York and New Orleans, right through
Washington, D.C., and Montgomery. It was the most
luxurious exclusive Pullman train that ever ran on the
Southern Railway lines. Plessy was head porter within a
year, shuttling back and forth across the country, but he
must have chafed under that yoke. Delsey used to say that
his dream was to write the Negro into the very bedrock
of the United States Constitution. I try to imagine what
it must have been like, an educated man having to rely
largely on tips, on the generous whim of White folks for his
livelihood. People who were less educated than him and so
demeaning."

Sylvia could feel the thin film of sweat beginning to
coat her skin. Midmorning Mississippi summer dew. She
reached up to pull the cord on the ceiling fan above the
table.

"You mind?" she asked.

"Help yourself," Faith replied. "You want me to turn on the cooler?"

"No, not yet. I'll acclimate."

Sylvia went to the refrigerator and brought the pitcher of iced tea back to the table, poured herself a cool drink. "So how did they meet? I mean if Delsey was in Hattiesburg, and he was in New Orleans or D.C. or wherever."

"By luck, apparently. Although that is the mystery that makes you wonder about an unseen hand in things. Somehow, she ended up on his train, which ran along the Gulf coast on its way to Montgomery, and he found a seat in her passenger car that night, as he came off duty as a porter. However it happened, they found each other and Delsey said it was as if they had been looking for each other all their lives."

"Come on, Faith." Sylvia protested. "Are you saying it was destiny? Fate?"

"You can call it what you like, synchronicity or providence or just plain coincidence, but there's something, isn't there Sylvia, some mysterious weaving together of things. A tapestry of lives," Faith replied.

Sylvia shrugged. "And McLeod was their son?"

"Yes, although you're jumping ahead a little." Faith rose and went to the counter, poured herself another cup of coffee. She swirled in an extra measure of cream. Returning to the table, she added a dash of sugar.

"They courted for a year and then got engaged. Somewhere about that time, Plessy got recruited by Asa Philip Randolph to work as a labor organizer for the Brotherhood of Sleeping Car Porters. I remember this because it was one of the few times I ever heard your grandpa and Delsey fight. I couldn't have been more than eight or nine years old. It was a lazy summer evening and Mama had sent me down to the store with a lunch pail full of fried chicken and mashed potatoes for Daddy and Delsey who were doing inventory and would not be home for supper. I rode my bicycle the mile or so from the house to the store, their supper strapped onto the cargo rack of my Hawthorne Flyer De Luxe. God, I loved that bike, candy apple red with a real electric light. I was always looking for an excuse to run an errand for Mama just so I could ride that bike. I can still see the fireflies as I rode back that night, a blinking swarm all around me.

Anyway, when I got to the porch at the store, I heard them talking loudly. Delsey was saying that Plessy was only fighting for what was fair. Bargaining and collecting, things I didn't understand. Daddy said everyone had fallen on hard times and Plessy was being uppity, asking for special treatment for Negroes. Delsey said she respectfully disagreed, and that Mr. Hardee might just want to ponder on the pittance he had paid her compared to what he would have paid a White accountant. Suddenly it was quiet. I stood in the doorway and watched. They were frozen there looking at each other, like a couple of cats with their backs up. Daddy said in a low growl. 'Well if the Coloreds are lookin' for a fight down here in Mississippi, they're sure gonna get one.' It must have been the creaking of the floorboards under my feet as I held myself, rocking back and forth there on the porch, which turned their attention. I guess I started to cry because Delsey held her arms out to me. Daddy took the lunch pail, and I ran over to Delsey. She pulled me close, into her body. 'Don't worry, Faith, your daddy and I were just discussing politics and it always stirs the air.'

A few days later, I went back to the Trading Post and waited until I could speak to Delsey alone. I asked her more about what she and Daddy had been fighting about and why he was mad at Plessy. That's when she told me about the Brotherhood of Sleeping Car Porters."

"Sounds intense. Did they work it out? You know, Hardee and Delsey?"

"Somehow they brokered a delicate truce. They still needed each other then. But Delsey had changed. With Plessy, she saw other possibilities. The family she wanted, the chance to go to a teacher's college. I think your grandpa could feel the ground of Southern society shifting and knew he might lose Delsey. He didn't like it. Delsey and Plessy got married the next year. She told me they had planned to move to Florida so she could begin her teaching studies at Bethune-Cookman University. But Randolph begged Plessy to stay in Mississippi to head up the southern region's labor organization. Then Delsey got pregnant. Not more than a couple of months after they were married. They had a son and named him McLeod after Mary McLeod Bethune, the mentor she hoped to meet someday. So, you see, McLeod was a dream holder from the day he was born."

"Did she ever meet Mrs. Bethune?"

"Oh, yes. She told me about it in one of our letters. She kept in touch after they left Mississippi. First with Mama, then I picked it up after Mama died. We wrote to each other over all these years until a couple of years ago when the letters came back "Mail unclaimed." That's when I realized she had probably passed. It's why I want to change the Will to name McLeod as beneficiary instead of Delsey."

Sylvia stared at Faith, waiting. "But what about the time

between them leaving Mississippi and two years ago?"

"Let's do these dishes," Faith replied, standing up from the table. "I'll tell you more after you take me into the grocery store this afternoon. I decided to wait until you got here before I stocked up."

Sylvia held her hand up, like a traffic cop, as Faith started to clear the table.

"Please, let me do these, OK?" she said, her voice softening as she took the dishes from Faith's hands. "Why don't you rest a little. I have a couple of calls to make, some loose ends to clear up at work. I want a clean plate, so to speak, for the next couple of weeks."

"Hmm, good idea. I could use a little nap. But only thirty minutes, OK? You'll wake me up in thirty minutes?"

"Sure," Sylvia replied. "Thirty minutes."

Sylvia put the plates in the sink. Sweat was now rolling down the hollow of her spine as the sun marked its zenith. Her shirt clung to her like a damp washcloth. Faith watched as Sylvia pulled her shirt away from her body, flapping it to fan herself. Without looking back, Faith made her way to the bedroom.

"The switch to the cooler is in the hallway, by the way, once you're acclimated and ready to turn it on."

Without seeing her face, Sylvia knew that the right corner of Faith's mouth had lifted into a half smile, the hint of a dimple trying to emerge.

Later that evening, as they harvested the garden, Faith recounted more about Plessy, Delsey and McLeod. It turns out they moved to Washington, D.C. a few years after McLeod was born. Faith didn't recount all the details, but she said that Mr. Philip Randolph, with the help of Plessy and many others, had been successful in elevating the

Brotherhood of Sleeping Car Porters into a true political force. They had successfully negotiated a labor contract with the Pullman Company, the first contract in history between a Black labor union and a major corporation. It brought the porters a pay increase, but more than that, it let the porters raise their heads and negotiate their working conditions, rather than beg as another man's supplicant. It was a first heroic step towards full civil rights. However, with such progress came a backlash, and Plessy became the target of that backlash. He had been severely beaten. The real and immediate threat to Plessy's life caused them to leave Mississippi. Maudie and Delsey stayed in touch by letter for a long time, which is how Faith came to learn that McLeod had settled in Clarksdale.

Faith and Sylvia walked back to the house with a basket brimming with tomatoes, okra and green onions, the sun throwing sprays of peach and gold across the western horizon.

They enjoyed the next two weeks together, those late summer days filled with the easy flow of cooking and chores around the house. The business of the Will took only a couple of days to settle. Their conversations grew more intimate as they worked together. They harvested the garden daily and spent the last weekend together preserving that harvest. Faith reminded Sylvia how to can all sorts of vegetables; the extra care needed in the hot preparation of the beans.....

"I prefer not to die of botulism poisoning," Faith quipped as she stood at the stove over a steaming pot of Kentucky Wonders. "I'll bloat soon enough after I die, no sense doing it before."

"God, you're sick," Sylvia said.

"I meant…. I meant your humor," she added.

"Comes from tending the ill, I suppose. And in places you would not believe. I remember working years ago in Burma, or Myanmar as they call it now, where palliative care consisted of thin broth and a warm towel. Maybe a little opium if you were lucky. When I gave up on prayer, God taught me the saving grace of hard laughter."

"You gave up on prayer?"

"Oh, many times but never for good. Hard to explain really, but some…. I do not know what else to call it, some Presence…. would not let me go, through all my anger and doubt. Guess I finally stopped seeking relief or understanding. I had to give up on ready answers."

Sylvia grew quiet and Faith let her stew for a while. She turned off the beans while Sylvia scrubbed the last of the glass Ball jars in hot soapy water and rinsed them. The ceiling fan clicked rhythmically in the endless expanse of the lazy summer afternoon.

"This batch of beans is ready for the jars. Since we are hot packing them, they won't shrink much. You can give them a little breathing room," Faith told her.

"Oh……OK." Sylvia said. A momentary tremor made her fumble one of the jars, as she tried to place it in the rack that would nest inside the pressure cooker.

"Actually, let's fill the jars with the beans and the steamed juice first, then we'll rack them," Faith offered. "You want me to do it while you wash the next batch of beans?"

"No, I can do it," Sylvia replied, her forehead knit in earnest, like that of a ten-year-old child.

Faith stopped tending the beans and relaxed, letting her attention come to rest on her own breathing, the rise and fall of her chest. She watched as Sylvia continued to scurry about the open kitchen transferring the clean Ball jars from the dish rack on her right to the white-tiled countertop of the breakfast bar on her left. A little gray squirrel full of industry and intensity.

"Sylvia?" Faith tried to meet her eyes.

Sylvia would not relent. She continued her task until she assembled a small regiment of pint jars into three neat little rows.

'Onward Christian Soldiers' began playing in Faith's mind. She smiled, let the song float through, then returned to the rhythm of her breathing. As Sylvia paused over the open mouths of the jars, pondering what to do next, Faith reached over and touched her shoulder, then gradually took Sylvia's hand in her own.

"Whatever it is, Sylvia, it's OK to talk to me about it."

"Well, I just don't remember how to do this. I mean the pressure cooker and all...."

Faith waited. When Sylvia started to pull away, she did not let go. She waited until a blush of pink arose on Sylvia's cheeks. When Sylvia tried to turn away again Faith let her go and handed her the pot of beans, which Sylvia promptly started gathering into piles with a pair of tongs.

"I was just thinking about how, you know, how you said a... a Presence wouldn't let go of you," Sylvia said.

"Yes."

"Faith, I wish I could believe in God. Believe me, I wish I could believe in some benevolent Creator, but I can't. Not when I see a kid sitting in juvie court for stealing groceries or a pair of shoes because his mother is gone, working two jobs that still doesn't pay the bills."

Sylvia was ramming beans into the jars like bullets into

a revolver. Her face was deep red, her gaze cold and fixed. She filled six jars in a couple of minutes.

"How can a supposedly compassionate God, some great architect, allow such injustice?"

"That is the question of the ages, isn't it?" Faith replied. "Sylvia, I am so grateful that you are there in the flesh and blood to care for these children and I know it must be excruciating for you to see the distrust in their young faces. How can they survive in such an unfair world?"

She helped Sylvia pack the rest of the jars and load them into the warm water bath of the pressure cooker.

Faith continued, "I wish I had the answer you want, Honey. What I know is more of an experience than an answer. Set the pressure cooker to twelve pounds and then come out here in the yard. I want to show you something."

Sylvia clamped the thick, stainless-steel lid into place. After the pot had steamed for a few minutes, she turned the burner on low and dialed the valve on the Presto to twelve. She wiped her hands on the green checked dishtowel lying on the counter.

A gentle breeze greeted her as she stepped out onto the front porch. The cooking had made the kitchen hotter and more humid than the out of doors. Faith was in the garden pinching the eager budding heads off the basil plants.

"I can hardly keep up with these guys as fast as they are trying to bolt."

Faith tossed the pruned bits of basil into the compost bin at the east side of the garden, then looped her arm around Sylvia's elbow and guided her to the small grove of fruit trees just down the hill from the garden. They came to an old peach tree whose trunk was split down the middle; the two sides splayed on the ground. The splintered insides suggested that a violent cleaving had occurred some years before.

"Twister barely touched down here about five years ago. I was incredibly lucky that the house was spared. But this old girl was split in two, snapped in a second."

Sylvia looked at the dead gnarled half trunks that lay on their backs, the places where they touched the earth already reabsorbed into its substance. They formed two beautiful arcs bowing to the ground, like a buried heart with only the top half exposed. The brown bark was coarse and lifeless except for the lichen that scavenged the surface.

"What do you see?" Faith asked.

"I see a dead tree," Sylvia responded.

"What else?" Faith asked.

"You mean the new tree?"

In the center, at the crux of its shattered base, a new trunk had risen. It was almost six feet tall now and the leaves of its branches were a hearty green. At the tip of one branch was the first fuzzy nubbin of a new peach.

"So what did you do, Faith, plant a new tree when the old one died?"

"No, I didn't do anything," Faith replied. "Its own life did that."

Sylvia was quiet. Faith stood next to her in silence for a full minute.

"I guess what I am saying is, I don't know how a person cannot believe in God when there's resurrection around us all the time," Faith said. "That may not be an answer, but it is what I know, even if I don't understand how or why it happens."

MISSISSIPPI 1931

Delsey inked the last of the month's receipts into the green lined ledger and stowed it, with the locked cash box, in the steel floor safe. She heaved the door closed and heard the resonant clunk as she swung the handle down. Dust danced like glitter in the late afternoon sun streaming in from the high windows of the Trading Post office.

It had been a year since she moved to Hattiesburg, and it looked like Hardee's business might begin to break even by January. She had worked hard and felt she was part of something here, even if it was not the family of her own she so vividly imagined. Delsey took dinner most days at the Wiggins' table, flanked by Faith and Grace and the circle of the other sisters. Schools and businesses in Hattiesburg took an hour and half break in the middle of the day for the main meal. Walking to and from home fired the appetite and aided the digestion. Brett would arrive at the last minute, just in time to join hands for the blessing and then excuse himself early to get to his afternoon job. His senior year in high school took him to early classes in the morning and vocational education in the afternoon. He earned a small amount of money as an auto mechanic apprentice, a practical skill he sought in pursuit of his dream to become a pilot and aeronautical engineer. Delsey recalled one summer afternoon earlier that year when she was outside with Brett as a barnstormer flew over.

He looked up and proclaimed with absolute certainty, 'I'll be up there someday!' He believed he could declare his destiny, and she watched as he prepared, of late, to test his wings and fly his parents' nest.

Today, Delsey had skipped dinner, packing herself an apple and two egg salad sandwiches instead. She was in a hurry to finish her work. She turned from the oak desk to the bed in the corner of the office. A battered black leather suitcase was already packed for her trip. Next to it rested a wooden milk crate, filled with jars of butter beans and black-eyed peas that she and Maudie had put up just the day before. They had canned the last of the garden's fall harvest, and with the balance of the summer's bounty and a little care, it should last them the winter.

Delsey had intended to find a nice room in a boarding house as soon as she was settled in Hattiesburg. But all the Negro houses were situated in an isolated quarter north of town, a good three miles from the Trading Post. It was too far to walk each day and the thought of hopping a freight car morning and night didn't sit well with her. She contented herself to stay in her office bedroom at the store. This saved her money and effort but cost her a keen loneliness blunted only by the companionship of her books and the alley cats that moused for her in exchange for water and occasional scraps of food.

She finally convinced Hardee to give her two weeks off to go back to Montgomery for Thanksgiving. Delsey had not seen her family since she left Macon County and she was as thirsty for them as a honeybee for nectar. She wrote to them weekly and got the occasional letter back. Jesse and Tobias had managed to bring in a record cotton crop that year through a combination of daring and luck. First, they had decided to sharecrop an extra forty acres. Then they experimented with an early maturing variety of cotton developed to outrace the boll weevil to harvest. When God blessed them with the best weather conditions in recent memory, they ended up with nearly a hundred pounds of cotton per acre, almost double a normal season. The final stroke of luck was that they had secured an advance contract for their crop from the eager owner of a new ginning mill in early May, just before the glut of cotton on the market sent prices plummeting. Tobias finally realized his lifelong dream that summer when he put a down payment on his own piece of land. Delsey was going home for the biggest Thanksgiving celebration in Clemons history.

With her purse slung over her shoulder, she gathered her suitcase and the crate from the bed and placed them in a small wooden wagon. She looked around to reassure herself that she had left everything in good order for Hardee, picked up the note she had written him and walked to the front of the store. The cash register rang a loud brassy call as it opened. She tucked the note in the twenty-dollar slot, knowing that was the first place Hardee would look, so familiar were their ways of working together. Delsey turned out the lights, found the handle to the wagon and locked the door behind her.

Standing at the ticket booth of the Southern Railway depot minutes later, she was told that the train to Montgomery via Selma had lost its engine and a replacement wasn't likely for two or three days. Two passenger cars, one for Whites and one for Colored, were being added to a freight train down to Gulfport on the old Gulf and Ship Island line and would be switched there to the tail end of the renowned Crescent Limited. The exclusive green and gold, all-Pullman train from New Orleans to New York had agreed to pull two extra cars as far as Montgomery. She could buy a ticket on that car, but it would not arrive in Montgomery until early the following morning. There were no sleeping berths, and Negro passengers were forbidden from leaving their car except at the stations along the route.

Delsey fished through her coin purse for the two dollar and fifty cent fare. She had heard about the Crescent Limited with its dining cars and club cars, the Pintsch gaslights ornamenting the halls, and hot and cold running water throughout the train. There was even a library car with black walnut bookcases lining the walls. People would gather in the club car to smoke and converse in salon-like fashion. She tried not to linger over the knowledge that, had she been White, she could be sleeping in a berth and dining in one of the most luxurious trains in America for just a dollar more. The silver coins jingled as she dropped them into the tray below the cashier's window.

"Okay, a ticket to Montgomery then, please," she nodded. She asked if he would store the wagon until her return.

"Glad to, Ma'am. Sorry about the detour. I hope you have a nice trip," the young station clerk smiled from beneath his green visor as he pushed the ticket into the tray. His olive skin and taut brown curls betrayed an immigrant's face.

"You never know," he added with a boyish wink, "This may be your lucky ticket."

Delsey waited on a wooden bench in the shade of an old oak next to the boarding platform. The smell of the coal-fired engine stung her nose as the freight train pulled into the Hattiesburg station. From behind the half-opened doors of boxcars and perched on the tops of flatbeds loaded with lumber, peered the hungry eyes of displaced teens wandering through the aftermath of the Great Depression. They carried with them only a bindle of their belongings and the hope that work awaited them just around the bend. Delsey had come to know many of these young hobos, who would show up at the Wiggins' back porch at dinnertime, looking for a job or a meal. Maudie always fed them, if only a lump of buttered bread to take with them. But sometimes, if the family had finished eating, Maudie would invite the young man to sit down at the small table on the back porch while Delsey did the dishes. With a mother's heartache, she would listen to his story, as he spoke of the hardship that had driven him from home, parents grown short-tempered by lack of food or work, or pleading for forgiveness as they kicked their young from the nest at the age of fifteen. When he had finished eating, she would hold the grimy cups of his hands and ask him to pray with her.

The old bull at the Hattiesburg station was now patrolling the boarding platform, billy club swinging loosely at his side. In his case it was just for show, too softhearted to enforce his policing function with these young men. If the hobos did not panhandle in plain view and were not drunk, he turned a blind eye. By unspoken agreement, he would leave them alone if they kept to their cars and set up their camps down the line, out of sight of the depot.

It had been a vastly different story for nine young men in Paint Rock, Alabama last spring. A posse was waiting to round them up, arbitrarily arresting all the Negro stowaways on a freight train from Chattanooga to Memphis just because they had won a fair fight against some white-skinned fellow nomads, who they had tossed off the train a few miles up the line. In a matter of two weeks, the nine boys had been tried and sentenced to the electric chair in Scottsboro, Alabama for raping two White girls they never even met. A national outcry arose. Championed by the NAACP and International Labor Defense, they had won a stay of their execution by June, but their fate was still uncertain. What had become clear, though, was that a young Negro man risked his life riding the rails in the South.

Delsey watched from her bench as the train pulled all the way through the station, the caboose stopping at the near end of the boarding platform. A yard switchman jumped down from the platform and motioned to the engineer, who craned to see him from his cab in the distance. He levered the pin loose from the knuckle coupler and waved his hand again. The train jerked free. It pulled forward a couple hundred feet past the junction to a spur of rail that ran along the backside of the station. The yardman flipped the switch and the long load of cars lumbered back along the alternate track until it reached the two extra passenger cars waiting there. Twenty minutes later the cars were added and the caboose reattached, and Delsey was making her way down the aisle of the Colored car to a worn leather seat in the back. The young station clerk who had sold her the ticket offered to help when he saw her struggling with her suitcase and crate. Delsey accepted, letting him carry her crate, grateful for his kindness.

The screech of steel and lurch of the cars announced their departure. Slowly a soothing rhythm, ka thump ka thump, ka thump ka thump, set in as they rolled out of town and past the hobo jungles. She watched the lean form of an agile boy leap from the ground onto the train, snaking its way to his next great adventure. The last burst of sun radiated through the window, warming her as she grew sleepy in the rocking embrace of that old car. As she closed her eyes and drifted off, she patted the purse next to her, felt the sandwiches tucked inside. A sense of well-being enveloped her, some hint of being unusually blessed that day.

She dropped into a deep sleep and dreamed of standing in a doorway inside a plain yellow farmhouse. Her left hand rested on the shellacked maple doorframe to the dining room, and she knew she had sanded that piece of wood. She felt the gentle grasp of a toddler's arm around her right knee and reached with her right hand to stroke the soft curve of his ear. The men gathered around the table were speaking in fervent tones. The man at the head of the table glowed as if in a spotlight. He was mythically beautiful, the cut of his jaw both strong and elegant, his nose broad but elevated and the fullness of his lips almost succulent. Looking at his dark brown complexion, Delsey felt a throbbing in her womb and knew at once that he was the father of the child at her side. This doorframe, in fact, this whole house had been fashioned from the love of their hands working together. He looked at her, the urgency of the conversation swelling around him, sweat beading on his forehead. Then he smiled in private recognition, reassuring her with his warm brown eyes that everything would be all right.

She awoke to the force of gravity pulling her forward in her seat as the great iron horse pitched to a stop then slowly resumed its forward motion. It was dark outside, the moon having yet to rise, but Delsey could tell from the smell of saltwater that the train had arrived in Gulfport, the tracks winding closer to the harbor and to the station, which anchored a node of converging commerce. As they approached the lights of the boarding platform, the putrid smell of crab and shrimp greeted her from the cleaning stalls of the adjacent wharf. Lanterns illuminated a boardwalk that led to the painted hulls and weathered cabins of fishing boats.

Delsey stood up and braced herself as the train came to a final halt. Her legs needed stretching since it would be a bit of time before the Crescent Limited arrived and the cars were transferred to that train. She took her purse with her as she waited her turn to step into the aisle. A portly, ruddy-faced conductor approached from the platform as she and the other passengers exited the car. He handed them special transfer tickets as arranged and told them he would lock the car and secure their luggage until the train departed again at midnight.

She found the restroom designated for Colored women and washed her hands and face over the porcelain washbasin next to the toilet. Outside, she drank from a water fountain until her thirst was slaked, then headed to the boardwalk and the pungent pulse of moist air rolling in on the surf. A small shack that offered fresh fried fish and potatoes was still open. She splurged and bought a Coke for five cents plus the two-cent deposit and kept walking until she reached a pier at the far end of the network of walkways. A lone tugboat, dark and uninhabited, was tethered nearby. She sat beneath a lantern swinging slightly in the breeze and unpacked one of her sandwiches. She uncapped the Coke with a bottle opener nailed to the side of the pier and took a long drink, enjoying the refreshing bite of bubbles. She leaned back against the lamppost and gazed at the gibbous moon that was just rising. The remnants of her dream resurfaced, and she let herself tarry awhile with the memory of that face and the feeling in her body. She wanted to enjoy the company of her conjured lover for a bit longer before he disappeared into the subterranean vault of vanished dreams. She ate her sandwich slowly, tasting each bite. An hour or more elapsed and as the night deepened, she found herself walking the boardwalk again, the waves of high tide lapping below. The lights of a train approaching from the west illuminated the tracks ahead. She began to feel the excitement of seeing her family again, Toby and Jesse and her other siblings. A year was a long time to be without them.

A shrill whistle summoned her to the Crescent Limited, arriving from New Orleans. She watched the train pull into the station, light pouring from the windows, the frames of cozy families in sleeping berths flickering by like a movie reel slowing to a stop. The two extra passenger cars from Hattiesburg were soon attached to the back of the train behind the library car, and she stood there mesmerized peering into its opulent chamber. She could see the bookshelves faced with leaded glass doors. She reached her hand up as if she were inside the car and about to retrieve a book from the shelf.

"Best car on the train," said the rich, deep voice next to her. "It's the one place where I remember who I am."

She felt him before she saw him. She turned to face him. Although they had never met, he seemed familiar.

Beneath the round black box of his cap, its polished silver plate proclaiming him a Pullman porter, she caught the outline of his jaw, so gracefully defined. At six feet and a few inches, he had the long sinewy look of the naturally muscled, leaned by work and spare rations. The light from the car reflected the soft brown of his eyes.

"And who would that person be.... Mr. Walker?" she added after reading his name badge. Her own boldness surprised her.

"Well it certainly isn't some fellow called George, who shines the shoes of the overindulged." He removed his cap and rubbed his head, teasing loose the tight-coiled curls of his sweat-laced hair. He held the cap under his left arm and began to unbutton the blue woolen jacket of his uniform. "That fellow is just coming off duty."

"I'm Delsey Clemons and pleased to make your acquaintance."

"Sorry. Plessy, Plessy Walker." He replied, reaching out his hand and taking her in for the first time.

She was no timid slip of a woman. She came to within five inches of his height, her broad shoulders tapering to a narrow waist. Her muscled forearms betrayed a childhood as a field hand. Yet, there was something in the delicacy of her cheekbones and the elegance with which she offered her hand in return that suggested a keen intelligence. Her hazel eyes were steady, welcoming.

Gazing at her and with a light bow of his head, he added, "And I assure you, the pleasure is entirely mine."

They paused in the awkward tension of mutual attraction.

"You know, for a minute there, I felt as though I was actually inside that library car," Delsey continued. "I imagined myself standing there as the person I am meant to be. The one who would teach."

A second whistle blew announcing the final call to board. The ruddy-faced conductor waddled toward them at the end of the platform, collecting transfer tickets from the passengers from Hattiesburg. The white car boarded first. As the conductor began boarding Delsey's car, Plessy fell in line behind her.

"Coming off duty, Walker?"

"Yes, Mr. George," Plessy replied.

Delsey frowned. She thought the name George was reserved for porters named after George Pullman in the tradition of slaves named for their owners. Plessy noticed her expression.

"It's his real name," Plessy whispered into her ear, smiling, and pointing to the name badge that read George M. Bartlett, Conductor.

"How far are you headed then?" Bartlett continued.

To D.C.," Plessy returned. "Thanksgiving with my sister and her kids. And her husband, too, if he is not on call."

They walked down the aisle, all the way to the back of the car. Plessy reached up, opened a concealed compartment above the last bench, and pulled down two blankets and a worn pillow.

"You'll need some sleep, I imagine," he said, his words warming her even before he wrapped the blanket around her shoulders. "Where are you going, may I ask?"

"To Montgomery. My father just bought his own farm, only twenty acres, but a dream come true. It's going to be a real Thanksgiving this year." Delsey was wide-awake.

"You know, I'm not at all sleepy," she said, settling in next to Plessy as the train crawled out of Gulfport. "We could talk for a while."

"Or all night," he smiled softly.

"So, you never answered my question back there," Delsey ventured.

"What question was that?"

"When you are in the library car, who is it that you remember? Who is that man?"

"Well, Miss Delsey Clemons, he is a lawyer. He is a lawyer who knows that the thirteenth and fourteenth amendments to the United States Constitution were just the beginning. He's a man who knows that you and I deserve to manifest our own destinies and that it will require writing the Negro into every weave of the legal fabric of this country." He sat upright, took a deep breath then leaned back a little. He reached his right arm around Delsey and tucked the blanket around her, pulling her ever so slightly closer to him. "He's a man with big dreams."

"Go on," Delsey encouraged him. "I told you I am not the least bit sleepy. And I believe in dreams." She nestled closer as the image of the yellow farmhouse danced forth from her memory, mesmerizing her like the warm flames of a fire in the hearth.

MISSISSIPPI 1931

Maudie walked into the bedroom for a second time only to find the younger girls still snuggled together beneath the quilts, the frame of the large brass bed dwarfing their small bodies. She walked to the end of the bed and grabbed one leg of each and shook gently.

"You girls are going to be late for school if you don't get up right this minute," she admonished with half-hearted seriousness. Truth was she could seldom muster any real anger towards these two.

Faith popped her head out from under the covers and rubbed her eyes, her long blonde eyelashes amplifying their deep blue.

"OK, Mama, I'm getting up," she chirped as she slid out of bed, searching the floor with her feet for her slippers.

Grace opened one eye, then closed it and rolled over with her back to Maudie.

"I don't go to school," she tried.

"Well, yes you do, little Missy. Kindergarten is school and the tardy bell will be ringing in less than an hour, so get up and bathe and come to breakfast or I'll just have to throw you in the washing machine with those quilts this morning." Maudie tickled her until Grace finally started to laugh and sat up in the bed.

Faith loved school. Her third-grade teacher remarked to Hardee and Maudie at the last PTA meeting that Faith was clearly gifted with intelligence, as her IQ tests showed. The teacher had prepared a long list of rather challenging books for her to read at home and Faith relished them. Grace, on the other hand, was none too happy about leaving the warm comfort of her mother's skirts to venture into the world of concrete demands. She preferred the dreamy realm of her dolls and their teapots to the rigors of the three R's. Faith tugged the slippers onto her feet and walked around the end of the bed to the other side. She pulled the covers back from around her little sister and put her arms out to help her down.

"Come on Gracie, let's go get a bath. You'll like it when you get to school, remember?" she encouraged.

"No, I don't remember, and I don't need help," she replied as she spun her legs toward the side of the bed, then rolled over onto her stomach and slid off, holding on to the sheets until her tiptoes touched the ground.

Maudie smiled as she watched the two pad off to the bathroom, Faith's hair in an angry mess at the crown of her head and Grace's nightgown hitched up over her bottom.

"Don't forget to brush your hair, Faith," she added with affection as she turned and walked into the hallway leading to the dining room.

"OK, Mama," the bright little voice called back from the other room.

In the dining room, Hannah sat in her highchair corralling her Rice Krispies into a little posse then eating a handful at a time, half of them spilling back onto the tray. The older girls, Claire and Delta, were finishing their breakfast, in a hurry to catch their bus to the junior high school. Brett was already gone, having left with Hardee at dawn to help him with some crates at the Trading Post before going to class.

Mornings were always a little chaotic in the Wiggins' house. Maudie would get up first, in the last of the still dark night, to start breakfast. Hardee had promised her a gas stove even before they had left Alabama, but that was before the run on the banks and the collapse of the economy. Such a luxury had not even been a thought since moving to Hattiesburg. The Trading Post had not turned a profit yet. Tough times meant hard work, and Maudie got up early to bring in the wood and fire up the old cast iron stove. The spent ashes from the night before had to be shoveled out and carted off. Paper and kindling had to be coaxed to a flame and wood judiciously added before a sufficient fire was roaring. Often, Delsey would come down from the shop for breakfast and she would end up helping Maudie, but she had left the day before for Alabama to celebrate Thanksgiving with her family. Maudie always served breakfast in waves, eggs and bacon for Hardee and Brett, then cereal and biscuits for the girls in two separate shifts. Classes at the junior high school started a half hour earlier than the primary school, so Claire and Delta ate first, then Emma, Faith and Grace. Their staggered schedules gave Maudie extra time to get everyone ready for the day.

She and Hardee were both working from early morning until late at night just to survive. There were nine mouths to feed, and Ava, her husband Cecil, and the baby would drop by at mealtime more often than not, making it an even dozen. Maudie rejoiced in having all her children around her despite the extra work, but she was seeing less and less of Hardee as he spent long hours at the store.

When he did come home, she could smell the bootleg whiskey on him as soon as he came near. They had more than one argument about the sin of intemperance. She genuinely believed that whiskey was a tool of the devil. She already felt the wedge of it driving her and Hardee apart, especially when he bent forward to kiss her at night with his stale breath. Between her fear of getting pregnant again, now that Hannah was toddling, and her abhorrence of Hardee's drinking, she had begun to leave the marriage bed and sleep most nights by herself on a small cot in the screened-in porch. She was not sure how they had come to this. As she emerged from the long hall into the dining room, she tried to push the troubles with him out of her mind.

"Thank you for watching Hannah, girls," she said to Claire and Delta. "I got the little ones up so y'all get on down to the bus stop. I love you so much and you be careful, OK? By the way, have you seen Emma?"

"I think she ran over to Miss Ruth's," mumbled Claire, as she stuffed the last half of her biscuit into her mouth and picked up her books to leave.

"Lawd, I will never tame that child," moaned Maudie.

She walked out the front door with Claire and Delta and waved as they turned right onto the sidewalk. Maudie started across the street to Ruth's but just as she reached the curb, she saw Emma hightailing it home from the field next to the Moody's house. When she got within earshot, Maudie let her have it.

"Young lady, you get in this house before I have your hide. What have you been doing? You are supposed to be dressed and ready for school."

"Nothin'. I ain't done nothin' and I am ready for school.

Just need my breakfast."

Maudie looked at her closely and could see that she was dressed in the plaid jumper and cotton shirt that Maudie had ironed for her the night before, but Emma's collar was askew, and the sleeves of her shirt were full of fresh wrinkles. One of her mud splattered saddle oxfords was missing its shoelace.

"First of all, it isn't 'ain't', and if I find you've been hiding overalls in the Moody's field again, we're going to have another come-to-Jesus. Where is your shoelace?"

"Dunno."

Maudie had no way of knowing that Emma had used it to tie up her handkerchief, full of new marbles procured just that morning. The handkerchief and marbles were stuffed in a new hiding place, along with her overalls. Emma traded Buck Beasley an old pocketknife that Brother had given her, freshly oiled and honed, for five Cat's eyes, two aggies, a purie, an oxblood and the new shooter, a big round steely. She loved the cold smooth feel of that steely, the heft of it propped on her thumb and nestled atop the curved knuckle of her finger.

"Don't know," Maudie admonished. "Well you'll just have to tie up your shoe with twine this morning because I don't have any spare laces. There's a roll of it on the workbench under the carport. You can get it after you eat. Now go on inside and get your breakfast." She gave her a firm but painless pat on the rear as she ushered her onto the sidewalk and into the house.

Although Maudie understood the point of 'spare the rod, spoil the child' she had never been able to abide the tenor of it. Her faith in Our Heavenly Father was stronger because it had been negotiated by free will, and she believed that a child's moral compass should be oriented not by the fear of God, but by the love of her earthly mother.

Back in the dining room, Faith and Grace assembled themselves at the table and were teaching Hannah new words.

"Light!" Grace said as she pointed to the lamp hanging over the table. "Say Light."

"Yite," Hannah parroted, holding up a lone Rice Krispy between her plump thumb and forefinger, as if to feed it to the inanimate brass and glass fixture suspended overhead.

Maudie and Emma walked into the dining room and Emma plopped down in the seat next to Grace.

"You smell like a cat's patootie," Grace said, wrinkling her nose. She had heard the phrase on the playground at school, used to taunt one of the country kids who carried the fetid smell of the chronically unbathed, who lived in a house with no indoor plumbing. She was not sure what a 'cat's patootie' was or what it smelled like. Grace was simply responding to the scent of Emma's ripe, prepubescent sweat after the sprint across the Fletcher's field and whatever else she had been up to.

"Shut up," piped Emma.

"You shut up."

Faith looked at them from across the table and held up her right index finger to her lips and whispered,

"Shush. Don't let Mama hear you." It wasn't clear if she was protecting her mother from the bickering or her sisters from a scolding.

Maudie had disappeared into the kitchen and returned momentarily with three steaming bowls of Cream of Wheat. She put the pink porcelain bowls on the white linen placemats in front of each girl, then carved a generous slab of butter from the block in the middle of the table and dropped equal portions into each bowl. She used her fingers to crumble a light sprinkling of brown sugar onto the top of their cereal.

"Emma, would you please pour everyone a glass of milk," Maudie instructed, "and I'll go get Hannah's cereal and the rest of the biscuits and honey."

Emma complied, silently but willingly, grateful that she had apparently gotten off light for her morning's transgressions. She felt fairly sure that Maudie would never find her overalls, hidden in the hollow of an old oak, so she planned to sneak over after school and change clothes before she went to play in the woods by the creek. That is, if she didn't have homework that her mother discovered first. Emma was plenty smart for the work of fifth grade and could complete her homework in short order. It's just that she had better things to do. The Jasper boys had built a tree house deep in the woods with a rope ladder that could be pulled up after they climbed in. But she knew the magic whistle and they always let the rope down for her when she called. She had won their favor by bringing them the plundered treasure from her father's collecting dish on the hall tree that stood in the small foyer of the house…. the trimmed remnant of a half cigar, a pocketful of peppermints, or the gleaming copper from a new roll of pennies. Hardee ignored the minor thefts. Emma put the glasses of milk in front of Grace and Faith and they each poured a little into their bowls of Cream of Wheat, stirring it into a wet swirl. They ate with hearty appetites.

Maudie reappeared from the kitchen again and set the plate of biscuits on the table. Then she sat down and fed Hannah from the small baby bowl full of cereal and applesauce. For a few minutes, the dining room was quiet except for muted ring of spoons against bowls, or the occasional smacking sound when a large bite of biscuit proved too big for an eager little mouth. When they had all finished eating, the girls wiped their hands and mouths and went to their rooms to collect their schoolbooks. Maudie slid the tray off the highchair and unclasped the strap around Hannah's waist. She lifted her out of the chair and perched her on her right hip. She met the girls at the front door and inspected them to make sure they had their sweaters on and books in hand. The elementary school was only a few blocks away and the girls always walked to school. But the temperature was beginning to drop now that November had arrived.

"Now keep together on the way to school and don't dawdle on the way home for your dinner. I love you, love you, love you," she said, giving each girl a kiss as she balanced Hannah. "See you at noon."

"Mama, will Delsey be here for dinner?" Grace asked.

"No, darlin', she went back to Montgomery to see her family for a little while. Remember? She'll be back soon."

"What are you going to do this morning, Mama?" Grace asked, stalling.

"I'm going to have my devotional, Sweetie, like I always do, every morning."

Maudie was already relishing the hour she would have after she put Hannah down for her morning nap. In that blessedly still time of morning, with the children in school and Hannah asleep, she found an hour, a whole hour, to read the Bible and listen for guidance from her Lord. Before the chores and cooking and the return of her flock with homework and skinned knees and stories of their day, she took one hour for herself.

"Mama?" Grace twisted the toe of her right shoe into a crack in the green floorboards of the front porch.

"I know what you're doing, little Gracie, but you have to go to school anyway," Maudie said, with a twinge of guilt. "Emma, I want you to hold Gracie's hand all the way to school today."

Emma took Grace's hand and led her down the steps to the sidewalk. Faith waited a moment until the others were just out of hearing range, then she pulled on her mother's sleeve.

"Mama," she said with a look of deep consideration, "Now, I know why you named me Faith."

Maudie met her eyes but didn't answer.

"You named me Faith because your devotional is the most important thing in the world to you. Nothing matters more than your faith in God."

Maudie smiled because it was true. It was her anchor and Faith knew that. Although parents purport they never have favorites among their children, there is often one they are hopelessly in love with. And just as Delta had curried her father's favor, so Faith had won Maudie's heart from the moment she was born.

"Well, I think you may be right, and I think you are a very smart and wise girl. I love you with all my heart. Now go catch up to your sisters and have fun at school."

She watched Faith skip down the sidewalk until she reached Emma and Grace, watched them until they rounded the corner at the end of the block and were out of sight. Then she went into the house with a dozing Hannah on her hip to find her coffee and her Bible, and her hour all to herself.

~

"Can we hurry it up, Dad? I need to meet with Mr. Bullard before class this morning."

Brett fought to blunt the edge in his voice as they brought the last of the crates in from the loading dock. The fabricated meeting with his physics teacher was a ruse to buy a little time with his girl, Justine. Between school, his afternoon job, and Hardee's baffling new possessiveness, he felt like he never saw her. She was a dark-haired Cajun gal, full of Tabasco and filé spice and he felt certain he was going to marry her one day. He longed to walk beside her this morning, to brush against her hip as he draped his arm around the curve of her waist, his body rising to full attention.

Why had his dad insisted on his help this morning? It did not seem necessary. The rail hands would drop by on their way to work soon and, as always, were willing to trade their brawn for the prospect of a little of Fletcher Moody's home brew that Hardee kept stashed at the store. Ever since Brett applied to the Georgia School of Technology aeronautical engineering program, Hardee had been fussing over him like a mother hen.

"You know Delsey's gone, and I have to make a list of all this stuff!" Hardee groused back. "I'm here from dawn to dusk as it is, son. I ain't asking for much, just a helping hand now and then."

"I know Dad, but I gotta go. The guys from the rail yard can help you unpack the crate."

The crate held the booty Hardee gleaned from the recent estate sale of another bankrupt cotton merchant, who had risked his profits on the market and lost. Hardee purchased the best remnants of an entire life's work for a song. The salvaged parts of a new International Harvester, a thrown rod having crippled the engine; ornate chandeliers and wall sconces; mule harnesses and gang plows; the diaphanous drapes from a lady's sitting room and a claw footed tub with its brass fixtures. Hardee was close to turning a profit within a year of opening the Trading Post, by working deals just like this against all odds. He worked sixteen hours a day and seldom saw his wife or kids awake except at dinnertime or supper. At night, after the evening meal, he would return to close the shop and take his time nursing his three fingers of whiskey. Fletcher Moody had a gift for turning corn mash into gold and he and Hardee had become friends. He sold a little of Fletcher's brew from the shop in exchange for his free share. At first, he had been careful, allowing himself only a little taste each night, one neat finger. But over the year, as he worked longer and harder, one finger became two, then three until he was a little sloppy by the time he locked up the Trading Post and headed home to his sleeping family. He had to wrestle with the devil every morning, but at night he found refuge in the bottle. It soothed the ache in his aging muscles and the growing loneliness in his heart.

"All right, go. Get on out of here if you're in such a damn hurry. But don't be late for your mother's supper tonight."

The bell jingled as the front door opened. Hardee turned away from their bristling conversation and went to greet the visitor.

"Jeez-us," Brett muttered under his breath and turned in the opposite direction.

He walked into the back office to retrieve his coat, glad to think the guys from the Southern had arrived and would occupy his dad while he slipped past them and out the front door. If he ran fast enough, he would be able to catch Justine before his first class.

But as he approached the front of the store, he was surprised to find the alluring figure of a well-heeled woman bent seductively over the front counter, a round mahogany bar Hardee had confiscated from an old speakeasy. His father was standing on the other side unlocking the cash register. She stood on her right leg with her left knee bent at a coy angle, her elbows resting on the counter, her gloved hands clasping the far edge. The calf of her left leg tapered exquisitely to its delicate ankle, extended in submission to the high heels she wore.

Hardee looked up without lifting his head and met her gaze, unable to suppress the boyish grin tugging at the corners of his mouth. Then he glanced past her to see his son returning from the back of the store, shock registering on Brett's face. Hardee stood up and assumed a business-like stance, telegraphing his caution to the woman, who glanced back to see Brett off to her side. She shifted her weight equally to both feet and pushed back from the counter. She smoothed the imaginary wrinkles out of the front of her dress as Brett watched, mesmerized.

"Mr. Wiggins," she ventured, smiling demurely, "I was just hopin' to see that candelabra you told me was comin' from Vicksburg. You know the electric one that hangs from the ceiling?"

Brett lost track of time standing there next to the crates in the front office, watching Hardee's spirits lift in front of this woman.

"Well, it is most certainly in one of those crates, Miss Styles," Hardee said, motioning in Brett's direction, "but

I won't have it unpacked until late this morning if you want to come back then." Hardee emerged from behind the counter and came around to her side, gently grasping her elbow as if to usher her out of the store. But she lingered.

"I was also hopin' you would be able to come by the house yourself and hang the thing, seein's how I don't know a thing about electricity and all."

Brett's mind and body were a conflagration of confusion. He could not take his eyes off this woman, the perfectly symmetrical opposing curves of breast and bottom, beckoning from beneath the red silk dress clinging to her like a jealous lover. And was he imagining it or did his father seem to know this woman? Maybe she was a good customer. She clearly had means. But he detected something else.

"I'll do it," Brett blurted out. "I could come by this afternoon after work and wire the chandelier myself." He thought of his mother at home getting the girls ready for school, stealing an hour for her devotional before spending two hours in the kitchen preparing dinner for the nine of them.

"I can do it today, Miss....is it Styles?" Brett continued.

Hardee and Miss Styles stood next to each other and stared at Brett with bewilderment. Their bodies had stiffened into mannequin-like poses and they were equally mute. Brett suddenly remembered Justine and their promise to meet before school. He pulled the watch on its chain from his pocket.

Hardee finally spoke from his frozen stance.

"That's OK, son, you run on to school before you're late. I'll get one of the rail hands to help Miss Styles out this afternoon." He could see the worry in his son's eyes, the fear that Hardee had betrayed his marriage.

"I promise," Hardee added with weak reassurance.

"OK, Dad, OK. I'll see you at dinner then. And it was nice to meet you, Miss.... Styles," he added. He searched his father's eyes for the briefest second before heading for the door.

"Tell Mr. Bullard to get that letter off to the Georgia Tech today," Hardee commanded, having resumed his fatherly posture. "And tell Justine to join us for Sunday dinner this weekend," he smiled. "She a wonderful girl, Brett."

Brett didn't look back, the bell jangling loudly as the door closed behind him.

MISSISSIPPI 1998

The two-lane highway stretched straight and taut across the flat alluvial plains of the Delta. Sylvia passed field upon field of spent cornstalks, parched brown and ready for harvest. They evoked thoughts in her mind of soldiers caught stock-still in the exact moment of their deaths.

She drove with one hand on the wheel, her left arm draped loosely over the driver's door, fingers tapping out the rhythm of the radio's blues beat against the side of the car. She was savoring the past two weeks with Faith. Their time together had expanded to the point of forgetfulness, where the luxury of conversation amidst the leisurely pace of tending house and garden had knocked the hands right off the clock. They had gardened and cooked, repaired screen doors and faucets, all the while pondering the unsolvable. As usual, Faith had displayed an easy mix of empathy and humor and a firm conviction that one can trust in the unseen. Sylvia was not so sure. She still considered religion a self-soothing invention that dismissed all suffering as a part of some bigger plan. How could the hungry faces and empty shops in ghost towns like Yazoo City be part of anybody's plan? But what was it Faith had said about resurrection being around us all the time?

Sylvia decided to take an extra day to drive home, angling towards Clarksdale before heading south. She wanted to stand at the crossroads of US highways 61 and 49 and imagine the strains of "Dust my Broom" flying off the strings of Robert Johnson's guitar some sixty years before. To find deliverance in the sung soul of that ramblin' man and his mentor Son House. She had heard of a juke joint outside of Clarksdale and resolved she would allow herself a beer or two to accompany an evening of music. She reasoned it was safe after her two-week abstinence at Faith's, but the memory of her night in Baton Rouge, the recklessness, still spooked her. It had been more than concern about Faith, or the rugged parting with Joe.

Sylvia missed Joe today. He would understand her detour here. This music was as alive in him as it was in her. They had talked every couple of days while she was in Florence, and he was warm, listening deeply to her stories. Flying down the road to Clarksdale, Sylvia wanted him by her side, wanted to find a cabin with a clean bed and make love all night long. She needed to wake up to the sound of him playing harmonica on the front porch, his steady calming tunes drawing her in, embracing her, jagged edges and all. Her passion for him came in spurts like this, when she knew in the deepest part of herself that she would not find a better man. Sylvia had met him a few months after returning from New York, just after her thirty-ninth birthday, fresh off the skids of having brokered her future for the sake of a man whose self-interest was supreme. Joe was the opposite of Jack; interested, and supportive of Sylvia. But early on he had pushed her to have a family. Sylvia would never consider it. She had her chance to be a mother when she was eighteen, and she had passed on it. Even after five years, Joe persisted, in a quiet sort of way. Sylvia knew she was keeping him from being the father he was meant to be. But how could she let him go? She pushed the question aside and focused on the road ahead.

When she came to a small town, consisting of a traffic light and a couple of grain elevators, Sylvia pulled into a gas station, stopped next to the pump and put the nozzle in the tank. She left it to run while she stepped off to the side to call home. Joe didn't answer and she was just leaving a message telling him where she was and what she had been thinking about, when he picked up the phone somewhat breathless.

"Hello."

"Hey Hon, it's me," Sylvia said.

"Hey. I didn't hear the phone. I was outside unloading the truck."

She could imagine the sweat coursing down his lean muscular arms.

"God, it's good to hear your voice," she gushed, surprising them both. "I wish you were here with me right now. We'd have ribs and beer for dinner with a side of blues and then each other all night long."

"Is that a real invitation?" he asked.

"Yes, come right now!" she replied in a tone somewhere between plea and command.

"Nothing like absence to make the fond grow harder," he chuckled. "How about this, I'll come with you next trip."

"Good idea! Are you busy?"

"Yeah. I'm slammed today finishing up the new corral but it will give us a couple of free days when you get back."

"I love you, Joe."

"I love you, too, Sylvia, and I'm glad you're almost home."

"See you tomorrow night."

"OK, Babe, I'll be here."

Sylvia turned back towards the car and saw the gas station attendant replacing the nozzle in the pump.

"This your car?" he asked.

"Yes. I was just making a call."

"Well, you can't just leave it unattended like that. You need to pay up and move it. There's other people needin' the pump."

Sylvia looked around. There was not another car in sight except for the old truck parked next to the gas station. And she saw that the pump registered only six gallons, half a tank.

"And that will be two dollars for the service. I washed the windows and finished pumping the gas for you."

"What?" Sylvia was puzzled. She hadn't requested any such service.

"Two dollars lady, plus eight for the gas."

"But I didn't ask you to wash my windows."

"What, you want me to wait on you for free?"

"No, I...."

"I ain't your boy." He stood up taller, daring her response.

She suddenly knew she was unwelcomed here with her Ray-Bans and sports car and implied privilege. But she was defiant in her innocence.

"I would never say or even think that sir! And could I be permitted to finish filling up my tank?"

"Nope. Pump's shut down. That'll be ten dollars," he said, not budging.

She stood there, frustrated, unable to bridge the distance between them. He held out his hand and she placed a ten-dollar bill in it. He turned and walked back into the office, never looking back.

She felt a wave of nausea as she drove off the gravel onto

the pavement. Her very being seemed to have offended the station attendant, although her defensiveness certainly had not helped. She ruminated about it, trying to dismiss her growing humiliation by understanding that this was the consequence of a near century of Jim Crow. It was her turn to feel unwelcome. It made some sense, but she could not stop wrestling with herself. She worked every day to fight for the neglected, she told herself. She found ways to preserve families who had to choose between parenting and a paycheck. Over half of her clients were Black or Hispanic. She wasn't the bad guy here. She did not discriminate. Right? So why did she feel so guilty? Why had it been so hard to thank the guy for his service and simply pay him for it?

The speedometer registered almost eighty miles per hour before she realized she was speeding. The heaviness in her stomach solidified into a leaden lump. She pulled to the side of the road and turned off the engine, looked out over the fields planted with cotton and felt the hardship of this place. This land held the suffering that stretched back over three centuries to the bitter roots of slavery, a living hell her people had wrought. The violence against the Black body could be felt in these fields. She wanted to wiggle out of that feeling, banish the human sadness buried in this soil, fertilizing this very crop of cotton. But she sat there instead until the constriction in her chest eased. She let the sadness wash over her. Her mother's ancestors never owned slaves, primarily because they didn't have the wealth. But they treated their 'Colored help' as servants. They were as culpable for their demeaning beliefs and for turning a blind eye as were those who inflicted physical cruelty. She understood the debt Faith wanted to repay, even if it was impossible. When her breath began to flow again, she whispered something akin to a prayer. 'May justice be served and healing found'. She did not try to contemplate what she was praying to. She pulled back onto the highway, determined to do her part by honoring Faith's wishes.

It was just past six p.m. when Sylvia finally arrived in Clarksdale. She wondered if Faith's recollection of McLeod Walker's whereabouts was current. 'Last I heard he was living near Clarksdale'. Sylvia decided she would look him up in the phonebook, not that she intended to call him tonight. Having made no reservation ahead of time, Sylvia needed to find a room for the night. She followed Highway 49 into the center of town, passing under a concrete railroad trestle. She turned off the main road and meandered through side streets, past houses lacking for trees or hope of renewal. The streets had a quiet, vacant feeling. There was no cozy sense of families sheltering themselves from the late summer heat or gathered in kitchens to cook supper in a humble, but beloved home. Standing out among the houses on the right was a plain red brick building, framed by a box hedge. A wooden sign reading 'Hellbound Hotel' swung leisurely from the porch. A smaller "Vacancy" sign hung from the right corner. Sylvia pulled up to the curb and looked it over. Not her typical digs but the spirit of the place, some faint music on the wind, attracted her.

She parked on the street and walked up the grass path to the hotel. The screen door creaked as she opened it, the front door propped open to let a breeze through the building. An office was tucked in an alcove down a short hallway. The proprietor sat behind a roll top desk, a green shaded lamp on the top. When Sylvia appeared, he stood to greet her. The bit of hair he had left was a soft gray, matching his neatly trimmed beard.

"May I help you?" he asked. His smile was genuine, amplified by the fine lines at the corners of his eyes.

"I need a room for the night," Sylvia replied, looking around.

"Well we specialize in rooms and have one available if you want to see it."

"Yes, please," she said. The runner beneath her feet emitted a faint mustiness, the smell of time passing.

"This place must have quite a story."

"More stories than I could tell you in a month of Sundays, Miss...."

"Barbarino."

"Raymond, Raymond Jackson," he said extending his hand. "Yessum, Miss Barbarino, this place is downright alive with stories. It has been home to some of the greatest blues players ever to gather at the crossroads. John Lee, Muddy, Sonny Boy, B.B. Even Bessie, herself."

He escorted her down a hallway to the left and stopped at the door to room eight. He slipped the brass key into the lock. The latch opened with a clunk, the door swinging back under its own weight and the slight tilt to the floor. The room was simply appointed with a double bed covered in a chenille spread, a bedside table and lamp and small rocking chair in the corner.

"Sounds like you know some of those stories firsthand," Sylvia said.

"Yes indeed, Miss Barbarino, yes indeed. I have lived in this house for sixty years, been running the hotel for twenty, since my mama suffered her first stroke. But she's a fighter, God bless her. Still gets around."

"I'll take the room," Sylvia said, without hesitation, not even sure if she had a private bath. "And you'll have to tell me some of those stories."

The old man's smile filled his face.

"You may not want to get me started," he laughed, then returned to the business at hand. "There's a shared bath with room seven, but nobody's in there tonight, so you get yourself a private bath."

"Now that's a luxury, id'n it?" she said, an ancestral accent slipping from her tongue.

"Pure luxury," he replied.

As they returned to the front desk, Sylvia inquired about a place to eat, preferably brisket, and the whereabouts of the juke joint she'd heard of. The hotel owner told her about Boolie's Barbeque, a restaurant a couple of miles out of town along the railroad tracks and Maizie's bar another mile or so past that. He told her that the music at Maizie's would not really get going until about ten o'clock, not 'til night started to cool things down. He suggested Sylvia might want to go eat, then come back and rest up a bit before her night out.

She thanked him and paid in advance before heading out. She drove the short distance past the edge of town and found Boolie's with no problem. The place was hopping, being a Saturday night, and she was told it would be at least a half hour before a table opened up. She ordered a brisket plate to go and found a small park nearby where she polished off the meal with surprising hunger. Sated and a bit sleepy, she headed back to the hotel for a bath and a nap before going to Maizie's.

By the time she arrived at the blues bar, the sun had

long relented its hold on the day and the band was warmed up and stoking the crowd. The audience was a mixed lot, some locals, and a fair number of pale-skinned pilgrims. She paid her five-dollar cover and took a seat at the bar.

"Thanks for coming out tonight," crooned the lead singer, bending over his guitar into the microphone.

"Umm huh," the crowd murmured back.

The drummer began a slow one, two, one, two beat. "You ready for some music?" the guitar player continued.

"Yeah."

"You ready for some blues?"

"Yeah!"

"OK, well we're going to start off with a little B.B. King, then see where we go from there."

He slid into the first plaintive rift of "The Thrill is Gone" and Sylvia ordered a beer. The bartender pulled her a draft with a perfect one-inch head. She enjoyed the icy bitter taste of the first sip. She settled onto the hard wooden seat of the stool and leaned into the leather covered bar rail as the music began to swell and fill the room. A woman in her late sixties, perhaps straddling seventy, pulled up a stool in front of her. It had a padded, albeit compressed, seat atop the wooden frame.

"Lost most of my own natural cushion," she smiled, patting her backside as she settled onto the softened stool.

The woman's hair was as thick as winter wheat and plaited in a perfect French braid, the ample swaths of lustrous silver carefully partitioned by small colored clips. As she turned to introduce herself, her smile unmasked a much younger beauty still visible through the loosening that comes with age.

"I'm Louise," she said, offering a sturdy hand.

"Your hair is beautiful," Sylvia replied, returning the handshake, and wishing for a moment that her own name was Thelma, because certainly this character before her could have inspired that movie of a few years back. For a flash of a moment, Sylvia wondered what mischief the two of them might get into together. "My name is Sylvia."

"Well thank you, Sylvia. Nice to meet you." Louise lifted her hand and swept a stray silver strand from her forehead, patted it against her temple and on back to the crown of her head.

"It's my trade," she paused. "Hair. Had my own shop back in Florida."

"Well, you are certainly good at it," Sylvia said.

They settled into the shifting moods of the music. The lament of B.B. King gave way to a more upbeat, foot tapping rendition of Keb Mo's "Muddy Water", then the rambling roll of Robert Johnson's "Terraplane Blues".

When the band paused to drink and retune, Sylvia picked up the conversation again. "So what brought you to Clarksdale?"

"This," Louise replied, encompassing the entire club with the sweep of her arm. "Sold my business in Florida and bought a little place here in Clarksdale so I could discover every juke joint left in the Delta before I die. Course, most of the original places are gone, but the spirit and the music live on and a lot of the clubs have tried to keep the feel of the old spots. I end up here at Maizie's when I'm back home, resting up from my latest road trip."

"You mean you just picked up like that and left your life in Florida?" Sylvia was fascinated and a little envious.

"Well, not just like that. I had to give my customers almost a year's notice, especially the old gals who came in every week for the same shampoo and set. You woulda thought they were losing their only daughter. But it was time."

"For what? Time for what?" Sylvia sensed that Louise was closer to unraveling some mystery that Sylvia was still pursuing.

"Time to stop making excuses for not doing what I want."

"Which is to travel the Blues Highway?"

"Exactly. And to take the music into my bones again. Most folks don't know, but I used to play a little myself, back when these fingers could still take a lick to my old Gibson. Grew up playing piano, though."

"My boyfriend plays piano."

"That so? I had a few of those."

"Pianos?" Sylvia had never known Joe to own more than his secondhand Baldwin upright.

"No, boyfriends, darlin', boyfriends." Louise chuckled, again displaying that bewitching smile of hers, warm enough to melt the rocks right out from under a good bourbon. Sylvia guessed that Louise had always had her pick of the litter when it came to men.

"Yeah, can't live with them and can't live without 'em," Sylvia quipped, feeling quite open with this stranger. She motioned to the bartender. "I'll have another," she said as she tapped the bottom of the glass on the oak countertop.

"Well, live with them while you can, darlin', 'cause they'll be gone soon enough. For better or for worse."

"I guess that's true."

"Buried two myself. One not soon enough, crazy bastard. But the other, dear God still occupies the lion's share of my heart. Feels like half of me is buried in a little cemetery back in Dothan, Alabama."

The band was joined by a female vocalist, a local favorite, who started into a sultry version of "Cool Drink of Water".

Sylvia hesitated but decided to risk a more personal question. "So which came first, the bastard or the love of your life?"

"Oh, the crazy one came first, for sure. God, what a temper he had, and it seems like I was born to bring it out in him. I can see now that a tangle like that is always a two-step."

"What? Did he hit you or something?"

"Oh yeah, hit me hard. And I hit him back. Then an hour later, we would be up in the bed trying to bang our way back to love. It was a sad, sorry passion play."

"Almost sounds like you forgave him," Sylvia said with a whiff of indignation.

"After I left him, yes." Louise's eyes were gentle, unfazed by Sylvia's response. "I forgave us both, once we finally realized the best way to love each other was to say goodbye. By the time he got sick, we were mended enough that I was able to visit him. I sat vigil at the end. I'll admit it took a good bit of prayer to get there."

Sylvia softened, thought about the families she had worked with back in Texas, the confounding complexities of their tattered lives. "So I know I'm digging in a little deep here, but may I ask how you were able let yourself fall in love after that?"

Louise caught the bartender's attention. "Another club soda and lime, please, Mike."

"Coming up," he winked at her.

Louise turned back to Sylvia and met her eyes with an unfettered kindness. "You can ask, hon. I'd say a lot of humble pie, a good dose of the blues and the grace of God."

"There is something about the blues, isn't there?" Sylvia responded, skirting the tougher remedies mentioned.

"Well, they'll never leave you for good, will they?" Louise laughed. "Funny thing, that so many of us White folk, having lost God, go looking for our soul in the blues. A gift from a whole family of people we still owe. Thing is you can't take God out of the blues. It's those early sorrow songs that gave root to gospel, which birthed the blues. And maybe when we can understand another's suffering, appreciate another man's blues, well maybe then we are on to something."

"And maybe that begins at home," Sylvia murmured, not sure if she wanted to be heard.

"Oh, it most definitely begins at home," Louise said softly. "So who is this piano man of yours? And why can't you say yes?"

"His name is Joe. And how do you know I can't say yes?"

Louise shrugged. "Intuition?"

The bartender reappeared and asked Sylvia if she wanted another beer.

"No thanks, two's enough," Sylvia replied. "I'll try one of those club sodas."

"Well the night is young if you want to talk about it, and I'm all ears," Louise said.

Sylvia proceeded to bend both of Louise's ears for most of an hour, through several refills of her club soda. She talked about Faith at first and why she had come to Mississippi. Then she told her about Joe, that he was a musician, had been a Philosophy professor and now worked as a caretaker on a ranch outside Austin. How he was content with a simple life that included his ongoing love for Sylvia. Only problem was, he wanted kids and she didn't. She also talked about Jack, that it had been easy, day by day, to let herself fade into the fabric of his life, until she did not even know what she wanted for herself.

Louise, as a hairdresser, had learned how to apply the therapeutic question when necessary or risk hearing the same story over and over for years. She prodded Sylvia into talking about her parents and was painted a picture of a typical 1950's marriage, except for some elusive shadow that Sylvia hinted at but seemed to avoid.

"So your parents, Phil and Grace, right?"

"Right."

"So you think they were happy together?"

"Well I always thought so, growing up. I mean there were no big fights. Well, maybe one. I guess they were happy, but my mother was so damn docile."

"Docile how?"

"Just quiet. Always getting a good dinner on or ironing his clothes or bringing him the newspaper and a beer."

"Yeah?"

"I never saw him hit her, but I have always wondered if she feared that. He had a temper. He would come home tired from the restaurant, pissed about something. The suppliers or the staff or the landlord. He could just give her a look and she'd leave the room."

"King of the castle, huh?"

"Yeah. But he could be wonderful, too. I remember going to the state fair with him. He closed the restaurant and took all of us out for the whole day. He went on all the rides with my brother and sister and me and bought us candy apples. He won some big stuffed dog for Mom at the ring toss."

Louise just kept her eyes on Sylvia's face and nodded.

"I found it in the trash the next week, the stuffing ripped right out of it. I can tell you; it wasn't my mother who tore it up. She treasured the stupid thing."

"My guess is she treasured your father."

"For what good it did her. She was always begging for money for groceries or our clothes or school supplies. I can't imagine living like that."

"And you don't, do you?"

"And never will!"

The band was winding up the last song of the night. At almost midnight, the crowd was thinning out.

"So has Joe asked you to do that? I mean compromise any important part of yourself for him?"

"I don't know. In a way, yes, because he wants me to have his child. I refused. Has he made peace with that? I don't know. He also wants me to work a little less and be around for him a little more."

"I bet he does."

"But..."

"Yes, but. Sounds like it's been 'yes but' for the last five years, Sylvia."

Louise's use of her name made the exchange suddenly more intimate.

"Look Sylvia, I know I'm being forward, and chances are we'll never see each other again. And I like you. We can swap phone numbers, but you know how it goes. Life gets busy. So let me indulge in a little advice here. Go home and jazz the socks off Joe. And every time you get scared, like when he loves you even more, do it again. It will be difficult and wonderful and more complicated than necessary. But there is no nobler path to God than learning to truly love another person, for who he is, because we finally have to get ourselves out of the way. And if after all the work of loving, if the lack of a child is too much for him, then you gave it your best."

Sylvia looked at Louise, listening, and nodded in understanding. She pulled two business cards from her wallet and handed them to Louise.

"OK, advice considered. But please take my phone number. And would you write yours down on the back of the other card? I'd like to have it, even if you are right that we won't see each other again. Who knows?"

"All I've got is a landline," Louise offered. "I don't need to be so accessible as to have a cell phone. And I'm on the road a lot."

"That's OK. I'll take it," Sylvia said, gathering her things to go. "And Louise, thank you. Really. Thank you. Promise me you will call if you ever need help. Any kind of help."

"Sure." She winked and conferred the blessing of one last smile on Sylvia.

As Sylvia turned to leave, Mike came around from behind the bar to sit next to Louise. The club was closing. It was clear that Louise was beloved in this town and would not be wanting for any help, should she ever need it. Sylvia felt free of concerns for the first time in a long time, as she walked toward the parking lot where the Miata waited under the light of a lone lamppost.

Despite her late night, Sylvia woke by seven o'clock the next morning and felt surprisingly refreshed. She found Raymond at his desk in the small office when she went to check out.

"Good morning, Raymond," Sylvia said, yawning unexpectedly then smiling. "Excuse me!"

"Good morning, Miss Barbarino. Glorious morning

actually," he replied.

"Are you always this happy at seven a.m.?" Sylvia asked.

"Mostly," Raymond smiled back.

"I was wondering if you could tell me where I could get breakfast this morning," she said.

"Not much open around here on Sunday morning, with church and all. What do you like to eat?" he asked.

"Oh, just eggs and toast and a cup of coffee" she replied.

"Well, I'll tell you what," Raymond offered. "It's slow this morning. Don't expect any early checkouts. How 'bout you come on back to the kitchen and have breakfast with me. And I'll tell you one or two of those stories you were asking for yesterday afternoon."

Sylvia jumped at the offer. He escorted her through a door at the back of the alcove. Behind it were his modest living quarters – a bedroom and a combination kitchen and living room with a vinyl-topped dining table. He began talking as soon as he opened the refrigerator, retrieving a carton of fresh eggs and a loaf of bread. He regaled her with stories of his youth, how his grandmother used to baby-sit McKinley Morganfield, later known as Muddy Waters, who lived with his grandparents in Clarksdale. He told how his older brother and B.B. King once caught two dozen channel catfish in a single afternoon in an oxbow of the Mississippi river down near Greenville.

The hotel had become a kind of familiar home on the road for these bluesmen who shuttled back and forth between New Orleans and Memphis and later Chicago. Their presence was palpable, as though they had sung their souls right into the walls of the place. As Sylvia drank her coffee and mopped the yolks of her eggs with a piece of toast, Raymond excused himself to answer the telephone.

The stories transported Sylvia back to her own childhood. She recalled the annual summer trips to Hattiesburg for family reunions, a weeklong gathering of aunts and uncles and some twenty cousins. Most lived in the area and stayed at their own homes, but since her mother, Grace, had moved away she was treated like royalty when she returned to the fold. Sylvia's parents were given a guest bedroom in Maudie and Hardee's house and Sylvia and her brother and sister got special cots on the screened-in porch.

She remembered a particular afternoon from one of those summers, appearing in her mind's eye like a pentimento against the picture Raymond had painted. She must have been twelve or thirteen years old.

Sylvia had cajoled her father, Phil, out of two quarters and joined her older sister and three of her cousins as they walked the four blocks to the corner store. It sat next to the railroad tracks, a line that marked the boundary between the White and Negro sections of town. She had always been forbidden to cross those tracks. She presumed it was because of the danger of being hit by a train, but her parents had other fears. The children opened the front door to the store, a sign in the window saying, 'Whites Only' and went in to buy their candy. When Sylvia emerged from the store with a quarter's worth of chocolate drops and jellybeans, she heard music calling to her. It felt familiar even though she had never heard that kind of music before. She looked out across the tracks and saw a ramshackle storefront on the other side. There was a Black man sitting on top of a large wooden barrel, playing the guitar. Sylvia felt as if her feet did not even belong to her. She started to cross the railroad tracks. Her sister and cousins called out to her not to go, but she was deaf to them. As the rest of the group turned to go home, her sister pleaded one more time. 'Come back here, Sylvia. Don't go. I am gonna tell Mama and Daddy.'

Sylvia had made her way cautiously across the tracks, careful not to wedge her foot between the rail and the ties. When she got to the store, she stepped up onto the porch, the music from the man's guitar and the dance of his hands holding her spellbound. The music slid and jumped and made her sway as he glided the sawed-off neck of a whiskey bottle, slipped over his left ring finger, up and down the fret board. A frayed guitar case sat at his feet, a few odd coins littering the bottom. As he finished his song, Sylvia remembered the quarter she had left in her pocket. He smiled at her and nodded his head.

"Looks like you love the blues, Miss...?"

"Sylvia," she replied.

"Well, the blues belong to everybody. And the blues is for free."

"Thank you," she said and slipped the other quarter from her pocket into the guitar case before she turned and walked back across the tracks to home.

The sound of Raymond's voice brought her back to the moment.

"I said do you want another cup of coffee?" he asked.

"Sorry Raymond, I was just remembering... uh, no. I've had enough coffee but thank you for breakfast and for sharing your stories. You've nourished my body and my soul."

She stood up to help him wash the few breakfast dishes.

"It's nice to be able to talk about the history of this place with someone who is really interested," he said.

"Well, I am, and I think I'm beginning to remember why," she said.

"The blues are in your bones, aren't they?" he winked.

"I guess they are," she replied.

They went back to the front desk where she had left her suitcase. She insisted on paying for breakfast, but Raymond refused. She wanted to linger but she needed to get an early start back to Austin. He said he hoped she'd come back again to visit. There were plenty of blues clubs around and he had another two days of stories to tell. She thought of McLeod Walker and what lay ahead.

"I promise I will be back, Raymond. And when I come next time, I'll bring you some homemade gumbo."

"Oowee, girl. I'm gonna hold you to that."

They laughed and she picked up her suitcase, preparing to return to a world that seemed a million miles away.

MISSISSIPPI 1932

Plessy rolled over onto his side and slipped his arm between Delsey's breasts. The warmth of the flannel sheets enveloped them. He pulled her closer, the fullness of her body melting into his chest and belly. He was instantly aroused as the first veil of sleep began to dissolve. She reached back, silently, her hand stroking the curve of his muscled thigh. She pulled his leg over her as she turned to face him. They looked at each other, a moment of unspoken intimacy, then he pressed his lips against hers. The dance of their bodies lifted them into that place of suspended time where all that existed was the joining of body and soul. When they finished making love they rested in each other's arms, basking in the first light of day.

Delsey decided that this was how she wanted to wake every day for the rest of her life. In sunrise anointed lovemaking with Plessy Walker, a blessing beyond her wildest dreams.

"Good morning," he whispered into her ear, which fanned the flame still burning in her body. She almost started up again, but this was Wednesday. Plessy had to be on the early train to New Orleans today.

"I can't stand it that I have to leave you this morning," he said.

She held his face in her hands and paused to look at him a moment longer before she kissed him. Her eyes traced the distinct line of his cheekbones, etching them into her memory, the gentle flare of his nose poised above his lush lips. Reluctantly, she tossed the covers off their naked bodies, a filigree of pearled sweat still clinging to her skin. She would not let herself miss him until he was gone.

"Me too, Love, me too. But it is only ten days this time. And we'll just have to celebrate Thanksgiving a couple of days late," she said.

They rose and stood next to the bed for a moment, watching the sun slip through a rent in the horizon. Plessy put his arms around Delsey, kissed the nape of her neck. Outside the window, a red camellia opened imperceptibly to the first rays of light.

"We'll go cut the Christmas tree that Saturday, too, when I get back," he said, lingering.

She slapped his bare ass playfully, rousing him from desire and spurring him towards work.

"Well you can't come back unless you get going. And if you don't work this Crescent run, how are you going to afford a little surprise for me under that tree?"

He smiled, finally relenting, and reached for his pants. He pulled them on, thumbing the suspenders over his chest. They walked into the adjoining room, which served as kitchen, living room and makeshift bathroom. It was hardly bigger than the bedroom, its walls rough-hewn pine logs. Plessy had removed the crumbling old chinking and filled the gaps with fresh limestone plaster smoothed to a fine hand finish.

A few months after Delsey returned from her trip to Alabama she had moved out of the Trading Post office into this shanty north of town. She and Plessy had welded an enduring bond that night on the train from Gulfport to Montgomery. They wrote to each other every week, their letters passing in the mail. When Plessy came to Hattiesburg on New Year's Eve, during a three-day leave from work, their friendship ignited into a full-blown romance. They made love for the first time in the rickety twin bed in her room at the Trading Post. It took a bucket of bailing wire to strap its tottering frame back together after they were finished, and Delsey immediately set about finding them a more private place to meet. She had originally considered renting a room in the Negro quarters not far from this cabin, but she surmised that a shared bathroom in a women's boarding house would pose more problems than her office room. When she confided her true lodging needs to the manager of the boarding house, she was pleasantly surprised to be met with clandestine kindness rather than suspicion. Mrs. Howard was a widow, still warmed by the lasting traces of her husband's love. She told Delsey about a cabin in the woods a half mile up the tracks. It belonged to the owner of the boarding house but was in a bit of disrepair. She figured she could arrange for Plessy and Delsey to rent it for next to nothin' if they were willing to fix it up.

This morning, as Delsey stoked the still live coals in the wood cook stove, she thought about how familiar her life with Plessy had become. Memories of life before him seemed distant. She threw some small sticks of pitch pine onto the embers and the fire caught immediately, crackling like bacon in a frying pan. She fed it wood until it was roaring, then put a bucket of water and the teakettle on top of the stove. It heated quickly. Plessy had thrown on a jacket and was outside pumping water through a hose attached to the spigot. The hose ran through the window to a small tub in the corner of the kitchen. He had plumbed the tub and kitchen sink to drain out through the floor and down the hill that sloped to the nearby creek. But he had not managed to run a pipe from the pump to indoors yet. There was a lot still to do on their little home in the woods.

Delsey carefully poured hot water from the bucket into the tub until it was warm enough for a bath. She motioned to Plessy through the kitchen window. He stopped the rhythmic rocking of the pump handle and the last spasms of water gurgled from the hose. When he returned to the kitchen, he shed his clothes and eased into the tub. Delsey made them some coffee while he doused himself with warm water, then lathered a washcloth with soap, scrubbing vigorously from top to bottom. The smell of the coffee mingled with the hint of lemongrass from the soap. When Plessy was finished, he stood up and lifted a towel from its peg.

"This job is bleeding my soul, Delsey. Bleeding me dry," he said in a quiet voice, a question lingering in the air.

He didn't want to complain. He made decent money as a Pullman porter, considering the times. Close to one hundred and fifty dollars a month, including tips. He, more than most in the brotherhood of porters, garnered generous tips from the wealthy White patrons catered to on the Crescent Limited. His intelligence was clear and his reputation for discretion unparalleled, and he was rewarded accordingly.

She came over to him but said nothing. She took the towel and gently wiped his chest and arms. She turned him around slowly as though orienting someone who was lost and wiped his back in one slow full sweep of the towel. Then she wrapped the towel around his waist and hugged him, leaning her face against the broad bridge of his back.

"You can leave it today if you want to Plessy. We will find our way together. I might be able to squeeze a little more out of Mr. Wiggins."

"Oh, Dels, I can't let you do that. You work hard enough as it is. And you should be teaching, not bookkeeping."

He walked back to the bedroom to dress for work. He tucked his starched white shirt into the blue wool pants, accented with a black stripe running up the seam. He cinched his belt and donned the matching vest and jacket, fastening the brass buttons all the way to the neck. He dusted the wrinkles from his sleeves. Plessy felt confined in these clothes, straight jacketed into a wrong life.

"There are just so many more beds I can change or squalling brats I can tend," he said when he returned to the kitchen. "It may pay well to guard a man's infidelity while his wife dines in another car on the train, but it's not what I ever intended to do."

Delsey listened as she fried eggs and cracklins, a thick slice of bread toasting on top of the stove. Plessy was right that he had been born for another destiny. Just months older than Delsey, he graduated from a private high school in Virginia in 1925. He had won an academic scholarship to Howard University and had thrived in the political climate of Washington, D.C., excelling in his study of history. This Freedman's Bureau university drew him by the inspiration of its inception.

The long march from emancipation to a legal framework that guaranteed rights for Negroes was proving to be a road littered with landmines. The equal protection promised to freed slaves after the Civil War, by the Fourteenth Amendment to the Constitution, had been bargained away in 1876 when Rutherford B. Hayes exchanged those rights for the South's electoral votes. He won an illegitimate presidency against the prevailing will of the people, and a flurry of laws designed to institutionalize segregation blew across the South. The mocking minstrel image of Jumping Jim Crow became the directive to Negroes from Texas to Maryland. 'Know your place and keep to yourselves or risk the rope.' In train cars and schoolrooms, restaurants and cemeteries, the Jim Crow laws turned the shared company of Whites and Negroes into a criminal offense, while President Hayes turned a blind eye.

Plessy's parents had never escaped their own indentured life as tenant farmers. Hoping to mark their son for another possibility, they named him Plessy, after Homer Plessy, a thirty-year-old shoemaker who refused to give up his seat in the White car on the East Louisiana Railroad. Homer Plessy became a beacon of dignity even though the United States Supreme Court ruled for the railroad in 1896, ushering in the era of separate but equal.

Plessy Walker carried that legacy inside him. A trust had been passed to him, a call to work for justice. An uncle who migrated north at a young age had gained an education and met with modest success as a book merchant. He found a patron in Virginia who agreed to pay for Plessy's education. Plessy went to live with his uncle when he was fifteen. He seemed headed toward great things and had just begun his first year of law school at Howard Univerity when the stock market crashed. The endowment securing his scholarship suddenly vanished. Stunned and jobless, he accepted work as a Pullman porter on the prestigious

Crescent Limited, a recently chartered luxury line of the Southern Railroad. The demand for educated Negro men to staff the trains was great and the line ran right through Washington D.C. Plessy's older sister had moved there a couple of years earlier to pursue her own teaching career. She married a young doctor, recently graduated from Howard's Medical School. The three of them moved in together and made a home that pulsed with the vibrancy of fresh ideas and youthful activism. Plessy continued to use it as his home base, gone for days working long trips and eighty-hour weeks. He planned to save enough money to pay for his tuition and return to law school.

That had been three years ago. Sitting down at the small kitchen table with Delsey this morning, Plessy felt the sting of the wool collar scratching his neck. He and Delsey held hands. She blessed their food, then they ate their breakfast in the poignant silence of the soon to be parted. He gathered his suitcases while she rinsed the dishes in the sink and damped down the fire in the stove. They pulled on their coats and walked the short distance through the woods to the nearby tracks of the Southern line. The engineers knew to slow at this stretch each morning to allow Delsey to hop aboard for the short ride to the Hattiesburg depot. Because of Plessy, Delsey now warranted free passage to and from work every day. This morning they huddled together and shared their warmth on the rear platform of the caboose for the ten-minute trip into town.

They kissed one last time as the brakes squealed to a stop, then dismounted the train and turned away from each other. Plessy headed to the depot and Delsey to the Trading Post. Neither looked back. They knew the unnecessary pain of it. They had to trust that reunion would follow.

~

It was past noon when Plessy's train, a weary freighter, rattled into New Orleans. The Crescent Limited was scheduled to leave for New York at eight thirty p.m. He grabbed his bags and headed to the local porter house; quarters provided by the railroad for the Pullman porters.

He was planning to partake of a meal and an extended afternoon nap, having learned to be rested and well fed before undertaking the two-day trip from the Crescent City to New York. When he arrived at the house, the packed living room buzzed with conversation and excitement. The Baker Heater League was just adjourning to the dining room. These porters' societies gathered around potbelly Baker heating stoves in porter houses across the country to share stories and carry messages. In the center of the crowd was a tall, lean man with aquiline features accenting a receding hairline, a hint of gray at his temples. Plessy recognized the man not so much by his features as by his presence, confident but quiet; his passion tempered.

"Hey, Plessy, my man. Come over here," waved Henry Boatwright, a fellow porter.

Plessy wove his way through the clump of men steering themselves toward the dining room.

"Plessy, you missed all the excitement today! The Baker Heater League stopped jabberin' about our lives long enough to start talking like a real Brotherhood. You'd been proud. More socialism than socializing. I was just talking about you to Mr. Randolph here. I think you are exactly the man he is looking for."

The gentleman extended his hand and Plessy shook it.

The firmness of Randolph's grip heartened Plessy.

"I'm Philip Randolph," the older man said. "Or A. Philip, if you ever read my byline in the *Messenger* before it went out of print. Or in the *Black Worker*."

"Oh, I know who you are, Mr. Randolph," Plessy responded, hesitating before continuing. "I must say I greatly admire your stated mission to organize us into the first, as you say, 'Black' labor union. I admire this despite your complete ineffectiveness."

Randolph smiled. He could feel the cool floorboards through the worn soles of his shoes. The last seven years had left him hungry and humbled, and manifestly more resolute. He knew that Plessy spoke a certain truth, even if incomplete. Asa Philip Randolph had learned from his mistakes, especially his initial failure to descend from the lofty realm of socialist rhetoric to the stark reality of a porter's life. He appreciated Plessy's spine.

"Well, Mr. Walker, is it?"

Plessy nodded.

"I trust a man who is not afraid to be honest. And I am glad to take my share of responsibility for the disappointment you must feel. I want to hear your grievances. But understand that we are David fighting Goliath. The reach and influence of the Pullman Company is inestimable, capable of purchasing the editorial soul of the *Chicago Defender* and the *Pittsburg Courier*."

"I'll grant you that Pullman has the money to buy influence, but we have the power of numbers. Why did you call off the strike in 1928?" Plessy asked. The bluntness of his question was matched by its abruptness.

Randolph relaxed his shoulders, took his time before responding.

"How long have you been working for Pullman?" he asked, a genuine curiosity softening his angular face.

"Three years. Signed on in October 1929, after the Crash."

"And before that?"

"I was at Howard. Just starting law school after getting my degree in history," Plessy replied.

"So you were following the events of the Brotherhood of Sleeping Car Porters before you started working for the Pullman Company?"

"To be honest, Mr. Randolph, I have closely followed your union efforts ever since I visited Harlem in the summer of 1925, before going off to college. I read the *Messenger* back then and even passed myself off as a new Pullman recruit so I could slip into that first meeting at the Imperial Elks Lodge."

"God, what a steamy night that was," Mr. Randolph said.

"Yes, it was," Plessy said. "I was so full of hope that night. I knew that the Black labor movement was the door to our own self-determination. It was to be my focus in law school." His shoulders drooped as he gazed at his feet.

"Well, lift your gaze for a second, Mr. Walker. Can I call you Plessy?"

Plessy nodded.

"You *are* the man I've been looking for. And I will let you in on all the inside details of the last few years. The struggles, all the successes and setbacks. And I'll answer your question about calling off the strike."

He reached his arm around Plessy's shoulder. "But let's get some dinner first and get you some sleep. I'll be in the segregated coach just behind the engine on your train back to New York tonight, so we'll find time to talk."

Randolph reached into his pocket and jingled the coins that the porters had collected to pay his fare back to Harlem.

"I know we have a long way to go, son, but the Brotherhood of Sleeping Car Porters is poised for a comeback. Mr. Roosevelt's election is an answer to a prayer." An irrepressible smile rose on Randolph's face. "The tide is turning, Plessy, but I need some help getting these men down here organized. As I am sure you know it requires a more discreet approach than up north. I've got big plans for you if you're willing."

They turned and walked toward the dining room, where a couple of seats had opened at the table. They filled their stomachs with mulligan stew and buttered biscuits. Then Plessy bid Mr. Randolph farewell until evening and found his way to the nearest empty bunk. His mind was buzzing as he lay his head on the worn cotton pillowcase. But the ride from Hattiesburg, and the soporific effect of lunch soon overcame his body and his breathing took on the slow deep rhythm of sleep.

~

That night Plessy arrived early to the Crescent to make sure all the berths were turned down and beds made while the passengers dined. Sometime around midnight, after most of the passengers were tucked and tended, he had met Randolph in the Negro passenger car. He had secured a thermos of coffee and some leftovers from the dining car. They had talked nonstop, sitting on the hard wooden benches, luggage stowed at Randolph's feet.

"Did you grow up in Harlem?" Plessy asked.

"No, son, I was raised in Jacksonville, Florida. Quite a

progressive town once upon a time, back when I was a kid. The town changed but the sturdy crucible of my parents' love, and expectations I might add, gave me a chance to make something of my life, despite the extreme poverty we faced."

"What were they like?"

"Well, my father, James, was an African Methodist Episcopal minister. His congregation was mostly sharecroppers, without a penny to spare for the collection plate. And my mother, Elizabeth, instructed me and my brother, James, in the classics to supplement our regular classes at the Cookman Institute. My father used to tell me stories about the dignity of Negro self-reliance and the men who exemplified it. Men like Nat Turner and Toussaint-Louverture. We were expected to hold our heads up, to master the English language and articulate our words."

"Not to bow and scrape."

"Absolutely. Their guidance came from a faith in God and social justice. And they demonstrated the risks and rewards of that faith by their actions; facing down lynch mobs and refusing to participate in Jim Crow institutions. They preferred to walk than ride at the back of the bus. I would do the same, rather than ride in this car, if it weren't thirteen hundred miles from New Orleans to New York. They told us we had the same intellect, talent and potential of any man and we need never defer to the color of another's skin."

"So how did you end up in New York?" Plessy asked.

"By stumbling around for a bit. Life seldom moves in a straight line. I would say it was a combination of a certain aimlessness in Jacksonville and the call of the wider world. Because of the way my parents taught me to speak and this baritone voice I inherited, I developed a talent for oratory. That led me to acting, of all things! College was out of the question financially, but my talent needed a platform. Acting was a way out of the dead-end jobs I took to clothe and feed myself. Turns out I was rather good at it. Started getting lead roles with an acting company. New York was a logical next step."

"So, you moved to New York to be an actor. I had no idea. No wonder I was riveted when I heard you speak in 1925."

"Glad I made an impression, so you're willing to give me a second chance." Randolph responded. "I did move to New York with the intention to pursue acting, but it was more than that. My father inspired me with his ministry of social justice, instilled in me a passion for ideas. When I discovered W.E.B. Du Bois's *The Souls of Black Folk,* my mind opened to a bigger dream. New York was a gateway to new possibilities, and it was irresistible. I had just graduated from Cookman, having studied hard and done well. I couldn't bear to tell my parents I was leaving Florida for good, so I suggested it was a summer jaunt when I hired on as a hand on a steamship headed North. But it was a one-way ticket to a destiny that was beyond even my own imagination."

As Randolph went on with his story Plessy learned that after settling in Harlem, Randolph had taken a job as a switchboard operator at a hotel and enrolled in City College. He embraced acting again, with a natural affinity for Shakespeare. Poised for a career in the theater, Randolph made a fateful choice in response to the heartsick pleas of his father. Asa's rejection of a life in the ministry was hard enough for the Rev. James but for his son to aspire to a life in the theater was unthinkable. Randolph assented to his father's wishes and pursued his other muse, politics. He focused on classes in history and philosophy, and Socialism became his new foundation. His eyes opened to another world where reality was limited only by the possibilities not imagined. He saw that economic as well as racial barriers would have to be surmounted before Black people would know real freedom. He thrived in the activist environment of Harlem, began going by Philip instead of Asa, his childhood name. He adopted the New Negro language of 'Black' in his conversations and writings on race relations.

"Sounds like Harlem is where you found your true calling," Plessy said.

"You're right. It wasn't acting in the end. My passion for oratory found a greater cause, encouraged by the people I met in that remarkable community. My wife, Lucille, is as kindred a soul as ever there could be. What an amazing mind. And Chandler Owen was a true comrade and friend."

"I remember reading some of his articles in *The Messenger* when I was at Howard in 1925," Plessy said, "Then it seemed he disappeared. What happened?"

"Hard times. I think he lost faith in what we were doing. We started the *Messenger* in 1917 and it took off. Quickly became the premier forum of the radical Black press here in the U.S. if I say so myself. We were promoting trade unionism and the magazine had its heyday, but the prevailing events and shifting moods of the times failed to sustain it. Unionization of Black workers stalled amidst the strength of White resistance. The rising Harlem Renaissance began to prize art and literary accomplishments over the flagging efforts of the Socialist party. By 1925 Chandler was fed up with politics, so I found myself without a viable magazine or my longtime collaborator. Chandler moved to Chicago. Hard as it was, it honed my focus, strengthened my dedication to sow the seeds of economic liberation by unionizing Black workers. An opportunity presented itself later that year when a handful of Pullman porters, defecting from the company's sham union, approached me about forming a new union."

During their long conversation on the train, Plessy listened intently as Randolph talked about the early days of the Brotherhood. Randolph explained that the union members had anticipated the threat of company spies in their midst, and employed stealth in their communications, resurrecting the *Messenger*, which porters hand carried across the country. In barbershops and bars, kitchens, and alleys, they collected dues and passed literature to each other, their wives' active agents for the Brotherhood. They had limited their demands to what was reasonable and possible: a maximum work schedule of two hundred forty hours a month, a doubling of wages with time and a half for overtime, no doubling out for second runs without time off, and a place to sleep on long runs.

The Pullman Company fought back with carrots and sticks. They instituted a seven percent pay raise, then fired union members and hired Filipinos to take their jobs. Some Brotherhood members were physically beaten. And in its most pernicious attacks, the company manipulated Black ministers and the editors of the *Chicago Defender* and the *Pittsburg Courier* to denigrate Randolph, lining their coffers with cash.

But Randolph was a shrewd and worthy adversary. A talented wordsmith, he slowly won back the Black press by eloquently advocating for the independence of the Brotherhood union. He recruited men, tough and trusted, from among the porters' ranks to organize the community and expand the union's roll. Randolph even managed to get the mediation board created by the Railway Labor Act (RLA) to recognize the Brotherhood of Sleeping Car Porters as the union that represented the majority of porters, supplanting the Company union. But he had his failings too. In an attempt to force a pay hike out of the Pullman Company, he had shown his ignorance of the law and of the true plight of porters when he petitioned the Interstate Commerce Commission (ICC) to ban tips on the trains; this, despite the opposition of the porters themselves. Without tips, he had reasoned, the Pullman Company would have to raise salaries. But he had not done his homework, or he would have known that the ICC could not set salaries nor could the RLA mediation board arbitrate a solution. When he couldn't negotiate a pay hike, the only loophole he could find was a strike option. If the Brotherhood threatened to strike and the mediation board declared it an emergency, they could ask the President Coolidge to intervene.

Through a massive effort, Randolph and his liaisons organized most of the porters to support a strike vote in the spring of 1928. Soup kitchens were prepared, and munitions procured in case of retaliation. But the Pullman Company outmaneuvered him, convincing the mediation board that few porters would risk their coveted jobs, and more than enough strikebreakers were available if needed. The board let Randolph know that no emergency would be declared, and the president would offer no redress for their grievances. His calculation having failed, Randolph called off the strike and the result was utter deflation. Men left the Brotherhood en mass and the public called for his resignation. His remote ideological leadership style had caused his men to lose faith in him and their movement. The vehicle for his voice, his beloved *Messenger*, finally gasped its last breath. Spent and chastened, he learned the wisdom of humility. When the Depression hit the next year, all goals became concentrated into the simple act of holding on.

"I told you that I heard you speak at that Brotherhood rally in 1925," Plessy said, "You convinced me of your leadership because you knew that economic independence was the key to our full freedom. Frankly, you became a role model for me; educated, articulate, infused with passion. That's why I was so disappointed when you called off the strike in 1928."

"I understand and I'm sorry, but I had to do it. When I got the letter from the RLA mediation board saying they supported the Pullman Company, I knew the strike would fail. And I'm sorry I disappointed you personally, Plessy," Randolph replied.

"I thought you permanently crippled the movement. The depth of my disillusionment shook me to my core," Plessy said.

Randolph did not defend his position.

"I've tried to learn from that experience, Plessy, and it's why I wanted to talk to you tonight. With your legal mind and your experience as a porter, I think we can resurrect the union. But I need your help."

They spent the next hour plotting a path toward the horizon to which they both aspired – a union of Black workers who could open the door to greater economic and social opportunities. When Plessy finally looked at his watch it was almost three o'clock. He thanked Randolph for his offer and excused himself, returning to his quarters to get a couple hours of sleep before starting his day.

The train rounded a curve and pitched sideways rousing Plessy from his thoughts. He grabbed the steel curtain rod above his head to catch his balance. He pulled a blue blanket off a shelf in the small sleeping compartment and sat down on his cot. Plessy was exhausted but still too excited to sleep. He had not yet decided what to say to Randolph. He picked up the New York Times from the top of the stack of discarded newspapers that he had gathered from the club car. He stretched out on his cot, using the extra blanket as a pillow.

FRANKLIN D. ROOSEVELT WINNER IN LANDSLIDE!

proclaimed the front page of the week-old Times. Plessy had not been allowed to vote, since he had not lived in Mississippi long enough to pay poll taxes for two years running. He felt a glimmer of hope as he read about the plan for a National Labor Relations Act. Roosevelt was no foe of segregation, but he believed in collective bargaining. It was a foot in the door as Plessy saw it.

He opened the paper and found a small headline above a three-column article on page four.

Scottsboro Decision Overturned

It chronicled the legal battle of Ozie Powell, one of the Scottsboro boys and his recent Supreme Court victory calling for a new trial. The court held that the due process clause of the Fourteenth Amendment to the Constitution had been violated when the defendants had not been provided with adequate counsel. Ozie and his eight co-defendants would face a new jury in the spring, and it was rumored that the famous New York City criminal attorney, Samuel Liebowitz, might be enlisted to take the case. Meanwhile, the young men would remain in their cells in Kilby prison, within easy earshot of the sounds arising from the death chamber housing Alabama's electric chair.

Plessy felt the muscle of regret twist inside. He could not put it out of his mind that he should be clerking for someone like Liebowitz right now. He would have been fresh out of law school if his scholarship at Howard had not evaporated with the Crash. Instead, he was spit polishing the shoes of men less educated than him, most of whom did not care a whit what happened to nine innocent boys rotting in the bowels of an Alabama jail. His jaw clenched so tight the muscles started to twitch with fatigue. Plessy thought again about Philip Randolph's offer to him. Plessy would be the principal labor organizer in the South for the Brotherhood of Sleeping Car Porters. There was no money in it to speak of and there was the very real threat of violence against him and his family if the locals caught wind of his involvement with the union. This would not help Plessy save money to return to law school and it would mean more time away from Delsey, at first anyway. But he was burning to make a difference in a color-coded world that had conspired against his destiny. He needed to feel he had a hand in his own life, and sooner than later.

He glanced at his watch as he pulled the worn wool blanket from the foot of the cot up over his legs and chest and rolled over. He could catch a two-hour nap before early breakfast if he fell asleep now. He determined, as he closed his eyes, that he would wake up Mr. Randolph before the other passengers and tell him 'Yes.' Yes, he wanted this job!

MISSISSIPPI 1932

The savory scent of sage and thyme greeted Brett as he opened the door from the back porch into the kitchen. Maudie turned around, her calico apron cinched round her waist. She let out a squeal of joy when she saw his face.

"Hallelujah, hallelujah," she exclaimed. "My boy is home!"

He stooped over so she could wrap her arms around his neck and squeeze the living daylights out of him. It was early morning, with a hint of winter coming, and the Thanksgiving turkey, stuffed with cornbread and giblet dressing, had already been cooking for a couple of hours. This was Brett's first trip back to Hattiesburg since starting his freshman classes at Georgia Tech. He had been rattling along from Atlanta since yesterday morning, having switched trains in Birmingham about suppertime. His body still reverberated with the rhythmic sound of steel on steel.

"Let me get you some breakfast."

"Oh, Mama, have I missed your cooking," he said with a smile, reveling in the comforting smell of home. "And your little bitty self."

"Shorter than little, I 'spect," she said, gently patting her hips. She moved the pot of boiling potatoes to the back of the stove and retrieved the slab of bacon from the icebox.

She sliced two thick pieces for Brett and placed them in the frying pan. The grease began to sizzle and crackle.

"How do you want your eggs, fried or scrambled?"

"Fried."

A basket of eggs, gathered at dawn, sat next to the stove. Maudie chose three and broke them against the side of the frying pan.

"I want to hear everything, Sweetie. What is Atlanta like? How are your studies? Have you made new friends?"

"I'm sorry I didn't write more, Mama. I have been so busy, so wonderfully busy. And you know I have to write to Justine every week or some other guy's likely to come along and sweep her off her feet."

She tried to hide the loneliness she had felt for months. Maudie had grown remarkably close to her son during the winter and spring of his senior year in high school. He had been more attentive than usual, almost protective of her, and had made a point of bringing Justine home for Sunday dinner every week. He even accompanied Maudie to church all that spring to compensate for Hardee's absence from the pew.

"Forgive me?" he added, kissing the top of her head before sitting down at the small kitchen table behind her.

"Oh hon, there's nothing to forgive. I'm just so glad to have you home." Maudie put the bacon on a towel to drain and scooped the eggs onto a plate.

"How about, after you finish your breakfast, you help me shell those pecans for a pie. Then you can tell me all the things you would have written about." She placed the plate with the eggs and bacon and a piece of toast on the table.

"Put me to work. I am all yours until noon. That's when

I told Justine I'd pick her up for dinner," he said between bites. He was hungrier than he had thought and was grateful to be served breakfast as soon as he got home.

"You know, it's ROTC that's got me as busy as anything else. Besides the physical training, I have aviation classes. And that's in addition to my engineering courses. But they like me, Mama. My professors say I'm a natural born leader and my Cadet Wing Commander thinks I will be ready for field training next summer. That's a whole year early."

Maudie poured herself a cup of coffee. She came and sat next to him at the table.

"You've always had that quality, Brett." She had never adopted his nickname, Brother. "Even when you were little, the other children looked up to you, whether it was at school or on the sandlot."

"I guess I never really thought about it. I mean, I joined the Air ROTC because I want to be a pilot. What I am figuring out is that it's about a lot more than just flying. I feel like I am part of a whole new family there. And yet, Justine and all of y'all are back here...."

He grew quiet as he finished his breakfast, the mix of excitement and melancholy puzzling him. Maudie reached over and squeezed his hand, refraining from a quick response. Her son was thriving. The Army Air Corps was his launching pad and she had always known he was meant to shepherd a larger flock than roosted here in Hattiesburg. This was the real love of motherhood, to let your child leave you and encourage him towards his own intended life. She pushed the bowl of unshelled pecans into the center of the table and handed him the nutcracker. She picked up two shells and cupped them in her palm, closed her fist and felt them break gently against each other.

"Well one doesn't necessarily have to preclude the other, does it Brett?" she said, after a while.

"I guess not," he smiled.

"Seems to me there are things we are called to do. Ever since that first barnstormer caught your eye at the county fair, you have been determined to fly. I swear, I thought you might sprout wings if you did not eventually get yourself into the cockpit of a plane. And as I said, I have always seen that people have looked to you for guidance. From where I sit, it looks like the Army Air Corp is the best place you could be to do both. What do you think?"

"Oh, I'm happy, Mama, I'm happy," he said, cracking pecans and putting them on the newspaper beside the bowl. "You are right about flying. When I went up with my flight instructor for the first-time last month, it was as if I had been waiting all my life to feel that free. And I like looking out for my fellow cadets, especially the guys who aren't so sure of themselves. But some days are hard."

"Why's that?" She began plucking the meat from the growing pile of cracked nuts, careful to remove the shell remnants from the pleated centers.

"I don't like being so far from home," he said, a boyish expression on his face, "so far from Justine. And from you."

"How does Justine feel about it? I don't mean to pry, but I assume you two have had something to say about this in those weekly letters."

"She says she loves me, Mama, and I think she really does. She says she will wait for me, but I don't know. How long can I expect her to wait?"

"Wait for what, son?" Maudie asked, knowing the answer, and helping him voice it.

His face flushed suddenly. He looked up from the pecans

with a shy smile.

"Wait for me to ask her to marry me."

Maudie smiled. She dusted off her hands then looked into his blue eyes, a twinkle in her own.

"How about you stop shelling pecans and go ask her right now?"

"Ha!" he laughed, having to catch his breath from the surprise of her response. He wondered how she could embrace his proposal with no reserve, particularly when she and Hardee seemed so estranged these days. The memory of that morning at the Trading Post when Miss Styles walked in still haunted him.

"Maybe I will. I want to, and I think I am ready. But I do not take it lightly. I mean, marriage is a rest of your life deal."

Maudie's face became more thoughtful. "Yes, it is Brett. And sometimes amidst the comings and goings, there can be wanderings. But like you said, it is a lifetime deal. You do not leave it. No matter how hard it gets, you do not leave it, because it is a covenant. It's a covenant with each other and with God."

"I know, Mama. I know."

"So the question is, do you want to look across the table at Justine's face for the rest of your life?" Maudie was smiling again because even she appreciated the magnitude of Justine's beauty.

"Oh, Lord, yes!" Brett replied. "I should be so lucky."

"Well then come on back to your father's room with me. We've been saving your grandmother's engagement ring for this very day."

"Well shouldn't I tell Dad?"

"Yes. I think it would be a good idea for you to stop by

the Trading Post on your way to Justine's and show him the ring. And could you remind him that dinner is at one o'clock today?"

"Sure, Mama. I'll make sure he is here on time. I'll pick him up on my way back."

"Oh, and Plessy is out of town so I invited Delsey to dinner. Can you pick her up, too?"

"Yeah, I'll get them both."

They walked into Hardee's bedroom and Maudie pulled a small red velvet box from the toe of an old sock hidden in the back of the bottom drawer. She opened the box and unfolded the jeweler's cloth holding a half-carat emerald cut diamond in a four-post gold setting. She handed it to Brett. He stared at the ring.

"Oh my gosh, I can't believe this. Really, Mama?"

"Yes, son. We agreed a long time ago that this would be yours when the time came."

"Thank you," he said. "Thank you for this ring.... and for helping me get up my courage."

He polished the ring carefully and returned it to the box, clicking the lid closed.

"You didn't really need help, Brett. Just a little nudge. Now you go on and I can't wait to see that girl's face when you bring her back here to dinner."

"OK, see you soon," he said, wrapping the box in his handkerchief and tucking it deep in his pants pocket, trying not to race out the front door.

"Love you, son."

"Love you, too, Mama," he called as he skipped down the front steps and headed to his father's Nash.

Maudie walked back inside, returning to the kitchen where she found Emma shelling pecans at the little table.

She was immediately suspicious. Not that Emma wasn't a willing worker when prodded, but she seldom volunteered her help. She was so different from nine-year-old Faith, who had risen at dawn to help her mother gather eggs, then asked what else she could do to get ready for the big Thanksgiving meal. Maudie had put Faith to the task of getting Grace and Hannah bathed and dressed while she unpacked the silver service from the China cabinet. Thanksgiving and Christmas were the two occasions when the pieces were used for dinner, the big fat gravy boat having waited all year for its sterling performance. After the younger girls bathed, Maudie covered the dining room table with newspaper and set the silver polish and two rags to one side.

She showed Faith and Grace how to carefully remove all traces of tarnish from the silver bowls and tray until they shined like a mirror. Hannah was parked at the end of the table with her coloring book, contentedly absorbed. Maudie had dispatched the older girls, Claire and Delta, to Ava's house a few blocks away. The kitchen here was too small for more than one cook, so Ava was preparing the candied yams, cornbread, and green bean casserole at her house. Maudie had just assumed Emma would make herself scarce, which frankly would be easier than trying to harness her energy into a constructive contribution to the day's feast.

"Hello, Mama, I thought I could help with the pies," Emma offered, with a sheepish smile. Maudie decided to take her at her word. She reached over and gently patted Emma's cheek.

"I would love to have your help, and your company. I think we probably have enough pecans for a pie so could you go to the pantry and get me that special can of pumpkin for the other pie?" It had only been the last year or two that Maudie had the luxury of buying Libby's canned pie filling instead of having to make it from scratch.

"Then you can help me with the crust."

"Are we going to have apple pie, too?" Emma asked, almost a plea. "It is my favorite. The way you make it with the cinnamon and raisins."

Maudie fought the sense of mounting pressure to get everything done in the next three hours. What would it matter if dinner were fifteen minutes late? She probably needed a third pie, anyway, since she had invited Ruth and Fletcher to dinner at the last minute.

"OK, go pick out four big apples from the root cellar and the raisins from the pantry. I really am going to need your help now if we're going to make three pies." Maudie gathered up the spices for the pies. Cinnamon, cloves, and vanilla. She opened the canisters of sugar and flour and spread wax paper on the small kitchen counter, then retrieved the butter from the icebox.

They made short work of it after Emma returned with the other ingredients. Maudie quickly made the pie dough and left Emma to roll it out, while Maudie prepared the fillings in three separate bowls. In less than an hour the pies were tucked in the oven and filling the house with an aroma of festive sweetness.

"You can make a jelly tart with the scraps of pie crust if you want Emma. But wait for me before you put it in to bake. I need to go check on your sisters." Maudie took the potatoes off the stove and put the pot in the sink to cool. She went to the dining room to see how the silver polishing was going.

Emma took the leftover dough and a small apple she had hidden in her dress pocket and put them in a pot she found in a cabinet. She added a handful of raisins and a pinch of cinnamon then quickly slipped out the back door. She jumped off the porch and ran around the side of the house. She found the little hinged door in the lattice apron that skirted the front porch and crawled under the house. Everything was ready for her to bake her own apple pie.

It had taken her most of the morning to make the preparations. Two bricks held a discarded oven rack. She had paper and twigs wedged underneath, ready to light, and larger sticks piled against the porch post. The mid-morning light was bright, filtering in though the latticework. She opened her pot and pulled out the apple, carefully slicing it with a paring knife she took from the kitchen and letting the pieces fall back into the pot. Then she picked up the pie dough and pressed it against the inside of the lid until she had flattened it into a crust. She put it in her lap and filled it with apples and raisins. She pinched the crust closed at the top and put the whole round dumpling back in the pot. She could hardly contain her joy as she sat back and admired her work. After a minute, she fished a pirated match from her pocket and struck it against the side of the brick. The paper smoked at first, then caught fire. The twigs began to crackle. She added the bigger sticks, feeding the flame, and soon the fire was leaping around the bottom of the pot. The dumpling began to pop and sputter and the lid to the pot began to shake. It scared her. She jerked back, kicking one of the bricks over. The pot fell off its rack and the fire jumped its ring and caught the sticks lying nearby.

Emma scrambled out from beneath the house, panicked

now. Smoke crept from beneath the porch and the base of the post began to smolder. Emma saw Ruth across the street in her front yard. She ran towards her waving her hands and calling her name. Ruth immediately ran to meet her.

"I didn't mean to..." Emma choked, the tears running down her cheeks.

"Don't explain now, Honey, just go grab as many buckets as you can from the shed."

Ruth ran to the pump in the side yard and quickly filled the bucket that hung on the handle. She pumped ten strokes in half as many seconds and raced back to the front porch, emptying the bucket onto the fire, slowing its advance. She ran back to the pump where Emma met her, carrying two empty buckets. Ruth filled them quickly and hollered at Emma.

"Now go get your mother, quick, quick!"

Emma froze, her tears overtaking her.

"Don't worry hon, it's OK," Ruth said, more calmly. "I know you didn't mean to. But quick, quick now. Go get your mama."

They ran off in different directions. Ruth hurried back toward the fire. She poured both buckets onto the flames now climbing up the post. The water beat the fire back to the base of the charred beam. She and Maudie passed each other as she returned to the pump, Maudie with two full buckets of water at her side. By the time Ruth brought the next round of water, the fire had retreated. The last buckets extinguished it completely. The three of them stood there looking at the steaming porch post. The latticework was burnt for a stretch of three feet and the edges of the floorboards were scorched. Maudie looked down and saw the overturned pot and half-baked apple dumpling lying on the ground under the now exposed recess of the porch.

"If God had not given me the patience of Job, child, you would be dead by now," she said with as much restraint as she could muster. Her face was beet red, a rare occurrence that only Emma could elicit.

"What in God's name were you thinking?" This was as close as Maudie came to blasphemy.

"Mama, I'm sorry. I didn't mean to start a fire. I just…"

"You just what? I made an apple pie especially for you. We did that together and you very clearly intended to make this fire. Intended it from the moment you came in the kitchen to help me. Emma Jean, I am too angry to talk to you right now. You go in that house, take a bath, and wait in your room until I come get you. I've got to calm myself down."

Emma slinked off into the house, the dirty sash of her dress dragging like a little tail between her legs.

Ruth stood silently next to Maudie.

"I'm so sorry to lose my temper like that, Ruth. Thank you. Thank you for saving my house and my daughter."

"She's a good girl, Maudie. Just a little wild."

"I know, Ruth, I know. But she tries my patience past its breaking point. I don't think that I will ever understand that one, much as I try."

"You can always send her over to us for a spell when she gets to be too much."

"Oh, I do. And I cannot tell you how grateful I am that you and Fletcher have taken her under your wing. She actually has been more respectful to me in the last year than I have ever known her to be."

"Fletch and I try to talk to her, help her see that all that you ask of her is for her own good. She even reads some scripture with us."

"Bless you, my friend," Maudie said as she opened her arms to embrace Ruth. They turned back to the porch and saw that the post had stopped smoking. "Where is Fletcher? It's not like him to miss a fire," she chuckled. Fletcher always enjoyed the thrill of an emergency.

"Oh, he's down at the Trading Post with Hardee," Ruth replied. "Said he wasn't going to let him work past noon today. He said it was because he wanted to enjoy your fine cooking at a leisurely pace, but I think the truth is he's a little worried about Hardee, working so hard and all. They've become good friends."

"Well, I'm glad. I think Hardee needs a good friend these days." Maudie took a deep breath as if she had more to say, but instead she exhaled, smiling faintly.

"Oh, my gosh, the pies!" she suddenly remembered.

"You and Fletcher come on over as soon he gets home," she shouted over her shoulder as she ran back towards the kitchen.

~

Fletcher knocked on the door to the Trading Post and let himself in, without waiting for an answer.

"Hey, Hardee, it's Fletch," he yelled.

He pulled up a cane bottom chair, part of a dining room set on display at the front of the store and sat down. He straddled it backwards, his chin resting on his hands on the back of the chair. For a minute, he let his eyes close, still tired from his night shift at the lumber mill.

"Hey, Fletcher," Hardee said with genuine delight as he returned from the back office. Now that Delsey had moved into the cabin with Plessy, he had more room for storage in the office. "You're a pleasant surprise. Wouldn't have expected you to be up this early. I was just sorting out some car parts. I got some great stuff off a couple of salvaged wrecks."

"You're smarter than a back-alley cat, Hardee, and just as gutsy. I'm breaking my back as a sawyer down at the mill for three and a half bucks a day and you're feeding a wife and eight kids on scrap metal and other folk's junk."

"Hey, that's salvaged steel and antiques! And I am working seven days a week, but I'm not complaining. Feeds my family and there's even a little left to send to Brett at school," he bragged.

Out front, a car horn honked twice. "Speaking of whom, that may be him. I sent him a train ticket last week so he could surprise his mother for Thanksgiving."

The two men walked out the door onto the front loading dock to find a stout, red-faced gentleman standing next to the driver's door of a late model Cadillac. Despite the cool day, a ring of sweat marked the armpit of his white shirt as he reached up to push a thick lock of silver hair from his forehead. His cheeks were flushed and his thick neck spilled over the collar of his shirt. His stomach bulged from beneath his gray vest.

"Mornin'," he said nodding to Hardee. He wiped his forehead with a handkerchief and reached for his straw hat resting on the driver's seat. His suit coat was draped over the back. A woman leaned forward from the passenger side, waved, and smiled graciously from beneath the lace netting of her black hat. "This darned thing just stopped running on me a quarter mile back," he said, motioning toward the front of the car. "Had to push it from there. We are on our way to the coast to see my sister. Sure could use some help but looks like everything's closed up around here."

Hardee descended the steps, while Fletcher watched from the dock.

"Hardee Wiggins," he said, extending his hand. "I'm glad to help you if I can. You think you need gas? I've got a five gallon can in my truck."

"Roscoe Pittman," the man responded, returning the handshake. "No, I filled up just outside of Laurel."

"Well then tell me what happened," Hardee said as he went around the front of the car and popped the hood.

"We took the back road down from Laurel. I wanted to catch the last of the maples turning. Anyway, nothing particular happened. We rattled along on some washboard roads. Then the car started missing a little, then more, and then it just stopped up the road a bit."

Hardee began his inspection under the hood of the car, checking the oil and the fan belt. He wiggled battery cables and spark plug wires and finally found the problem, a loose clip on the side of the distributor. He bent it a little and snapped the cap closed, then lowered the hood and wiped his hands on a rag he pulled from his pocket.

"Try her now," he instructed Roscoe.

Roscoe got behind the wheel of the car and turned the engine. It started immediately and purred without hesitation.

"Distributor cap came loose. Should be fine now, I tightened the clip."

Roscoe and his wife were visibly relieved. "I can't thank you enough Hardee," he said, smiling. "I think we'll make it to Gulfport in time for dinner. What do I owe you?"

"That'll be two bucks."

"Two dollars?" Roscoe responded, incredulous. "That took you five minutes!" But he dug his wallet out of his coat pocket and pulled out two crisp bills.

"Well, Mr. Pittman, you are not paying me for my time, you're paying me for what I know." He smiled and took the money, folded it neatly and put it in his shirt pocket.

The Pittmans drove off, disgruntled but relieved to be back on the road.

"You are the best damn businessman I have ever seen," Fletcher laughed, slapping him on the back when Hardee returned to the dock. They walked back into the Trading Post.

"Well, you've done all right by yourself the last year with your corn mash and your still," Hardee reminded him.

"Because you tripled my customers by selling it from your store."

"You've paid me back, in kind. I would say we both profited. Come to think of it, we should share a little of the profits right now. I've got a couple glasses in the office."

"I don't know, Hardee, it's kind of early. And Ruth will shake me senseless if I come to Maudie's Thanksgiving dinner with whiskey on my breath."

"Oh, come on, grab a chair and come back to the office. That little deal out there deserves a celebration. I've got a couple of clear Havanas I have been saving and they'll mask the smell of a couple sips of whiskey. Come on, Fletch, it's Thanksgiving."

"Oh, all right, but just a sip. Sometimes I think if I were a better friend, I wouldn't be supplying you with so much hooch."

Hardee shrugged. They crossed the long expanse of the front room and entered the office in the back. The potbelly stove was well stoked and the room warm. He sat down at the desk and opened the bottom drawer. Hardee pulled two Ball jars from the drawer and set them on the desk. He retrieved the jug of whiskey from the recess beneath the desk and poured some into both jars. They each took a sip of the smooth brew.

"You do have a talent," Hardee said. He closed his eyes, sipped again, and let the whiskey linger on his tongue.

"You know, I read in the paper that now that FDR's been elected, Prohibition's likely to be repealed. Probably within the year," Fletcher mused.

"It always was a bad law. You can't legislate morals."

Hardee took two cigars from a wooden box in the same bottom drawer of the desk and pulled a clipper from his pocket. He inhaled deeply as he slowly drew one of the cigars beneath his nose.

"Still good."

He smiled and quickly clipped the tip off the end of the cigar. He handed Fletcher the other cigar along with the clipper. Fletcher repeated the ritual.

"Funny thing is, Hardee, it's got me a little worried. Repealing Prohibition, I mean, because I need the extra money. I been tryin' to put savings aside in case things go bad at the mill. It don't look good. Hardly anybody's been building the last three years and the land around here is pretty much timbered out."

Hardee snapped a thick cedar splinter off a log and opened the grate to the stove. The makeshift match lit and flamed. Hardee held the cigar above the flame until the edges blackened then took it into his mouth, puffing slowly and rotating it to get an even burn. He handed the cedar match to Fletcher.

"But you're skilled, Fletcher, as a sawyer. Not just some laborer," Hardee said, exhaling a cloud of smoke.

"But if the trees are gone..." Fletcher paused to get a good burn on his cigar, the end now glowing orange.

"What about the union? Wasn't there a union? The IWW?" Hardee pressed, hoping to find a bright spot in the darkening economic picture Fletcher was painting.

"Oh, the lumber operators association broke it years ago. And frankly, I think the International Workers of the World was just as much at fault. Spreading their socialist views and integrating the workers. I mean, you can't have Negroes and Whites meeting together in the South. They brought it on themselves. I ain't no believer in the Lost Cause or anything, but you have to have some social order. If people don't understand their place... I mean, especially in these hard times, you'll have a riot on your hands."

"Never did have much use for the unions myself, being a business owner." Hardee said. "And I don't wish the Coloreds no harm. Hard times hit them like everyone else. But a man's gotta make his own life with his own two hands. You can't be expecting the government to save you. Those socialists don't understand that big government makes a man impotent."

Fletcher blew a perfect smoke ring. "Yeah, and they've got radical ideas about Whites and Coloreds and men and women all being equal. Getting equal pay. My God! We all know that women and Coloreds aren't born with the same intelligence as a White man. And them Negroes shouldn't be poaching our jobs." Fletcher took a deep puff on his cigar, rocked back in his chair a little and exhaled.

"Well, I think you are right about one thing. The mixing of the races is only going to bring on another war down here in Mississippi," Hardee nodded, nursing the last of his whiskey.

"But what about Delsey?" Fletcher needled.

"What about her? She is an employee who works for cheap. That's good business." Hardee was a little annoyed at the direction the conversation was taking.

"But you serve her dinner at your dining room table, don't you?" Fletcher was persistent.

"Hell, Fletch, Maudie would have her sleeping in our back bedroom if I didn't put my foot down. You gotta remember I hired Delsey when she was only sixteen years old. She moved with us from Alabama and, frankly, I don't know how I'd run the business without her. She's practically a second mother to those girls. And Maudie, well…. I'm never going to change her mind." Hardee was determined to steer their discussion in an easier direction. "By the way, how's Ruth? Didn't she take sick around Halloween?"

"Yes, but luckily it was just a bad cold. Almost turned into pneumonia but the mustard plaster pulled it right out of her." Fletcher took one last short puff on his cigar and laid it in the ashtray on Hardee's desk to die out. He relaxed into his chair. "Thanks for asking about Ruth. You know I worry about her. And thanks for that cigar. Can't remember the last time I had one like this."

"Only share 'em with a good friend." He winked at Fletcher.

The bell attached to the front door clamored when it opened wide.

"Hey Dad, you here?" Brett's voice resonated from the front room. "I have something to show you."

Hardee nearly bolted from his chair with excitement when he heard his son's voice but stopped before he got up. He waited to see if Fletcher would excuse himself without prompting.

"Well, I need to get going Hardee. Ruth put me to the task of gathering camellias and bayberry leaves for the dining room table. So I need to start walking back."

"Look forward to seeing you both at dinner, my friend," Hardee said. The men stood and walked toward the front of the store. They met Brett outside the office door, the fat cigar still wedged between Hardee's fingers.

"Hello, Mr. Moody," Brett said when the men entered the front room.

"Good to have you home, Brett," Fletcher replied. "I'm just on my way out, but I'll catch up with you at dinner. I think your old man here might want some time with you. He's been like a hen on eggs waiting for you to get home."

"Go on now, Fletcher," Hardee laughed.

"Bye, Mr. Moody," Brett said.

Hardee hugged his son. When they let go, Brett took a small step back and reached into his pocket.

"I need to tell you something, Dad. I already talked to Mama."

He pulled the handkerchief from his pocket and unfolded it carefully.

When Hardee saw the red velvet box, he immediately knew what Brett had come to say. He cleared his throat to keep from tearing up.

"Congratulations, son," he said, then lifted the cigar to his mouth, puffed twice to refresh the burn and offered it to his son.

"Don't mind if I do," Brett smiled, expanding his chest as he inhaled the smoke. He coughed immediately and handed the cigar back to Hardee.

"You will never find a finer girl, son. And I could not be prouder of you than I am right now. I want to hear all about Georgia Tech and the corps. But I suspect you have other things on your mind at the moment. You run on and find Justine and I'll see you at dinner. We can take a long walk tonight after sunset and have our talk then."

"OK, that'll be great. I have a hundred stories to tell you, Dad." Brett turned to leave, then paused and turned back. "I missed you out there in Georgia."

"I missed you, too, son." Hardee returned.

"I'll come back by and pick you up in a couple of hours. I promised Mama you wouldn't be late. And Dad, please...."

"Don't worry, son, the jug's been corked for the day. I will be as clean and respectable as this day calls for. See you when you get back."

~

By one o'clock, everyone had gathered in the Wiggins' dining room. Ruth had made a centerpiece of bayberry branches surrounding a bowl of red and pink camellias. Maudie placed it in the middle of the long dining room table covered with a hand-woven Irish linen tablecloth. Two silver candlesticks, spotlessly polished, held long white tapers, ready to light. The silver service including the gravy boat and relish tray, sugar bowl and cream pitcher sat at one end of the centerpiece. The steaming, perfectly browned turkey sat at the other. Fourteen places were set with Haviland China and sterling silverware. Cut glass goblets were filled with tea. A highchair near one end of the table held Ava's daughter, June, now 18 months old. The table teemed with other dishes, mashed potatoes, giblet dressing, candied yams, green bean casserole and cornbread. There was also creamed corn and fresh broccoli.

Delsey walked in from the kitchen with the last of the pies and set them on the buffet, while Hardee lit the candles. The circle closed as they joined hands to say grace. Ruth was to Maudie's left.

"That's awful nice of Delsey to work for you on Thanksgiving," Ruth whispered in her ear.

"Oh, she's not working for us, she's our guest, like you and Fletcher," Maudie whispered back.

Ruth stiffened and almost let go of Maudie's hand. The air between them chilled. But Maudie would not let go and instead squeezed Ruth's hand tenderly.

"It's OK Ruthie, we are all God's children. I am privileged to have all of y'all at my table today."

Delsey stepped into the circle between Maudie and Faith and joined hands for the blessing. It was a prayer of great gratitude for the health and love of those gathered, and the ample harvest to feed them.

Maudie ended saying, "Bless this food to the nourishment of our bodies and us to thy service. In Christ Jesus name. Amen."

"Amen," sang the Wiggins chorus and the room was suddenly filled with talk and noise as chairs scraped back from the table and serving spoons clinked against dishes. Ruth and Fletcher couldn't resist the warm feeling of family and joined in, despite their discomfort with Delsey's presence. Hardee began to carve the turkey, then paused and looked up, catching Maudie's eye across the length of the table. She was radiant, and the warmth in her eyes was directed especially at him. Her smile was word enough. Despite all his transgressions, love would abide. Come what may, Hardee knew, he would never leave her.

MISSISSIPPI 1998

The first of the shocked, red-rimmed oak leaves skated on the wind, descending to the ground. Autumn had arrived overnight and the morning chill had caught Faith by surprise. She turned up the collar of her lilac terrycloth robe and pulled the sash tighter around her waist. Standing at the kitchen sink, filling the tea kettle with water, she watched an updraft play with a leaf, suspending it in midair. A kind of infinity opened up inside of her and she rested there, savoring the stillness. These moments were coming more frequently she noted. They seemed odd, yet familiar too. This telescoping of time. After a seemingly endless breath, the leaf continued its fall. Faith turned to the stove and lit the gas burner under the kettle. She thought how hard it was to articulate the numinous quality of these moments, how words had failed her when Sylvia had come to visit seeking some evidence of a greater Presence in the world.

She picked up the flashlight from the counter and fetched some matches from the drawer. She carried them to the living room where, on her knees, she wrestled the grate from atop the floor furnace. She turned the black knob to the right and a whiff of gas let her know the pilot was ready to be lit. She wedged the end of a wooden match into the tip of a long slender metal rod next to the furnace and struck it. Careful not to extinguish the flame, she lowered it toward the pilot light and watched as a small blue plume ignited. She turned the knob back to center and heard the faint roar of the burners coming on. Replacing the grate left her a little breathless and she paused before standing up.

The kettle let out a plaintive whistle and Faith hoisted herself up, using the back of the couch for leverage. She brushed her hands against the front of her robe and smelled the pungent scent of the year's first gas heat rising from the dusty furnace coils. Soon the house would be a toasty refuge against the swirling cold.

Faith returned to the kitchen and turned off the burner under the kettle. Looking out the window, she wondered how Sylvia was faring back in Austin under the full load of her job. Sylvia had been gone for over a month. Their time together had been so full of love for each other. Faith knew that Sylvia had begun tiptoeing her way toward a spiritual path.

A bluster of wind rattled the kitchen window. Faith watched as the wind whipped the falling oak leaves into dancing eddies of red and gold. She knew Sylvia had returned home still searching for an elusive peace. Faith didn't fully understand Sylvia's restlessness, but knew it was beyond her power to resolve it. Gazing out the window, all she could do was offer up a prayer of love for her niece. She turned back to the stove and picked up the tea kettle. Faith poured the hot water over the coffee grounds in the French press and waited a few minutes, then poured herself a cup of coffee. She added two dollops of cream and the usual teaspoon of sugar to her cup. The warm air from the floor vent billowed her robe and lifted her spirits. She raised her mug, enjoying the first taste of coffee. It was as full and rich as a good lover's kiss. She glanced outside one more time. The leaves had settled. She watched an orange-breasted bluebird squabble with a huffy cardinal for the sunflower seeds she had tossed out the night before.

Faith felt her attention settle on her breath again without any undue effort. The noticing allowed a sense of clarity to develop, as though the silt of a stream were settling into the still presence of a large pool. When she had worked in the missionary medical clinics in Burma in 1968, she had strayed from her Nazarene roots finding refuge in the teachings and practice of Theravadan Buddhism. Mindfulness practice, the friendly attention to her breath, had become her daily bread. It had not supplanted her faith, only expanded it. In a sudden flash, she realized that she had not really talked to Sylvia about this part of her life. Maybe meditation could serve as a spiritual compass for her niece.

Faith carried her mug of coffee into her bedroom, the rubber bottoms of her slippers slapping against the hardwood floors. She stood before the bookshelf that held her Bibles and devotionals and meditation books and took another sip of coffee. She sat the mug on the bedside table and picked up her reading glasses, perching them on top of her head for later use. She felt a thrill as she ran her fingers along the spines of the books. They were not organized in any specific way. Certainly not by author, and only vaguely by subject because after all, how do you classify the subject of God? Finally, her hand came to rest on the white binding of a small volume. She pulled the book from between its nearest neighbors and donned her glasses. The soft butter cream cover featured a ghostly image of a tree emerging from the mist. The title "A Gradual Awakening" was printed beneath the author's name, Stephen Levine. She sat on the edge of the bed and leafed through the yellowing pages. Just reading the chapter titles recalled the comfort she had found in these words, the comfort of being at peace with not knowing.

She took her coffee and the book back to the kitchen and sat at the small table in the dining nook. She read the first pages, then reached for the stationery pad and pen that were always on this table. She began a letter to Sylvia.

"I know how hard it must be for you to trust in something greater, that bears witness to our suffering as humans, especially the suffering of the innocent that you see in your work every day. And I know it is natural for the mind to become afflicted with indignation. But I do not think cynicism is born from the suffering, but from the disappointment of being too certain in our beliefs. We must be able to tolerate the absence of answers...."

When she finished the letter, she tucked it inside the front cover of the book, then dropped it in a large manila envelop. She addressed the package to:

Sylvia Barbarino, Esq.
5928 36th Street
Austin, TX 78705

MISSISSIPPI 1932

Plessy could hardly sit still on the train ride home from New Orleans. Though sleep deprived, he churned with excitement at the prospect of seeing Delsey and telling her the news. Philip Randolph had been thrilled when Plessy said he would accept the job with the Brotherhood of Sleeping Car Porters. They had disembarked the train together in New York, discussing the details of the work. There would be no salary initially, but Randolph promised to find some money for Plessy if the union grew. Plessy would organize the Pullman porters by distributing pamphlets at stops along his route and attending meetings of the Baker Heater League in New Orleans, Birmingham, Atlanta and Washington, D.C. He was authorized to assign tasks to the other union members then report his progress to Randolph.

The Crescent was scheduled for a twelve-hour layover in New York before it returned to New Orleans the next morning. Randolph invited Plessy to spend the night at his home in Harlem. As the two men left the train platform, Plessy felt flush. He had collected a handsome twenty-dollar tip for finding a woman's lost wedding ring on the train. The two men crossed the large open halls of Penn Station and made their way through the tunnels to the subway. Plessy paid the nickel fare for both himself and Randolph and they boarded the new 8th Avenue train to

125th Street. Minutes later, they stepped out of the subway car and ascended to the street above. As the cool evening air greeted Plessy, he felt lighter, unchained from some great weight. Black couples, elegantly dressed, were getting into their new roadsters while the strains of Duke Ellington pulsed from a nearby club. He was home.

They walked the five blocks to Randolph's flat in a brick rowhouse, where his wife Lucille had a home cooked meal waiting for them. After dinner, the couple insisted that Plessy join them at a friend's party. He declined, saying he had to be on the Crescent by five a.m. to prep the sleeping cabins, but they persisted, promising to introduce him to the people who were the lifeblood of the Harlem Renaissance. Plessy reconsidered, not able to resist a chance to step out of the shadow of the South for an evening. The party had reminded him of his time at Howard University, the thoughtful conversations of people envisioning a cultural reformation. He was especially taken by Zora Neale Hurston, a woman whose intelligence and fearlessness reminded him of Delsey.

That had been a week ago and he had traveled over four thousand miles since then. The brakes squealed as the train pulled into the Hattiesburg station. Plessy was almost there, almost back with his Delsey, the woman he knew he wanted to marry. He was dressed in a fine, blue gabardine suit he had purchased with his leftover tip money. He bought it because he wanted Delsey to see the man he was meant to be. He picked up his suitcase and leapt from the train as soon as it reached the platform, stopping to gather a bouquet of purple asters and goldenrod on the short walk to the Wiggins' Trading Post. He approached the door to the back office, then paused and knocked.

"Just a minute," replied Delsey, her voice instantly sending his body into a riot.

He straightened his wide maroon silk tie and held the flowers out in front of him.

When she opened the door, her jaw dropped, and she gasped in delight. "Sweet Jesus! And I thought you were handsome before! Come in this office and close the door before I make a fool of myself in public."

She took the flowers from his hand. He drew her into his body, closing the door behind him until the latch clicked. She put both arms around his waist and tilted her head back to receive his kiss. The wet fullness of his lips eased the longing that had been growing in her for days.

"I missed you so much Love," she whispered in his ear, "Missed you something fierce."

He scooped her up and began to waltz in slow big circles, her arms clasped around his neck, still holding the flowers. Her feet lifted off the floor as they twirled around the room.

"Marry me, Delsey. Please marry me," he said, his warm brown eyes impatient for an answer.

"Yes!" she said, "Yes, yes, yes!"

He lowered her until her feet touched the ground. They continued to dance, spinning faster in a small circle, a pas de duex. After a minute of exhilarating dizziness, they stopped and looked at each other.

"I love you, Plessy Walker, like the God's sweet earth loves rain. And I will marry you heart and soul," she reached up and kissed him hungrily, "and body." They laughed and Delsey leaned into him, her head resting against his chest just beneath his chin, his arms draped around her waist.

The accumulated exhaustion finally caught up with him and Plessy leaned on Delsey a little. "Oh, Dels, I have so much to tell you, such wonderful news. I want to spill it all out right now, but I don't want to rush it. When do you get off work?"

"Soon, just let me post these bills and I'll come home. It is Saturday and it's kind of slow. Hardee won't mind. He's already closed up shop for the day," Delsey stroked the side of Plessy's weary face. "You run on and catch the train. I'll walk home and stop at the grocery on the way. It'll give you a chance to sleep before supper."

He wanted to lay down with her on the floor right then, to pour himself into her then fall asleep in her arms. But he gathered the energy to push the last few miles toward home. He opened the back door to leave and saw his suitcase sitting where he had dropped it. He remembered the present tucked inside.

"I've got something for you," he said, reaching down and unsnapping the locks on the case. He pulled out a soft bundle wrapped neatly in tissue paper. He turned back around and handed it to Delsey. She removed the paper. Inside was an exquisite dress, unlike anything she had ever owned. She held it up to herself and let it unfold to its full length. Made of wine-colored silk crepe, it had a V-shaped back that plunged to a fitted waist, sleeveless with a high collar in front, accented with black beading. The ankle length skirt billowed slightly in soft folds. Plessy had bought it for five dollars when he got his suit in Harlem.

"Oh, Plessy," Delsey was speechless for a moment. "How can we afford....?"

He stopped her by putting a finger to her lips. "I received a sizable tip for finding a passenger's lost ring on the train.

I wanted to buy you an engagement ring, Delsey, but I knew what you would say. So I waited before spending our savings. We can talk about it tonight."

"But Plessy, it is so beautiful. I've never...." Delsey was on the verge of tears. She thought how happy her mother would have been for her today.

"Not half as beautiful as you, Dels. And we deserve good things in this life. I can't wait to tell you about Harlem and Philip Randolph and...." The warning whistle signaled that the train was about to leave the station.

"Run, go catch the train, Love. I'll see you at home in a couple of hours," Delsey said as she grabbed one last kiss and pushed him out the door.

After he left, she cleared her desk and carefully smoothed the tissue paper, meticulously folding her new dress and rewrapping it. She tucked it into a large canvas bag that served as her purse and grocery bag. Then Delsey gathered the bills to carry to the mailbox and locked the office door behind her. She stepped out into a perfect autumn afternoon. The golden slant light warmed her against a faint cool breeze that whispered in the red russet oaks and bronze hickory trees lining the road home.

The leisure of the walk put Delsey in a reflective mood. She had kept to herself for most of the first year after moving to Hattiesburg, holed up in her office living quarters with the occasional refuge of the Wiggins' home. She had always been treated well by Maudie. Delsey was not sure whether Maudie felt a particular sympathy for her as a young woman who had lost her mother by the age of ten, or whether Maudie recognized the Lord's work in every face she beheld. Regardless of the reason, Delsey was grateful. It made the transition from Alabama easier, but she missed her family and the company of other Black people. After she met Plessy, a nesting instinct in her began to take hold. Once they moved into the cabin, she started to make friends in her new neighborhood. The first was the near blind, gray haired Otis Jenkins, parked in a rocking chair on the front porch at the local grocery store. He was there every day, a local fixture, and a sort of country ambassador, greeting everyone by name. But to know your name, he had to get your story first, and that was the beginning of Delsey's induction into the fold. She later joined the local Baptist church, and its worship hall and members became welcome company on those long stretches when Plessy worked the rails.

Delsey dropped the letters in the corner mailbox in time for the three-p.m. post and followed the dirt road along the railroad track leading north toward their cabin. She welcomed the exercise and the unfettered hour it would take to get to the grocery store. There was plenty of time to savor Plessy's proposal, to daydream about their life together. She drifted back to their first meeting on the train platform outside of Gulfport. The lure of the library car had called them both and her immediate feeling had been that Plessy's incarnation as a Pullman porter was a mistake, an error of casting in some great play. She suddenly remembered the dream she had on the train just before arriving in Gulfport. The plain yellow farmhouse, the shellacked maple doorframe, the toddler's grasp around her knee. But who were the men gathered around the table? She now recognized Plessy as the man at the head of the table, but what had they been talking about? She let the questions go, focusing instead on the image of the farmhouse. In her dream, it was a simple structure, nearly square but a little wider than long with a porch fronting the house. Large windows on all sides beckoned to those who passed, the warm light of oil lamps flickering in the front two windows.

Walking home, Delsey floated between her fantasy of the house that she and Plessy would build and the call of the sights and sounds around her. This Saturday afternoon there were few cars on the dusty road. A couple of tow-headed ruffians ran barefoot one last time before winter set in. Where the tracks forked a couple of miles from the depot, a farmer rode into town in a horse drawn cart filled with bales of cotton, the last of the year's harvest. The slow steady clop, clop of the hooves echoed in the lazy afternoon sunshine. She came to the Negro quarters a half mile from the cabin and passed a graying pine plank house where the Tucker brothers sat on their porch, playing checkers on makeshift tables. She stopped at the corner grocery store and Otis greeted her warmly.

"Evenin' Miss Delsey," he said, eyes uplifted, gazing blankly toward the late afternoon sun.

She was not sure whether he recognized people by the sound of their steps or the scent of their approach. "Evenin' Mr. Otis," she replied, more chipper than usual.

"What'sat I hear?" he smiled. "Yo' man come home?"

"Well, yes," she felt a flush of shyness. "You're some kind of seer, aren't you Otis?"

He smiled, the dense cloudy cataracts of his eyes suddenly opalescent. "When the Lord takes one set of eyes, he gives you another."

"He brought me somethin' from New York City, Otis," she said.

"Umm huh?" he mused.

"A dress, like I never seen." Delsey pulled the paper bundle from her bag and worked one corner loose so Otis could feel the material.

"That silk?" he asked.

"Yes sir!" she said proudly.

"What'sa color?" He loved to remember the joy of seeing the world in brilliant hues.

"Deep dark red," she replied. "More like burgundy."

"Um um um, beautiful," he exclaimed rolling the material between his thumb and fingers. "I reckon this means he'll be asking you to marry him soon."

Delsey was so startled by his clairvoyance she could not respond. She and Plessy had barely spoken their intention and it was too soon to share it with anyone.

After a pause, Otis eased her on her way. "Well, I guess you better buy those groceries so you can get on home to him. Tell him to drop by and talk to old Otis sometime."

"I will, Otis, I will," Delsey said. "You want anything from the store?"

"No, thanks. Got everything I need," he said, then smiled. "Sunset's a comin'."

She went into the store and gathered what she needed to make a chocolate cake for Plessy, his favorite. A bar of baking chocolate, a pound of butter and a quart of milk. Then she splurged and bought a three-pound pot roast to go with the potatoes and carrots from the garden. Tonight they were going to celebrate. She gave the cashier two dollars, the equivalent of a day's pay for her. With the change, she purchased a peppermint for Otis. He was dozing when she came out of the store, so she dropped the candy in his shirt pocket, letting him rest.

Delsey walked more briskly as she neared the cabin.

She crossed the railroad tracks and ducked through the opening in the bushes, following the little path Plessy had cut for them. When she got to the door, she opened it quietly, careful not to wake him. The blue suit hung neatly on the bedroom door, which was propped open. She could see him lying there under the covers, his back rising and falling with the deep rhythmic breathing of sleep. She put her bag on the counter and pulled the dress out, the paper protecting it from the groceries. She unwrapped it and hung the dress on the door next to Plessy's suit then stood back and looked at the two of them there together. As quietly as she could, she fired up the stove and put the roast and vegetables in to cook, then opened the canisters of flour and sugar. She measured the ingredients carefully, mixing in the eggs, milk, baking powder and butter. She set it aside to cook later.

Finally, Delsey did what she had wanted to do since Plessy walked through the door to her office two hours ago. She took off her clothes and silently slipped into bed with him. He moaned slightly as she curled up to his back, resisting the urge to wake him with the stroke of a hand. She closed her eyes and soaked in the warmth of his body, then drifted off into a deep sleep.

When he awoke, twilight had settled in. He was hungry, the smell of roast and onions and carrots filling the house, but his thirst for Delsey was greater. He rolled over and pulled her supple body on top of him, waking her slowly, at first, with soft kisses. Within minutes, though, they were rocking at a feverish pitch and their lovemaking was over much too soon for either's liking. They considered starting again after a pause, but hunger was calling them both.

"Let's eat supper," Delsey said, "We've got all night."

They put on their flannel robes and stepped from the bedroom into the warm kitchen. Plessy lit the oil lamps and set the table while Delsey served their plates, then put the cake in to bake, stoking the fire with fresh wood to make it hot enough.

"It's so good to be home with you, Shugs. I'm sorry I was so tired. I was going to cut us a Christmas tree this afternoon, but..." Plessy said.

"No 'sorrys' tonight," she said, placing a hand on his chest to quiet him. "We have a lifetime to worry ourselves over troubles, both little and big. But tonight.... tonight's for dreaming."

"And celebrating," he said, as they sat down at the table. He lifted a fork to his mouth and took a bite, the juiciness of the marbled roast whetting his appetite. They took their time enjoying the meal.

"The way you cook, Delsey Clemons, I do believe I would marry you even if you weren't so good lookin'," Plessy said when he had finished.

"Well, I don't know that I can say the same, Mr. Walker," she sassed, "because as smart as you are, if you think my value lies in my domestic abilities you need a gorgeous face to go with that fat head." She smiled playfully. "I have never worked as a domestic, and I don't plan to start now. I will make my living with my mind, not my back."

"We both will Delsey," he said, the dream visible in his mind. "You will be teaching while I practice law. Someday soon, we'll get there. I promise. And I guess I'm gonna have to learn how to cook."

"I'll teach you. We'll do it together," she said. "Now tell me your news. Tell me all about New York and this, who'd you say? Somebody Randolph?"

"A. Philip Randolph," Plessy said, "head of the Brotherhood of Sleeping Car Porters, the union that really represents the porter's interests. Not like the sham Pullman company union, the Employees Representation Plan." He was suddenly animated, his eyes clear and the cadence of his voice gathering speed. "He offered me a job, Delsey. He wants me to organize the union here in the South."

Delsey could see something rising up in him, some parched possibility watered by hope. She wanted to be excited for him, but a foreboding lurked inside her.

"Can he pay you anything?" she asked, leaning forward, and taking his hands in hers.

"There's no pay for now, but once the union grows, maybe, I don't know. I'll keep working my run on the Crescent. But Dels, I think it is my way back, to the life I intended. I can make a difference here," he said.

Delsey took a deep breath and sat up straight, letting go of his hands. It was clear that Plessy was being called to a cause that was bigger than he was, bigger than both of them. And he was asking her to accompany him through a life's work. She got up to check on the cake in the oven.

"Well Love, like I said, tonight's for dreaming. Sounds like this job could open a whole other world for you."

"For us, Delsey, for us."

She closed the door to the oven and turned around. His eyes were pleading.

"OK, for us. When I said I would marry you, Plessy Walker, I meant it. Through all the twists and turns. So tell me more about the job and where you see the road leading. Then I'll tell you my dreams and we'll see how we get there together," she said as she sat back down.

His face took on a youthful earnestness as he unveiled

the plan. "Like I said, I'll keep working for Pullman, but I'll meet with men along the route and pass along information and plans. I'll have to be in New Orleans a little more, at first, to organize the guys there." Plessy watched Delsey to gauge her response. "We hope to make it a regional headquarters. Once it gets going, though, maybe I can get the men together up here. It may be safer."

A shudder ran up her spine as she recalled the dream, the men gathered around the table in the yellow farmhouse, their words urgent, insistent. She remembered the image of Plessy reassuring her with his eyes.

"What do you mean, safer?" she asked, glancing quickly to the window and back.

He stood up from the table and reached out, pulling her up into his arms. He breathed in the scent of her hair, a scent that smelled like home. He let his enthusiasm wane to allay her fears. "I won't do anything that will endanger us, Delsey. I promise. Randolph hired me because of my discretion and my judgment of character."

Delsey felt the strength of his arms, the ferociousness of his love. Her apprehension settled as her own toughness asserted itself. "You have to be careful, Plessy," she demanded, but in a calm tone. "I know you must answer to your own soul, not mine, but I could not survive seeing you swing from the branch of a hanging tree."

He continued to hold her in his steady embrace. "Nobody's gonna lynch Plessy Walker, I promise you," he said, "and it's only until the union is established down here, Delsey. I don't see myself as a union organizer all my life. I see myself as a labor rights lawyer. I see myself writing the legislation that will turn the freedom we won sixty some years ago into a reality." He let her go and looked into her eyes.

"What do you see Delsey?"

She smiled and held his hands. "I see a yellow farmhouse that we have built with our own hands, and a child. And in the distance, I see me teaching. But right now, I see me frosting you a chocolate cake."

She kissed him for a moment longer than usual, then opened the oven and removed the cake placing it on the kitchen counter while she whipped up butter and chocolate and sugar in a bowl. He unpacked his suitcase while she washed the dinner dishes. After the cake cooled, she frosted it, sprinkling pecan pieces over the top, then cut them each a generous slice. They sat together at the table savoring their dessert, passing the rest of the quart of milk back and forth between them as they dreamed on late into the night. They designed their house, and their pathways back to the vocations that called them. They discussed the savings they had each cobbled together over the last few years, almost eight hundred dollars between them. Their dreams seemed more and more like a reality waiting for their direction. Sated by food and shared imaginings, they finally wandered back to bed.

"Let's go cut the Christmas tree, tomorrow," Plessy whispered to Delsey as he held her in his arms.

She propped herself up on one arm and looked at him, "There's another foreclosed farm up for auction tomorrow afternoon, selling in parcels I hear," she said, eyes dancing like a child's on Christmas eve.

"Well, let's go buy us a plot of land tomorrow, Shugs," he replied. "We've got a house to build."

She hugged him tightly then rolled onto her back, pulling him with her. This time they were in no hurry. Tomorrow was Sunday and they could sleep in. They had no one to work for except themselves, nothing to do but buy their own land. They let their bodies revel in joining again, in soothing touches and heaving passion until dawn finally came and they surrendered to sleep.

MISSISSIPPI 1933

The sweet scent of blue and yellow jasmine rose from the basket Delsey had filled with fresh cuttings. Plessy stood inside the front door of their new house, nailing the last of the maple trim to the doorframe.

"We have to go, Love, or we are going to miss the eleven-thirty train," she said. "I don't know about you, but I don't feel like walking all the way to the Trading Post this morning."

"Done!" he said pounding the last nail into place. "And not a spot of dirt on my suit." He held his arms out from his sides to reveal his pressed white shirt and blue gabardine pants. He put down the hammer and picked up his suit coat from the back of the chair next to the door.

"You look especially fine today, Mr. Walker."

"Well thank you, Mrs. Walker."

It had been four months since Plessy returned from Harlem and proposed to Delsey. The week after he got back, they had managed to buy a small farm, a ten-acre parcel sold at auction. They purchased it for the price of back taxes and a nominal settlement fee, since the four-room farmhouse on the land was uninhabitable. For a few dollars more, they bought the rights to the well. The roof of the house had been leaking so long that most of the floorboards had rotted, and the plaster walls inside were flaked and peeling. But the foundation was solid and the wood planks of the outside walls salvageable. The stone chimney along the west side of the house stood securely among the sturdy rafters, a lone sentry over the abandoned structure. They had to tear it down to the bones and rebuild it, but they had the materials and more than enough resolve.

Plessy had been busy through the winter working hard from New Orleans to Washington, D.C. to bolster the shrinking membership of the Brotherhood of Sleeping Car Porters. The great enthusiasm that swelled the rolls to almost five thousand members in 1928 had dissipated after Randolph's miscalculation led to the failed strike that year. As the economic depression hit, then deepened its hold on the country in 1932, the fear of unemployment pared the union's ranks further. Now, in the spring of 1933, there were less than seven hundred members of the union nationally.

Plessy had no illusions about the difficulty of his job; to inspire hope in such hard times, and to ignite a passion for the Black labor movement as the bridge to full civil rights. Even harder was the task of restoring faith in the Brotherhood as the seminal vessel for this transformation. But Plessy was undaunted. He felt a new sun had risen since the inauguration of Franklin Delano Roosevelt just three weeks before, and Plessy trusted that Philip Randolph had learned from his mistakes. Randolph now listened to the leaders of the local unions. He also recognized the need to move beyond tenuous alliances with predominantly White unions like the American Federation of Labor and instead focus directly on writing legislation in Washington, D.C. This is what had excited Plessy the most, that Randolph had consulted him for help crafting language to amend the Railway Labor Act, so it finally had teeth to enforce its mediation role. The latent lawyer in Plessy awakened once again.

In addition to his profound satisfaction with work, he brimmed with joy for his life with Delsey. She embraced his dream and nurtured it, even hosting fish fries and bake sales for the Ladies Auxiliary of the Brotherhood. But she refused to be relegated to helpmate. She, too, had dreams of helping steer the country in a new direction by ensuring that Black children received quality education. And she wanted a home and family with Plessy. So every moment he was back from the rails they worked on their new house. They slowly but surely removed the salvageable lumber from the outside walls and loaded it onto Hardee's truck. By some sleight of hand, Hardee managed to get Fletcher Moody to run all the planks and timbers through an industrial planer at the sawmill. It had been Maudie's idea to help Delsey and Plessy with the house as a wedding gift, but Hardee willingly collaborated. He could not let Fletcher know where the wood had come from because Fletcher's anxiety over the specter of unemployment seemed, increasingly, to be channeled into a bitterness toward Negroes. Hardee just told him it was a batch of lumber for the Trading Post, and that had ended the matter.

Around Christmas time, word began to spread in the neighborhood that Delsey and Plessy needed help raising their house, thanks to Otis Jenkins. Plessy made a formal trip to the store a few days after he had proposed to Delsey in November, just before leaving for his next work stint in New Orleans. He bathed and shaved before going to meet Otis for the first time. Delsey told him that Otis had insisted on the meeting. Despite his failing sight, the old man sized up Plessy in the span of a half hour over a game of checkers, which he won easily, his fingers lightly brailling their way across the board. His pieces were filed to a smooth edge to identify them. He counseled Plessy during the entire game.

"Now you know you done ruin't her for any other man, Mr. Walker," Otis blurted out after they had scarcely made their introduction and sat down at the table.

Plessy was caught off guard by the swift frankness of the remark, but he could tell the old man meant no offense. He was just being protective of Delsey.

"And I'm not talkin' 'bout flesh and bone, 'cause she got a shape on her hittin' ninety-nine that any man's gonna notice, no matter what you done. Nope, what I'm talking about is you've gone and stole her heart beyond any chance of reclamation."

Plessy waited for Otis to have his say and make his opening move on the checkerboard. The silence softened the air between them.

"Mr. Jenkins," he said, soberly, "I assure you, she has done the same to me." He confided in Otis that he and Delsey planned to marry and they had purchased an abandoned farmhouse.

Plessy slipped his piece diagonally onto the next black square. Within a few moves, Otis had taken half of his pieces. They continued playing their game, exchanging a few bits of story, but Plessy had won Otis's affection the minute they had first shaken hands. By the time they finished their checker game Otis had given the marriage his blessing.

"I'll be recruiting some folks to help with your house," Otis added.

By the first of February, the house had been stripped down to the frame. The windows and doors were removed and wrapped in oiled canvas to repel the winter moisture. They were stacked neatly beneath a large oak at the edge of the property. The fine maple trim from the house's interior had been taken to the Trading Post for dry storage alongside the newly planed wood siding. Plessy had even found time to dig a cistern and line it with brick, trenching the ground to the house for the plumbing that would go to their new indoor bathroom. A few of the porters in New Orleans came up to offer their labor in addition to the locals who had responded to Otis's call. The rains finally abated in the last three weeks of February and the crew of volunteers made rapid progress on the house. Outside walls were wrapped in tarpaper and the siding replaced, after framing in the windows and doors. A tin roof was set over wood slats covered with tarpaper. Inside, the lath walls were replastered. By the eve of the wedding, the house was weather tight and lacked only a coat of paint and the inside finish work.

Maudie had hoped that Delsey and Plessy would marry in a private 'family' ceremony at the Wiggins' home. Delsey knew that Maudie had weighed the offer carefully before presenting it. Though Hardee accused Maudie of being naïve in her treatment of Delsey, Maudie was starkly aware of the Klan's resurgence over the last several years and the risks posed by having a mixed race gathering. Yet her belief in a just God told her to choose her friends on the virtue of their soul, not the color of their skin. Even before Delsey had come to work for them, Maudie had felt a call to care for the child. It began the day that Maudie had held young Delsey, sobbing, in her arms while her mother's body was lowered into the ground. Maudie had come to love Delsey as one of her own. For better or worse, she could not feel otherwise.

For weeks, Delsey had watched as Maudie cultivated the back yard in preparation for the wedding. She did not try to stop her because she knew that gardening had become Maudie's salvation since Brett had left for college, and with Hardee consumed by his business. By springtime, the yard was transformed into a riot of color. An arched trellis, dripping with pink wisteria opened to a small lawn, rimmed with azaleas and forsythia. Lantana was interspersed with nandinas and dogwoods.

But Delsey decided she could not accept Maudie's offer, despite their filial bond. Plessy pleaded with Delsey not to have the wedding at the Wiggins' home. He had no personal relationship with the family, although Hardee and Maudie had treated him well enough on Delsey's account. What troubled him was the real danger that the gathering would incite retaliation from the neighbors. He asked that they marry in their own little church north of town, which they had done yesterday with a large reception afterward. Delsey convinced Plessy to accept the invitation to Sunday dinner, today, at the Wiggins' house as a compromise.

They made it to the railroad tracks in time to catch the eleven thirty train into Hattiesburg. The engineers knew to look for them at this new place on the line. The train slowed again when it came to the spot near their old cabin. Waiting there by the tracks were Delsey's father and brother. Toby and Jesse had traveled from Montgomery two days earlier to join in the wedding party, and they had spent the night in the old cabin to give Plessy and Delsey some privacy on their official wedding night. Maudie had insisted that Delsey bring them along to Sunday dinner. Hardee picked everyone up at the Trading Post around noon and drove the short distance to the Wiggins' house.

When they arrived, Delsey went to join Maudie in the kitchen while the men wandered over to the dining table that had been moved into the back yard. Maudie was putting the finishing touches on dinner. A large pot of ham hock and beans simmered on the stove. She chopped the last of the cabbage for the sour slaw and mixed it into a large bowl on the kitchen table. Delsey knocked on the porch door to the kitchen and walked in.

"Can I help?" she asked, handing Maudie the basket of jasmine.

"What a heavenly scent. How about a hug first, angel," Maudie said, wiping her hands on a towel.

They lingered for a moment in the embrace, then Maudie stepped back a little.

"Let me take a look at you, Mrs. Plessy Walker."

Delsey could not contain her smile. "I do like the sound of that. And thank you for having us today, Maudie."

"Oh Delsey, I am so happy to have y'all for Sunday dinner. It would have been wonderful to have your wedding here, but I understand the quandary. I want you to know that."

"I appreciate that, Maudie."

"You can pull those pans of cornbread out of the oven if you want to and I'll just finish up these deviled eggs," Maudie said, sprinkling a little paprika over the tops of the creamy yolks. "When did Toby and Jesse arrive?"

"They came in day before yesterday on the late train from Montgomery," Delsey replied, then hesitated. "Maudie are you sure no trouble's going to come from having us to dinner. I mean, 'specially with the addition of Toby and Jesse."

"You let me worry about Mr. and Mrs. Moody across the street," Maudie said. "I know they don't approve. They're just scared for lack of money and the prospect of the mill closing."

"OK," Delsey said, "but I think it's best we don't stay too long after dinner."

"That's fine. Y'all go when you're ready. I don't want you worrying about any hurt feelings today. This is a celebration for you and Plessy."

The conversation was punctuated by the sound of boots mounting the porch steps. They both turned to see Brett open the back door to the kitchen, home from college on Easter break.

"Come in this house, my favorite son," Maudie said, reaching up and standing on tiptoes to hug him.

"I'm your only son, Mama," he smiled, kissing her on the cheek.

"And nonetheless my favorite," she said, briefly holding his face in her hands. "And more your own man every time I see you."

He let his mother take a good look at him before he greeted Delsey. "Congratulations, Delsey," he said, sneaking a deviled egg and popping it into his mouth. Maudie slapped his hand gently as an admonition to any further indulgence. "You and Plessy only beat me and Justine to the altar because she insists on being a June bride. I am a touch jealous, but I sure am happy for you two. I know how excited you must be."

Delsey was surprised but pleased by his enthusiastic blessing. Brett had always been closer to her brother Jesse than to her. Their interactions had been more polite than personal.

"Thank you, Brett," she replied. "Jesse's out back. I'm sure he'll be glad to see you again."

"Yeah, it'll be good to see him too." He started to reach for another egg.

"No more, now," Maudie said, catching his hand. "Those are for dinner."

"All right, I'll wait. I just can't resist your deviled eggs, Mama. You want me to carry out the ham hock and beans?" He nodded toward the stove.

"That would be great, Brett, and could you call everyone to dinner? And make sure your daddy set up the card table for the younger girls."

Brett took the large pot to the dining table outside then rang the dinner bell that hung from a tree nearby. The Wiggins clan began to congregate around the tables. Everyone had on their Sunday clothes for the occasion. Faith sat with Grace and Hannah at the little table, telling them a story about the time Brer Rabbit outsmarted Brer Fox. Emma came and stood next to Faith. She loved the stories about Brer Rabbit but she could not stop wiggling. She tugged at the slip bunched around her waist, then sat down. She couldn't bear the starched perfection of her Sunday dress. Claire and Delta sat at one end of the big table, poised in bonnets and white linen gloves. Claire had taken a leap into womanhood with the start of high school but had left Delta behind in the forlorn land of mid-adolescence. While Maudie and Delsey carried plates and bowls of food from the kitchen, the men gathered at the large table. Before they all sat down, they held hands in a circle. The younger girls scrambled up from their table to join the prayer. With bowed heads, they waited in silence for Maudie to speak.

"Dear Lord, we ask your blessing today on this gathering of family and friends. We come together to celebrate the marriage of our dear Delsey and her husband Plessy. We ask that you watch over them, that you guide and protect them. May they know the joy of their union, blessed in your name. And we are grateful, Lord, that Toby and Jesse could join us today. Please keep them safe in their travels back home. Bless this food to our bodies and us to thy service. In Jesus name we pray, Amen."

Conversation rose as plates were passed and heaped with food. Jesse sat down at the end of the table next to Brett.

"Been awhile since we were unloadin' Mr. Hardee's truck over yonder," he said, nodding toward the carport next to the house. He searched Brett's face for some recollection of that day two and a half years ago when he had moved Delsey from Alabama along with most of the Wiggins' belongings, back when he and Brett still had a boyhood kinship.

"Yep, been awhile," Brett replied, thinking how much his life had changed in that time. He smiled back at Jesse.

"How's the farm? I heard your daddy bought a little piece of it for himself."

"He did. We're getting' by. Drought took out most of the cotton crop last year, but we are holding on. You still working for your daddy?"

"No, I'm at Georgia Tech now, getting my degree in aeronautical engineering. And flying with the Air ROTC."

"Engineering? You some kind of genius? I didn't know you were even headed to college."

"Oh, I'm no genius, Jesse," Brett replied. "I just enjoy learning, like your sister Delsey."

"Yeah, she's the smart one of us Clemons," Jesse said looking down at the table.

They groped in silence for further conversation, muted by the stark difference of their lives. The words that finally surfaced fell leaden from their mouths.

"Nice day to celebrate a wedding," Brett said.

"Yep, sunny but cool," Jesse said. He looked up at the sky as if to make his point or gauge if he could fly away from the awkwardness between them. They both knew in that moment that their boyhood friendship couldn't hold them anymore. "Well, I better check on Dad. He hasn't been feelin' too good, lately."

Jesse got up and walked to the other side of the table. He put his hand on his father's shoulder and spooned another helping of beans onto Toby's plate. Toby tried to sit up straighter, fighting the stoop of age and overwork that claimed his body. At forty-five, he had already reached the life expectancy of a Black man in the South at that time. Jesse served himself a plate of food then squeezed in to sit next to his father. There was polite conversation around the table and Plessy and Delsey talked about their wedding and how the work on the house was nearly finished. Jesse and Toby ate their dinner quickly, unable to relax or join in the conversation. Delsey and Plessy were gracious and complemented Maudie on the food. But they too seemed in a hurry, eating their meal while sitting on the edge of their seats. Across the street, a face peered out of the front window, through a crack in the faded calico curtains.

"Come back over here, Fletcher Moody," Ruth scolded. "They're gonna see you."

"It's wrong Ruthie," he said, still watching the proceedings going on in the Wiggins' back yard. "It's just plain wrong and Hardee Wiggins knows better than to be having Coloreds over to his house."

"It ain't our business, Fletch."

"What goes on in this neighborhood is our business," he said, starting to sweat despite the cool day. He turned and looked at her over his shoulder, then turned back to continue watching.

"Calm down, Fletcher. You're just gonna get your blood up again if you don't stop."

"Ain't it enough they's got good jobs? Now they're mingling with the neighbors. Next thing you know, they'll be movin' in next door." His face was red now.

Ruth finally walked over and grabbed his arm, pulling him away from the window. She turned him around and looked at him, her face all worry and concern.

"I ain't gonna let it happen," he said. "You hear me?"

She hugged him and held on until his breathing slowed a little.

"We're gonna be OK, Fletch. We'll be fine." But even she knew they were only a couple of months away from the breadlines if the sawmill closed. She patted his back slowly until she felt him relax.

"Now come have some dinner, then we'll go take a little nap," she winked, enticing him with the only thing that could absorb his attention above all else.

He smiled weakly, weary from fretting, and followed her into the kitchen.

TEXAS 1998, NEW YEAR'S EVE

Faith pulled her down jacket closed, zipping it all the way up. She tucked the quilt around her legs and nestled into the lawn chair that Joe had unfolded. He had placed it in a prime spot to watch the fireworks over Lake Austin. The faint smell of wood smoke drifted up from the valley below. Faith loved coming up here to Mount Bonnell, a lofty name for the cliff outcropping that towered above this swollen stretch of the Colorado River. The arctic blast that had brought ice storms to Austin for Christmas pivoted such that the precipitation left, but the cold remained. The skies were crisp and clear, and she had spent more than one evening up here sipping hot cider or cocoa while watching the stars meander slowly overhead. Diamonds rolling across the indigo velvet of the night.

When Sylvia called at Thanksgiving and begged her aunt to come to Texas for Christmas, Faith had been delighted. She was in a celebratory mood. By luck and perhaps some favor with her oncologist, who knew of her work as a nurse, she was enrolled in a clinical trial for patients with chronic myelogenous leukemia testing the new drug STI571. The pill taken daily had few discernable side effects and was showing miraculous results. Like many patients, she was in a complete remission and had not required a transfusion in two months. She had even put on a little weight and her energy was almost back to normal. She had jumped at the chance to travel again even if only for a short jaunt to Austin. She and Sylvia had grown closer over the last three months through a steady stream of letters, mostly expounding on Sylvia's life at the Juvenile Probation Commission and her relationship with Joe, but also occasionally touching on the inscrutable nature of God. It was time for them to have another face-to-face visit and time for Faith to meet Joe.

The past week had afforded them a chance to get acquainted. She liked him. He seemed gentle, quiet. And when she coaxed him into conversation Faith discovered his deep intellect. Mostly she liked him because he clearly loved Sylvia. She wanted that for her niece.

Sylvia returned from the car with an extra blanket and a picnic basket.

"What? More food?" Faith asked.

"Just a few things in case you're hungry," Sylvia said. She had been trying to fatten Faith up during the visit.

"OK, well let's see what you've got," Faith said, lifting the top of the basket with a gloved hand. She wasn't hungry but she didn't want to dampen Sylvia's good mood.

"There's scones and guacamole," Sylvia said.

Faith looked over and caught Joe's eye. They exchanged a puzzled look of mutual affection for Sylvia's eclectic culinary tastes.

"I hope that means you also brought chips and jam," Joe smiled.

"And the best part," Sylvia continued, ignoring the teasing, and holding up a large thermos, "Eggnog and brandy." She leaned over and kissed Joe's cheek then sat down in the chair next to him.

She fished three mugs from the basket and handed

one to Faith, the other two to Joe. Steam rose from the eggnog she poured into the mugs, the sharp bite of nutmeg registering as she tasted it. A first renegade burst of red sparked the night sky, a test firing before the official fireworks show.

"This is the best New Year's Eve yet," Faith said, stretching her arms out to embrace the moment.

"Really?" Sylvia asked, her voice rising.

"We're so glad you came for the holidays," Joe said. "I've been waiting a long time to meet you."

"Likewise," Faith replied, dipping a corner of her scone in the eggnog. She considered her next question before speaking.

"Joe, I wanted to continue our conversation about Plato and the pursuit of virtue. But I am also curious about your teaching experience at the University. Would I be prying to ask why you left?"

He paused before answering, taking time to articulate his thoughts. An owl hooted from a nearby tree.

"Faith, from you it is not prying though as you sense it is deeply personal. And it has everything to do with Plato's ethics."

"I figured as much," she said.

"As you know, Plato recognized that ethics is grounded in virtue and reflects the soul of the man or woman."

"Who one is, not what one does," she replied.

"Exactly," said Joe, "The foundation of one's being gives rise to intention which leads to action. Being is the source of the Good."

"Or soul is the ground of God, from a Christian perspective."

"God?" Sylvia began but stopped when Joe reached over

and squeezed her hand.

"Yes, you could argue that," he continued. "I see the pursuit of virtue as a more primal call than Kant's call to duty, although both hold to a moral absolute."

"Aha! But who decides what is moral? Doesn't it depend on the cultural values you inherit? Isn't morality simply fidelity to your values?" Faith said. She didn't try to hide the sly provocation.

"Absolutely not!" he said with a smile.

"There you go again with that absolute thing," Faith said, wagging a teasing finger at him.

"I don't deny the moral relativist's premise that the ego, conditioned by culture, filters our perception of the Truth. I personally have wrestled with the mind's infinite capacity for rationalization and self-deception. But that is the very argument to not give up the pursuit of the Good. To accept moral relativism is to abdicate the hard work of building character, of looking deeply within for an answer as to who we are as human beings. It requires more than accepting what our common society tells us."

Hoping to move the conversation from the professorial realm to a more personal one Faith gently asked, "Can you live without knowing the answer?"

"Yes. But I can't live without the quest and that is what the University asked me to do."

Faith sensed his vulnerability.

"I have found that the more certain my views, the farther I am from understanding, especially when it comes to God. Only when I give up the need to see the face of God do I have any sense of Presence."

"Such is the spiritual journey, yes?" Joe said.

"And what other journey is there?" Faith smiled.

Sylvia looked for a way to enter the conversation.

"I never thanked you for sending me that book "A Gradual Awakening," she said.

"Does it resonate?" Faith asked.

"Very much," Sylvia replied. "I'm doing sitting meditation in the morning now."

"And?"

"Well, Joe says I'm easier to live with."

Joe smiled.

"And it makes me curious about what you call Presence."

"Just keep sitting. The curiosity is all you need," Faith said. "I look forward to hearing what you discover."

Faith was careful not to push the matter, trusting Sylvia to find her way. She paused before changing the subject.

"By the way, Joe, I meant to thank you for letting me stay in your caretaker's cabin for the week."

"Truth is it's no sacrifice, Faith. The boss and his family are off skiing in Colorado, so I've got to stay in the big house anyway."

"Well, just the same, it has been a welcome refuge," she said. She especially enjoyed the piano, its bench well worn by Joe's hours at the keys. "Has Sylvia's mother Grace ever heard you play piano?"

"Yep, a couple or three years ago, last time she was invited for a visit." Joe grinned, nodding towards Sylvia.

"Hey guys, don't start ganging up," Sylvia bristled. "New York's a long way off and Mom doesn't like to travel since Dad died."

"I'm not ganging up, Babe, really," Joe said, reaching out to pull her close. "Truth is I'd like to see more of your mom. She's a good soul and even if she does have her own beliefs, it's clear how much she loves you."

"Humph," Sylvia muttered.

"He's right, you know," Faith said. "And I think she misses you."

"That woman thinks I'm going to Hell," Sylvia said. Joe let go when she pulled away.

The first pyrotechnic volley exploded in the sky before them. Green and yellow and red starbursts followed by shards of light falling back to the lake below.

"That woman?" Faith said. "I'll remind you that 'that woman' is your mother. And my sister."

"Please don't start, Faith. You don't know what it's like. I'm forty-four years old and every conversation still starts with her harping that I should marry Joe and stop living in sin."

"Fine with me," Joe piped in.

"It's not about getting married, Joe. Even if I did there'd still be the other problem," Sylvia's voice was weary, worn down by the subject of the conversation.

"So what's the other problem?" Faith asked, as though she had not heard it a dozen times.

"The problem is Mom cannot rest until I say I accept Jesus Christ as my savior and the only son of God, so that we can spend eternity together. Jesus! That would be Hell. I'm sorry, but my salvation as the key to her everlasting peace? No thank you. That's too big a burden." Sylvia said, standing up and rubbing her arms to warm them.

The cold night turned her breath into a small cloud before her face. A round of eight booms rose from the ground below just before the sky was set on fire again. The show dazzled them all into a temporary silence.

"Believe it or not, she just wants you to be happy," Faith said softly, after the climax of light faded to dark.

"I don't know about that. I think she wants to love me but she doesn't know me. Doesn't seem to want to know me. And ultimately, I think that her ideology is stronger than her love for me. That's what I believe and I think it's a shame." Sylvia was spent. She wanted to tell Faith about the real rupture in her relationship with her mother, the secret that her mother would have found unforgivable.

Faith got up out of her chair and turned to Sylvia. She took Sylvia's hands and looked into her eyes. Another flurry of fireworks filled the air above them.

"Honey, I think the shame is that a forty-four-year-old woman cannot find her own relationship with God, or whatever you want to call that thing we come from, because she is still rebelling against her seventy-three-year-old mother." She held Sylvia's cheek in her hand for a moment then turned back to the lawn chair and, still standing, began folding the quilt she had left there. The silence enveloped them like a heavy cloak. They watched as the last volley of fireworks exploded above in a brilliant display.

"Happy New Year, Faith," Joe finally said, standing up and walking to Faith's side. He leaned over to hug her.

"Happy New Year, Joe," she said, hugging him back. She tucked the quilt under her arm and pulled a small flashlight from her jacket pocket. "I'm going to head on down to the car since it takes me a little longer. I'll meet you two down there. See you in a few minutes," Faith said as she reached over and brushed Sylvia's shoulder with the fingertips of her gloved hand.

"Wait, we'll go with you," Joe said.

"Thanks, but I'm fine," Faith replied.

"Here, take the keys. We'll be right behind you," he said.

They watched as Faith carefully picked her way down the stone steps. Joe walked over to Sylvia, her arms now slack at her side, eyes downcast after her outburst.

"Love you, Sylvy," he said and kissed her. She took it in, prolonging the kiss, his familiar taste soothing her. She had never been able to fathom his patience with her. Joe lifted the lantern from beside the picnic basket to light their way down the path.

"I love you so much, Joe," she said, searching his eyes. They were a light blue, contrasting with his brown hair, close cropped and peppered with gray. His high cheekbones accentuated the slight hollow at his temple. Sylvia loved that he was over six feet, a good three inches taller than she was. She rested into his lean, muscled body and wrapped her arms around him, the heft of their down jackets cushioning the space between them. She nestled her face into his neck.

"How did I come to deserve a love like yours, Joe Lambert?" she whispered.

"Well," he smiled, "they say the Lord works in mysterious ways."

"Now don't you start working on my salvation, too," Sylvia chuckled, poking him playfully in the ribs.

She hugged him a minute longer before bending over to gather the mugs and leftover snacks into the picnic basket. She pondered what Faith had said, knowing it was truer than not and wishing she could see things differently. Perhaps with meditation she could find a way out of her old thinking. The most she could hope for was to trust in the Mystery. She stood up with the basket in one hand, a blanket and the thermos in the other. She shivered against a gust of cold wind stirring the oak leaves around her feet.

Joe gathered the folding chairs and took the basket from Sylvia, offering his arm to her as they walked down the hill together. The space between them was soft and quiet. Approaching the car, they saw Faith nestled into the back seat, having arrived just moments before they did.

"Are you warm enough?" Sylvia asked, as she slipped into the front passenger seat.

"Yep, just got here a minute ago. But I will take another mug of that special eggnog of yours."

"Coming right up," Sylvia unscrewed the top to the thermos. "Last cup is yours." She stumbled towards an apology.

Joe put the chairs and the basket into the back of the Jeep and closed the hatch.

"I'm sorry about my little fit back there," Sylvia said as she handed the cup of eggnog to Faith.

"You don't need to apologize, Sylvia," Faith replied, taking a sip. "I'm just sad for you and your mother. Seems like a long time to have been at odds with each other."

"I know," Sylvia said softly. "Truth is I miss her, too."

Joe got into the driver's seat and started the engine. He could tell that Sylvia was mending her fences, so he stayed quiet. He pulled out of the parking lot and began the long winding descent back toward the highway. The heater purred, warming them. It would be a good forty-five minutes before they reached the turnoff to the ranch. They rode in silence for some time.

After finishing her eggnog, Faith spoke up.

"Grace is coming to see me at Easter. I'd love it if you joined us, Sylvia. I'm sure I could scare up a fourth hand for Bridge." She suddenly had a great idea. "How about you, Joe? Do you play Bridge?"

"I do," he said.

"Gerber or Blackwood convention?"

"Blackwood."

"Alright, my kind of man. Not afraid to bid up," Faith said, becoming more animated. "You'll be my partner and we'll take Sylvia and her mother to the cleaners."

"Ganging up again, guys!" Sylvia interrupted.

"Penny a point?" Joe asked.

"Maybe a nickel if I can goad Grace into it," Faith chuckled.

"Well, I could take a few days off and come at the end of your visit, if you decide to go Sylvia," Joe looked over at her and winked. "We could stop in New Orleans on the way back."

"I'll think about it guys," she said. "But you might have to sleep on the couch while you're there, Joe, because..."

"Couch is fine with me, Babe. But maybe you just need some time alone with your mom."

"I'll think about it, really, I will."

Faith hummed a soft tune from the back seat, the brandied eggnog having warmed her from the inside out. "That moon will be full in a couple of days," she said, looking out the window. She paused. "Isn't it remarkable what we take for granted; that morning will follow night? Here we are living on a miracle, a revolving ball that is the perfect distance from the right star. How did elements conspire for us to find ourselves living in paradise? Makes you wonder."

It made Sylvia wonder too and, for once, she did not grasp for an answer. Faith resumed her humming, and Joe reached over to hold Sylvia's hand. As Joe steered the Jeep toward home a stray meteor entered the atmosphere in the distance ahead and burned an exclamation mark into the night.

~

Sylvia hung up the phone after the conference call with the Chance House Board of Directors. It was good to be back at work after the holidays. She lifted her briefcase from the floor and looked around her office one more time before leaving. The Miata was already packed for her weekend getaway to the Hill country. Joe had left for a horse auction in Amarillo that morning. His boss had agreed to a new cutting horse after the old Paint, Picasso, came up lame. Sylvia would miss Joe terribly but, sadly, she needed time to think things through. Since her trip to Mississippi the dreams had become more explicit, their meaning transparent. She could no longer escape the reckoning with her own past.

She walked the short distance to the car, which was parked on the street and threw her briefcase in the passenger seat. There was just enough daylight left to make it to Canyon Lake for a sunset walk on the dam, which was close to the cabin she had rented. She pulled onto Interstate 35 and felt herself relax as she hit the outskirts of town. Sylvia need this weekend to begin facing her feelings, in a place with enough open sky and beauty to hold them. The turnoff to San Marcos arrived before she knew it. The flat grassy fields gave way to gentle rolling hills of limestone studded with juniper and scrub oak. She arrived at the dam just in time for the short stroll across and back as the sun set. The gravel lot was sparsely populated this evening and she met few people on her walk. Without any clouds for reflection, the sun set without fanfare. But Sylvia was too deep in thought to notice. Perhaps it would be easier to sort through her feelings if she could share her secret with someone. But who? She still considered seeing a therapist but hadn't made an appointment yet.

On her way to the cabin she pulled into a roadside café offering flame-grilled burgers and sides and got some nourishment to go. She unpacked quickly when she arrived and took her dinner outside to the table on the back porch, overlooking the Guadalupe River. She ate a couple of bites of her burger and reached for a tablet in her briefcase. She began a letter to Faith.

Dear Faith,

I am still relishing the gift of our time together. Thank you for letting me drag you to all the places that have become touchstones, for witnessing my life with such compassion and understanding.

I have thought a lot about our discussion on New Year's Eve atop Mt. Bonnell. I wasn't completely forthcoming about the reasons that I remain estranged from Mom. I must take responsibility here. It's not just about God or her need for me to be saved. Or maybe it is, because of something I have kept from her all my life, for fear I would never be forgiven.

She may have talked to you about her frustration when I dropped out of college half-way through my freshman year. You remember they had moved to New York the summer before so Dad could take over the family import export business when his father retired. John, of course, moved with them as he was still in high school. My sister, Sophie, had just received her degree from University of Texas and landed a plum teaching position in Connecticut so she could be near them. I left Dallas at the same time to go to UT, happy to be on my own. I loved Austin, the expansive world of ideas at a large university. I felt released from my cloistered suburban world, arriving in this diverse new country. Having slipped the leash of my parents, life became an experiment in discovery. I said yes to everything, including my love for a man named Antwan Chatman.

We met in my only elective that fall semester, Intro to Drama. I sat in the back of the auditorium, wall flowering. He on the other hand stood out, not only for his stunning beauty but also because he was the only Black student taking the course. I just watched him the first couple of days as we practiced monologues before the rest of the class. Then we were paired for the first duo exercise. The skit was simple. Taking turns, we each played a teenage panhandler approaching a passerby on Guadalupe Street. For the first round I was the passerby. I was avoidant, fearful but polite. I pulled the largest bill from my purse and handed it to him, barely making eye contact. The intention was to move along without shaming him. Obviously, the scene didn't last but a couple of minutes, even after he called out to me to say thanks and perhaps open a conversation. I just nodded, waved, and kept walking. It was an entirely different scene when I was the panhandler. Antwan stopped when I approached him. He looked deeply into my eyes with a compassion that left me breathless. He asked me my name and where I was from. How did I end up in Austin? How was I getting by and did I know about the youth shelter on Congress Avenue? Only after that lengthy conversation did he reach into his pocket and give me all his spare change. I was in love with him from that first improv exercise, but I wrote it off to theatrical transference. But a chord had been stuck and we went for a beer after class. Pretty soon it became our routine and transference or not, our attraction grew.

He was my first lover, Faith, and even now I feel blessed by him. It was more than sex. His tenderness, the thrill of his scent, the safety I felt in his arms. We tried to deny where we came from, such vastly different worlds. We would dwell in the present, in the musky smell of autumn. It was all we could do to keep our class schedules and study for exams. By Thanksgiving, I was three weeks late for my period. He almost always used protection, but our passion made us reckless a couple of times. When I told him, he held me gently. I tasted the salt from his tears as he silently rocked us in that embrace. He said he loved me, that he would marry me. We could be a family, he insisted.

Faith, you must remember that was 1972. The Texas miscegenation law had only been overturned five years earlier by the US Supreme Court case, *Loving v. Virginia*. Unimaginable that our love, but for a handful of years, would have been a crime. The law may have changed but racism in Texas had not. We stayed together until the spring, but I couldn't see our future. How could I ever tell Mom? Can you imagine her response? I was the one who ended the relationship. I was terrified of the racism we would face, and shamefully, more concerned for myself than the violence that might come to Antwan. But I never considered aborting our child. Not Antwan's child. He still lived in me even if I had sent him away.

I obviously wasn't traveling in Mexico in the spring and summer of 1973. I dropped out of school and lived with a friend, waitressing to pay the bills. I had Terrell Antwan Barbarino on July 4th and gave him up for adoption through the Home of the Holy Infancy. Maybe now you can understand the distance that has grown in my relationship with Mom. I am finally owning up to my part. Secrets preclude a trusting relationship. But I also find her relentless quest for my salvation, through confessions of my sins, unbearably painful. She has no idea of the forgiveness I seek, the redemption I long for after abandoning Terrell. Every time I think of him, I wonder 'Would I have raised him if he was White?' I don't know how to live with that. It is why I could never have another child, not even Joe's. He doesn't know why I will not give him the family he wants. Where that leaves us, I don't know.

Sylvia looked up from the letter she had written, the river babbling beneath the oaks. A mockingbird trilled in the branches overhead. She felt the constriction in her throat, the banished grief, the unspilled tears. A drink of water loosened the knot enough for her to pick up the letter and read it again. She knew she could never send it. This was Sylvia's work to do. She had never been able to tell Joe about this part of her past and her dilemma was now acute. She knew she would not find peace until she reached out to Terrell, which was allowed by the adoption agency once the child reached adulthood. But that meant she had to level with Joe. Ironic that just as she was admitting to herself how much she loved Joe, she might have to let him go, while he could still have a family of his own. But she had to reconcile with her own son, or at least try if there was the slightest possibility. The knot of thoughts and feelings was too much to untangle alone. Sylvia vowed to make an appointment with the therapist who had helped her through the rough patch after New York. She was scared. But she could no longer deny what she needed to do.

MISSISSIPPI 1934

The wind howled in concert with Delsey's contractions, coming every two minutes now. Gusts of air whipped around the sturdy yellow farmhouse as if trying to get in to see who was being born. A thin stream of light from the waning crescent moon peeked through the bedroom window.

"Keep breathin' Sugar, it'll be time here soon enough to start pushing," said Lettie Burris, a silver-haired rail of a woman who had birthed more babies in the north end of Hattiesburg than most of the doctors in town.

Plessy had drawn two big pots of water from the kitchen tap and was warming them on the stove, as instructed. A small blanket was draped on a chair nearby, close enough to absorb the heat from the stove. A week shy of their first wedding anniversary, Plessy and Delsey were about to welcome their child into the world. Miss Lettie had guessed it was a boy because Delsey carried the baby low, but she readily admitted that she was not a hundred percent in her prognostications. She was closer to fifty-fifty. Predictions were not her specialty; perfect timing of a delivery was. And she rarely had a mother or baby suffer injury during childbirth.

Plessy and Delsey had finished the interior work on the house by early summer the year before, the last coat of lacquer applied to the maple trim of the doorframes on

June 19, Juneteenth, an appropriate day for what had felt like their own personal emancipation. They now had running water pumped by the new windmill to a raised holding tank. The bathroom had a tub and a flush toilet. It was a luxury beyond Delsey's greatest expectations and now, with the pain of childbirth homing in, she found respite in the comfort of their new home. A fire flickered in the woodstove in the bedroom.

"I gotta push Lettie. I gotta push," Delsey insisted.

"Not yet. Breathe, breathe. He ain't started down yet."

Delsey puffed like a locomotive at full speed while Plessy paced in the hall outside the bedroom. He poked his head through the half-closed door.

"You OK, Shugs?" he said, hands fidgeting from forced idleness.

"No!" she hollered, another contraction pushing the baby deeper towards the birth canal.

"She be OK, Mr. Walker, she be OK," Lettie said, reassuring the expectant father. "You can go get that water shortly and some towels. But keep that blanket by the stove so's it's warm when the baby's washed up."

Delsey caught her breath when the contraction subsided and looked at Plessy who still stood in the doorway, his brow furrowed and slightly damp.

"It's OK, Love, I'm OK," she said, forcing a smile. "Do what Lettie tells you."

"I love you, so much," he said, a question in his voice somehow asking forgiveness for his part in the pain she was bearing.

"I love you, too," she replied, then lay her head back, resting. Positioned at the foot of the bed, Delsey alternately sat up or reclined back against a mountain of pillows. Her knees were bent, her feet gripping the edge of the bed. A slightly longer pause preceded the next contraction.

"OK, Sugar, let me see where that little fella is." Lettie reached two fingers inside Delsey and felt the baby's head at the fully dilated cervix.

"OK, you can start pushin' with the next big pain," she instructed, "but only for long as you got the urge. You gotta pace yourself now. He's gonna be here soon. You push as long and hard as you feel like, but when it starts to burn you're gonna slow down, OK?"

Instinct took over and Delsey eased into a natural rhythm of intensely painful work, then rest, work and rest. She could feel her child inching his way down, out of her body and into the world. An abiding sense of peace and gratitude tempered the physical pain. Nothing in her life had prepared her for this, the sheer magnitude of the experience. Plessy came to the door every five minutes to inquire in whispered tones as to the progress of the birth. He wanted to be by Delsey's side but did not know if custom, much less Miss Lettie, allowed such a thing. Finally, after an hour of pushing, the small head began to crown, and Lettie called for the water and towels. When Plessy entered the room, it was clear he was not going to leave. He closed the door behind him with his foot and carried the pots of water over to the foot of the bed. He had towels draped over each arm. The mix of blood and fluids did not bother him. He was mesmerized as the baby's forehead appeared. He watched, speechless, as Lettie coached Delsey to slowly ease the baby's head out. Once the head emerged, Lettie cradled it in her hands. She gently angled it down, tugging slightly, until one shoulder slipped out then the other. The child slid into her arms and let out a robust cry. A small stream of urine shot into the air announcing his relief to be out.

"It's a boy, Delsey, it's a boy," Plessy shouted.

"Told you she was carrying him low, didn't I," Lettie piped in, pleased to have chalked up another accurate prediction. "Now, let's tie off that cord, Daddy Walker, and get this boy cleaned up."

Plessy reached for two lengths of string already cut and waiting on the bedside table. The table also held the tools from Lettie's bag: scissors, gauze, rolled cotton, vinegar and alcohol. There was even a needle and thread in case Delsey tore herself as she pushed the baby out. Lettie tied the cord securely in two places, an inch apart, and let Plessy cut it. She then quickly began cleaning the blood and buttery film from the baby's eyelids and skin, first with a flannel cloth soaked in castor oil, then with warm water.

"You can go get that blanket now, Mr. Walker," she said, directing him with a sense of calm focus. She could see the blood still streaming from Delsey's womb into the basin.

"And Miss Delsey, you gonna need to start pushin' to deliver that afterbirth." She washed the baby once more with warm water, then positioned him in the crook of one arm and began massaging Delsey's belly with the other hand. A gush of blood landed with a loud plop into the basin below.

"What was that?" Delsey asked. A shiver of panic grabbed her for the first time since her labor had begun.

"It's OK, Delsey, just give me some pushes now."

Plessy returned with the blanket and Lettie quickly wrapped the baby up and placed him into his arms. She had no time to reassure him.

"Now, you take that baby over to see his mama," she said, an urgency showing in her eyes. She needed his help.

Lettie soaked a clean towel in vinegar and placed it into the opening of the birth canal, squeezing the vinegar in. She checked for any tears in the perineum, but Delsey was intact. The delivery had been smooth as silk, but the womb was not clamping down after the birth, as it should. She massaged Delsey's belly again.

"OK, now give me another push. I'm gonna tug on the cord here, see if we can get this afterbirth out."

The maneuver worked and the placenta emerged intact, with no apparent pieces retained in the womb. But the bleeding continued.

"Is everything alright?" Delsey asked, her voice shaking.

Lettie shot a look at Plessy before she answered. "You're gonna be fine, Sugar." She reached into her bag and retrieved a small glass vial. "I want you to chew a little of this horn seed while I keep massaging your belly. You're gonna be fine."

Lettie carefully measured out three pieces of a black seed-like material each cut to a precise size. Delsey chewed the seed, wincing at its bitter taste. She looked up at Plessy who was staring down into the face of his new son who was quietly and intently looking back.

"Is HE OK?" Delsey asked.

Plessy smiled a smile so wide that his teeth filled most of his face.

"He's wonderful, Shugs. He's perfect."

Plessy met her gaze with a softness she had never seen before. He sat down on the bed next to her and placed the boy in her waiting arms. Delsey felt a sudden cramp in her womb as the herbs went to work, followed by a softer tightening. The bleeding slowed and Lettie cleaned her with warm towels. Delsey looked at her son for the first time and was flooded with joy. She was surprised at how familiar he appeared to her, like seeing the face of a long-lost love again after so many years.

"What should we name him?" Plessy asked.

Delsey pondered the wonder of those wise little eyes looking back at her. "McLeod," she replied. "McLeod Tobias Walker. After the mentor I intend to study with, Mary McLeod Bethune, and after my father." She paused and looked up. "I mean if that's OK. I guess I used up all his names. We could name him after your family if you want, or..."

Plessy laughed and shook his head. He could not stop looking at his son.

"No, I love it. McLeod T. Walker. It is a strong name, a man's name. The name of a man who can leave his mark on this world."

Plessy placed his hand next to McLeod's and extended his little finger under the tiny open palm. McLeod grabbed it and held on.

"We got ourselves a family, Shugs," Plessy said, kissing Delsey. "We got ourselves a family."

MISSISSIPPI 1937

The dust was finally settling from the whirlwind of President Roosevelt's New Deal initiatives. The spring and summer of 1933 had ushered in an unprecedented presence of government in peoples' lives; lives that had landed on the flat resolute plain of subsistence following the Depression. The government's new plans offered help to the unemployed and new rules of business for farmers and industry. But in the rush to act, the president and congress wrought changes that were as perplexing as they were relieving. In order to stabilize crop prices, farmers were being paid to let fields go fallow and plow their crops under. Sharecroppers were hardest hit, being left with no land to till. Those out of work were offered free food and clothing but the scrutiny required to apply for assistance proved humiliating. Many people chose to go without. Raised on the precept of bootstrap individualism, some people could not adjust to being paid for their idleness.

When the Civilian Conservation Corps and Public Works Administration offered these men jobs, they were thrilled, as they were for the new federal loans that let them save their farms and homes from foreclosure. But not everyone was happy with the new wage and price controls the government was imposing. Although they were guaranteed a minimum wage, people could no longer work more than forty hours a week. The push to limit production in many industries meant fewer jobs and higher prices for food and clothes.

Slowly the engines of factories began to rumble awake and by 1935 it appeared the country had found some strength on the wobbly legs of its economic recovery. There were still plenty of men without jobs but there was a new spirit of confidence growing. A second wave of New Deal legislation revitalized the popular public works projects and established a remarkable new program. The Social Security Act of 1935 provided old age insurance to the elderly and allocated money for children of the poor in a program called Aid to Dependent Children. A safety net was being woven to lift the vulnerable from a sea of despair. But the racial disparity persisted as domestic and agricultural workers were excluded from Social Security.

At the same time, those with jobs were being encouraged to raise their voices about workers' rights. The Wagner National Labor Relations Act passed in the late summer of 1935. It cemented the right of workers to collectively bargain and required employers to recognize and negotiate with employee-elected union representatives. Company unions were outlawed and the National Labor Relations Board was created to oversee and certify union elections. As automobile factories and steel mills shuddered back to life, the production lines that had turned ghostly during the Depression reanimated with men returning to work. The clang of their muscled efforts echoed their newfound power. Just as the desperation of unemployment had forced them to abandon the unions and take any job available in 1930, so the resurgent economy empowered workers to make demands on companies. Those companies were now dependent on the workers returning to the factory floor to meet the rising demand for goods in late 1935.

John L. Lewis, head of the United Mine Workers, was poised to leverage the moment and vault the labor unions into a powerful new political force. Shortly after the passage of the Wagner Act, he broke with the elitist American Federation of Labor and formed the Committee for Industrial Organization. Its objective was industrial unionization because Lewis knew that power lay in numbers. The result of this new union activism, spurred on by the American Communist movement and the fledgling economic recovery, meant an explosion in union membership. That same summer of 1935, the Brotherhood of Sleeping Car Porters beat out the company-sponsored union by a four to one margin to become the legal representative of the Pullman porters. Within two years, they won their contract with the Pullman Company, the first Black union to negotiate a labor contract with a major American company. They secured a fifteen percent pay raise, the guarantee of overtime pay for time worked past two hundred forty hours in a month, and a four-hour sleep break for trips greater than twelve hours. But more importantly, they had won the confidence that their own determination could alter the course of their lives. The seeds of a broader civil rights movement had been sown and the landscape of a new social order began, ever so tentatively, to extend its first groundbreaking roots.

In the South, where cheap labor was the tool used to pry a slight economic advantage from the North, the unions met fierce resistance. Strikes failed amidst intractable unemployment. The specter of the Great Steel strike years earlier, when tens of thousands of Black men crossed picket lines to keep the red-hot metal flowing, stood to remind Southern workers that no job was secure when a hungrier man was around the corner and ready to work. Companies readily exploited racial tensions to further undermine the unions, tensions that flared as Congress began to confront the blatant violence used to preserve the Jim Crow system of the South. An anti-lynching bill passed the U. S. House of Representatives in 1937 only to languish in the Senate where the seniority of powerful Southern Democrats prevailed. The seismic shifts in the established social order served only to calcify the resentment of some Southerners.

Just as the Pullman porters were celebrating their new gains and showing their muscle, the country began to slip into another recession. In Mississippi, the closing of the lumber mills was a last blow and proved that even the strongest man had his breaking point.

~

Fletcher stumbled into the kitchen, his red-rimmed eyes avoiding the late morning sun streaming through the windows. The cut over his right cheek was swollen and bruised, the edges knit together by a thin line of dried blood. The pot scraped as he dragged it from the stove and poured a cup of day-old coffee.

Ruth was gone and had been for weeks. She had moved in with her mother after months of denial, then cajoling, and finally fighting to pry the bottle loose from Fletcher's hand and their lives. But nothing had worked since he lost his job at the mill six months ago. Nothing had been able to stem the flow of bitterness that was eating like acid into the core of the man and destroying his marriage and his body. This morning as he sat at the bare kitchen table, the bedrock of his anger cracked. He slumped in his chair, elbows resting on the table, and let his face fall into his cupped hands. A stray tear escaped his fingers and rolled down a muscled forearm.

Fletcher could not find a new footing once he lost his place as the breadwinner of the house. He had not been able to create a child with Ruth, but he had always been able to provide for her. At least he had been able to give her the basics and occasionally a new dress or a grand prize, like the secondhand piano. After being laid off at the mill, he forgot who he was. He spent the first weeks attending to needed repairs on the house but once those tasks were completed, aimlessness took over. He woke up later in the morning and would wander over to Stinson's garage in the afternoon for a game of cards with his unemployed pals. None of them were union guys and most had signed yellow dog contracts to get their jobs in the first place. The contract stipulated, as a condition of employment, that the worker could never join a union.

When the mill closed, their severance package consisted of a pat on the back and the advisement that 'the fish are bitin' near where that old truck is sunk in Thatcher creek.' It wasn't long before the fish stopped biting and the men gravitated towards Stinson's garage. Occasionally old Ralph Stinson would have enough work to spare a sawbuck to whoever worked for him that week. But mostly the men played cards. Poker, pinochle, canasta; it was always the dealer's choice. The whiskey started getting passed around earlier and earlier in the day. It fueled the growing resentment that was their main conversation. Talk of how some people were winning new advantages while others like themselves were going hungry. The porters' union had won a new contract with the Pullman Company, turning everything upside down. Who would have believed that a Negro could buy the foreclosed farm that used to belong to your cousin?

Mississippi, like most of the South, had remained a stronghold against organized labor. Yellow dog contracts were routine. Fletcher Moody had grown up in a union family and, at first, he had been filled with the optimism inspired by that collective voice. But the American Federation of Labor's own legacy of failure had left him with a bitter taste. The AFL was organized to protect the interests of skilled craftsmen, which is to say native-born White Americans. It had briefly experimented with industrial unionism when it attempted to organize a strike of steelworkers across all skill levels in 1919. Initially the strike managed to shut down half the mills from New York to Chicago and across the Appalachian Mountains to the mines of Colorado. But the steel industry leaders had crushed the union's effort by pitting skilled workers against immigrants. The failed strike left Fletcher's father, a skilled melter, jobless and broken. Having no other particular skill, he had moved his family to Mississippi where he worked in the lumber camps of the thriving pine industry. He had instilled in Fletcher an unrepentant self-reliance and a distrust of unions. He made sure Fletcher acquired a skill as a sawyer and taught him to guard his job above all else. Now, that was gone.

Fletcher lifted his head from his hands and ran a finger over the cut on his right cheek. He winced at the memory of the pointless bar brawl from the night before. He and the poor Okie passing through town had more in common than not, including a short fuse to the blinding anger of humiliation that each felt. He couldn't even remember how the argument started and it had consisted of only a half dozen good blows, just enough to knock the stink out of each other. Fletcher took a drink of cold stale coffee and pondered his fate. He had no job, no children, and his wife had left him. He had done everything his father told him to do; worked hard, been fair to other men and devoted to his wife. Although he supported segregation, he refused to don the sheet. He had lived by the rules of the times and what did he have to show for it? An aching head, a thin dime, and a pig wallow full of pity.

This morning he finally accepted that even if the rules kept changing under his feet, he had to pull himself up. He wanted Ruth back more than anything in the world and he knew the only way for that to happen was to give her back the man she had married. He walked over to the kitchen sink, reached beneath it, and retrieved the half-empty fifth of whiskey. He hesitated as he began to pour it out, his hand showing the first signs of tremor. He tilted the bottle forward and watched as the last of the sweet amber liquid swirled seductively down the drain. He turned and walked over to the phone, cranking the handle three times.

"Lily, I need to speak with Doc Tatum," he said into the mouthpiece when the operator came on the line.

"Alright, Fletcher," she replied, "You OK, any emergency or anything."

"No, Lily. No emergency. Just a little matter I been needin' to tend to."

"OK then," she said and connected the line on the switchboard to Dr. Tatum's office. It rang four times before the comforting deep voice answered on the other end.

"Doc Tatum here."

"Hey Doc, it's Fletcher Moody. You answerin' your own

phone these days?"

"Hello, Fletch. I'm just holding down the fort so Nora Mae can go to lunch. She is too good of a nurse to lose. What can I do for you Fletch?"

Fetcher swallowed hard. "I think I'm gonna need that medicine you told me about. That para... What did you call it? Paral...that stuff that helps..."

"Paraldehyde," Dr. Tatum replied. "I'm glad to hear it, Fletcher. Is Ruth going to be there at the house with you? This could take a couple of weeks."

"No sir," Fletcher replied. "I'll be doing this by myself."

"Well I don't prefer it that way, but alright. This will not be easy you know. You are going to have to stay well hydrated, Fletcher. It is crucial. I will get Dixie's kitchen to send over some soup. Get yourself a couple gallons of apple cider and mix it one to four with water. I want you drinking at least a half-gallon a day. And I'll send Nora Mae over on her way home in the evenings to check on you."

"OK, thanks, Doc. I'll come by this afternoon for the medicine."

"See you then, Fletcher. We'll get you through this."

A slight crackle marked the end of the call as Lily disconnected the line to Dr. Tatum's office. Fletcher could hear her breath against the silence.

"You there, Lily?"

"Yes, Mr. Moody, I'm here."

"Not a word of this to Ruth, you promise?"

"I promise, Mr. Moody, I promise."

～

Delsey stood on the front porch of the farmhouse and watched as the clouds mustered themselves into an angry clinched fist of darkness. A bolt of lightning slashed through the heart of the storm, finding the ground a couple of miles south towards town. A shiver ran up her spine as she called McLeod in from the yard where he chased after the ever-elusive barn cat. She wasn't sure if it was the storm or the morning squabble with Plessy that had her on edge. When she thought about it now, she realized the feeling had been building for some time. Months? Maybe a year? Life had changed after McLeod was born. His birth had fostered a division of labor between his parents that coincided with a divergence in their dreams. Delsey still wanted to teach someday and could imagine herself getting her degree under the tutelage of Mary McLeod Bethune at the Bethune Cookman Institute in Jacksonville, Florida. In fact, her son's name helped carry that dream. For now, though, she was content to raise her rambunctious three-year old, and continue to support, financially and emotionally, the foundation of her family.

Plessy's fire was lit elsewhere. He didn't lack for love of his wife and son nor feel his call was separate from their welfare. In fact, Delsey and McLeod were the refuge from and reason for his growing activism. Ever since the Wagner National Labor Relations Act had passed and the Brotherhood of Sleeping Car Porters had emerged triumphant, he had become a man possessed. Emboldened and unflinchingly focused, he had spent many more hours on the rails helping Philip Randolph organize the men. Randolph had been instrumental in getting the Wagner Act passed and now a contract with the Pullman Company was in the offing. The sense of impending celebration was almost more than Plessy could contain. The course of so great an endeavor had shaped him into a new man, steeled him against compromise and made him willing to take the fight to whatever quarters necessary.

Delsey had watched, first with surprise then with alarm as a growing anger began to fester in him, boiling over in quick flashes of controlled violence: the pile of firewood transformed into a spray of splintered wood; the old tractor rendered to salvage with a sledgehammer when the engine seized up for the last time; the sharp tone in his voice this morning when he realized Delsey hadn't paid the property taxes, due last month. These moments confused her because his tenderness always returned after he had a couple of days at home with her and McLeod. In fact, their lovemaking was slower and gentler than ever. She was learning about the breadth of this man. He could be moved to great anger by the frustration of his ideals but also to vulnerability in a moment with his son, like last night. Delsey had caught a flicker of a tear as Plessy tucked his son into bed by candlelight, lulling him to sleep with a bedtime story. She could not resist leaving the dinner dishes to peek around the corner and watch these quiet moments between the two of them. She had dashed back to the sink before he returned to the kitchen table.

"When did he start climbing that little pine tree?" Plessy asked, settling into a chair, his voice unable to hide the regret of milestones missed. He had watched his son hone his climbing skills earlier that afternoon.

"That surprised me too. He learns so quickly. Remember how he went from pointing at the oatmeal box and saying 'Waneee, waneee' to 'Mama, I want oatmeal'"?

"He's growing up too fast," Plessy said, shuffling the saltshaker from one hand to the other across the smooth worn surface of the table, his brow furrowed.

Delsey folded the towel and placed it on the dish rack. She walked over to him and pulled him close, cradling his head in her bosom.

"I don't like being away from y'all," he said. "Somehow I thought it would be different by now, working for Randolph and all."

She hesitated. Part of her wanted to scream. 'Yes, me too! I don't know how much longer I can stand it. Please just leave it and come home.' But she knew that he would wither without the work. She released her embrace. She stood next to him, resting one hand on his shoulder and the other on the table. She finally found the calm voice that had held them through more than one rough patch.

"How about McLeod and I come with you on your next trip. Mr. Wiggins can spare me for a few days and Lord knows he's beholden to me. Truth is he can't say no to me when I finally get around to asking for something."

Plessy stood up and hugged her.

"That'd be great! I'll see if I can get a sleeping berth and..." his voice trailed off. He thought of the near misses he and his fellow porters had faced ducking down dark alleys after union meetings to avoid Pullman's retaliation squads. "Let me make some arrangements first. Not this trip but the next. OK, Shugs?"

"That's fine," she said. "It'll give me time to write a letter to Jesse back home. Maybe he can drive Daddy to the station in Montgomery to meet us when we pass through. I would love to see my daddy's face again, even if only for a few minutes." Her head rested on Plessy's chest, his reassuring scent surrounding her.

Plessy did not let go of her but his embrace softened. "I'm going to figure out a way to be at home more Delsey, I promise. I am going to talk to Mr. Randolph about it. Once the contract with Pullman is signed, I want to turn in my porter's uniform and work for the Brotherhood full time. A paid union representative, that's what I want to be. I think I've earned it and I think Randolph will agree."

~

Plessy turned up the collar of his wool jacket and pushed his Pullman cap down tighter on his head as he passed into a shady spot along the road next to the railroad tracks. Despite the nip in the air, he decided to walk home from the depot. His train from New Orleans arrived in Hattiesburg at four in the afternoon and the sun was inviting, setting the red and gold oak leaves ablaze from its lower position in the autumn sky. He smelled the smoke of potbellied stoves warming the insides of thin-walled cabins against the season's first cold snap. He thought about his recent conversation with Philip Randolph at dinner two nights before. His 'job' with Randolph to organize the southern region of the Brotherhood of Sleeping Car Porters had proven to be a non-paying position, which he saw as an investment. His call to the work was so irresistible that he never complained, but now the goal had been reached. It was a month to the day since the Pullman Company had signed the contract with the Brotherhood of Sleeping Car Porters. Plessy was now ready to walk through the door that had opened to a wider civil rights movement. He had asked Philip Randolph for a paid position as a union liaison to the National Labor Relations Board.

Randolph had been effusive in his praise for Plessy at dinner that night, but he was noncommittal in his promise of a paying job. Milton Webster, another porter and union member, had organized the biggest and most influential local of all in Chicago. Randolph told Plessy he had already promised the liaison job to Webster.

Plessy didn't feel hopeless, but he was subdued as he walked home that day. He had envisioned a celebration with Delsey and McLeod, announcing his new position and handing them the tickets he had purchased for them on the Crescent's run to New York over Thanksgiving. He had hoped for a coincidence of timing that could have made the holiday an especially personal moment of gratitude.

He looked up from the road where his eyes had focused as he walked along, pondering what to say to Delsey. The wilted faces of last night's jack o' lanterns, perched on the porches of houses, taunted him with their sooty smiles. He noticed a group of men gathered at Stinson's garage on the corner up ahead. Their conversation seemed to take on the posture of an argument as three men stood and looked in his direction. They stopped and turned back to a fourth man who appeared to resist whatever they were saying. Plessy, immediately wary, could hear the anger in their voices, though he could not make out their words. He looked around for a place to run but the cotton fields to his left, just across the tracks, wouldn't hide a rabbit much less a grown man. The voices turned to shouts. Plessy considered what to do next and determined it would be safer to seek refuge in the store next to the garage than to make a run for it.

Fletcher Moody stood in front of Stinson's garage, trying to calm his old friends. His face was pale and gaunt but his hands were steady. It had been a month since he had endured the nightmare of the shakes and fits, his skin crawling with imaginary insects as he slowly rid his body of the whiskey poison. The hot burning taste of paraldehyde lingered in his memory but it had saved him from madness with its hypnotic powers. Ruth had gone to church with him the last two Sundays and there was hope that she might come home again by Christmas. He still came down to Stinson's garage, mostly out of habit but he was finding it harder and harder to spend time with his old buddies as the bottle and their bitterness tightened its hold on them.

"What happen? Did ya' lose your balls when you quit drinkin', Fletch?"

"I'm just sayin' don't go lookin' for trouble. It finds you soon enough," Fletcher said. He lifted his bottle of Coke and took a deliberately slow drink.

"I ain't lookin' for trouble. He's the trouble!" one of the men said, pointing towards Plessy who had just crossed the street, heading for the store.

"Yeah, you hear what they got," said another. "Pay raise. Overtime pay. You see any such thing for our kind? Hell, with this here Roosevelt's recession, we ain't even got jobs."

"He's right, Fletch," said the third man. "How you gonna get Ruthie back without a job."

Fletcher felt his jaw clinch as he thought of the possibility of losing Ruth for good.

The man grabbed Fletcher by the arm and pulled him toward the street. Another hand pushed him from behind. He suddenly found himself face to face with Plessy, the group of men surrounding them.

"See him there. He's climbin' up, makin' a better life for his wife and kid. What you got to show your wife, Fletch?"

His forehead beading with sweat, Fletcher wondered if he did have anything to offer.

"Excuse me," Plessy said, trying to push through the

crowd, but stumbling against Fletcher. He stepped back.

"Keep your hands off him," someone shouted and shoved Plessy back into Fletcher.

Fletcher pushed back. Plessy kicked and elbowed his way out of the crowd, landing a sharp blow to Fletcher's groin.

One of the men shouted, "You find your balls yet, Fletch? Maybe that's why you can't give Ruth no kids." The other men hooted with laughter.

The next thing Fletcher knew fists were flying. He threw the first punch, aimed more at the cackling voice challenging his manhood than anything else. But it landed on Plessy's left cheek. The other men let loose in a flurry of blows they had been longing to unleash, knocking Plessy to the ground, kicking, and pummeling him with their fists. Fletcher retreated to the edge of the fight. A group of people from the store and surrounding houses began to gather. Ralph Stinson hollered for the men to stop, but they were deaf and blind with anger. He went inside to call the sheriff. Finally, the men paused and Plessy heaved himself up, finding his feet. Fletcher walked toward him and reached for Plessy's elbow, trying to steady him. Plessy looked up and spat in his face, blood spattering down the front of Fletcher's shirt. One of the men leapt forward and grabbed Plessy's arms, wrenching them behind him.

"Hit him, Fletch, hit him," the man said as he squeezed harder.

Fletcher heard the sickening pop as Plessy's left shoulder was ripped out of its socket and watched as his body fell limp. Fletcher pushed his old drinking buddy back with one hand and caught Plessy with the other. He fell to his knees under the dead weight as they both collapsed on the ground covered in blood.

"Oh, my God," Fletcher kept whispering, "Oh, my God," he prayed. "What have I done? Help me. Help us both."

～

The sharp smell of ammonia shocked Plessy back to consciousness. A bright light buzzed overhead and flooded his vision, making it difficult to see the faces that went with the voices he heard. Plessy lay on the padded gurney in Dr. Tatum's back office, his left arm in a sling across his stomach. The searing pain that had shot from his neck to the tips of his left fingers, dropping him to the ground at Stinson's garage, had changed. What remained was an immense dull ache in his left shoulder and a phantom-like numbness where he should have felt an arm. Transient tingling like summer heat-lightning flickered in the limp limb. Doc Tatum had waved an ampule of smelling salts under his nose to rouse him. Now as he took a deep breath and considered sitting up, a spasm of pain seized the right side of his chest. He lay still again waiting for the pain to subside and tried to focus on the words coming from the darkness beyond the cone of light circumscribed by the lamp.

"No major broken bones as far as I can tell. I got the shoulder back in its socket but it is hard to know how much nerve damage there is. Time will tell," said a deep calm voice.

Another voice, weak and distant, came from behind the doctor. "Thank you, Doc. I didn't know what else to do but put him in the truck and bring him over. I'll find a way to pay you for all this."

"Fletch, I will take it from here. You hurt?" Doc Tatum said with the same calm sense he afforded all his patients.

"No, not really. Busted lip and a little bruised. Nothin' like him." He paused. "I didn't mean to hit him, Doc. I just started swinging and ..."

Both men turned to Plessy as he struggled to sit up on the gurney and coughed.

"Where am I?" he asked.

"Whoa there Mr. Walker," Dr. Tatum said, easing Plessy back down on the gurney. Fletcher hung back against the wall.

"I'm Doc Tatum and you're in my office. You are pretty torn up but you're going to make it. Stitched up your cheek and the back of your head. You probably have some cracked ribs. I gave you some chloral hydrate before I put that shoulder back in so you're likely to be woozy for a while."

"I want to go home," Plessy said, his eyes darting to the door as though his legs could follow. The musky sweat of fear rose from his body.

"OK, but just hold on a minute. I called Miss Lettie and sent her to fetch your wife. They'll be here shortly," the doctor replied, as he poured a glass of cool water and held it to Plessy's lips. "I need to tell you a couple things before you go."

Plessy sat up slowly and took a sip of water, looking at the doctor with a provisionary trust.

"Now those stitches on your head need to stay in for a week. The ones on your cheek can come out in five days. Miss Lettie can do it for you. You put this salve on your cuts twice a day," he said, waving a small tin of ointment between his thumb and forefinger and tucking it in the breast pocket of Plessy's coat. "It'll fight back infection before it starts."

Plessy ran the fingers of his right hand over the back of his head feeling the prickly ends of the clipped sutures. Then he touched his left cheek and suddenly realized he was only seeing the light with his right eye, since the left was swollen shut. The full extent of the trauma to his body began to register. For a moment, he let his guard down. "I can't feel my arm, Doc." The question was implied in his tone.

Doc Tatum leaned closer so Plessy could see his face. His eyes reflected his concern. "Mr. Walker, I wish.... I wish I knew the answer to your question, Plessy. That is the other thing I need to tell you. When your shoulder was ripped out of the joint, that fellow tore the nerves, the brachial plexus, going to your left arm. Some might just be stretched, others torn clean apart. You might get some use back in that arm, Plessy, but I cannot promise you. I'm very sorry."

They both fell silent as the truth of the matter sunk in.

"I'll give you some codeine for the pain." The doctor held up a glass vial of white tablets, tucked them in the same pocket that held the salve. "One or two pills up to three times a day if you're really hurting. But try to make them last. It'll be hard to get you more."

Fletcher squeezed back further into the shadows knocking a tray of used suturing instruments to the floor where they landed with a loud clang.

"Is that peckerwood in here?!" Plessy shouted, sitting up further, and raising his right fist.

"Easy, Plessy," Dr. Tatum said. "You'll hurt yourself if you move too quick."

The crunch of gravel and skid of tires announced the urgent arrival of a car at the front of Dr. Tatum's offices.

It was not clear whether it was Miss Lettie and Delsey or the sheriff.

Like a cornered cat, Fletcher dashed across the room and out the back door, making a beeline for the alley. If he cut across the cemetery, he could make it to the Wiggins' house in under five minutes.

"You better run, you yellow belly," Plessy called after him, collapsing back onto the gurney.

Fletcher looked back for a split second, part of him wanting to explain, but the instinct to save his own hide pushed him forward into the alley and over the rock wall to the cemetery. Heart pounding, he ran with the quickness of a much younger man.

It was pitch black outside when Hardee Wiggins heard a rap on the back door. Maudie and the girls had already gone to bed and he was enjoying a quiet moment alone at the kitchen table with the newspaper and a cigar. He was not expecting anyone, and the intensity of the knock startled him.

"Who is it?" he asked through the closed door.

"It's me, Fletcher. Hardee, let me in!"

Hardee opened the door and gasped when he caught sight of his friend and neighbor. He was pale and shaking, his clothes covered with blood.

"Good Lord, Fletcher Moody, what the hell happened to you. You been in another bar fight?"

"No Hardee, I'm sober. Sober as a judge. But it was horrible. A horrible thing down at Stinson's garage. I, I...." he fought to catch his breath after the run from Doc Tatum's.

"Come on in and sit down, Fletch."

Hardee looked around in the darkness behind Fletcher,

then closed the door and locked it.

"I think the sheriff is after me." His eyes were glassy.

"Sit down, man. Let's just calm down, now. You're safe in here."

Hardee took a better look at Fletcher. It appeared that he had not received the brunt of the fight. There was a slight cut on his lower lip but no other marks. It did not explain the amount of blood on his clothes, which made Hardee think that someone else was in much worse shape. From the look on his friend's face, he was worried that Fetcher might have sent someone to meet his maker that night. Hardee stirred the coals in the wood stove and added some fresh sticks of wood, trying to think of what he should do.

"What you drinkin' instead of whiskey? How about I heat you some cider?"

"Okay. Alright. That sounds good." Fletcher said. He was hugging himself, rocking slowly back and forth in the kitchen chair.

"Want to tell me what happened?" Hardee asked.

Fletcher recounted the story in detail, emphasizing his confusion and how he had tried to avert the fight in the first place. He broke down crying,

"I didn't mean for this to happen, Hardee. Oh my God. What is Ruthie gonna say when she finds out? What is she gonna do if I get arrested?"

Hardee thought he heard the pat of feet in the hallway and when he looked at the doorway between the kitchen and the hall, he thought he saw a movement. But then everything was quiet, and when he looked again, he could not see anyone there. He rubbed the back of his neck trying to figure out what to do. He couldn't bear to see Fletcher in trouble with the law, not after all he had gone through to get himself sober for Ruth. Hardee knew the torment Fletcher had faced in giving up the bottle.

"Get those clothes off, Fletch. I'll heat some water so you can clean up. I've got an old shirt and pair of trousers you can have."

"I don't know why I hit him, Hardee. You gotta believe me. The guys started teasing me, telling me Ruthie would never come back, that I couldn't give her a child. I just went crazy, started swinging and…"

"Shhh. Don't worry. Just get those clothes off, Fletch."

Fletcher stripped down to his underwear, while Hardee stuffed the blood-stained garments in the stove, making sure they burned down to an ash. While Fletcher took a sponge bath over the washbasin, Hardee headed toward his bedroom to retrieve the clothes he had promised.

At the far end of the hall skittered the swift-footed Faith. She slipped around the corner into her room just before Hardee reached the hallway. Faith was not sure what she had just witnessed but she knew it was bad. Mr. Moody had done something very wrong, and Hardee was hiding it.

～

By the time Christmas arrived, Plessy was pretty much healed up except for his left arm, which hung limp at his side. He could at least shrug the shoulder now, suggesting the nerves were showing some recovery. But the gain in muscle strength came at the cost of a knifelike pain that ran from his neck to his elbow as the sensory nerves reawakened in random bursts. Miss Lettie had seen a few children born with Erb's palsy, a similar but milder condition in babies whose necks were stretched during childbirth. She was able to help Plessy with physical therapy exercises to keep his joints limber and encourage what movement the arm could still manage.

Delsey received an extra bonus from Hardee that Christmas, an unexpected but welcome surprise. Plessy had been unable to work since the injury. When Milton Webster heard through the porters' grapevine what had happened to Plessy he called Philip Randolph with the news. Both men decided that a position must be found for Plessy in Washington, D.C. Randolph spent days searching for a solution. If not a union representative, certainly there must be a clerk's job at the National Labor Relations Board for Plessy. He knew that Plessy had enrolled in Howard University's law school almost a decade earlier only to lose his scholarship.

The NLRB was hiring legal staff as fast as it could find applicants now that the Supreme Court had upheld the Wagner Act in *NLRB vs. Jones and Laughlin*. This case had involved ten men fired from the Jones and Laughlin Steel Company in retaliation for their union membership. The steel company had argued that since the court had previously ruled that the 1933 National Industrial Recovery Act was unconstitutional, they were not subject to the rulings of the labor board on behalf of the workers. The Supreme Court reversed itself and upheld the new 1935 Wagner National Labor Relations Act, which specifically forbade discrimination against union members. It was a huge victory for organized labor, but also for the NLRB, which began a rapid expansion of its overworked legal staff. It took some maneuvering but Randolph finally landed Plessy a job as a legal assistant. He sent a telegram on Christmas Eve.

When the Western Union messenger arrived at the Walker's farmhouse that night, the amber glow of kerosene lamplight shone through the windows. He knocked on the front door. The smell of honeyed ham and mulled cider greeted him when it opened.

"Telegram," he announced.

Plessy stared at him a moment, uncertain what the envelope held, but he took it with his right hand.

"Thank you," he said.

"And Merry Christmas," the delivery boy added, waiting with a hopeful smile.

Plessy reached into his pocket to fish out a dime. He handed it to the boy with a quiet nod of his head.

"Oh, yeah," he said flatly, "Merry Christmas."

He closed the door and took the telegram to the large table in the front room. Delsey was just clearing the plates from the late holiday dinner. The ham had been a gift from the church and she had gathered yams from the root cellar and green beans from the pantry to prepare a huge feast for family and friends. Miss Lettie Burris and Otis Jenkins had joined them for Christmas Eve and were sipping their mugs of cider, the room now quiet after the big meal. A small pine tree stood in the corner of the room, its young branches garnished with strands of popcorn and cranberries. McLeod had fallen asleep on the cloth skirt beneath it, nestled among a few wrapped presents. Plessy sat down and struggled to open the thin brown envelope with one hand.

"Dammit!" he growled under his breath.

Otis reached over into the veiled void between them and held the envelope still while Plessy snagged a finger beneath the flap and ripped it open.

"What the Lord brung you now?" Otis asked with not a hint of fortune or fear.

Plessy unfolded the paper inside and read the words out loud.

PLESSY WALKER=
SOUTHERN   RAILWAY   DEPOT   HATTIESBURG MISSISSIPPI=

JOB WAITING   NLRB LEGAL THIRTY DOLLARS A WEEK AWAIT REPLY=

PHILIP RANDOLPH.

The squeals of jubilation from Delsey and Miss Lettie woke McLeod from his nap. Otis chuckled, a private little prayer of gratitude. He remembered when Delsey had come to him years back with a dream that had scared her, a dream she later realized was about Plessy and the Brotherhood of Sleeping Car Porters. It had seemed clairvoyant, foreshadowing grave danger for him. Otis, who knew the pain of prophecy, had tried to reassure her.

"Not everything you see means it's gonna be," he had said. But he, too, had worried.

Plessy read the message aloud again to convince himself it was real.

JOB WAITING   NLRB LEGAL THIRTY DOLLARS A WEEK AWAIT REPLY=

"Lordamighty," he cried, his radiant smile returned for the first time in weeks. "Await reply. What do you say, Dels?" he said, standing up from the table.

She grabbed him and kissed him full on the mouth,

forgetting they had company.

"I'll tell Mr. Wiggins to find himself another bookkeeper. I'll tell him day after tomorrow. I never doubted your destiny, Pless, because I know your strength resides in your character, not your body."

Otis patted Miss Lettie's hand. "Sounds like it's time for you to drive me home, Miss Lettie," he said, a hint of a sparkle in his old, clouded eyes.

~

Delsey arrived early at the Trading Post on the morning after Christmas. She buttoned her coat for the short walk from the train depot. The sun was rising and the early light revealed the frozen dew, shining like tiny glass slippers on the blades of grass. She entered the Trading Post through the back-office door as she had for seven years and immediately went to build a fire in the small woodstove. As the crackle of flame consumed the wood, she took off her gloves and looked around the room. This had been her home for a year after she arrived from Montgomery. The stinging memory of loneliness pierced her. How had she managed without Plessy and McLeod, with only the alley cats and her books to comfort her? She shuddered as though a ghost had passed by.

She had decided to give Hardee a month's notice so he could find an accountant to take over the store's ledgers. It would give her time to finish the yearly inventory and ready the receipts for taxes. Plessy wired Randolph on Christmas day saying he was immediately available for the job in Washington. He'd start the first week of January and was at the Southern depot at this very moment calling the Pullman Company with his formal resignation. Delsey heard the front doorbell jingle announcing Hardee's arrival.

She swallowed hard and practiced her words, then walked to the front of the store.

"Good morning, Mr. Wiggins."

"Mornin', Delsey," he said, walking to the front counter with a spring in his step. "Hope you had a Merry Christmas." He unlocked the cash register behind the counter.

"We sure did, Mr. Wiggins. How about you and Maudie and the girls?"

"Wonderful Christmas, Delsey. Brett surprised us and came home for the holiday."

"Oh, my goodness. Brett's home?"

"Yes, but just for a couple of days. Ever since he graduated from Georgia Tech and enlisted in the Army Air Corp, we're lucky to see him at all. He's doing his advanced flight training over at Kelly Field in San Antonio these days." Hardee beamed. "You ought to drop by the house for dinner today and say hello to him and Justine."

Delsey hesitated. She didn't know if she could ever join the Wiggins table again.

"I appreciate the invitation but I need to get dinner on for Plessy. He needs more help these days," Delsey sad.

"Oh, I understand," Hardee replied, looking down into the cash register.

"Mr. Wiggins, I do have some good news to share with you."

He looked up and nodded, waiting for her to go on.

"Plessy has been offered a real good-paying job with the government in Washington, D.C. He'll be moving up there next week and McLeod and I will follow him in about a month."

The smile faded from Hardee's face, but he made an attempt to get it back. He knew Plessy would not stay in

Hattiesburg after what happened to him.

"Well Delsey, I will force myself to be happy for you. But Lordy, after all these years, I don't know what I'll do without you." Delsey was surprised by his acknowledgment. She had never heard him say he depended on her. "You will come to dinner today, won't you? I think Maudie will want to hear it from you, not me."

"I can't stay for dinner, Mr. Wiggins, but I'll come by and tell Maudie."

Delsey walked over to the Wiggins house later that morning and found Maudie in the kitchen preparing the noon meal. She knocked on the back door.

"Oh, good, you can join us for leftovers," Maudie said when she opened the door.

"Oh, that's kind of you but I can't stay. I need to get back to Plessy and McLeod."

A part of Delsey had already left Mississippi and the Wiggins.

"I understand," said Maudie. "How is Plessy?"

"He's still on the mend. It was a terrible injury. He can move his shoulder a little. He's got some feeling back, almost to the elbow. But his spirits are still pretty low."

"I'm so sorry about what happened to him, Delsey. I keep prayin' over him. Every morning and every night."

"Thank you, Miss Maudie. I hope it helps." She continued after a moment's pause. "I need to tell you something, Maudie. Mr. Philip Randolph got Plessy a job with the national labor board up in Washington, D.C. I'll be leaving next month."

They were both silent as their tears welled up, then retreated.

"I'm happy for y'all, Delsey, truly happy." Maudie put

the leftover ham and potatoes in the oven to heat. "You must be really proud of Plessy. He's a brave man. And Washington, D.C. is bound to offer you and Plessy all sorts of new opportunities. I can understand why the Lord opened this door and I think you are both headed to greater things."

A sound came from the dining room.

"Faith, you don't have to hide behind the door. You can come on in since you're listening anyway," Maudie said.

"I didn't want to interrupt y'all," Faith said.

"I'll go put the plates on the table so you two can have a minute to talk," Maudie said. "And Delsey, I want to come say goodbye to Plessy before he leaves."

Faith stepped into the kitchen as Maudie left. She had turned fourteen in July and had emerged from puberty with the petite hourglass figure that blessed all the young Wiggins women. Her blue eyes were soft and open. A faint line formed in the middle of her brow. She bit the inside of her lip for a second before she spoke.

"You're leaving?" she asked.

Delsey smiled gently. "Yes, Faith. I think it's time. Everything has its time."

"Is it because of what happened to Mr. Plessy?" It was a question that needed asking.

"Uh huh. You could say that."

"What did happen, Delsey?" Faith wanted to talk to someone about it.

"Some men beat him up, Honey. Beat him up bad."

"What men?" Faith persisted.

Delsey's eyes narrowed as she tried to decide whether to continue or let the conversation die. Faith had always been the kindest of the Wiggins girls.

"Some men from down at Stinson's garage."

Faith's eyes went back and forth from left to right as she thought back. Delsey watched Faith working a puzzle.

"What night?" she asked. She remembered the sight of Fletcher at the kitchen table, his clothes splattered with blood.

"November first, the day after Halloween." Delsey said. She was going to give Faith the pieces and let her figure out for herself who had injured Plessy. Plessy had recognized Fletcher that day, having seen him before at the Trading Post. Plessy had told Delsey that Fletcher was one of the men who hit him, but not the one who dislocated his shoulder.

"How come they beat him up Delsey? Was there an argument?"

"No, Faith. He was just walking home. There was no argument and he didn't do anything."

"Why Delsey, why would they do that to Plessy?"

Delsey's warm brown eyes suddenly darkened. She was not prepared to speak it, but Faith was insistent.

"Faith, you're smart enough to know the answer to that. He was beaten for nothing more than the color of his skin."

Faith had always known the world was divided into Colored and White. She had even questioned it, but she had never faced the cruel violence that kept it that way. Suddenly, a curtain was pulled back on a world she did not want to see, opening a chasm between them, one that had not been there before. It seemed unbridgeable.

"Oh, Delsey. I'm gonna miss you."

WASHINGTON D.C. 1941

The sidewalk was littered with spent cherry blossoms, clustered in pink drifts at the curb. Plessy paused at the corner of Fourteenth and Constitution and gazed up at the Washington Monument, a few hundred yards to his right. Even though he had rounded this corner five days a week for the past three years the sight of that massive spire still commanded his view. The new Main Labor Building sat across from the National Mall, an expanse of green lawn hemmed on north and south by thick rows of elm trees and confined to the east by the U.S. Capitol. The mall abutted West Potomac Park and boasted monuments at both ends: the obelisk at which he now stared, and in the distance, the Lincoln Memorial perched on the banks of the Potomac River. He could not believe how much had changed for him personally over the past three years.

Plessy remembered arriving to freezing rain and a shroud of fog that descended upon the nation's capital in the first days of 1938. The stark contrast to the temperate Mississippi winter had only compounded his physical disorientation. Already dizzied by the buzz of city traffic, and sorely missing the sight of a horizon, Plessy's mind had seized up. His view was obscured in all directions by the grand architecture of federal buildings. He had not yet become accustomed to the paralysis in his left arm and in those first weeks of 1938, while Delsey and McLeod were still in Mississippi, he was overwhelmed with bouts of fear and doubt. The injury had left him with more than a flail arm. It had shattered his confidence. He had finally confided his concerns to Philip Randolph one night over dinner at the Whitelaw Hotel, where Randolph was staying on a visit to Washington.

"Mr. Randolph," he said, "I'd like to address some personal matters that I think you should know about."

Randolph leaned back in his chair and untucked the napkin from the front of his shirt. "This isn't a court, son, and I'm no judge. Friends don't require such formality. And you're talking to a friend."

"Thank you, Brother Randolph," Plessy sighed. "I guess I'll just say it then. I'm afraid I may not be the right man for this clerk job at the NLRB."

"Why's that?" Randolph reached for his water and took a long, slow drink. He set the glass back on the table and waited.

"Well, I don't know. I barely finished two months of law school before the money ran out and I had to go to work for Pullman. I am the only Black face in the building far as I can tell, except for Henry who works the lunch grill. And now that I got this handicap..." He shrugged his left shoulder and looked down at his trouser pocket where his left hand disappeared into its perpetual repose.

Randolph remained quiet until Plessy could finally look up and meet his eyes.

"I wouldn't have recommended you for the job, son, if I didn't think you were up to it. You were hired for the strength of your mind, not your left arm which was injured through no fault of your own."

Plessy nodded, silently taking in the encouragement.

"Now, I'll grant you that working over at the NAACP with Professor Houston and young Thurgood would be a more congenial culture. I am just not convinced that they can end the discrimination that keeps Black people from getting good jobs and serving alongside White folks in the Armed Services. I have big dreams Plessy and I think you are destined to play a part in realizing them. It requires access to the inner workings of the federal government, where laws are written and enforced. That's why I need a man like you inside the National Labor Relations Board."

"But am I the man to work on the inside? I feel mute there and at the same time I'm burning inside to speak up about the specific needs of Black labor," Plessy said, sitting up straighter in his chair.

"You are exactly the man for this job," Randolph replied. "It is your experience organizing the porters' union in the most dangerous part of the country that gives you an advantage. You know when to speak up and when to be quiet."

Plessy thought about what they had accomplished at the Brotherhood of Sleeping Car Porters. "We did win our contract, didn't we, Brother Randolph?"

"We sure did, Plessy. And it is just the beginning. I intend to see to it that President Roosevelt desegregates the military and opens jobs in the defense industry to Black people, at equal pay and benefits. And Mrs. Bethune is working very successfully with Mrs. Roosevelt over the same issues."

"Mary McLeod Bethune?" Plessy's eyes widened. "You know it's always been my Delsey's dream to work with her. We even named our son for her."

"Well, Mrs. Bethune is living in Washington, D.C. these

days, running Mr. Roosevelt's Black cabinet. She's still president of Bethune-Cookman College but her principal endeavors are here. Tell you what, you call me after you wife arrives, and we'll arrange for Sunday dinner together."

"Thank you, Brother Randolph," Plessy said, as he stood up and reached into his right pocket to retrieve a five-dollar bill for dinner.

Randolph stopped him. "This is on me tonight."

"Thank you. I mean for everything; the job, this dinner and....and for talking to me tonight."

"It's a pleasure, Plessy. I know a good man when I see him, and we would never have won that contract with Pullman without your help."

Plessy felt like lead weights had been removed from his feet as he walked the two blocks to his room at the Twelfth Street YMCA that night. The doubts left and he was back to himself by the time Delsey and McLeod arrived in February of 1938. He secured a two-bedroom apartment in the basement of a row house at Ninth and U streets for forty dollars a month. It was a couple of blocks from Howard University hospital, an area he knew from the days when he lived with his sister and brother-in-law. They had since moved to Harlem, seduced by the new cultural Mecca.

Plessy and Delsey were never more contented than in the summer of 1938. They created a wonderful new home in that apartment. McLeod had his own room for the first time, and he relished it with the swagger of a four-year-old. It was the rare night that he would find his way into their bedroom and climb up into his mother's arms. Between the university and the community of rising political activists, the neighborhood pulsed with activity. Sometimes on a still evening, you could hear the pure crystalline voice of

Ella Fitzgerald radiating from the nearby Howard Theater or the jubilant sound of swing rising from Duke's piano. They thrived in their new life.

Randolph quickly delivered on the Sunday dinner meeting with Mary Bethune, who lived only a few blocks up on Ninth Street. She and Delsey took to each other like long lost friends, walking arm and arm in front of Plessy and Randolph as they strolled Howard University's campus after dinner. Mrs. Bethune invited Delsey to join the National Council of Negro Women, which she headed.

As Delsey fought alongside Plessy to overturn segregation, a new world opened to her, a world so unlike the one in which she had grown up. When McLeod entered kindergarten in the fall of 1939, she started her first courses toward her teaching degree. Though Mrs. Bethune was not her professor, she had indeed become her mentor. Plessy settled into his new job at the NLRB, patiently earning respect and eventually being trusted to draft briefs for pending lawsuits. He drew satisfaction in the incremental progress of his work, but he longed for something more revolutionary.

In late 1940, he got his chance. After three years of trying to persuade Mr. Roosevelt to desegregate the military and open defense jobs to Negroes, Philip Randolph finally had enough of waiting. In September of that year, shortly after another failed meeting with the president, he invited Plessy to join him and Milton Webster on a New Year's Eve trip to visit the southern locals of the Brotherhood of Sleeping Car Porters. In the course of their conversations that night, as the calendar flipped from 1940 to 1941, they launched the March on Washington Movement. They would organize ten thousand Black people to march to the grounds of the White House and make their demands known. They would sit there peacefully until their voices were heard.

That had been over four months ago, and the movement had mushroomed into a march of one hundred thousand people, with headquarters springing up from New York to St. Louis and even San Francisco. Plessy was in charge of organizing the southern states where he had contacts from his Brotherhood days. As he now looked up at the Washington Monument, he felt proud of what the Black community had been able to accomplish on a national level. There was a palpable excitement about the march, scheduled for July 1, less than two months away. He looked at his watch and realized he was late for work. Plessy prided himself on being the first into the office each morning. He quickened his step, rounding the corner to his left. He walked past the towering colonnade of the Main Labor Building and found his boss, Stanley Glasser, beneath the limestone archway marking the building's entrance. Glasser was taking a last puff on his cigarette.

"Hey Plessy, nice work on the intermediate report on the Weirton Steel case. Halliday was impressed. Says the case should be decided on the merits based on your report."

He snuffed out the ember of the cigarette butt beneath the toe of his shoe. Stanley Glasser was the chief clerk at the Board and Plessy's immediate supervisor.

"Did Paul mention me by name?" Plessy replied, unable to mask his surprise. He knew the care with which he had researched the case, but he was not sure if Paul Halliday, the assistant general counsel assigned to it, had noticed. It was the kind of case Plessy loved to investigate, a coercion case where justice would be applied to company thugs who had been wielding clubs against union organizers. A twinge of pain shot through his left elbow, an infrequent but startling reminder of his own beating.

"Yeah. Singled you out. 'Walker's thorough, attends to the details,' is what he said."

"Good," Plessy said, nodding, his lips slightly pursed.

"Hey Walker, at least you're valued, if not compensated," Glasser said with a shrug as they walked across the marble floor of the foyer. They turned down the hall to the clerks' offices and paused at the door to Glasser's office. "Let me know if you need any help on the New York Merchandise case," he added and disappeared behind the mahogany and glass door with the title Chief Clerk stenciled on the frosted pane.

Plessy proceeded down the hall to the large open office at the end. The room was filled with a dozen metal desks, each occupied by a Remington typewriter resting on a leather desk pad. Most of the desks were still empty, but soon a concert of clicks would rise to animate the air as clerks tapped out the reports that awaited their attention. Plessy walked to his desk along one wall and removed his coat, draping it over the back of his chair. He retrieved the coffee mug he kept in the bottom drawer. The electric percolator was burbling away at the small table in the corner, a sign that Ellen had already prepared the pot. He smiled as the smell of coffee greeted him.

"Good morning, Ellen," he said, when she returned from the ladies' room. "Thanks for making the coffee."

"You're welcome Plessy," she smiled. "I confess I do it selfishly. I can't take the black swill you guys pass off as coffee." She blushed slightly, realizing the potential offense in her words.

"Well, black is fine with me," he smiled, "but I will admit your coffee tastes better than mine."

He returned to his desk, set his cup down and leafed through the papers in the wooden inbox. They were mostly Labor department memos of no particular significance to him, just more bureaucratic redundancy. His mind wandered to the pending details for the March on Washington. He wanted to call Delsey and ask her how much money the National Council of Negro Women had raised this week. He still needed to talk to the Twelfth Street YMCA about places to house all the marchers when they descended on the city next month. First, though, he had to type up his notes on the New York Merchandise case and get them to Glasser by this afternoon. It would take a while to type it, one key at a time. He eased a piece of paper into the platen of the Remington with his right hand then reached for the knob to roll it into place. He heard the soft crunch as the paper wrinkled behind the roller.

"Damn it!" He whispered under his breath. He wanted to be marching at full stride with a placard in his hand, not fumbling with some cantankerous machine. He rotated the knob backward and released the paper, turned it upside down and tried again. As the paper slipped into its slot on the second try, the voice of a young man who had entered the office startled him.

"Telegram for Mr. Plessy Walker," the messenger said.

The rest of the clerks had slowly trickled in, and the desks were mostly full now. Plessy raised his hand like an eager student and waved the young man toward him.

"That's me, I'm Mr. Walker," he said.

He took the envelope and placed it beneath the

paperweight on his desk. He slipped a letter opener beneath the flap and neatly ripped it open.

PLESSY WALKER=

MAIN LABOR BUILDING   WASHINGTON DC=

NEW DEVELOPMENTS M.O.W. COMMITTEE MEETING HARLEM YMCA   JUNE 7=

PHILIP RANDOLPH.

Plessy was apprehensive. What new developments? He had worked hard to prepare for the march. The next three weeks dragged on at an insufferable pace, exacerbated by sweltering heat in the last week of May. Plessy boarded the train to New York on Sunday morning, the day of the meeting. He paused on the platform to hug Delsey one more time before he boarded.

"Stop worrying," she said. "It makes you look like an old man."

"But what if he's going to call it off? What if something's wrong?" Plessy said.

"I promise you that Brother Randolph is committed to getting fair labor practices enacted. The March on Washington is the way he is going to do it." There was a schoolteacher's firmness beneath her reassuring manner.

"OK, then I promise to take you dancing at the Savoy Ballroom to celebrate after the march," he smiled as the whistle blew, announcing the last call.

Plessy and his family had visited his sister in Harlem several times in the last three years. He had succumbed to Delsey's pleas to go dancing on their very first visit. The spirit of renaissance that filled the clubs and theaters of the neighborhood had helped him heal from the injuries he had suffered to both body and soul. He had managed to perfect a right-handed version of the Lindy Hop, having just enough strength in his left shoulder to barely raise that arm and guide Delsey back to him at the end of the swing. He committed to this labor of love because of the thrill it brought her. The smile of total abandon on her face when she was dancing was irresistible to him.

Today, though, Plessy could not shake the weight of worry. The sun blazed overhead when he arrived at the Harlem Y. He found his way down the hall to the gymnasium. The door, propped open by a metal folding chair, held a hand painted sign saying "M.O.W. Comm. Mtg." with an arrow underneath pointing into the room. The men were sitting in a loose grouping of chairs along the opposite wall, beneath the open windows. A large fan stirred the air, providing a hint of a cool breeze. Plessy picked up a chair from the stack next to the door and went to join the other men.

Philip Randolph cleared his throat and spoke. "Well, gentlemen, we should probably get started."

The hum of conversation fell into quiet whispers as the men pulled their chairs into a circle.

"Mrs. Mary Bethune sends her regrets that she cannot be here today, but a prior commitment required her to be in Jacksonville to attend to her presidential duties at the college there," Randolph continued. "She asked that I convey the substance of her communications with Mrs. Roosevelt over the past month."

"Communications about the March on Washington

Movement, I assume," one of the men said.

"Exactly," replied Randolph. A fly buzzed against the hot windowpane behind him.

"Were these official communications, Philip? Letters?" asked another man, whom Plessy recognized to be Walter White, president of the NAACP.

"No Walter, these were private conversations. Tea amongst ladies."

Randolph seemed to consider his words before continuing. The whir of the fan droned on above them.

"The president has made it clear that he will not tolerate a large-scale demonstration of Black men and women on the White House lawn while he is trying to prepare this country to defend Great Britain, in case of war. He suspects an invasion by Hitler is imminent."

"But isn't that the point of the march?" Plessy bristled. This is precisely what he had feared, that Randolph would buckle under presidential pressure. "Isn't the point that we be allowed to fight side by side as Americans, Black and White, in the war against Fascism?"

"That's right" and "Amen, brother" rose from voices around the circle.

"Yes, Mr. Walker, desegregation of the military has been a primary goal, but the president is not going to budge on this, I promise you. I am more concerned right now about getting access to defense jobs. It is part of what we need to talk about," Randolph said. "I think we need to focus on a single achievable act that will crack the walls of segregation. Integrating the armed services is too big a bite for the president to chew right now."

"I don't care what he can chew or swallow for that matter." The veins in Plessy's neck were bulging as he held his breath against a bigger outburst.

"Hold on, hold on," White broke in. "Before we begin conceding any legislative demands, let's be clear on how serious Mr. Roosevelt is about interfering with the march. What do you mean when you say he 'will not tolerate' a demonstration?"

"The president can't stop us from marching," another man said, starting to rise from his chair.

Randolph motioned him to sit down. The sun had dropped a notch in the sky and the rays were streaming through the windows, bearing down on the men.

"Well, he could literally stop the march if he chose to bring in the National Guard, but I assume he wants to avoid that. Mrs. Bethune was not specific but said only that Mrs. Roosevelt used those words. 'He won't tolerate it, Mary.' There are more subtle methods than force to pressure us not to march you know. There is the threat of jail. The word is that Mr. Hoover over at the Bureau is watching our organization very closely."

"Looking for what?" Plessy asked. He pulled a handkerchief from his back pocket to wipe the sweat from the back of his neck.

"Communist influence. And though we all know he will find no such evidence, Mr. Hoover is giving the president a weight to leverage."

A chorus of voices rose, insisting that the march must go on.

"I agree, I agree," Randolph said above the commotion. "But we must decide on our response to this situation. It is not going to go away. I understand that Mr. Aubrey Williams will draft a letter next week on the president's behalf formally asking me to call off the march."

"No!" they shouted over the screech of scraping chairs as they rose to their feet.

Mr. White's clear, calm voice coaxed the men back to their seats. "Let him speak, brothers, let him speak. What response do you suggest, Philip?"

Randolph moved to the center of the group. The room was ripe with the smell of angry sweat.

"I think we demand a meeting with Mr. Roosevelt. We make it clear that we will not be appeased by charming words. We demand equal access to defense jobs, at equal pay!"

White considered the proposal. "I could talk to Fiorello. I know the mayor has the president's ear. I think we can get his help."

"And what if the president refuses?" someone bellowed.

"Promise me you will NOT call off this march!" Plessy blurted. He needed the assurance. He needed to know that he had not been working in vain for the last six months.

"I promise you that I will not abandon the enactment of a fair labor policy that prohibits discrimination by race." Randolph replied, with a steely-eyed look that seemed to be staring down a ghost. The ghost was his past, when he had deflated the Brotherhood of Sleeping Car Porters by calling off the strike of 1928.

Plessy remembered the words Delsey had spoken to him that morning on the train platform in Washington, DC. 'I promise you that Brother Randolph is committed to getting fair labor practices enacted. The March on Washington is the way he is going to do it.'

"And what if the president won't meet with us or concede to our demands?" Walter White repeated the question.

"Then we march," Randolph said. "We march."

~

Delsey leaned against the edge of the soda fountain bar atop her swivel stool and put her lips around the paper straw. She took another sip of her Coke, the burn quenching her thirst. Plessy wiped the tight ringlets from her wet forehead. Delsey always danced with enough energy for both of them and Plessy was glad for this brief break. He kissed her long and lovingly then took a drink of his Rheingold beer.

"Well, I'll take more of that," she said, referring to his open affection on this rare date night at the Savoy Ballroom. The culture of the Savoy fostered this public show of tenderness. McLeod was already fast asleep at his aunt's house a few blocks away. Delsey never wasted a night like tonight. She kissed Plessy back, slowly, teasing him closer, then sliding off the stool just enough to press herself against him.

"You are intent that I celebrate tonight, aren't you?" he smiled. "I'm doing the best I can given the circumstances."

Philip Randolph had received the letter from Aubrey Williams on June 13, formally communicating President Roosevelt's appeal that the March on Washington be canceled for July 1st. Randolph had already drafted a response of refusal and it had worked. The president invited him and Walter White to a meeting at the White House on June 18. The meeting included various members of the Defense Department, including the War Office of Production Management. The president's garrulous charm had no effect on Randolph who tenaciously held to his single objective. A. Philip Randolph insisted that Mr. Roosevelt issue an executive order banning the exclusion of Negroes from jobs offered or contracted by the United States government. When the president refused, Randolph graciously acknowledged their differences and made it clear that the march would proceed as planned. Perhaps he was stronger for having led the Brotherhood for a decade and a half, or maybe he saw the expanding economy made the opportunity ripe. Whatever wisdom he had accumulated told him that he must seize this moment and not back down. In the subsequent week, New York City Mayor Fiorello La Guardia intervened to help the president see that he was beaten. On June 25, 1941, Executive Order 8802 was issued. It forbade discrimination based on race, creed, color or national origin in any government or private defense industry employment or training program. It established the Fair Employment Practices Committee to enforce the order. Randolph's right-hand man, Milton Webster, was appointed to the FEPC.

But the desegregation of the military would have to wait for another day. Although Executive Order 8802 represented a watershed moment, Plessy could not see it. He felt betrayed when he received Randolph's telegram calling off the march for July 1st. Randolph had convened another meeting of the March on Washington committee in Harlem for today, the Fourth of July. Plessy had been quiet on the train ride up from Washington, D.C. while McLeod danced up and down the aisle with excitement. Delsey gave Plessy breathing room, understanding the cauldron that boiled within him. She took McLeod to the dining car for breakfast, celebrating another newly won right to equal accommodations on trains, thanks to a recent Supreme Court decision. After ten years of traveling on trains, Delsey took her first bite of a warm meal served in the ornate dining car. She knew that she and Plessy would have the night together at the Savoy and she knew when and how to soothe him.

Randolph rallied the men at the meeting that afternoon, saying that the March on Washington Movement would not die. He said they had proved the potential power of mass demonstration and it would be leveraged to full capacity in the future. Still, the words had not quelled the fire in Plessy's belly. He had been ready for this fight. The chance to unleash his anger had suddenly imploded. But he had promised Delsey a date night at the Savoy and he refused to ruin it. After the meeting, he summoned his will, changing his mood as he walked back to his sister's house.

Now, as he caught his breath between the band's sets, he felt a release of energy from the exertion of dancing. As Delsey drew him closer, he turned his passion toward her.

"I guess I should be celebrating our night out," he said.

"We ARE celebrating!" she whispered in his ear.

"It still feels like a defeat," he replied.

"Plessy, winning does not always mean a fist fight."

"But the march was our chance...." he trailed off.

"Our chance to shape government. And we DID!" she said.

His face had twisted into a frown, but he knew she was right.

"You have a blind spot, Love," she said, pulling him even closer. "When those men knocked you out, they damaged your vision as much as your arm."

He winced, then his face softened.

"You lost the long view, Love. This battle that Brother Randolph is leading is not about what happened to you. It is about weaving Black people into the very fabric of this country, as equal members.”

“But the march...” he protested weakly.

“The march will happen, I promise you,” she said without a hint of hesitation.

“How do you know?” he scoffed.

“Because I dreamed it.”

“You and your dreams,” he said, shaking his head.

“Now listen, old man, you know better than to doubt my gift of prophecy.”

“Yes, I do,” he smiled.

“I dreamed that the lawn in front of the Lincoln Memorial was filled, with twice as many people as you thought would be there. Brother Randolph was there but he was introducing someone else. A much younger man with a voice as resounding as Gabriel’s trumpet. You were standing next to me and when this man spoke, you looked at me and said, ‘We’ve met our Moses, Shugs, we’ve met our Moses.’”

He kissed her quickly, before she could see his tears, then he pressed his cheek against hers. He was blessed by her love. The drummer tapped an opening riff, and the band broke into full swing again.

“Dance with me, Delsey” he laughed. “Dance me ‘til I drop.”

ALABAMA 1941

The train rocked along; a low rumble punctuated by the rhythmic click-clack of wheels traversing rail joints. Brett rode all night from Hattiesburg on his way to Savannah, where he was assigned a commission as Headquarters squadron commander for the 27th Bomb Group of the Army Air Corp. There was a six-hour layover in Montgomery while the train took on munitions from the ordnance plant in Talladega.

Even before he left Hattiesburg Brett decided to pay his respects to Jesse, a young man whose memory was an indelible part of his childhood. For a brief time they had almost been friends, but their worlds could never be reconciled. He drifted into an easy reverie that morning as the train rolled across the countryside, the images of his childhood forming against the expanse of the fields outside the window. It had been eight years since Brett had last seen Jesse Clemons, when Jesse had come to Hattiesburg for his sister's wedding. Delsey had moved to Washington, D.C. four years ago with her husband and son but she had kept in touch with Maudie Wiggins. Maudie had passed along the news that Tobias Clemons had died three months ago, the day after he and Jesse had finished putting in the spring cotton crop.

The train pulled into the Montgomery station around noon. Brett grabbed his things from the rack above his seat and asked the conductor for directions to Highway 80. It took him five minutes to walk the few blocks to the edge of town. He had barely stuck out his thumb before a truck stopped to pick him up.

"Where you headed soldier?" a gray-haired farmer in dungarees asked.

"Cubahatchee creek," he replied and threw his load into the back of the truck. They talked about the war in Europe and the Japanese encroachment in the South Pacific for most of the half hour drive.

"I've been of a mind like most folks around here that Hitler and his Jerries are none of our business," the old farmer said. "But the Brits have been getting pounded for over a year now. I don't see how they are gonna hold him off on their own. And I like that Mr. Churchill. Bit of a bulldog if you ask me."

"A bulldog on lean rations," Brett replied. "I understand your thinking. The war is on the other side of the world, but some things you have to stand up for regardless of self-interest."

"Maybe you're right, but Lord, I hate to see you boys go to war."

"I am afraid it'll take a miracle to prevent it. President Roosevelt is doing all he can with the Lend-Lease act to get Mr. Churchill the tanks and planes and weapons he needs. But I don't think it's going to be enough, not with Hitler's tanks plowing into Russia. The Japanese are in cahoots to take over Indochina and the Dutch East Indies while the Russians are busy fighting the Nazis."

"You saying we're headed to another World War?" the farmer responded.

"I don't know. Hard to avoid it," Brett said. "I mean, if

the Japanese take the Indies, what stops them from taking Hawaii? And with the alliance between them and Germany and Italy, it's possible that all of Europe and Asia could fall."

"My God. Well, guess it's better that we join the Allies before we're fighting on our own soil."

"Yeah. But I also think it is the right thing to do. We have a responsibility to stand up to the bullies of the world," he said, excited to tell the farmer about his flight training and his new command in Savannah.

When they reached the bridge over Cubahatchee creek, the driver pulled off onto the rutted farm road that led to the Clemons' farm. Neither man seemed quite ready to end the conversation, but they had arrived at their designation. Brett reached into his pocket to give the driver a dollar bill for his troubles, but the old man refused.

"You're the one payin' the price young man. You just be careful up there," he said pointing past the windshield to the blue sky above.

"I will, sir," he said. "I promised my Mama I would." He raised his hand, prepared to salute but caught himself halfway and just waved as the old man drove off.

The red dirt from the road billowed around his feet, coating his combat boots in a rust patina. The rim of his garrison cap darkened with sweat as the fifty-pound duffel weighed upon his shoulder. Brett walked a few hundred yards along the red clay road in blazing heat until he finally reached the shade of a blackjack oak. He dropped his duffel, which landed with a thud against the low bank of the road beneath the tree. The road meandered beside the creek, no houses in sight, just farmland. He removed his jacket, carefully polishing the two brass bars on the shoulder epaulettes with the cuff of his sleeve. Then he neatly folded and tucked the jacket inside the duffel. He pulled out his canteen and took a long drink, wishing he had been passing through Montgomery two months earlier. The dewberry vines that sprawled in thick thorny masses along the banks of the road would have been chock full of plump fruit. Now they offered only the dried brown receptacle where the berry once beckoned. He rested his back against the trunk of the blackjack oak and took another drink of water.

A smile crept across his face as he pictured Justine, the way she had looked at him when he told her he was taking her on a second honeymoon before he shipped out to Hunter Field in Georgia. He thought about their wedding eight years before. After the preacher pronounced them man and wife, Brett had lifted Justine's bridal veil to kiss her. She had whispered, "Can we ditch the reception and go straight to the honeymoon?"

He remembered how his body had pulsed at her eagerness. He loved her beauty, her Cajun hot bloodedness. They had spent their first honeymoon in New Orleans, and he had taken her back there last week. They had only returned to Hattiesburg a couple of days ago. It was going to be hard to be away from her. He tried not to think about it.

He took a last drink of water before stowing the canteen, then shouldered his duffel again. As he rounded the last bend in the road to the Clemons' farm, the old fishpond came into view. A flood of memories swept over him. He could see himself, as a child, holding a cake tin on his lap as the old model T Ford bounced along this same washboard road to the Clemons' cabin. The sun had been baking down on him back then too, and the smell of clay dust mixed with chocolate suddenly resurfaced. Brett had only been five years old when Maudie brought him along to pay her condolences after Lucy Clemons died. That was the day Jesse had brought him down to this pond, the first time he had felt the thrill of a swift tug on the line, when a fish takes the bait. He could still see Jesse's tear-stained cheeks and the brave face he made as he wiped them dry.

Now, two decades later, Jesse had already buried both his parents. Brett considered the good health of his own mother and father and briefly pondered the unfairness of the circumstances. Beyond the pond, he could see a small farmhouse. It was surrounded by fields of white that looked like popcorn hovering above the red earth. Jesse stood on the front porch, overalls draping his tall frame. He waved to the approaching soldier. The friendliness in the gesture caused Brett's shoulders to relax as he walked up the driveway to the house.

"Well, what a surprise. It's good to see you, Brett," Jesse said, handing him a Mason jar full of lemonade as he stepped onto the porch. He took a long drink then set the glass on the porch rail. He reached out to hold Jesse by the shoulders, looking into his eyes.

"I'm sorry about your daddy," he said, giving Jesse a firm pat before letting go. They stood there a moment in awkward silence. What a vast distance between the innocence of their childhood bond and their segregated worlds as men. But losing a parent had a way of crossing all barriers.

"Crop looks good," Brett said, nodding toward the fields as he took up his glass of lemonade again. "You got help to bring it in?"

Jesse relaxed into the comfort of everyday conversation, not yet able to touch with words the abyss left by Toby's passing.

"Yep, Miles Fitch said he and his sons can help me out. He put in corn this year, so we can harvest for each other this fall."

"That's good, that's good," Brett said.

"I got lucky this year, but I don't know how I'm going to keep the farm going by myself next year." Jesse said. "I try not to think about it."

"You sure do look official," he said, changing the subject. "You're flying for the Army now?"

"Yeah. I've got a command in Georgia. I am on my way to Savannah right now. In fact I've got to get back to the train station in a couple of hours, but I wanted to come by on my way and well, pay my respects."

A knot formed in Jesse's throat, but he guarded against the grief, just nodding.

Brett breathed in the scent of honeysuckle drifting from the trellis next to the porch. He noted Jesse's silence and the set of his jaw.

"Justine sends her regards," he smiled. "We just got back from a week in New Orleans."

"You're a lucky man, Brett," Jesse replied. "You couldn't find a better wife."

"That's for sure, Jess. She's the kind of woman a man wants to grow old with."

Jesse sat down in one of the cane rockers on the porch and nodded his head toward the other as an invitation for Brett to rest for a while. "How are those sisters of yours doin'?"

"They are all fine. Claire and Delta have each fetched

themselves a husband and could not be happier. Emma's working for Daddy at the Trading Post. She's good with numbers, but not as good as your sister, Delsey. Grace has a steady high school beau and is much more interested in her Delta Sigma Theta activities than her studies, much to Mama and Daddy's consternation. And Hannah just finished primary school. It's Faith who seems to want to fly farthest from the nest."

"How's that?" Jesse asked. He lifted his jar of lemonade and took a drink.

"Well, she's enrolled to start nursing school at Charity Hospital in New Orleans in the fall. She's already moved into a boarding house there and has a secretarial job for the summer. She does not show the slightest interest in finding a husband. I think she'd try to get into medical school if she could find a place that would accept a woman." Brett's brow furrowed as he talked about Faith, unable to fathom how she could navigate the world without a man by her side.

"I don't think you need to worry about your sister, Faith." Jesse said, resting his head against the top of the rocker and pondering the pattern of the wood grain in the porch ceiling. "If the Lord was ever going to look after one of his children, it would be Faith Wiggins."

They looked out at the browning stalks of cotton, the air shimmering in the afternoon heat.

"You're right, but you know how a brother worries."

"That I do, that I do." Jesse replied.

"How about you?" he asked. "You hear from Delsey?"

"Every week. She's much better at writing letters than I am. She and Plessy have made a wonderful life for themselves and young McLeod up in Washington, D.C."

"You must miss her something awful."

"I do, but they're better off up there. That's what matters. She's planning to come down with McLeod for a visit next month. That's what keeps me going these days." Jesse stood up and gave Brett a gentle pat on the shoulder. "Come on. Let me show you around the place. I've put in some fruit trees, and I've got a small hatchery going down at the pond."

The men spent an hour walking the fields and following the creek to the pond, lapsing into childhood recollections. It was clear how much Jesse loved the farm, but it was also apparent that it would be a huge task for him to maintain it alone. The sun had moved past its high point by the time they walked back to the house. Jesse offered to drive Brett to the train station.

"If you can give me a lift to the highway, I can thumb a ride from there. Everyone stops to pick me up when they see the uniform."

"That uniform is something to be proud of Brett. You are serving your country and you are a pilot to boot. Can't be much more of a hero than that."

They climbed into the cab of the flatbed truck, which finally coughed and sputtered to life after a few tries at the ignition. The afternoon with Jesse rekindled a feeling in Brett from childhood. Socially sanctioned or not, they ought to be friends. Or able to help each other out. At least that.

"Jess, I know you're real attached to the farm, but have you thought about what you want to do after the fall harvest?"

"No, I've been avoiding it. Why do you ask?"

"Well, I had an idea."

"What's that?"

"Look, Jess, you're every bit as much hero material as I am. You've broken your back helping your daddy buy this farm and supporting your family after your mama died. Have you thought about enlisting once the crop is in?"

The truck rattled along the uneven dirt road. Jesse paused as the possibility of a whole new life began to dawn on him.

"Can't say that I have."

"The Tuskegee Airmen just graduated their first cadet class. Moton Field is just a few miles from here and..."

"Yeah, but those guys have been to college or at least finished high school." Jesse felt his pulse quicken at the thought of joining a band of brothers.

"You're a smart man, Jesse. You could pass the qualifying exam. And I am sure Delsey would love to help you study."

The highway came into view as they rounded the last curve in the road.

"You're serious about this, aren't you," Jesse said. "You really think I could pass the exam?"

"I do. I definitely do."

"Well, you've given me something to think about."

He downshifted, slowing the truck as it approached the highway.

"You know, when Delsey and Plessy moved to D.C. I thought it was the bravest thing she had ever done, settin' out into the unknown like that. But I never thought that I'd be able to do the same. Always figured that I'd breathe my last on this little patch of dirt that I've always known." Jesse pulled over to the side of the road when they reached the highway and kept the engine idling.

Brett put his hand on the door handle but paused. He felt awkward as he struggled for words. This might be the last time he saw Jesse.

"Jess, there are so many divisions separating men – rich and poor, officers and enlisted men, Negroes and Whites. It is a shame we couldn't have been friends growing up. I'm actually sorry for that."

"It's the way the world is, Brett," Jesse said.

Brett got out of the truck and closed the door. He put his hand on the window frame and leaned in to say one more thing.

"Think about what I said. You'd be a good airman."

"I'll consider it," Jesse replied.

"Even if you couldn't be my wingman, Jesse, it sure would bring me comfort to think of you up there flying for the Army Air Corps, that we'd somehow be fighting together."

The hard lines around Jesse's mouth softened. He knew that Brett meant it.

"You be careful up there, Brett," Jesse said.

"I will," Brett said as he grabbed his duffel from the bed of the truck. He slapped the roof of the cab, then turned and walked toward the highway.

Jesse watch for a minute then set the handbrake and stepped out of the truck.

"Hey, Brett," he shouted, raising his right hand at a forty-five-degree angle to his forehead. He waited until Brett turned around and returned his salute. And he watched as Brett crossed the highway and stuck out his thumb, catching a ride in scarcely ten seconds.

MISSISSIPPI 1999

Faith lifted a photograph from the page of her scrapbook and gazed at the faded faces of Brother and her sisters, grouped into two neat rows from eldest to youngest. The edges of the picture were yellowed except for the ends tucked into the gray corner mounts. The black and white image captured the mostly bare branches of a maple tree Maudie had planted shortly after they arrived from Alabama. The tree was nearly twenty feet tall, and Faith estimated the photograph must have been taken when she was a freshman in high school. She ran her fingers lightly over the surface of the picture, then turned it over to find her mother's penciled note – "Christmas 1937". She thought of the care that had gone into making this scrapbook, a gift Maudie gave to each child on her eighteenth birthday. Faith slipped the corners of the picture back into the mounts and remembered what had been happening then. Brother would have graduated from Georgia Tech the year before and must have been in flight school. He and Justine were married, and Justine was working in Hattiesburg while he did his military training. The Wiggins girls were also living in Hattiesburg, immersed in various stages of their education from college to grammar school.

Faith picked up the next photograph on the page. She and Delsey stood side by side, her arm around Delsey's waist. She was wearing the same dress as in the previous picture. Delsey's posture was stiff, and Faith thought her own smile looked a little sad. As she lingered over the picture, her memory came into focus. It was the day after Christmas, just before Delsey, Plessy and McLeod moved to Washington, D.C. She remembered standing in the kitchen with Delsey after dinner, hearing the words 'He was beaten for nothing more than the color of his skin'. Her youthful notion that Jesus loved all the little children of the world had suddenly met the harsh reality that men did not necessarily feel that way. At age fourteen, she had begun to see that the world was ruthlessly divided into Red and Yellow, Black, and White.

Faith always felt closer to Maudie than to her father, but her distrust of him settled into a fixed place after the night she saw him burn Fletcher's blood-stained clothes. Two days later, when they learned of Plessy's injury, she had tried to talk to Maudie about what she had seen. But Maudie stopped her, stunned into silence. She said all they could do was pray for Plessy to be healed. But Faith wasn't satisfied. She knew that Fletcher had something to do with Plessy's injury. She wanted to tell Delsey but was afraid. Faith had squirmed uncomfortably each night as she knelt by the bed. She needed to do more with her hands than lift them in prayer. But what could a fourteen-year-old girl do? If she pushed Maudie to confront Hardee, she figured the fight would break them for good. The dilemma was too much for her. She decided she would give her life to helping people, regardless of where they came from or what they looked like.

Faith had wanted to become a doctor but quickly learned that the world was also divided into what was possible for men and what was allowed for women. After much advice from teachers, friends, and family about how ill-suited the temperament of women was for the rigors of medical school, she decided to enter the field of nursing and enrolled in a program at Charity Hospital in New Orleans at the age of eighteen. She ended up specializing in pediatrics and went on to a career in international nursing. In the end, she had found her own way to love all the children of the world. But she had never been able to reconcile what she had seen the night of November 1, 1937.

At the back of the scrapbook was a manila envelope stuffed with letters. Most were from Delsey to Maudie, a correspondence that continued for over thirty years after Delsey and her family moved to D.C. Faith had read through them long ago, having learned that McLeod settled in Clarksdale. One of the letters was postmarked July 22, 1972, and it was addressed to Faith.

Dear Faith,

Thank you for your letter letting me know of Maudie's passing. I had suspected that her time was near when she wrote to me in April. She said the recent heart attack had left her too weak to get out in her garden. I knew she wouldn't be long for this world if she couldn't wander among the jasmine and gardenias. She wrote in that last letter about what a comfort you were to her, not only as a loving daughter but also as a skilled nurse. 'Who needs a doctor when I have Faith?' she said.

Plessy and I are doing well but feeling our age. He retired from the NLRB last year after working there for thirty-four years. They eventually promoted him to assistant legal counsel some years after he finished law school. He graduated in 1954, having taken night classes after McLeod started high school. Other than some rheumatism, he feels healthy, thank the Lord. It does keep us from traveling down to see McLeod as much as we would like.

Our son followed in his father's footsteps and went to Howard Law School. He is now a civil rights attorney in Clarksdale, as well as an accomplished musician. He still plays that Stella you found for him in 1942.

I'm well enough and considering retiring from teaching next year, although I still love the kids. You may remember that I always wanted to study under Mary McLeod Bethune in Florida. As it turns out, I came to know her through the D.C. community. Though I got my degree at Howard University, like the rest of the family, she has been a guiding light to me after all.

I am so happy to hear from you, Faith. Of all Maudie's girls, you are the most like her. Recognizing that we are all God's children and equal in his eyes. I still remember you coming down to the Southern Railway depot with Maudie to see Plessy off to D.C., bringing him a loaf of banana bread. You were so respectful to him.

I hope to hear more from you and will let you know the next time we are coming to Clarksdale. Would love to see you in the flesh.

Love, Delsey

It was sometime the next year when Faith finally got a chance to see Delsey during a visit to Mississippi. It was a balmy spring day, and everything was in bloom, as if Maudie were making her presence known. Plessy and McLeod had gone fishing to give the women some time alone. Over coffee, Faith broached the subject she had wanted to talk about all these years.

"Sounds like your nursing career has allowed you to travel the world," Delsey said, lifting the cup to her lips.

"Yes, I feel blessed," Faith replied, "But I was ready to come home, especially after Mama's health began to fail."

There was a natural pause in the conversation. Faith took a sip of coffee and summoned her courage.

"Delsey, there is something I have wanted to say to you for a long time. An apology really."

Delsey was wise enough to remain silent, letting Faith find her words. Faith swallowed hard, then began.

"The night that Plessy was beaten, I heard a knock at our back door. I got up and walked down the hallway. Voices were coming from the kitchen. Daddy was talking to someone and when I peeked around the door, I saw it was Fletcher Moody. He was frightened and covered in blood. He said something like 'He didn't know why he did it. That he thought the sheriff was after him.' Daddy helped him wash up. He burned the bloody clothes and gave him something to wear. I'm sure Fletcher was the one who beat Plessy. I have always felt horrible that I didn't tell the police. Or that I didn't tell you. I am so sorry, Delsey."

"Sounds like you have been carrying this around for a long time."

"I have and as time passed, I wondered if I would just hurt you more by telling you, now that justice cannot be served."

Delsey looked down at her hands, the knuckles knobby, fingers curled with age. She rubbed the back of her left hand and stoked the fingers gently.

"You know as well as I do that justice was never going to be served," she said.

Faith was silent. She had no response.

"I suspected you knew something because of the questions you asked when I came by after Christmas to tell Maudie we were moving to Washington, D.C. I also knew you were a young teenager and caught up in a storm too big for you to navigate. Truth is you could have made it worse by going to the police. Could have unleashed a lynch mob. I'm not saying you are guiltless, but at the time I think you were powerless."

"Well, I am sorry, nonetheless."

"Thank you for saying that."

The awkwardness lingered until Delsey suggested they go for a walk.

"How about we walk for a spell, and I will tell you the story of how Plessy and I came to live our dream."

The two women kept up a monthly correspondence that mirrored that of Maudie and Delsey. A deeper connection emerged as they shared the stories of daily life. After Plessy died in 1978, Faith decided to leave her estate to Delsey. Here was her chance to attempt reparations. She had the Will drawn up. Now that Delsey was gone, the estate would go to McLeod.

Faith closed the scrapbook and put it in the 'Sylvia' pile at one end of the table. Outside, bluebirds and cardinals were chirping their urgent mating songs, announcing a new sun risen as they built their nests. A warm morning breeze fluttered the curtains of the kitchen window. Faith bent over to pull the next cardboard box from beneath the table. She blew a fine layer of dust off the top. 'Textbooks' was printed in large black letters, the faintest scent of permanent marker still present. Only a few weeks earlier she had sorted through her study, having boxed most of its contents. She was now past the sorting stage and into the getting rid of stage. This was not a task to leave for Sylvia.

"Odd," she thought, opening the box, "that these books have a longer shelf life than me."

It wasn't a complaint, simply hard to imagine. The promise of the miraculous medicine, STI571, had not proven true for her. Although Faith had achieved a complete remission with the medicine, the effects had waned. She had a relapse after five months and was now on hydroxyurea to slow the progression of the leukemia. She still felt well most days, which is why it seemed odd to wonder where these books would be when she was gone. Gone where? She could not imagine feeling any less alive, wherever that might be. The phone rang, interrupting her musings.

"Hello," she said.

"Hey, Aunt Faith, we're just leaving New Orleans," Sylvia said, her voice a strange mix of excitement and exasperation. "We're a little late getting off."

"What do you mean, late? It's only ten o'clock," Faith replied. "You know it's less than two hundred miles, Honey."

"I know, but Mom wants to go through Hattiesburg. It could take all day."

Faith paused before responding.

"There's no need to rush, Sylvia. Let Gracie have her wish today, OK? Whatever it is," she said. "I promise you won't regret it."

"OK, you're right," Sylvia replied, the edge in her voice softening. "I'll just enjoy the day, wherever it takes us."

"That's my girl. See you when you get here."

"Love you," Sylvia said.

"Love you, too."

Sylvia had taken her New Year's conversation with Faith to heart and made an effort to reach out to Grace. She had suggested they make the Easter trip to visit Faith together after Grace visited her in Austin first. Grace had initially resisted, and Sylvia considered dropping the matter. But after calling Faith in February to tell her she wasn't sure about coming to Jackson at Easter, Faith insisted.

"She resists everything at first, Sylvia," Faith had said. "Don't take it personally. It took me a year to pry her away from your father for a five-day trip to the Grand Canyon. Some people are just more timid than you and me. Don't give up. I really want to see you both, OK?"

Sylvia did not give up. She offered to make all the arrangements for her mother to come stay with her for a week in Austin before they drove to Mississippi. And she agreed to pay for the trip. As a final enticement, Sylvia had promised a weekend in New Orleans, a city that held special significance for Grace for reasons Sylvia didn't understand. Grace finally relented and Sylvia sent her a round trip ticket from New York to Austin, arranging for her sister, Sophie, to shepherd her mother to and from LaGuardia airport. Grace arrived in Austin in remarkably good spirits and the first three days together had been fun as they meandered the old mission trails around San Antonio. But that was over a week ago. They had begun to wear on each other's nerves.

This morning, Sylvia wanted to get an early start and head up Interstate 55, the fastest route to Jackson. She was in a hurry to get to Faith's. Grace asked if they could go through Hattiesburg instead, have lunch there near the old train depot. Maybe they could see if the Trading Post was still standing. They sat in the car in the parking lot of their hotel off Jackson Square in the French Quarter, having not yet settled on which way to go. Sylvia clicked her cell phone closed after talking to Faith. Grace overheard the conversation and hoped they were headed to Hattiesburg. She opened her purse, rummaging around for something. Sylvia turned toward her mother and noticed the growing translucence of her skin, the deeper set of her eyes.

"Now where did I put my reading glasses?" Grace asked, as they hung from chain around her neck.

Sylvia tapped the glasses gently.

"Oh, my Lord, I think I've lost the little bit of mind I had left," Grace blushed.

"Hattiesburg?" Sylvia suggested, nodding toward the east as they approached Interstate Highway 10.

"Oh, yes!" Grace replied.

They were quiet for most of the thirty-minute drive to Slidell, skirting the east shore of Lake Pontchartrain before crossing the eleven-mile Twin Spans bridge. As a little girl, Grace had accompanied Hardee on business trips to New Orleans. Each time they reached the old Watson Williams Bridge he would designate her as lookout for the manatees that often migrated from the Gulf of Mexico through the Rigolets strait into the estuary called Lake Pontchartrain. His raucous praise when she spotted the wayward sea cows was one of her most treasured memories. It was Grace who spied the small pod of dolphins diving off to the left as they now approached the north shore of the lake.

"Daddy always loved the manatees that swam up this way," she said. "Called them the Siren Sisters."

"When did you and Grandpa come to New Orleans?" Sylvia asked.

"When I was little, shortly after Brother left for college. I think he was lonely in a house full of girls. Whenever he came home with the trailer loaded up with salvaged steel, I knew it meant he was going on a delivery run. I'd sneak out of the house and hide under a blanket in the front seat of the truck. He'd wait until we were past the edge of town before he would pat the blanket and say 'What's this? A stowaway? Well, it's too late now. I'll just have to take you with me, Gracie.' Sometimes we'd camp out on the lake before heading back in the morning."

Sylvia had never heard this story before. She was hungry to know more about her mother's life growing up, about Faith and the rest of the Wiggins. She wondered if her mother knew that Faith was leaving her money to McLeod Walker. Sylvia was struck by the rich family history in these stories, a history she had kept at arm's length for years, a history living and breathing beside her right now. The detour through Hattiesburg turned into a gold mine of memories, helping to paint more of the picture that Faith had sketched about growing up in the Wiggins' home. Grace remembered Delsey Walker, her kindness, and her sweet scent but she did not remember much else: no details of a life outside the Wiggins world. Grace mostly recounted her own carefree childhood, doted on by older sisters and cushioned by popularity at school.

After lunch at a café near the refurbished train depot, Sylvia drove her mother by the Trading Post, which was now an abandoned ramshackle warehouse. They wound their way through narrow streets of paved-over bricks that showed beneath patches of crumbling asphalt. The old house on Sixth and Main was gone, sold to the Baptist church years ago. At least that sale had allowed Hardee and Maudie to retire. Grace's high school, consumed in a fire a few years back, was a burnt-out shell of red brick. Two stone archways still stood along the east wall, the words "Boys" and "Girls" chiseled on their facade. Grace flowed with stories as they parked the car and got out to walk around the old schoolyard: stories of sororities and boyfriends, cigarettes, and papa's stolen whiskey. It was a side of her mother that Sylvia had never imagined, a bit of a bad girl tucked behind the skirts of her proper Southern manners. A warm curiosity grew as she listened to the tales.

Sylvia's aunts had all settled close to home. Claire and Delta lived within a mile of their old neighborhood, having married childhood sweethearts. Although there wasn't time to visit them today, they were planning to come to Faith's for the weekend. Ava was in a convalescent home in Jackson, having outlived Cecil. Emma never married and had gone on to veterinary school, settling in Vicksburg. Hannah had ventured the farthest away, marrying a fellow from Mobile, Alabama. Sylvia felt a connection to this place, some sense of ancestral longing or familiarity. Then Grace would mention how she preferred the Colored people in Mississippi to those in New York because they were humbler here. And Sylvia would cringe, repulsed by the entrenched racism that was also part of her legacy.

By the time they left Hattiesburg it was late afternoon. A few miles out of town, on old Highway 49, Sylvia reached for the dash to retrieve her cell phone. She hit the speed dial for Faith's number. After ten rings, she got the answering machine. She figured Faith was running some errands since they had left it open as to when she and Grace would arrive. When they were on the outskirts of Florence, Sylvia called Faith again. This time the answering machine sent her heart into a race of worry.

"She's not answering," Sylvia said to her mother.

"Oh, don't worry, Honey. Faith has always been able to take care of herself. I'm sure she would have called if anything were wrong."

"I don't know about that Mom. She is not as strong as she was. You'll see. Problem is she's still as stubborn."

As they turned onto the gravel road leading to Faith's house, Sylvia strained to see if the old pickup was parked off to the side of the house. She knew that Faith would have left the space under the attached carport for the Miata. Magenta redbuds and the white crosses of blooming dogwoods nodded in the breeze as they approached the house. The truck was gone but Sylvia saw a note taped to the back door as she pulled under the porte cochere. She parked and jumped out of the car to retrieve the note.

Sylvia and Gracie,

Sorry I am not here to greet you. I started running a bit of a fever. I feel fine but out of an abundance of caution instilled in me by Dr. Prentice, I have taken myself to St. Catherine's. Take your time to unpack. There is some supper on the counter. I will call when I know what Dr. Prentice intends for me.

Love you both, Faith

~

Faith sat on a stretcher in the emergency room at St. Catherine's, waiting for the results of her blood tests. The place was quiet in the late afternoon, so she had the luxury of being in a private room. Her mind retraced the events of the day. After the phone call with Sylvia that morning, Faith was covered in a fine sweat. Walking to the bathroom, she hoped it was just a hot flash. But when she unsheathed the thermometer, shaking the mercury down into the bulb and placing it under her tongue, she had felt a shiver. Three minutes later, she rolled the thermometer between her thumb and forefinger until she could read its silver strip. One hundred and one degrees. She did not want to interrupt the trip that Sylvia and Grace were on. It had been too long in coming. She left a note on the door, deciding not to call and drove herself to the hospital, hoping the note conveyed a sense of calm; a calm that, frankly, she was having trouble maintaining at the moment. Faith had felt blessed by a feeling of peace over the past year, being able to rest in the knowledge that she was not alone in her illness. She had felt accompanied by something benevolent as she began to face her death, reveling in those moments when time vanished, and the eternity of the present moment opened up. Even as she had sorted and discarded the accumulations of a lifetime, she had felt more ease than grief. But now, suddenly, she was not ready.

Sitting on the side of the bed, the dam of denial broke, flooding her with grief. She wanted to taste the ripe red juice of another tomato plucked fresh from the vine this summer, from the vine she had planted only yesterday. She wanted to watch the oaks turn from green to gold next fall, to see the red camellia bloom at Thanksgiving and the crocuses laugh at winter with their blue and yellow faces. She wanted to hear the summer swell with the song of cicadas and smell the fragrance of magnolias floating through the kitchen window. She was not ready to let go of this body that allowed her to see and hear and smell this most remarkable and singular earth.

There was a soft knock at the door.

"Come in," she said.

"Good afternoon, Faith," said a familiar voice. She looked up to see Dr. Prentice, his gentle brown eyes ever so slightly downcast, pausing a second before meeting hers.

"Hello, Dr. Prentice," she said, waiting.

He paused a moment longer.

"I'm afraid I have some...,"

"Bad news," Faith said, finishing his sentence.

He nodded silently as tears spilled onto her cheeks. Faith fought to keep them back, but it was useless. She reached for the box of tissues beside the bed.

"There are a few blasts on your smear which, as you know, means you've gone into an accelerated phase of the disease. But Faith, you are in no immediate danger. I want you to hear that." He moved closer and placed a hand on her shoulder.

Faith looked down at the sheets and took a deep breath, folded the tissue in half and gently blew her nose.

"In fact, your other counts are in good shape. You don't need a transfusion, but I do want to keep you in the hospital for intravenous antibiotics until your cultures come back. If they are negative, you can go home in a couple of days on oral antibiotics, OK?" Dr. Prentice knew how to walk the delicate tightrope of treating a colleague.

"I've got family visiting," Faith implored. But the truth was she needed a couple of days to adjust to this news and it would be easier in the hospital.

"Well, good. They will be there to take care of you when

you go home. And Faith, I also want you to think about a central line. There's a chemotherapy regimen that is well tolerated and I think it can buy you some good time."

Faith knew all about the permanent intravenous lines that could be implanted under the skin. The procedure was a minor one, but the idea of more aggressive chemotherapy was daunting.

"Let me think about it, Dr. Prentice," she said with the same calm mask she had worn for years as a nurse.

"OK, Faith, I'll see you upstairs in a few minutes. I'll get your admission orders in, and we can talk a little more after you get settled." He squeezed her shoulder gently before leaving.

She waited for him to close the door before she gave in to the silent sobs. She pulled the thin blanket around her shoulders and embraced herself, trembling in her own sturdy arms. She let the compassion showered on a lifetime of patients come to rest on her own broken heart, crying freely and shamelessly for several minutes, her eyes closed. She fell into a darkness until a Presence lifted her. She caught her breath and opened her eyes. She was not alone, even if she would not be spared. The words of Aeschylus came to her.

"He who learns must suffer, and, even in our sleep, pain that cannot forget falls drop by drop upon the heart, and in our own despair, against our will, comes wisdom to us by the awful grace of God."

Her equanimity of the past year slowly returned, even in her sadness. 'The awful grace of God?' she thought. 'That we might know the abundance of incarnation and have to let it go.'

"Thank you," she whispered to the ceiling, "Thank you

for my one true life," then grinned and added, "And I'll take a little more if you please."

She blotted her eyes with the tissue and pushed the button on the bed, summoning the nurse. The staff was changing shifts so she expected it would take a while for someone to answer. She wanted to go outside to call Sylvia and Grace, to speak to them while soaking in the last of the day's sunshine. Vivien, the ER nurse who had tended Faith the previous summer when she came to the hospital for transfusions, popped her head in the door.

"You need anything before I go?" she said.

"No, I'm fine Viv," Faith said, "but I'm going to sneak outside to make a call. My sister and niece just drove up from New Orleans."

"OK, Faith, I don't know a thing about your whereabouts if anyone asks. Just be back here in fifteen minutes," she smiled. "Promise me?"

"Promise," replied Faith. "And I don't need a wheelchair."

"Got it," Vivien said and closed the door.

Faith went outside in time to catch the peach-infused sunset painting the underbellies of a few flat clouds. She wheeled her IV pole over to the edge of the parking lot where the smell of honeysuckle rose from the vine-draped fence. Faith tapped Sylvia's number on the keys of her cell phone and waited through several rings.

"Sylvia?" she said when a voice answered.

"No, it's Grace. Is that you, Faith?"

"Yes, it's me. It's so good to hear your voice Gracie! How was your trip?" It had been a while since Faith had heard her sister's voice and it rekindled an ancient joy.

"Great. The trip has been great, but where are you? Are you OK?"

"I've got a little fever and need to stay in the hospital for a couple of days, that's all. I feel fine. I'm at St. Catherine's. Sylvia knows where it is."

"We'll be right there."

"But wait..." For a second Faith thought Grace had already hung up. "Visiting hours are almost over. You can wait until morning. I'll..."

"Oh, Faith, I want to see you tonight. I promise we won't stay long, just a minute to see your sweet face and grab a hug. Please?"

"OK, Grace, I'd love to see you too. Then we can have a longer visit tomorrow and I'll be home the day after that."

"See you in a little bit."

"Alright. Hug Sylvia for me."

"I will."

"I mean really, Grace. Give Sylvia a real hug."

"I will, Faith, really."

Faith took a few moments to enjoy the sunset before returning to the ER.

It took Sylvia fifteen minutes to drive as many miles from Florence to Jackson. She had squirmed out of her mother's embrace when she heard that Faith was staying at the hospital. Sylvia hustled them both into the Miata, flustering Grace, who tended to move with glacial speed in even the most urgent situations. As Grace began digging through her purse for her lipstick, Sylvia whipped the car into reverse. It did not matter that Faith said she was fine. Sylvia shifted into her lawyerly crisis mode. Once on the highway the Miata burst forward in full throttle. Sylvia ignored her mother's plea to stop and put up the top on the convertible, which she had lowered when she unpacked the car. The feel of a seventy-mile an hour wind in her hair matched Sylvia's adrenaline-charged mood, but for Grace it proved an irreparable catastrophe to the coiffure she had received in New Orleans the day before. They arrived at the hospital in drastically different moods.

"I don't see how it would have hurt to take five minutes and raise the top on this sports car!" Grace said as she patted down the flailed ends of her fine silver hair, a slight palsy in her hands, the exasperation draining from her voice. She pulled a tissue from her purse, wiping her eyes.

Sylvia winced as she looked at her mother who was clearly shaken from the drive. The meanness in her own heart chilled her. She wasn't this way with anyone else. Whatever their history, it didn't warrant this response. Meditation was helping Sylvia see herself more clearly and sometimes it was painful. She realized that it was long past time for her to take responsibility for her own irritation.

"I'm sorry, mother," she said, "you are right. I should have pulled over and put the top up. Maybe we can find a restroom inside to freshen up."

They found the ladies room and Sylvia helped Grace locate the brush buried in her purse. She assured her mother that she would only be gone for a few minutes. She went to the emergency room and looked around for someone who might know where Faith was. Vivien was sitting at the nurses' station.

"Oh, thank goodness it's you, Viv. Do you know where Faith is?" she asked.

"Oh, hello Hon," Vivien said, looking up from her charting. "She just went up to the floor. Room 322."

"She's OK?"

"Yes, just a little worn out. But her vitals are stable."

"Worn out?" Sylvia took a deep breath, aware of her

clipped tone. "Sorry, Viv, I'm just so worried about her...."

"She's fine, Hon, really." Vivien stood up and reached over to pat Sylvia's hand. "I know she's waiting to see you and your mom. Hurry on up there before visiting hours are over. They'll give you a few extra minutes, I'm sure."

Sylvia returned to the restroom and found Grace talking to an elderly man in the foyer nearby. They seemed so at ease with one another that Sylvia wondered if the man was an old family friend. Grace nodded goodbye to him as Sylvia approached. Grace's face was soft and open as Sylvia told her what room Faith was in and when visiting hours were over. Grace took her daughter's elbow and tried to match her brisk steps as they headed to the elevator. Sylvia noticed that she was walking too fast for her mother and slowed down.

Once behind the shiny steel doors, Sylvia asked, "Who was that man you were talking to?"

"Let's see, he said his name was... Charles Purdue."

"Do you know him?"

"Oh, no Honey. He just looked like he needed a friendly face. Turns out his wife is in the intensive care unit. Heart attack. But the doctors think she's gonna make it."

Sylvia did not know what to say. She had always marveled at her mother's capacity to comfort complete strangers. People seemed to instantly relax in her presence. The elevator finally started with a jerk. Sylvia tapped her foot as it inched upward.

"It's OK, Sylvia. Nobody likes hospitals. Such painful places to visit. Worse for the family than the patient, don't you think?" Grace said.

Sylvia found herself calmed by her mother's voice and was reminded of her mother's loving nature.

"You know, you're a really kind person, Mom. To everyone. Kinder than me."

"Oh, not deep down, sweetheart," Grace replied, "You've got to have tough skin to do the work you do."

It was a moment of recognition that made Sylvia pause. Her mother did understand some things about her.

The doors to the elevator finally opened onto the third floor and a woman and her children stepped in. Sylvia and Grace got out and headed down the hallway to the oncology ward.

"Let's say a quick goodnight to Faith," Grace said, "then maybe we can go get some dinner. It's been nice having all this time with you. I'm glad you talked me into this trip."

Sylvia could tell it was a genuine statement. Maybe there was more to her mother than the story she had told herself all these years. The therapist she had finally seen was helping and had made it clear she was available while Sylvia was in Mississippi. When Grace and Sylvia arrived in Faith's room, she was reading a book. The picture on the front cover showed smoke billowing from the rose window of a church. She looked up over her reading glasses, laid down her book and reached her arms out to them both. Her face was as radiant as ever.

"I'm so glad you insisted on coming to the hospital tonight," she said, looking into Grace's eyes. "I realized how much I have missed you when I heard your voice." Grace bent over the side of the bed and kissed her sister on the cheek. Faith patted a spot on the bed next to her and motioned for Sylvia to sit down.

"Come over here, Sylvia. You can stop your worrying. I'm still here."

"What are you reading?" Sylvia asked.

"*Home Fires* by Margaret Maron. Lord, that woman can write a page turner! It's definitely what I need tonight."

"How are you?" Grace asked. Her voice was gentle and steady, devoid of strain or worry; the same voice Sylvia had heard in the elevator. It conveyed a quiet strength that she had not appreciated in her mother.

Faith had intended to wait until she returned home to tell them about the results of the blood tests, but the directness of Grace's question demanded a transparent response.

"The truth is I feel fine and Dr. Prentice doesn't think the fever is serious." Faith put her hand on Sylvia's back. "But the leukemia is advancing. He wants me to consider intravenous chemotherapy."

They let the silence sit there while the words sunk in.

"I've had my cry and my little talk with God. And right now, I'm all right. We'll see what the next moment brings, but for now, I'm fine."

"Well, I can see how Ms. Maron is the best medicine for you right now," Grace said.

"I didn't know you read mysteries," Sylvia said.

"There's a bit you don't know about me, Honey. But don't worry, we've got more time to talk." Then Grace turned and looked at Faith. "Don't even try to argue with me. I'm staying."

"But..." Sylvia started but stopped herself when she felt the extra pressure of Faith's hand on her back.

"It won't be easy, you know," Faith said, "And I can call Claire and Delta any time I need them. They're just down the road."

"I know they are. But you know I went through this with Phil. I'm the best one to take care of you Faith."

Grace's posture shifted, a steeliness of spine making her taller. While Sylvia seemed a little bewildered by this side of her mother, Faith had clearly seen it before.

"On one condition," Faith said, an impish twinkle in her eye.

"What's that?" Grace asked.

"That we go to New Orleans to buy you some summer outfits."

"Deal."

"And to get your hair done, Gracie. That's a fright of a do you have there."

"It's the Sylvia special," she said, patting the sides of her head with her palms and winking at her daughter. "What, you don't like it? It's the latest style."

Sylvia blushed and raised her hands. "Guilty. Cuff me now. I'm a coiffure killer."

The overhead speaker announced the end of visiting hours.

"You two better run along before they throw you out," Faith said, hiding the fatigue she felt. She gave them each a quick hug.

"You sleep well, and we'll see you in the morning," Grace said.

Faith lay back and closed her eyes, the book open across her lap.

As they were leaving, Sylvia turned out the overhead light at the door. Then she paused, turning around to look at Faith again. She held up a finger, silently signaling her mother to wait, and tiptoed back to the hospital bed. She reached down and lifted the reading glasses ever so gently from Faith's nose. She put them with the book on the bedside table and whispered,

"And a hug around the neck."

She returned to Grace at the door and offered her elbow to her mother.

"Let's go get something to eat, Mom," Sylvia said as they made their way down the hall, "And surprise me with something else I don't know about you."

MISSISSIPPI 1942

Faith adjusted the starched white cap on the crown of her head and pushed the bobby pins deeper into her hair. She picked up her suitcase, walked across the platform and entered the one room depot. The small station amounted to nothing more than a ticket booth and a couple of straight back chairs. It appeared to be unattended. The train from New Orleans to Hattiesburg had been half-empty and she had dozed for most of the trip only to awaken with her hair askew. She had freshened up in Hattiesburg before changing trains, taking the Bonhomie and Hattiesburg Southern some twenty-five miles to Wingate. Now here she was, in this little spot of nowhere. She wrapped her sweater snuggly around her shoulders and walked out the front door of the depot. She stood there waiting for her father, clad all in white from her nursing shoes and A-line dress up to her hat. She could have worn a more comfortable outfit for the trip home, but Maudie had requested to see Faith in her uniform, newly issued at the start of clinical rotations. Faith didn't mind. It felt like an anchor in a world now tossed at sea. The first stinging needles of an icy rain hit her cheek just as she saw the red cab of Hardee's new pickup rounding the bend in the road.

It had been a year since the explosion of Pearl Harbor catapulted the United States into full-scale war. The isolationist illusion that the Pacific and Atlantic oceans would somehow buffer Americans from world war was shattered. When Congress declared war on Japan on December 8, 1941, Germany foolishly responded by declaring war on the United States three days later. It allowed President Roosevelt and Prime Minister Churchill to finally join forces, publicly and unequivocally. The demand for the machinery of war being waged on two fronts had sent the country into a buzz of industry. Good paying jobs were plentiful, and people finally had extra money in their pockets. They were ready to spend it, but between the needs of soldiers and the disruption of imports, the supply of goods could not keep up with consumption. Commodity prices had soared, and the Roosevelt Administration had been forced to freeze prices and institute rationing of scarce resources. Rubber was especially scarce since the Japanese had occupied Malaysia and the Dutch East Indies. For the past six months sugar, coffee, and gasoline had been limited to weekly rations. Even shoes were restricted.

The need for high-grade steel had secured Hardee a tidy nest egg from his automobile salvage business. But wealth could not compensate for the real cost of the war. He and Maudie faced the unbearable loss of Brett who was missing in action. They had moved into a log cabin on a farm deep in the piney woods south of Wingate, hoping to find the ability to breathe again and some days wishing they couldn't.

Brett had been missing in action since May 14th, 1942, after flying a mission out of Port Moresby, New Guinea on a bombing raid of the Japanese at Lae. His plane never returned to the air station. Maudie chose to believe that her son was one of the American soldiers spotted on a small, deserted atoll in the Coral Sea some weeks later. She ignored the account of another B-25 pilot who said Brett's plane had been seen flaming its way into the Solomon Sea.

Hardee took Faith's suitcase and put it beneath a cover in the back of the truck. He opened the passenger door for her then walked around and got behind the driver's seat. He patted her knee as they pulled back onto the road. It was a while before they could find words to bridge their unspoken anguish.

"How's Mama?" Faith finally asked.

"'Bout to wear out her prayer bones, I'm afraid," he replied. "I 'spect those knees are permanently purple."

"Any word about Brother?"

"No, Honey, he's still officially missing in action."

"What about that story about the soldiers on the island in the Coral Sea?"

"It's just a story, Faith." Hardee's face fell slack. "Freddie Tanner told it to your mama when he came back in September. You know he lost his leg in the Battle of Savo Island, off Guadalcanal."

"I've seen pictures in the New York Times from that place. Gives me nightmares."

"I know, I know. You can tell from their faces that they are still just boys and a long way from home. Anyway, I think Freddie was just so glad to be alive he wanted to give your mama a wish to hold onto."

Faith was silent.

"I'm not so sure myself that hope doesn't make the cut that much deeper," Hardee continued, his voice growing softer. "But we all grieve in our own way and in our own time."

Faith recounted stories of nursing school as they drove

down the dirt road, strewn with the spent needles of longleaf pines. After about twenty minutes, they reached the farm, crossing beneath a rough-hewn pole entrance from which hung a sign, 'Plum Nelly'. A hundred feet ahead sat a four-room log cabin with a shed off to one side. A small Victory Garden lay in a clearing a little way from the house. It had been bedded down for winter.

Faith smiled when she read the sign and felt her shoulders relax.

"Plum Nelly?" she asked.

"Plum outa the county an' Nelly outa the state," Hardee answered, "That's what your mama asked for after we got the telegram about your brother. She asked me to take her away from Hattiesburg for a while, far away. So I went looking for a little farm. And here we are."

Faith paused to consider her father and the estrangement she had felt over the last five years. He had given up the bottle and reformed his appetite for other women shortly after Brother left for college, but the specter of that night remained. The stench of Fletcher Moody's blood-soaked clothes burning in the old wood stove had stayed with her. She struggled to reconcile her feelings. This man, through the shroud of secrecy, had played a part in the suffering of Delsey, abetting an injustice. Yet now, he was loving her mother in a fundamental and steadfast way.

"I love you, Daddy," Faith said, as he nosed the truck a few feet into the shed and turned off the engine.

"I love you, too, Honey," Hardee said, the question in his voice betraying that he had not expected to hear those words from her.

Hardee reached up and retrieved a large manila envelope containing a handful of letters from the visor overhead.

"Mail from home," he said waving the envelope before tucking it inside his jacket. "Ava and Cecil are doing a great job keeping things going in Hattiesburg and taking care of your little sisters. Frankly, I think Grace is thrilled to be finishing high school out from under the watchful eye of your mother and me. And Hannah is happy enough living with them, although we'll probably have her come down here for the summer."

"How about the Trading Post?" Faith asked. She opened the door of the truck and stepped out.

"Well, I had pretty much consolidated the business down to auto salvage seeing as how the money is in scrap iron and steel these days. Cecil is a good enough mechanic to tear a car down for parts, and we bought a crusher for the frames. So he's running the business and I let him keep most of the money. It works out, all around." He dismounted the cab of the truck.

"What about the rest of the stuff from the Trading Post?"

Hardee nodded his head toward the inside of the shed, stuffed with a chaotic arrangement of odds and ends.

"What I couldn't sell at clearance I brought down here. There may be a few valuables amidst the clutter in there."

Faith craned her neck then took a step forward to see what was in the shed.

"Tell you what," he said, "if you're willing to sort through that stuff, you can take anything you want and I'll take what's left to Carter Hill Church."

"Church?" Faith smiled.

"Your mother has adopted the church and let's just say we reached an understanding. I'll help the church out and drive her to services every week, as long as I only have to attend the sermon once a month."

"Well, wonder of wonders!" Faith laughed.

"Don't think that means I've been saved," Hardee cautioned, "at least not in your mama's eyes. You know her standards. Even whole-body baptism in the river don't mean much to her."

Faith recalled her mother's admonition against Baptists, 'They just go in a dry sinner and come out a wet one.' She made her way around the truck and reached for her father's elbow, walking arm in arm with him towards the cabin as the last of the daylight faded.

"So maybe you aren't saved, Daddy, but it doesn't mean you are beyond redemption."

"Well, we can only hope," he smiled.

Maudie turned around from the kitchen sink when they walked through the front door, wiping her soapy hands on a dishtowel before spreading her arms wide to embrace Faith.

"Thank you, sweet Jesus, for bringing my angel Faith home to me, safe and sound."

Even in the dim light of the overhead lamp, Faith could see how much her mother had aged. There were deep lines at the corners of her mouth, and she was thinner. Her hair, which had been more salt than pepper when Faith had seen Maudie in August, was now a snowy white. Faith held her mother in her arms and rocked her gently from side to side.

"I love you, Mama," she said as she let go.

Hardee dropped the mail on the kitchen counter where it landed with a plop.

"Another batch of mail from Ava," he said, kissing the top of Maudie's head. "Maybe there's some good news in there this week."

Maudie patted his cheek and gave him a weak smile. "We shall take whatever the Lord brings, rain or shine. Stew's just about ready if you two want some supper."

Maudie spooned drop biscuits from the bowl onto the cookie sheet and put them in the oven. Hardee went to the fireplace to stoke the flames and add some wood. The rain outside came down harder, pinging against the tin roof.

"You'll need an extra quilt on your bed tonight, Honey, with this storm blowing in," Maudie said, then stopped to take a good look at Faith.

"I don't know if I have ever seen a uniform more befitting a person. You look like you were born to be a nurse."

"Or a doctor! But I do love nursing."

"And what a beautiful woman you have grown into, both inside and out."

She put her arms around Faith, who was six inches taller than her mother. Maudie held onto her daughter.

"I can't wait to tell you about school, Mama, and what I am learning. The other girls in the dormitory are really swell. Did you know they are going to start a Cadet Nursing Program next year? It could pay my tuition."

"I want to hear everything over supper," Maudie said, "Why don't you unpack. You can take your Daddy's room. Supper will be ready in ten minutes."

Faith returned, having changed into a cotton shirtwaist dress. She set the table with napkins and spoons.

Maudie dished up three bowls of stew and put them on the table, then pulled the biscuits from the oven.

"Hardee, could you get some butter from the icebox on the porch?"

"Coming up," he said.

They ate their supper between talk of school and

country life and news from Hattiesburg. Faith avoided talking about the wounded soldiers who were returning from the Pacific front. The night unfolded in a slow parade of stories, until Hardee finally excused himself and retired to his chair next to the fireplace. He read his newspaper while Maudie and Faith continued their conversation.

"Why don't you grab that mail and let's see what's in it," Maudie said, needing Faith's company to approach whatever was contained in those letters.

Faith picked up the large manila envelope and poured the contents onto the table. There was a newsletter from the Nazarene church in Hattiesburg, a letter for Hardee from the Lions Club, a pledge card from the Shiner's Hospital and a letter from Justine, who wrote to Maudie every week. There was also an unexpected envelope with a postmark from Washington, D.C., the return address written in neat block print: D. Clemons Walker.

"A letter from Delsey!" Faith said, opening it without even asking her mother.

Maudie's face lit up. "What does it say?"

Faith read from the delicate onionskin pages.

"It says that Jesse read about Brother in the Hometown Heroes section of the Montgomery Advertiser last summer. Says she and McLeod are down for a visit with Jesse in Alabama and after he told her about Brother, she got hold of Ava who told her where you were."

Faith handed the letter to her mother. "She's coming to visit, Mama!"

Maudie's face was flushed from the mention of Brett and the prospect of seeing Delsey again. All that feeling had squeezed her heart into more action that she was accustomed to.

"Well the Lord is sendin' us some sunshine, child."

"And they'll be here tomorrow!" Faith said.

"Well we had better get ourselves some sleep then. Come on, I'll help you change the sheets on the bed."

The smell of bread baking in the kitchen woke her up. Maudie must have heard the rustling of the covers as Faith sat up in bed because she was in her room the next minute, pulling back the curtains to let in the sunshine. Faith stretched her arms above her head and let her hands drift back down to her side.

"What happened to the winter storm?" Faith yawned.

"Blew through overnight, looks like. And what a glorious day we've been given!"

Faith hopped out of bed, suddenly energized.

"That means you can show me around the farm this morning."

She had not been to the farm since her parents moved there. Faith had helped her mother close up the Hattiesburg house and pack some things for the move in August, but she had returned to nursing school before her parents had driven down to Plum Nelly. This was her first chance to get to see their new home.

"First thing after breakfast," Maudie said, rushing back to the stove before the bacon burned. She hollered from the kitchen back to Faith, who was putting on a flannel robe.

"Hens aren't laying much so just one egg each but there's plenty of grits and slab bacon."

Faith joined her mother in the kitchen and poured them both a cup of coffee.

"There's fresh milk in the icebox. I haven't separated

the cream on top if you want some in your coffee. I'll take mine black."

"OK, I think I will indulge myself this morning," Faith said, deciding a little cream was a fitting celebration.

She returned from the porch with the milk and sat down at the kitchen table, running her hand over the smooth tight grain of the oak before spooning some cream into her coffee. She took a sip and relished that first taste of the morning.

"Where's Daddy?" she asked, looking around.

Maudie brought the plates with bacon, grits, leftover biscuits and eggs, sunny side up, to the table. She handed Faith a cloth napkin before sitting down.

"Oh, he just left for the train station to fetch Delsey and Jesse and McLeod. He had to go by the feed and dry goods store first but it's later than you think. I decided to let you sleep in."

"No wonder I feel so good this morning. I slept like a baby. It was so cozy under that quilt with the rain tapping on the roof. Is that a new featherbed on the mattress?"

"Yes, Honey, just for you. I know you like a soft bed. It's that princess-and-the-pea skin of yours."

Faith reached over and kissed her mother on the cheek. "Oh, Mama, how did I get so lucky that God gave me to you?"

"I was just wondering the same thing," she said, her eyes showing a bit of her old sparkle. "Wait 'til I show you my nandinas. It's too early for the hydrangea and azalea blooms but you'll be able to imagine what my garden will look like this spring."

They finished breakfast and Faith changed into a cotton blouse and knit pants for her tour of her mother's garden.

It had become the favorite ritual of her homecomings. Last year when Faith returned from nursing school, the first thing she did was roam the yard in Hattiesburg with her mother. They would amble as if they had all the time in the world to see what little space had been culled of weeds or grass or flagging vines and replaced with a new flowering bush. Today the air was still, and the sun overhead warmed then. As they walked the five-acre grounds, Faith noticed for the first time that Maudie had developed a roll to her gait, a faint sideways limp when she stepped forward on her right leg.

"Mama, is your hip hurting?" Faith asked.

"Nothin' worth complainin' about. A body gets older if we're lucky! Come over here and see this camellia. Have you ever seen a prettier red blossom? God bless 'em for bloomin' in winter."

They spent almost two hours walking and talking, sitting for a spell at times, and finally tending the chickens before returning to the cabin. Around noon they heard Hardee's truck rattle across the cattle guard into the front yard. Faith felt her pulse quicken at the sound and tried to remember the last time she had seen Delsey. It must have been Christmas five years ago, just before she and Plessy had moved North. McLeod had only been three years old at the time. She wondered what he looked like now.

She and Maudie opened the front door and walked out onto the porch. They watched as Jesse jumped out of the back of the truck and opened the passenger door. Delsey and McLeod spilled out of the cab, giggling about something or other. Hardee closed the door on his side.

"Sorry about the dusty ride Jess, but I figured it was better than squeezin' you into the front."

"It's OK, Mr. Wiggins. The sun's obliging us today."

Faith found herself flying off the porch to grab Delsey and hug her, surprising them both. Delsey took a small step back to take in the sight of Faith.

"Good Lord, girl, you are a full-grown woman now," she said, patting McLeod on the back. He was holding onto the side of her skirt.

"McLeod, this is Miss Faith Wiggins and I think you two might come to be real fast friends. She's a nurse, you know."

"You doctor sick people?" he asked, letting go of his mother and looking up at Faith. He trusted his mother's sense of people and Faith, at nineteen, was at the tender beginning of womanhood and quite lovely to his eye.

"Sort of," Faith said, kneeling to look at him face to face.

"Well I might be a doctor when I grow up," he said, "or a lawyer. The name's McLeod T. Walker and I'm pleased to meet you." He stuck out his hand.

She took his hand, from her squatted position, and gave it a solid shake.

"The pleasure is all mine, Mr. Walker," Faith said. "How about you come on inside and help me make some sweet tea."

Faith nodded to Jesse as she stood up. "Thanks for coming all this way to see us, Jesse."

"Yes, ma'am, Miss Faith. I'm happy to."

Faith held out her hand to McLeod. "Want me to show you the cabin? Then we can make that tea."

"OK," he said, then looked back at Delsey to be sure.

"Run along," she said, "I'll be right there. I need to give Miss Maudie a proper greeting first."

He skipped a couple of steps before bounding up the

porch stairs and into the cabin with Faith.

"Maudie, Miss Maudie," Delsey said, folding the diminutive figure into her ample bosom. She whispered quietly, "I am so sorry for your worries."

"Thank you," Maudie said, "It's a mighty big kindness for you to come all the way to Plum Nelly to tell me that. A true act of friendship." They looked at each other for a long moment then Maudie resumed her manners and looked at Jesse and Hardee standing awkwardly in the yard.

"Come on in fellas. I was just putting a chicken in the oven."

Delsey kept her arm around Maudie's shoulder as they all walked into the cabin. Faith and McLeod were standing in the living room over by the fireplace. McLeod pointed to a bronze framed picture of a soldier on the mantel.

"Who's that man?"

"That's my brother, Brett," she said.

"Is he in the war?" McLeod asked.

"Yes, he's a pilot," Faith replied, keenly aware of the present tense of her answer.

"Uncle Jesse was going to be a pilot. Weren't you Uncle Jesse?" he said, turning towards the table where the rest of the grownups had gathered.

"That's right McLeod. That was the plan." His voice trailed off. "So much for plans."

Jesse pushed his chair back from the table slowly and stood up. "Miss Maudie, Mr. Hardee, I sure hope you won't find it rude if I take a walk before I eat. I've been sittin' on the train so long then the ride here. I just have to stretch my legs a little."

Hardee stood up quickly at the other end of the table, happy for an opening to leave the women folk to themselves.

"That's fine, Jess. I understand completely. In fact I need to chop some wood to replenish the pile I used last night." He nodded to Maudie and Delsey before leaving the table. "That is if it is OK with you ladies."

"You guys go on and let us talk," Maudie smiled. "Dinner will be ready in a couple of hours."

Hardee lifted his coat off the peg next to the front door and walked out, leaving the door open behind him. Jesse paused at the threshold then turned around. He came back to the table and stood next to Maudie.

"I meant to say to you first thing when I got here how sorry I am to hear about Brett's plane going down. His visit to see me on his way to Georgia last year was.... Well, it stayed with me and set me to thinking."

Maudie reached over and patted Jesse's hand. "I know he enjoyed the visit, too. He wrote to me about it. Don't you worry, Jesse. I 'spect he'll be coming home to us yet."

"Yes, ma'am," he said. "See y'all in about an hour or so."

Delsey waited before settling into conversation. She asked if Faith and McLeod wanted help making tea, but they were content to do it themselves. She turned to Maudie.

"How are you holding up?"

"Some days I'm beside myself with worry because there's no word from Brett. Then other days the Lord graces me with the 'peace that passeth understanding'. I still believe he's alive over there somewhere, Delsey."

Delsey was quiet and looked deep into her eyes. "I'd be privileged to pray with you, Maudie, if you like."

"I'd like that."

Delsey let Maudie do most of the praying, which went on for a good ten minutes. After they were finished, Faith and McLeod joined them at the table and the conversation turned from Brett to Delsey and her family. She told the story of how Jesse had been inspired after Brett's visit to Montgomery. He had decided to enlist with the Tuskegee Airmen, and she had helped Jesse study for three months in order to pass the qualifying exam. They had both felt he would be ready to join the cadet class in November 1941. When he went for the prerequisite physical exam, he was shocked to find out he had a heart murmur. The doctor figured that Jesse had developed acute rheumatic fever some years back. The illness left him with a damaged heart valve that disqualified him from military service. Delsey said Jesse was a bit lost after that and, frankly, ashamed, especially when he read about Brett. She and Plessy had finally talked him into coming up to Washington, D.C. for the winter. She had come to fetch him, hoping the move would be permanent.

She watched the lines in Maudie's face soften as she went on to tell stories about Plessy and McLeod and Washington, D.C. She bragged a little about McLeod's talent for music. She imagined it must be a relief to Maudie not to have to talk about Brett. McLeod began to squirm in his chair as the stories dragged on. Faith could tell that Maudie and Delsey had more to say to one another, so she offered McLeod an out.

"McLeod, would you consider helping me with a job?"

"Sure. What is it?' He jumped up from the table. "I'm good at chores."

"My Daddy asked me to sort through the stuff in the shed and see what can be thrown out. He said there might be a treasure buried in there somewhere."

"Can I Mama?" he asked, hardly waiting for an answer.

"OK, but mind your manners, and Miss Faith."

"I will," he said as he dashed for the door.

"We'll be back before dark." Faith winked at Maudie and Delsey, then followed him out.

They stepped off the porch and walked past the truck parked in the front yard. The wooden doors to the shed were propped open, a semi-permanent position ensured by the clumps of grass that had accumulated in the corners. The boards needed a good whitewash, but the wood was still hard and dry. Faith and McLeod ventured into the center of the shed, a twelve-by-twelve-foot space that was lined on all sides with various objects. She picked up a flashlight from a nearby shelf and turned it on. A gray squirrel scolded them as he scurried across a beam overhead, ducking out a knothole in the eaves.

"Where do we start?" said Faith.

"Well," McLeod rubbed his chin as he had seen his father do when he was thinking about something. "Let's make piles."

"Good idea. How about we put boxes in that corner for now," she said pointing to her left, "and loose stuff out front."

McLeod walked across the dirt floor to a pile along the back wall. There were several bags of clothes stacked on top of each other. He picked up a bag with both arms.

"Are these boxes or loose?" he asked.

"That's loose," Faith replied. "Goes out front."

"Yes, ma'am," he said and marched the bag out onto the grass in front of the shed.

They worked for a half hour with Faith doing most of the lifting while McLeod watched. After she moved the boxes, filled with linens and dishes, into one corner she started shifting lamps and chairs into the other.

"So you must be in third grade by now."

"Yes ma'am. I've learned my multiplication tables all the way up to my nines. One times one is one, one times two is two, one times three...."

She could tell that once the recitation had begun, he was going to see it all the way through. She stood and listened attentively as he chugged on like a little train going up a hill until he arrived at 'nine times nine is eighty-one'. He sat down on the edge of one of the boxes to catch his breath.

"I remember third grade," Faith said. "My favorite book was The Secret of the Old Clock. It was about a girl named Nancy Drew who was a detective. Mama used to get after me to read other books because there was a new Nancy Drew book every few months and that's all I ever wanted to read." She picked up a box that was sitting on top of a desk and moved it to the side. "Do you like to read?"

"Oh, yes ma'am. But I don't know that Nancy girl."

"Do you have a favorite book?" she asked, opening the top drawer of the desk.

"Oh yes, Hezekiah Horton!"

"Hezekiah Horton, who's he?"

"He's a boy who lives in Harlem and gets to ride in Mr. Ed's big red car."

"That sounds fun."

"Yep. But I just got a new book called 'The Fast Sooner Hound' and I think it's going to be my best book because it's about a railroad man, like my Daddy used to be, but his name is Boomer, and he has a dog named Sooner and the book has more words than Hezekiah Horton."

"Oh, I like railroad stories," she said.

She pulled the drawer out of the desk and brought it over to McLeod. They rummaged through its contents.

"Hey, look what I found," she said, handing him a small leather coin case. It was square with a zipper around the outside. Inside was a plastic holder with slots for coins.

"That's swell," he said.

"You keep it," Faith said. "Think you can help me move this desk now that I have the drawers out?"

"Oh, sure," he said, "I help my Daddy all the time with heavy things because he has a bad arm."

This reminder hit her like an unexpected bee sting. The two of them slid the desk out a few feet from the back wall.

"Look! The treasure!" McLeod said, pointing to the black case tucked between the two by fours of the shed frame, behind where the desk had been. The hourglass shape suggested it contained a guitar.

Faith picked up the case and blew the dust off the cover before placing it on the desk.

"Go ahead. You can open it."

McLeod flipped up the metal latch and held his breath as he opened the case. A real guitar! The body was a honey-colored birch swirling with dark brown grains. The surface, though dulled by age, had few scratches. A wreath of gold leaves was stenciled around the sound hole and just above the bridge sat a decal of two ladies in green dresses, sitting on a bough of flowers. "Can I touch it?" He asked in barely a whisper.

"Why, McLeod, you can take it out and hold it and play it if you wish."

"Oh, thank you, Miss Faith."

He lifted the guitar gently from its cradle and stood it on its tail. The steel strings were old but intact. Across the headstock in slanting script was the name Stella.

"It says Stella," he said.

"Tell you what, young man, why don't you bring that with you and see if you can make any music while I go check with our mamas about dinner."

They returned the items from the lawn to the middle of the shed. Faith turned off the flashlight and headed out the door. McLeod hoisted the guitar under his arm and followed her. When they got to the porch he sat down on the step and began to play with the tuning pegs. Faith slipped into the cabin through the front door and motioned for Maudie and Delsey to come look. They stood there in the shadows, just inside the door and listened to him strum a blues shuffle beat. Before long, he was singing a lamentation of pure invention. They closed the door quietly and retreated into the kitchen so as not to disturb him. Faith went into the bedroom and found her purse on the bedside table. She unzipped the pocket in front and pulled out a shiny new silver dollar. She put the coin to her lips and kissed it, then looked up toward the ceiling.

"Bless this boy, dear Lord, and let him rise."

She walked back through the kitchen and said to Maudie, "I'll be right back to set the table."

Faith opened the door without interrupting McLeod's concentration. She went and sat next to him, waiting until he had finished his song, then asked him.

"Do you still have that coin case?"

"Yes, ma'am."

"Well here's something to put in it," she said, handing him the silver dollar. "Looks like you're gonna need some string money to go with that guitar."

"You mean I can have it?"

"I don't see how that Stella could belong to anyone else."

He could not contain his joy as he hugged the guitar to his chest. Faith patted his knee as she stood back up and returned to the cabin.

Inside she opened the cabinets, taking dishes down from the shelf, humming the tune McLeod was playing.

"Is there anything else I can do other than set the table?"

"No Honey, Delsey has helped me take care of everything."

Maudie put her arm around Delsey's waist and squeezed her gently. Faith could see how nourishing the visit had been for her mother. The crackle of twigs in the front yard announced Hardee and Jesse's return. The sweet sound of McLeod's singing drifted through the window as Delsey called to him.

"Come on in and wash up, Baby. We need to eat dinner if we're gonna make that train tonight."

MISSISSIPPI 1999

Faith opened her eyes and shut them again. It felt so good to sleep, to rest without any hint of striving. She let herself drift back to the dream she was having. She was swimming in a turquoise ocean above a coral reef, the warmth of the tropical waters bathing her. Just beyond her reach, a school of dolphins jumped and whistled, inviting her to join them in deeper waters. The dream receded and she lay there, swaddled in the blissful liminality that precedes awakening. She fingered the bedspread, trying to recall where she was. The crow of the rooster drew her into the light of day. She opened her eyes and looked around the room. The first rays of dawn peaked through the window as her sister quietly pushed the lace curtains to the side.

"Good morning, Gracie," she said, the corners of her mouth lifting ever so slightly. Another day. She had awakened to another day.

"Mornin' Faith," Grace replied. "Thought you might want a taste of sunrise to go with your coffee and paper today." She walked to the bed and caressed Faith's cheek with the back of her fingers. She paused a moment to gaze into her eyes then collected the empty water glass from the bedside table.

"And maybe some Cream of Wheat?" Faith said. She felt surprisingly well this morning. Was it the morphine she had begun taking for the aching in her bones? No, actually she had not needed her pain medicine last night. She smiled at her need to explain her good feelings.

Faith had carefully considered Dr. Prentice's offer of further treatment. The concoction of chemotherapy was 'fairly well tolerated, even in the elderly' he had told her. She was as disconcerted at being considered elderly, despite her seventy-six years, as she was at the prospect of more intense chemotherapy. Faith had seen enough in her fifty years of nursing to know that 'fairly well tolerated' meant not dying of the treatment. It was not the vanity about baldness that had stopped her. The gain of a few months at the expense of more fatigue, nausea and mouth sores just did not seem worth it. As much as she longed for another season in her garden, she had never been one to cling. She and Dr. Prentice had decided to escalate her hydroxyurea dose slightly and Faith had entered a home hospice program. Grace, true to her promise, had stayed on in Mississippi limiting the need for nursing visits to three times a week. As spring gave way to summer, they settled into an easy companionship, the unspoken familiarity of sisters.

"Cream of Wheat sounds delicious," Grace said with genuine enthusiasm as she turned to go to the kitchen. It delighted her that her sister was showing signs of an appetite. It had been a couple of days since Faith had requested anything other than tea and soda crackers. She turned around at the doorway to the bedroom. "Do you want your breakfast in bed?"

"No, I think I'll catch the sunrise from the front porch this morning," Faith said, rising slowly and letting her legs dangle from the side of the bed before trying to stand up. She extended her right foot, curling her ankle around the walker and pulling it closer.

Grace started back toward the bed to retrieve the walker for her. "All you have to do is ask for help!"

Faith held her hand up to stop Grace's advance, but her sister was instantly at her side.

"And I will, if I need it. But I can get myself up and dressed this morning." She reached over and stroked Grace's arm. Her sister seemed utterly incapable of halting her hovering. In the past couple of weeks Grace had become more fidgety. Faith sometimes found it difficult to contain her own irritability at the unacknowledged anxiety. But she knew that Grace loved her and was doing her best.

"I will ask you a favor, though."

"Yes? What's that?" Grace said.

"Would you put the Times next to the rocker on the porch?"

"And your devotional?"

"No, I think just the Times this morning," Faith said. An equipoise descended to help her love her sister as she was, full of conviction in her own daily religious routine. Today though, Faith had no interest in the hereafter. She wanted to be of this world for just a little bit longer. She stroked Grace's arm again, then stood up and rolled her walker into the bathroom. After a brief shower, she donned her robe and decided she had the energy to navigate the house without her wheels.

Grace brought coffee and a bowl of steaming Cream of Wheat to the porch a few minutes later. She seemed to have made peace with the fact that Faith needed some time to herself this morning.

"I think I'll have my devotional time inside," Grace said. "Holler if you need anything."

"I will," Faith said. She peered up over her reading glasses long enough to see her sister's rounded backside disappearing through the screen door. She returned to her paper and continued reading with interest the news of the day.

It had been over three months since the impeachment trial of President Clinton had ended in his acquittal of the twin charges of perjury and obstruction of justice. The independent counsel law was set to expire by the end of the month. Ken Starr, true to his weasel-like nature, was still rooting around in the dirt for a morsel of trash to use against the sitting president. Faith wondered when it had come to this. It seemed that what now passed for news was not much more than a gossip column. Although it had been three months, the pundits could not stop drooling over the president's public humiliation. Was this a new aberration of the office? Some of the most revered presidents from Jefferson to Franklin Roosevelt to Kennedy had extramarital affairs. There was little mention of Clinton's accomplishments during his tenure; a historic economic expansion, greater college opportunities, and the development of a national infrastructure for the Internet. Faith recalled a time when a president was judged by the legacy of his policies, not by his personal indiscretions.

She laid the paper down and looked out across the east pasture. The faint pink of early sunrise gave way to bright gold as the sun broke the horizon. The cows had begun their slow saunter toward the barn for milking. Faith considered how her own life would stand up to scrutiny when measured by another's yardstick. She had diligently poured herself into her work as a nurse, to the point of exhaustion at times. She had generously given time and money to the congregation at Emanuel and many local causes. She had done good work and traveled the world. Nevertheless, she had had her dalliances. She had reconciled herself a long time ago that she need not be confined to a life of celibacy just because she did not want to marry, regardless of the church's teachings. There had been a handful of men she had loved, some for a matter of months and one for several years. But she had never compromised her principles. None of her lovers was married and all were clear-eyed about her intentions. She had always kept her love in confidence. Hearts had been broken, sometimes hers and sometimes his, but that has always been the price of love or attachment, as the Buddhists would say. Faith smiled at her remembrances. There was no reason to lament the comings and goings of her life.

She took a drink of her coffee, especially strong this morning with ample cream to blunt the bitterness. 'Grace has finally learned how to make a great cup of coffee,' she thought. She picked up the paper to resume her reading and felt something wet on her upper lip. She must have been sloppy with her coffee.

The first red splotch on the newspaper puzzled her. Red ink in the middle of an article? Then another spot formed on the page, and another and another. In the eternity between breaths, as she watched the crimson blossoms form, her mind fell still. Then, as though on a soft slow breeze came the thought, 'We fall like leaves from a sweet gum tree, carried away by an invisible wind.'

She reached into the pocket of her robe and retrieved a Kleenex to wipe the blood from her nose.

"Grace?" Faith called, trying to mask her own fear.

"Grace, could you bring me a cold washcloth?"

Her blood counts had been dropping for the past month. She let herself get another red blood cell transfusion last week to treat her anemia but her platelets, her clotting cells, had not been a problem. Now suddenly, in this suspended moment she knew that it was time to stop bargaining with God. Clearly, her platelet count had dropped. Soon her good white blood cells would be gone, and she would be defenseless against infection.

Grace appeared at the screen with the washcloth. Her eyes widened visibly when she saw the blood. Faith took a deep breath and regained her composure. Tears began to well in her eyes as she came to accept that her time was near.

"Gracie, see if I have some Neosynephrine in the bathroom cabinet."

Her sister nodded, momentarily frozen before she summoned the courage she had promised to find when Faith needed her.

"Now go call Dr. Prentice," Faith said when her sister returned with the nose drops, "And I think you might want to call Sylvia and tell her to catch a plane."

MISSISSIPPI 1999

Rain pelted the windshield. The wipers slapped frantically, unable to disperse the water sheeting across the glass. The slight drizzle in Vicksburg had picked up in intensity as Sylvia headed north, but she had continued on into the storm, wondering if she was crazy to take another detour to Clarksdale on her way home. This downpour had come on so suddenly and was so blinding that Sylvia did not have time to search for shelter beneath an overpass. She pulled over to the side of the road and felt her way to the shoulder by the sound of the gravel and the subtle drop off at the edge of the pavement. She rolled to a stop and turned off the engine. Another wave of grief washed over her as she thought about the past two weeks. She still couldn't believe how quickly Faith's health had declined.

Once Faith decided to stop her hydroxyurea and forego any transfusions or antibiotics, she had begun to let go in earnest. She had died ten days after Sylvia's arrival. In that last week together, Faith found time to talk to Sylvia about her wishes. She wanted three things. She wanted to be cremated and gave instructions for disposing of her ashes. She wanted her entire estate, other than some individual gifts she had set aside, to go to McLeod Walker, and she wanted Sylvia to hand deliver a letter to him. After that was done, and not before, Sylvia was to unlock a safety deposit box at the First Charter bank in Jackson. Sylvia had carefully scribbled notes onto a pad as Faith talked so Faith could witness her wishes being recorded. Once she felt sure they would be fulfilled, Faith had relaxed and turned to her memories of young McLeod Walker. A real music talent, that young man, she had said.

Even though she had never met him, Sylvia had developed a fondness for McLeod Walker from the stories Faith had told. She had done her best to simplify the transfer of Faith's estate to him, setting up transfer on death accounts for the cash and investments. However, the transfer of the title to the house meant the Last Will and Testament still had to go through probate. She knew she needed to meet with McLeod soon, but she could not do it today. Not until she had sent him a letter of introduction.

Sylvia and Grace had packed up the last of Faith's things, which she'd so carefully winnowed to the most valuable and personal. Together they had cleaned the house, just as they had washed Faith's body the night she died, as a last ritual of love. The memorial service was held at the Emanuel Congregational Church on Sunday afternoon and the sanctuary was packed with friends who overflowed onto the front steps. They had invited everyone back to the farmhouse for food and remembrances. The picnic table outside was filled with the dishes people brought, offerings of fried chicken and cornmeal crusted catfish, deviled eggs and potato salad, yellow squash, and fresh purple hull peas. A true Southern wake. It was well after dark before the last visitor hugged Sylvia goodbye.

The next morning she and Grace had tended the garden one last time, unable to turn the plants under just yet. Then they locked up the house and left. Sylvia had seen her mother off at the airport in Jackson early this morning.

Grace was going back to New York City and her life there. The parting had been hard for them both because of the intimacy they'd shared. It was one more rent in the tapestry that was unraveling now that Faith was gone.

It had only been a couple of hours since Sylvia had bribed one of the county workers at the abandoned Vicksburg Bridge to let her slip past the chain link gate and walk the three quarters of a mile to its midspan. There she let Faith's ashes fly, honoring her wish to fall into the arms of Old Man River and dance with him all the way to the Gulf of Mexico and beyond. Sylvia had asked Grace if she wanted to come along but her mother felt uncomfortable with the whole idea of cremation. Brimstone and all that, Sylvia imagined. So she had taken on the task alone. It left her a little wobbly at first, as though her compass had lost its North when the last of the ashes were whisked away. But some part of Faith's essence, her wisdom, must have breathed its way into Sylvia, who felt a sense of calm after letting go of her beloved aunt in this way.

Now she sat quietly in the car, waiting for the storm to pass. The rain eased up as the clouds moved off to the east. The weather had been fierce at times over the past week with a spate of tornadoes and floods wreaking havoc over much of central and eastern Mississippi, as though the earth itself was convulsed with grief at the passing of such a remarkable soul. Sylvia checked the rear-view mirror to make sure the road was clear before easing back onto the highway. She figured she would be in Clarksdale in little more than an hour.

The tires splashed against the wet pavement. She slipped Rory Block's 'Gone Woman Blues' CD into the dash of the Miata and fast-forwarded to the title song. The soft moan eased her deeper into the bucket seat until the lick of the slide guitar took over, infusing her with the only salvation she could feel at the moment, setting her left foot to tapping and her shoulders to shimmying. She let the album transport her all the way to heaven and then on to Clarksdale.

Sylvia had called ahead to make sure a room was available at the Hellbound Hotel. When she arrived, she found out that Raymond Jackson, the hotel owner, was on a much-needed vacation. The attendant greeted her kindly.

"Evening," she said, "You needin' a room for the night."

"Yes," Sylvia replied, "Just one night. Is room 8 available by any chance?"

"Let me look. You been here before?" The young woman flipped through a file of index cards.

"Yes, last September." Sylvia said, as she fought back tears. The past year with Faith had gone by so quickly.

"Yes, it's available. Shared bath you know, but there's a lady in room seven."

"I'll take it," Sylvia said, laying her credit card on the counter.

She took the key and walked down the hall to the left, opened the door then closed it behind her. She sat on the bed and rummaged through her briefcase until she found her cell phone.

"Hello," Joe answered.

"Hey, Love. I'm in Clarksdale."

She imagined him smiling as he paused before speaking.

"I thought you might end up there on the way home. How are you?"

"Sad and missing you."

"Me too, Babe, me too."

"How's the ranch?"

"Same old, same old. Baling hay and fixin' fences. I'm starting to realize that I am not thirty years old anymore. There comes a point when a body can't keep doing this work."

"You could play piano in Austin instead."

"Then I'd need to rent a house and buy my own car. You know how much a piano player makes?"

"You could live with me, at least until you get steady gigs," Sylvia said.

Joe laughed out loud, "What are you proposing, Miss Sylvia Barbarino?"

She paused before she responded, afraid to promise a future she couldn't deliver. "You know how much I love waking up with you, Joe. If you need a place to stay for a while you would be welcome. I really called to thank you for coming to the memorial service."

"You know how much I cared about Faith. I wanted to be there, for you and to say my goodbyes."

"I know," she said, "But it was still kind of a big deal for you to come."

"Like I said, I was happy to."

"I'm serious about you playing piano full time, Joe. Think about it."

"I will. But in the meantime, would you please get your sweet ass back home. My bed is cold and empty without you."

"Well warm it up as best you can. I'll be there tomorrow night."

"OK, drive carefully."

"I will."

Sylvia clicked the phone closed and put it back in her briefcase. She really missed Joe. Right now, all she wanted was to lie next to him, to rest in their love. But was that fair to him? The therapist she was seeing had displayed great empathy for Sylvia's situation as well as the impact on Joe's life. She had encouraged Sylvia to be honest with Joe about her past before taking any steps to contact the adoption agency. Joe needed to know how certain Sylvia was about not having another child and about her intention to find the son she had. Honesty was the first step toward any future, with or without Joe. Sylvia had tried to bring herself to have the conversation with Joe on a couple of occasions but hadn't found the courage. Then Faith had relapsed and she had turned to Joe for comfort, delaying any difficult discussions. Sylvia was suddenly tired.

She leaned against the pillows, thinking she would lie down for just a few minutes. She was out cold before she knew it, and when she awoke it was a little past seven o'clock. The string cheese and bag of peanuts she had eaten after stopping for gas in Beulah had whetted the small appetite she had. She decided to go straight to Maizie's instead of finding a restaurant. She knew the music would not start until later, but she needed to get out, and that juke joint was the only place she wanted to be.

When she arrived, Sylvia found Mike behind the bar. There was a momentary lull in the evening's business. He was wiping down the counter with one hand, holding a sturdy looking baby in the other arm.

"What can I get ya'?," he said looking up.

"Whatever you've got on draft," she said. "It's Mike, right?"

"Yep, I'm Mike and this is James Lucas," he said,

holding up his boy with both hands and letting his little round feet touch the freshly cleaned counter. The baby reflexively began a stepping motion.

"Well, Mike, I'm Sylvia Barbarino and I'm sure you don't remember me, but I passed through here last September."

"Sorry, Sylvia, I'm not so good with faces. Lots of folks come through here." He shifted James Lucas back to his hip and drew her a cold glass of beer. He placed it on the counter in front of her. "But we're glad you decided to drop back by."

"I didn't know you were a father."

"Yep, this is me and Rosie's first. Of many, I hope. She's in the kitchen grilling some burgers for dinner. Do you want one?"

"Yea, that would be great." Sylvia said, suddenly discovering her appetite again. "I forgot to eat dinner."

"Sure, I'll bring it out when it's done" he said, then nodded toward the stage.

"Those guys are just finishing up a jam session. Tonight's band won't start warming up for another thirty minutes. Right big guy?" he said, lifting his son over his head and dropping him back down, eliciting a belly laugh.

Sylvia looked over at the stage and listened to the two men improvising blues rifts on the guitar. One was quite a bit older than the other. The older man played with his eyes closed, fingers dancing up and down the fret board, keeping time with his right foot. The music he made was like the salve of cool water on a burn. The sound of a familiar voice turned her attention away from the men and towards the hall leading to the restrooms.

"Put another club soda on my tab, Mike. I'll get it myself so James Lucas can keep up his flying lessons there."

"Louise!!" Sylvia squealed and jumped off her bar stool. She had kept up a scant correspondence with Louise after they had met at Maizie's last September, but she had let it slip lately.

"Well, rocka my soul in the bosom of Abraham," Louise said opening her arms wide, "Welcome home, Miss Sylvia Barbarino."

Sylvia hugged her longer than she had intended and found herself crying. Louise did not flinch, prepared to hold the broken sparrow of a gal all night if needed. Sylvia finally let go and wiped her eyes with the bar napkin that she retrieved from underneath her beer.

"Faith's dead," she blurted out.

Louise looked into her eyes for a moment then nodded.

"I was wondering, after you told me she relapsed this spring. Figured you'd be in touch after the dust settled."

"I'm surprised how much it hurts," Sylvia said, wiping her eyes again.

Louise motioned to Mike to hand James Lucas over.

"Your Aunt Weezy wants you," he said.

"Mike, I told you I'm gonna have to shoot you if you call me Weezy again."

"You don't have a gun, but OK. Here you go, Aunt Louise," he chuckled, passing his son across the counter.

James Lucas settled onto her lap and nuzzled the side of his head against her breast. She placed her hand on his cheek and held him close.

"Lucas, I think I'm going to have to put you to work for a few minutes."

She kissed the top of his head then handed him to Sylvia.

Sylvia did not know what to do at first. She looked at

Louise, waiting for direction.

"Nothing takes the sting out of death like holding a baby," Louise smiled. "Just confuses the hell out of the brain having all that death and new life mixed up together. Like they're both true at the same time."

Sylvia took him from Louise and held him so that his head rested on her shoulder, his crown tucked beneath her chin. She stood up and began to rock gently side to side. She felt his body loosen in trust, the full weight of him against her. Soon she heard his breathing take on the quiet rhythm of sleep. She sat back down and closed her eyes, just holding this baby boy. Mike excused himself, letting the women have a moment alone.

"You know the hardest part," Sylvia said, her eyes still closed, "I was just starting to think that maybe I could trust in something, a Presence as Faith called it."

"And now?" Louise asked.

"Well, I don't know if I can find it without Faith around to point me in the right direction."

"Darlin' you don't need to understand the Mystery to have a relationship with it."

Sylvia was quiet. She breathed in the pure sweet smell of James Lucas and opened her eyes to see the two guitar players packing up their instruments. She waited for Louise to continue.

"It's where the music comes from. You can find it in the blues or in the forms released from Michelangelo's marble. It is in the roll of the tides and the love you make with Joe. It's in whatever brings forth life. At least that's God enough for me."

Sylvia reached over and held Louise's hand.

"Thank you, Louise. I knew I needed to come to

Clarksdale on my way home."

Mike returned from the kitchen with Sylvia's hamburger. When he saw his son sleeping in her arms, he decided to invite her to join them for dinner.

"Sylvia, why don't you eat in the kitchen with Louise and Rosie and me? Looks like James Lucas has decided to adopt you as his newest aunt."

The bell over the door jingled as the musicians from the jam session made their way out.

"See you tomorrow, Mike," said the shorter Black man, carrying his six-string.

"Sure thing, McLeod. You guys are the show next Thursday, right?"

"That's right, man."

Sylvia stole a glance at the man. The crown of his head was balding and there was ample gray in his well-trimmed beard.

"Did you say McLeod?"

"Yeah, McLeod Walker. He is a lawyer here in town. And the best blues guitar man from here to New Orleans," Mike said as she watched McLeod disappear out the door.

~

McLeod dropped his keys into the small brass bowl on the table next to the front door. The clear deep ring of it made him smile in reflex. He could hear Jasmine, his twelve-year-old lab, jumping off the bed in the guest room. He had long ago surrendered the furniture to her, finding dog sheets an easy quid pro quo for her faithfulness. The day's mail, delivered through the slot in the door, was scattered on the floor. He picked it up and walked into the open living room to his left, placed his guitar case in its stand next to the couch and sat down. He tapped the seat next to him inviting Jazz, who had padded her way through the dining room to join him there. The dog leapt up stiffly and nestled in close. She nosed McLeod's hand as he sifted through the mail.

"Hello, Jazz, old girl," he said, setting the mail on the end table, stroking her smooth round head. "You as tired as I am?"

She laid her head in McLeod's lap and let out a soft groan of contentment as she closed her eyes. McLeod was pleased with the practice session tonight. The two had really nailed their timing on a couple of songs and they had fine-tuned the amps so that the acoustics filled the room without overwhelming the stage. The Gibson L-00 reissue that he had bought a year ago had hummed, the frets smoothed in, and the strings loosened up. Though he was tired tonight, it wasn't weariness, just a day well spent.

McLeod had long ago settled into his life in Clarksdale. It was hard to imagine that he had lived here for over thirty years. He had turned sixty-five this past March and was beginning to wind down his law practice, but he still had every intention of continuing his work at the Delta Center for Justice and Opportunity. And to play as many gigs as he could book.

Jazz let out another groan as she shifted her weight on the couch. McLeod scratched her behind the ear.

"Let's go for our walk, girl. We've got to get your nightly business done before we hit the sack."

Jazz was reluctant, having just settled into the couch. She looked at McLeod and thumped the cushions with her tail.

"I know you're comfortable, but we have to go," he said.

They both got up from the couch and walked to the front door. He lifted the leash from the coat rack and attached it to her collar. They tread carefully down the steps to the sidewalk and began their circumnavigation of the neighborhood. The sun had set but the summer breeze still warmed him.

On nights like this, the loneliness would sneak up on him. He wished he could reach over and hold Nora's hand. He and his wife were still friendly since the separation five years ago, even intimate on occasion. There had been no great betrayal, just the years of his unrelenting absence, as he tended the mistress of his work. McLeod's career as a civil rights attorney in Mississippi had consumed him. As he and Jazz reached the park at the end of the street, the dog slowed down to sniff a row of bushes planted along the perimeter.

McLeod Walker had never intended to move to the Mississippi Delta when he boarded that train in Washington, D.C. in the summer of 1961. On the other hand, he had not hesitated to head into the Deep South as part of the next wave of Freedom Riders. It was a calling many had answered. Across the country small teams of men and women, Black and White, had taken their seats at the front of buses and crossed the lines of segregation in waiting rooms on their way to Jackson, Mississippi.

He had met Nora Davis, a teacher, three years later during Freedom Summer and they fell in love instantly. They were married by Christmas and had a son the next year, Darius, their only child. McLeod spent as much of his free time with his son as possible and supported him through medical school, but their relationship had always been more work than play, more preparing for life than enjoying it. Now that Darius was immersed in his own career as a surgeon in New York City they seldom saw each other. Nora had developed a life independent of McLeod's, getting her doctorate in Sociology at Fisk University. While Darius was in high school, she had commuted to Nashville for courses. After he left for college, she ended up moving there to teach at Fisk. Nora and McLeod still saw each other most weekends, but she no longer served as his other half. At first, he resented her independence but, over time, it made them truly appreciate the time they did have together.

Jazz tugged at the leash as they rounded the last corner towards home. Her nightly aspirin, wrapped in a slice of cheese, awaited her. She coughed as the collar tugged at her windpipe. McLeod walked faster.

"OK, OK Jazz, I'm hurrying. Don't strangle yourself for a bite of cheese."

The peaceful rhythm of the walk had soothed him but as he approached the house, McLeod missed Nora even more. Turning from the sidewalk toward the house, he looked at his watch. It was ten o'clock. He knew Nora would still be up. Maybe he would risk a call, see if she wanted to go to Memphis for a couple of days. Once inside the house he unleashed Jazz and picked up the phone.

"Is Dr. Walker in?" McLeod teased.

"Hello, Mac," Nora replied, "you're up late."

"Well, maybe I'm turning into a night owl like you." He tried not to sound defensive. The difference in their circadian rhythms always kept them a little bit out of sync. "How was your day?"

"Great," she said, becoming more animated, "I just put the finishing touches on the curriculum for the new course

I'm teaching this fall."

"About Black women and the abolitionist movement?"

"Yeah, it's called 'Black Women at the Forefront: The Abolition of Slavery'."

"I'd like to come up for the opening lecture."

"That'd be wonderful. First class is next Friday, 10 a.m.

McLeod hesitated. "I have a gig at Maizie's that Thursday night."

"Well, you're an early bird. If you hit the road by 5 o'clock you can make it."

"You're right. I'll be there," he said. His desire to see her overcame any thought of negotiating schedules.

"Thanks, Mac," her voice softened, "You could stay the weekend."

"I was thinking we might go up to Memphis for the weekend. A little Beale Street time."

"Lord, you courtin' me again?'

"Maybe. Now that I'm cutting back on the law practice, I was thinking I could book some gigs in Memphis. Maybe… Maybe stay with you in Nashville half the week."

Nora was silent. McLeod felt his face flush. He wondered if he had pushed too far.

"Do you know how long I've waited to hear you say those words?" Nora finally replied.

"So, that's a yes?" McLeod asked, not hiding his excitement.

"It's a yes to a weekend on Beale Street. We'll see about the rest."

"Can't wait. I assume Jazz is welcome."

"Always," Nora said, "See you, Friday.

"OK, good night, Boo."

"Good night, Mac."

MISSISSIPPI 1999

McLeod stepped into the shade of the awning that ran the entire length of the red brick storefront. Although it was still morning, the blazing sun had already generated a sweltering heat. He stopped at the door to the office, the name 'Delta Center for Justice and Opportunity' stenciled in gold trimmed letters across the upper glass panel. McLeod had chosen a downtown location to be more accessible to clients, but also because he liked to mingle with the locals at lunchtime, to talk music and politics over a bowl of gumbo. Since it was Saturday, the shops would not open for another hour. He opened the door and walked into the middle of the large open room, pulling the chain that dangled from the ceiling fan. It turned slowly, the old motor whining over the soft slap of blades stirring the humid air. By the time he finished opening all the windows, his forehead was beaded with sweat.

"I'm sure the guy over at Owens electric said he was going to install the new fan this week," he muttered to himself.

But by August even a good ceiling fan offered little relief from the Mississippi heat. McLeod had found just enough money in the budget to buy the new fan. In the 1970s he won a couple of high dollar verdicts for clients targeted by hate groups. The contingency fees had provided him some savings and enough money to open the Center, which now relied on grants and donations for funding. His private law practice overlapped with his work here. He provided legal services for most of the Black community in Coahoma County, doing everything from fighting discrimination cases to defense at criminal trials. His clients paid what they could and he got a small salary as Center director. Except for the single private room for client conferences, the office still resembled the old warehouse he had purchased years ago with its wide plank pine floors and unfinished brick walls.

McLeod went to his desk in the corner next to the conference room and sat his briefcase on top. He leaned his guitar case against the wall. Initially, the Center had only offered legal services. But after a few years it expanded to include social workers and a literacy project, including adult remediation classes and tutorial services to students.

For McLeod, though, the heartbeat of the Center was the mentoring program for at-risk-youth. He started the program fifteen years ago. He had wanted to find a way to redirect the despair that could turn to rage when kids lacked for opportunities. McLeod knew what it took to accomplish that; a deeply personal connection and patience until the child found a passion, some taproot to a creative instinct. If that passion was music, it was easy; McLeod was his man and could guide him through the feel as well as the theory of the art. If it was chemistry or building or writing, he had to work a little harder to find the right mentor for him. But the success of the program spoke for itself. Since the program started, none of the kids enrolled had gone on to a life of incarceration.

McLeod was aware of the paradox of having left his

own son at some risk by being so absorbed with work, but luckily Nora had more than compensated for this failing. Darius had thrived with a full-time mother and a part-time father. Most of the kids in the Center's mentorship program were lucky to have even one part-time parent. That was certainly true for Mose Cunningham.

"Is that Catfish Cunningham?" McLeod said when he heard the front door open.

"Mr. Walker, you know I'm never going to take the name Catfish," Mose replied as he closed the door behind him.

"Well then next time we go fishing, you better stop catchin' your limit before I even get my hook wet," McLeod jousted.

He extended his clinched right hand. Mose returned the greeting with a quick fist bump, and then lifted the guitar case in his left hand.

"Where should we set up?" he asked McLeod.

"I thought we'd try the acoustics in the conference room, today. See how she plays in a small space."

They entered the room, enclosed by glass panels rising from a half wall to the ceiling. Mose set the guitar case on the long table. The black tweed case was new, a minor investment on McLeod's part to protect the vintage instrument inside. He loaned this guitar to his best students. It was the Stella he had grown up playing and he had taken meticulous care of it over the years. The neck remained unbowed after years of use, due to his regular adjustments of the truss rod. He had long ago replaced the original frets thinned by natural wear. When Mose showed his skill at playing, McLeod had a new ebony bridge and bone saddle mounted. Mose carefully lifted the instrument from the case.

"I washed my hands before I came and I do it every time before I play, just like you said."

McLeod noticed the clean cloth in the bottom of the guitar case.

"And I see how careful you are at wiping her down each time."

"Yes, sir, Mr. Walker. I promised you I'd take care of your Stella."

"Alright, let's warm up with the E minor pentatonic scale and then your E blues scale."

He watched as the boy's fingers danced across the fret board, the pick in his right hand moving with quicksilver precision across the strings. Mose was starting to add vibrato to his ending notes. He ran through both scales several times before looking up from the guitar.

"I can tell you've been practicing," McLeod said, his smile revealing his obvious pride in this young man.

"Every spare minute I got," Mose replied.

"OK, now the A minor pentatonic and let's see if you can add a slide into the blues note in the A blues scale."

Again, Mose flew through the exercise with the effortless execution that comes from proficient muscle memory, the mind having loosened its reins on the body. He naturally moved into an extended scale up and down the fret board and then repeated it in an overlapping three-note pattern.

"Have you been reading the theory book I gave you?"

"Yes, sir. The tabs are easy to read but that treble clef still throws me. Truth is, once I get a feel for the pattern, I just start listening to the notes and my fingers seem to know what comes next. That's when I start playing around, remembering licks I learned at some of the jam sessions down at Maizie's."

He riffed a variation on the E blues scale, bending strings with a flourish of bravado.

"If you get any faster on that guitar, I'm going to have to rename you Lightning Cunningham."

"Now that's a name I could live with Mr. Walker," Mose grinned, "How about you teach me a whole song."

"OK and I'll show you a little about using this."

He held up the steel slide that he had pulled from his pocket.

"And I think it's about time you started calling me McLeod, don't you?"

"Alright, Mr. ... McLeod."

They passed the guitar back and forth exchanging the language of music until the morning was almost gone. For McLeod this was the only antidote to the disease of racism. The blues; and sharing it with a young man who could have been him fifty years ago. A body could forget the world for a spell when lost in the soul of this music. When McLeod finally glanced up at the clock, it was noon.

"Let's grab a quick lunch before you go home," McLeod said. "I have an appointment with an attorney from Austin at one o'clock and I'll need a few minutes to get my papers together." He always made a point of sending his students home with a full stomach. As Mose was packing up his guitar, he noticed a picture on the wall.

"Who's that?" he asked, nodding toward it.

"That's me with my mother and my father, and his mentor, Mr. A. Philip Randolph. And that's my uncle Jesse, standing behind my mother."

"Wow, you were young once," Mose said.

McLeod laughed.

"Yes, well that was August 28, 1963. I was only twenty-nine years old. It was a great day."

"What happened?"

"That was the day we marched on Washington, son. A quarter of a million people filled the National Mall from the Washington Monument to the Lincoln Memorial. My mother said it was the day the world finally met our Moses."

"Moses?" the boy had a tenuous recollection of the biblical character but could not figure what he had to do with some march on Washington.

"That's what my mother called Reverend King," McLeod said, surprised by a flash of sadness. She had been gone two years.

"So your Daddy had a mentor too?"

"Yes, and he was a great man," McLeod said.

"Who did you say he was?"

"Is my man Mose asking for a history lesson?" McLeod asked with a smile.

"If you can tell it without turning into Professor High and Mighty," he bantered back.

"OK. I'll do my best," McLeod said, placing a hand on the boy's shoulder.

"How about Ray's Ribs for lunch?" He knew it was Mose's favorite lunch. With his hand still on the boy's shoulder, he ushered him through the office and out onto the walk beneath the awning, commencing the story of A. Philip Randolph.

"There was a time when the railroads were the most luxurious form of travel in the world and the Pullman porters were the backbone of that industry. Now, Mr. Randolph had already been fighting for justice for our people for years when he recognized the opportunity for advancement that a porter's union offered. It was the first real chance to make a corporation respect the rights of its Negro workers."

"Negro?" Mose scowled.

"You know what I'm saying, Black workers. Remember young man, we are speaking historically."

"Yea, like ancient history," Mose smiled.

"OK, but you've got to understand all of this was occurring during the Harlem Renaissance so the world was ripe for change."

"The Renaissance? How far back are we going?"

"Not that Renaissance, the Harlem Renaissance of the 1920s and 1930s. I can see right now that we are going to need a lot of history lessons over lunch in the months ahead. You see, this was a golden time in your heritage and the Pullman porters, like my Daddy, were the front-line soldiers in the battle for civil rights....."

～

McLeod barely made it back to the Center by one o'clock for his appointment. Mose had been captivated by the story of Randolph and how he had helped McLeod's father, Plessy, find a job in Washington, D.C. McLeod felt bad that he had to cut the boy's questions short but he had promised to continue the story after their guitar lesson next week.

He stood at his desk and rifled through his briefcase until he found the folder marked Correspondence, S. Barbarino. He took out the letter dated July 15, 1999 and sat down as he read it again.

McLeod T. Walker, Esq.
Delta Center for Justice and Opportunity
145 East 2nd Street, Clarksdale, MS 38614

Dear Mr. Walker,

I am writing to you as the personal representative designated in the Will of my deceased aunt, Faith Wiggins of Florence, Mississippi. She died on July 4 of leukemia. As I am a member of the Mississippi Bar by reciprocity, I have chosen to act as probate attorney as well as her personal representative to expedite the distribution of her estate. I have filed a Petition for Probate of Will and Issuance of Letters Testamentary with the Rankin County Chancery Court and it has been admitted to probate. Hearing is set for Thursday, August 17. Other than certain specified items of tangible personal property that she has designated to be given to her sisters and myself, she has left the whole of her estate to you. I anticipate that the Order granting the Petition will be issued without incident at the time of the hearing but I would like to meet with you before that time to discuss your wishes regarding the disposition of her house in Florence and, more importantly, to give to you a sealed letter that she has instructed me to hand deliver. If you choose to sell the property in Florence, I have the name of a local realtor who can assist you.

I look forward to meeting you in the near future, at your earliest convenience. In the last week of her life, my aunt recounted her fond memories of you as a child. I am honored to fulfill her wish that you receive the inheritance she left to you.

Sincerely,

Sylvia Barbarino, JD

McLeod placed the letter back in the folder and put it on top of the desk. He picked up his other papers stacked there and tucked them into a filing cabinet, then set the briefcase on the floor next to his feet. Although the memory of Faith Wiggins had been rendered apparitional by the passage of fifty-seven years, her effect on him remained indelible. She was the one who had given him his Stella, the instrument of his music and the most faithful of friends. He had wondered about Faith at times, usually in the still moments after hours of practice as he put the old guitar back in its case. But there had never been a strong enough pull to follow his curiosity. They lived in vastly different worlds.

He heard the purr of the engine at the same time he saw the blue Miata pull into the parking spot in front of the Center. He watched as the lanky figure of a woman with auburn hair unfolded herself from the low-lying driver's seat. He rose to greet her as she entered the door, meeting her halfway across the open room.

"Sylvia Barbarino," she said extending her hand. "I am so glad to finally meet you, Mr. Walker."

"Please, call me McLeod," he said, shaking her hand. "I am happy to meet you, too, but I must say this whole situation has caught me by surprise."

"Understandably," she replied, "My aunt told me that though she kept up a correspondence with your mother, she never told her about the Will."

"Yes. Frankly, I'm a bit puzzled."

He picked up a chair from one of the other desks and motioned toward his small workspace in the corner.

"How about we sit at my desk," he said, "unless you think we need the conference table."

"Oh no, this will be fine," she said, taking a seat in the chair opposite him. "Do you think I can get some water?"

"Please excuse my manners," he said reaching to open a small beverage refrigerator behind his desk. He handed her a chilled bottle of water.

"Thank you," Sylvia said after taking a long drink.

She handed him two envelopes, one embossed with the large black letters "Last Will and Testament" and the other displaying his name in handwritten script.

McLeod opened the Will first and scanned it. The language was familiar, following a standard format. Faith had simplified her assets, consolidating most of her investments into bonds and keeping a single cash account. The total amounted to approximately $200,000. That, and the Florence property, comprised her entire estate.

"The administration of the Will should be quite simple," Sylvia said as she watched McLeod read the document. "She had no debts or liens and the house and furnishings are valued at approximately $100,000, so there should be no estate taxes."

McLeod nodded an acknowledgment of her statement but remained wordless as he opened the other letter. It was not dated.

Dear McLeod,

I hardly know how to begin. It may come as a shock to you to be named my heir, yet part of you must know the debt we Wiggins owe the Walkers. Your dear mother, Delsey, was as generous a soul as God ever breathed into a life. She made my father's business run like clockwork from her office hidden in the back of his store, keeping track of all the goods that passed his threshold, organizing receipts and expenses. But it was the way she treated us Wiggins kids, McLeod, that was so memorable. Many a morning, if Mama was down with a cold, she'd come by to brush my hair or straighten my collar as I readied for school. She wiped more than one tear from my young face after a scraped knee or a bruised ego. As you must know, she could soothe the sting out of the worst bite.

I kept up with her after y'all moved to Washington, DC; first, through her correspondence with Mama, then on my own after Mama died. I even got a chance to make my apologies to her when she came for a visit about twenty years ago.

McLeod, Delsey's gift to our family is reason enough for me to leave my estate to you, especially since I have no children. But it is more complicated than that. I grew up knowing that my father gave shelter to the man that injured Plessy on that dreadful night some sixty years ago. Our neighbor, Fletcher Moody, came knocking at the door, clothes bloody, crying that he thought the sheriff caught sight of him leaving Doc Tatum's where he had left Plessy. My father cleaned Fletcher up and got rid of the evidence. I have lived my whole life regretting that we never reported the crime. I finally talked to Delsey about it during that visit. I am sorry, McLeod, for the injury to your father and our silence about it.

I never told Delsey of my decision to leave my estate to her. When her mail was returned 'unclaimed' two years ago, I suspected she had died. I had my Will revised making you the heir to my estate. This is my stumbling attempt at reparations, way too late and impossible after all. I pray it doesn't strike you as blood money. I don't seek absolution and am ready to face my God. Hopefully, you can put the money to good use. Trusting that you are your mother's son, your father's son, I know you will.

Respectfully,
Faith Wiggins

He felt seasick, his mind swirling with a mix of emotions. He had only the vaguest recollection of his father lifting him up with both hands, to pluck an apple from a tree when he was three years old. Instead, the image that endured was of Plessy, his lifeless left arm tucked into the pocket of his pants, playing baseball with him after they moved in Washington, DC. Plessy would pitch the ball to him and then quickly pick up the glove from the ground to catch the fly ball or grounder that jumped from McLeod's bat, cheering his son's success with every hit. McLeod had taken it for granted that his father had only one good arm, but he didn't dwell on how that came to be. He had no memory of the day the injury occurred. The letter stirred a horror in him that he had effectively buried.

"I'm not sure how to respond," he stammered.

Sylvia squirmed. The room suddenly felt too small.

"Well, as the letter was sealed, I have no knowledge of its content so I'm not sure what you are referring to. I had assumed it would be welcome news."

McLeod handed the letter to her, feeling no need to conceal the truth that was being unearthed before them.

"If you'll excuse me, I think I need to use the men's room," he said, turning and walking to a door just past the conference room.

Sylvia read the message, trying to divine the reason for McLeod's distress. She and Faith had discussed the story of Plessy's injury when Sylvia had first come to visit almost a year before. They had talked about it again just before Faith died. It suddenly occurred to Sylvia that for McLeod this might be entirely new information. Rereading the letter, Sylvia saw that however imperfect the attempt, Faith was trying to make reparations for Hardee's complicity in the crime against Plessy. But she now also saw that Faith's attempt to make amends may have been a need to unburden herself before she died. That burden had been handed off to Sylvia and McLeod. She drank the rest of her bottled water and considered getting another from the small refrigerator but decided to keep her seat until he returned.

In the bathroom, McLeod turned on the cold water and splashed it on his face. He soaked a paper towel and placed it on the back of his neck, forcing down a wave of nausea. He leaned up against the wall and surrendered to the sorrow and joy of his mother's memory. The second anniversary of her death loomed, and today's events had amplified the loss. Delsey had died peacefully, without regrets, after a heart attack at age ninety. McLeod had been at her side.

"God, Mama, I miss you. What am I to think of all this?" he said out loud. He was answered only by the stir of a breeze through the bathroom window. He wiped his hands and returned to the office.

Sylvia stood up when she saw him emerge from the bathroom, her legs getting tangled beneath the chair and almost upending it. She caught the back of it in time to keep it from crashing to the floor.

"Are you OK?" she asked, "Do you need some water?"

"No, no. I'm fine, but feel free to help yourself," McLeod

replied waving his arm in the direction of the small refrigerator.

Sylvia retrieved more water and returned to her chair. She waited for McLeod to take his seat before she spoke.

"I can see that the letter from my aunt upset you," she said, nervously twisting the cap of the bottle.

"Well, yes, it did Ms. Barbarino," he said. "I understand..."

"It's Sylvia, please call me Sylvia."

"OK, Sylvia, I understand that your aunt Faith is trying to make amends, but..."

"But?" she could feel her face becoming flushed.

"Well, it's that.... uhh."

"Yes?"

She immediately regretted the urgency in her voice.

"I'm sorry," she said, pausing. "I hope this is something we can talk about."

He pondered how honest he wanted to be.

"Sylvia, with all due respect, this money is not reparations. It can't change what happened. And honestly, I didn't know the details of the circumstances of my father's injury. Or have any idea of your grandfather's attempt to obstruct justice."

There, he had said it. He did not know how he felt about all this and was not even sure he could accept the inheritance. Nonetheless, he had unlocked the door to a conversation. He hesitated whether to open it further.

Sylvia sat frozen, caught between her duty to fulfill Faith's dying request and her desire to honor McLeod's response to the news he had just received. Her pulse quickened. She remembered to breathe. As she relaxed, she heard a voice inside her. 'Just listen to him'.

"I'm so sorry. I didn't realize...." Sylvia said, then

paused. "You're right, McLeod, about the money and what happened. You've opened the door to a conversation and I would like to listen if you have more to say."

She seemed genuinely open. He wondered if he had the energy for this. He could dispatch her right now; tell her he needed time to think and would call in a couple of weeks. He thought about what Delsey might tell him. McLeod looked his watch. It was just past two o'clock.

"It may be a little early, but do you want to get a beer? Maizie's is usually closed at this time, but I know the owner, Mike. He'll let us in."

The invitation eased the tension between them.

"Yes, thank you. I love Maizie's. Do you want me to drive?"

McLeod looked outside at the Miata, visible through the office window.

"In that little thing?" McLeod said, nodding toward the car and offering a faint smile.

"Yeah. She's more fun with the top down. You're welcome to drive if you want," she said.

"OK, top down but you drive."

Sylvia asked questions about the Delta Center for Justice and Opportunity on the short drive to Maizie's. She was impressed by the Center's accomplishments at community development and especially interested in the mentorship program. He turned the conversation back to Sylvia. She talked about the frustrations of working in the juvenile justice system and her hope for programs like Last Chance House, with its community mentors. It soon became apparent that the spheres of their work overlapped. By the time they reached Maizie's their conversation had turned collegial. They parked in the nearly empty dirt lot and got out of the car.

"I still want to hear how you came to live in Clarksdale," Sylvia said, reaching behind the back seat to raise the top to the convertible.

McLeod helped her unfold the cover from the other side of the car.

"Well that is a very long story, though an interesting one if I do say so."

"I want to hear it."

"Alright. It will cost you a beer. We'll need to go around to the back door to get Mike's attention. They'll be in the kitchen about now."

"Lead the way."

Mike was glad to see McLeod and welcomed him in. He remembered Sylvia from her recent visit.

"You two want something to eat?" he asked. "I can throw some steaks on the grill."

"No, thanks man. We're just finishing up some business and thought a couple of beers sounded good."

"Coming up," he said. He pulled them each a cold draft and returned to help his wife prep the food for the evening's opening.

Sylvia placed a ten-dollar bill on the bar.

"OK, this round is on me, for the price of that story."

McLeod meant to start from the time when he went to work for CORE, just after finishing law school. But in the way that life stories tend to meander after one reaches a certain age, he soon found himself traveling all the way back to the earliest memories: the scratchy feel of his father's wool uniform against his cheek, men speaking in spirited tones across plates of food at a large table. He later learned that these were union meetings and realized his parents had engaged in important, and dangerous, work in Mississippi. He talked about how different it was living in Mississippi, then and now, compared to Washington, D.C. He skipped over his confusion about what had happened to Plessy and why they had to leave Mississippi in the first place. Washington, D.C. was like a wild dance compared to the lazy shuffle of the South. It pulsed with the vibrancy of new jazz and a growing activism for racial equality. It had formed him, nurtured by the likes of A. Philip Randolph and James Farmer. McLeod beamed as he spoke about crossing the stage at Howard University to receive his law degree.

"I was twenty-six years old and fresh out of Howard University Law School. It was 1960. I took a job at CORE, the Congress of Racial Equality, started by James Farmer. He was steeped in the traditions of the Fellowship of Reconciliation and the teachings of Mohandas Gandhi, and he took me under his wing. We were hopeful that President Kennedy's election meant the entrenched segregation of the South would finally be addressed. You probably don't remember those days."

"No, not really," Sylvia replied, "I was only six years old."

"Yeah, I do have a few years on you. Well, looking back, it was the idealism of youth that guided me. As you surely know, The U.S. Supreme Court ruled in 1946, *Morgan vs. the Commonwealth of Virginia*, that segregation on any interstate travel was illegal. Eight years later, *Brown vs. the Board of Education of Topeka*, did the same for public schools. But without federal enforcement it didn't mean shit."

McLeod looked up from his beer, his jaw clenched.

"Pardon my language."

"No need. Couldn't agree more," Sylvia said.

"It took the financial sting of a yearlong boycott of buses and retail shops in Montgomery in 1955 to get the attention of White business owners. E.D. Nixon and Rosa Parks put their bodies on the line to secure that early civil rights victory and launch Rev. Martin Luther King, Jr. onto the national stage. But progress only intensified resistance in the South. The level of violence unleashed by the first attempts to integrate schools was like war, barely stifled by the mobilization of the National Guard and U.S. Marshalls. The movement faltered."

"But it didn't die," Sylvia said.

"No, it didn't. I think it was the urgency of youth that spurred it on. CORE started trainings just after I got there. College students in Greensboro, North Carolina and Nashville, Tennessee learned the techniques of nonviolent direct action. Then they staged sit-ins at segregated lunch counters across the South. Reverend King joined them in Atlanta. Despite beatings and arrests, they persevered. Formed the Student Nonviolent Coordinating Committee, SNCC, and started recruiting support in the North. It was our passion at SNCC and CORE that resurrected the movement. Before long, there was a nationwide boycott of the Five and Dimes practicing segregation at lunch counters. It worked! Slowly the department stores began serving Black people. That was when James Farmer got the idea for the Freedom Rides. He had been hounding JFK to end discrimination in public housing, as promised, and to enforce desegregation in interstate travel. Farmer figured the Freedom Rides would compel federal action."

Sylvia was riveted, transported to the streets that McLeod spoke about, wishing she could have known that world. McLeod had been at the center of history being made. He had mattered! When Mike came to check on them, she smiled and pushed the ten-dollar bill on the counter towards him. He poured two more beers without a word, respecting the conversation in which they were absorbed. He pointed to the spigot indicating to Sylvia that she could help them both to another whenever they were ready.

The afternoon disappeared into the narrative that unfolded. When McLeod told her about his work at CORE, Sylvia was curious.

"So why did you leave D.C.?" she asked, "It seems that you were in the very cradle of the civil rights movement."

"You might think so, and I thought the same until I joined the Freedom Riders."

"You were a Freedom Rider?" She could not hide her admiration.

"Yes, although I wasn't in the first wave of the riders or even the second or third. After the first bus was firebombed outside of Anniston, Alabama on May 14, 1961, and the second group of riders attacked in Birmingham, it looked like the Freedom Rides had been stopped. Not for want of courage on the riders' parts. They were ready to continue, but there was not a bus driver to be found in Birmingham. That's when the Nashville chapter of SNCC stepped up. Three days after the firebombing in Anniston, a group of ten students boarded the morning bus from Nashville to Birmingham. They had signed their Last Will and Testaments the night before. That's how much they resolved to keep the ride alive."

"The White House finally had to respond," McLeod continued. "Attorney General Robert Kennedy negotiated with Governor Patterson of Alabama for the riders' safe passage out of Alabama, but in Montgomery the police ignored the directive, again stepping aside while an angry mob of three hundred attacked the bus. Even the U.S. Marshalls couldn't thwart the contagion that spread over the next days. Reverends Abernathy, Shuttlesworth and King converged on Montgomery to preach peace and persistence. After three days the Ride continued, escorted by Highway Patrols and National Guard, all the way to Jackson, Mississippi. But Robert Kennedy had made a bargain with the devil, meaning Governor Ross Barnett of Mississippi. As long as the governor assured the safety of the riders, he was free to arrest them once they arrived in Jackson. The riders were marched straight from the waiting rooms to the paddy wagons that took them to Parchman Farm. Incarceration in the state penitentiary for sixty days of hard labor was meant to send a tough message to the Freedom Riders. But it only galvanized the movement, expanding its reach. Those images of angry mobs on television just recruited more riders in a full-scale effort to fill Parchman Farm. It was that summer, in 1961, when I realized that the real hot bed of the civil rights movement was in Mississippi. James Meredith had just sued for admission to the Ole Miss."

"So this was before Medgar Evers was shot."

"Oh yeah, a couple of years before. The lunch counter sit-ins and boycotts had already forced Woolworth's and Kress to desegregate the dining areas up North. The pressure was building down here, and it finally boiled over that summer when the bus carrying the first Freedom Riders was firebombed in Anniston."

"When did you take the ride?" Sylvia asked.

"Not until August. By then people were headed to Jackson by bus, plane, and train. Parchman prison was filling up. I remember saying goodbye to my dad on the train platform in D.C. I was taking the Crescent to Greensboro, North Carolina to meet some students there for the bus ride. The Crescent was the same line he worked from New York to New Orleans as a Pullman porter. He said, 'I'll be riding with you in spirit, son, but this time we won't be riding to serve. We'll be riding for freedom.' "

McLeod stopped to take a drink of his beer.

"It was during my sixty days at Parchman that I realized I was back home."

Sylvia looked down, staring at her empty beer glass. She moved it in a slow circle, gliding it across the surface of condensed water that had collected on the bar.

"I was so insulated in our Dallas suburb, so caught up in my own world. I didn't start to understand what was happening until I went to college," she said.

McLeod got up from his stool and walked around to get them another beer.

"You want a fresh glass?" he asked. He looked at his watch. "Oh, my gosh, I've taken your whole day."

She looked up to see his smile, open and friendly.

"Oh, no. I'm glad to be listening and learning so much," she said, passing the empty glass to him. "Just another half, OK?"

"Sure," he said, drawing them both a half glass of beer.

"So did you stay on in Mississippi after Parchman?" Sylvia asked.

"No, I went back to Washington, D.C. to continue my work at CORE, but Mississippi had worked its way into my blood. Maybe it was some latent memory of my early childhood or maybe it was the assassination of Medgar Evers, which turned Mississippi into Ground Zero of the civil rights movement. But a force kept tugging at me, pulling me back here. Freedom Summer in 1964 offered me the opportunity. A voter registration project had been launched in the South and hundreds of volunteers flocked to Mississippi to open freedom schools and community centers and to organize voter registration. When three of the first workers were murdered, I moved to Clarksdale. I've never really considered leaving Mississippi. Of course, it could be that it was because I met Nora that summer."

"Nora?" Sylvia asked.

McLeod paused then went on in a quieter voice.

"Nora Davis, my.... wife. She's a sociology professor at Fisk University."

"In Nashville?' Sylvia asked.

"Yes, it's complicated," McLeod replied. "Sylvia, I've spent my life prosecuting hate groups, fighting for desegregation of public facilities and integration of state workers. I worked with state politicians to change legislation even if I did feel I needed to take a shower afterwards. I must admit I have been driven in the fight for justice. It never ends. When I think I can't take it anymore, I channel the rage into the blues. I tried to give my life to something, but I'm afraid it left me lacking as a husband and father. But that's a story for another night."

"I hope you will tell it to me someday," Sylvia said. She ventured her next question carefully.

"Can I ask?" she hesitated. "Did you ever know the circumstances of Plessy's injury?"

"Only vaguely," he said, shrugging his shoulders. "I guess I was too young at the time for my parents to explain it to me. They just said some men beat him up. And once we left Mississippi, they never wanted to visit the place or the subject again. Except that time we came to see your grandparents after your uncle died. That's when I remember meeting your Aunt Faith."

"So her letter was the first you knew about what happened that night?"

"First time I knew there was a connection to the Wiggins."

"She told me the whole story if you care to know more."

"No, at least not right now. I'm not sure if you can understand, but it might make it worse."

"Because no one ever paid for the crime?"

"It's more than that. Sometimes, I guess most of the time, I think that if you didn't grow up Black in the South, you'll never be able to understand...."

Sylvia took a slow sip of her beer. She thought of Terrell and wondered if he was safe.

"You're right. I have never had to face that level of violence, that hatred."

She looked him in the eye, and he didn't look away. She wanted to tell him about Antwan and Terrell, but it was getting late.

They finished their beers in silence.

McLeod put another ten-dollar bill on the counter.

"Shall we head back to the office?" he asked.

"Sure, then I should get on to the hotel. We can talk about the disposition of the estate in the morning before I leave town if you want."

"Actually, I'm going to need some time to think about all of this, Sylvia."

"You mean...."

"I mean I don't know if I can accept the inheritance. It

may have been Faith's wish, but it feels loaded. And we haven't really started that conversation about money and reparations."

"Oh…. Okay," she said, slipping off the barstool and reaching for her briefcase. Sylvia looked around the room as people started coming in and taking their seats.

"You looking for someone?" McLeod asked.

"Oh, I just thought Louise might be here."

"Oh, she's down at the Cajun Music Festival in Mamou, Louisiana. I'm headed there myself tomorrow."

"Well, I guess I'm going to miss her this trip. She's something, isn't she?"

"Wiser than Solomon."

The sun was just setting, fanning gold streaks across the western sky as they walked across the parking lot. At the car Sylvia paused before getting in. She rested her chin and arms on the convertible roof.

"How about this?" she said, "I'll get the probate hearing rescheduled for October and come back for another visit a few days before. You can tell me what you have decided then. And we can have a longer conversation about money and reparations."

"I would appreciate that," McLeod replied.

His voice relaxed. "If you want to make it the second weekend in October you can hear me play at King Biscuit Blues Fest. It's just across the river in Helena, half hour's drive."

"Really?"

"Louise will be there, dawn to dusk."

"Where do I buy a ticket?"

"Well, it's already sold out, but I think I can get you a pass," McLeod said with a grin, "Now give me those keys."

~

The trip to see McLeod in Mississippi had initially left Sylvia at loose ends. She had hoped to wrap up the disposition of Faith's estate quickly and the uncertainty about McLeod's decision weighed on her. On the other hand, she had enjoyed getting to know him and welcomed the chance to hear more of his story, not to mention hear him play at the King Biscuit Blues festival. A few days after returning to Austin, she finally summoned the nerve to have the conversation she had been avoiding with Joe. They had taken an afternoon walk along the upper reaches of Barton Creek, the water tumbling over large boulders as they talked.

"Joe, I need to talk about something that has been difficult to bring up."

"Is this about kids, because...?" Joe began.

"It's more than that," she said, pausing.

"There's no easy way to say this," she began, taking a deep breath, "Joe, the reason I am certain about not having a baby is not because I am too old. It's because I already have a son."

He was stopped in his tracks, stunned. He couldn't fathom that she had kept this from him; for over five years. She told him the story of Antwan, of being swept away by her first love; about her decision to give up Terrell because she couldn't face an interracial marriage. Joe had listened, trying to understand why that precluded them having a family together. It didn't make sense to him.

"I don't think I am punishing myself," Sylvia had said, "though I have wondered. The truth is, I want to find Terrell,

if possible. That is, if he is willing to see me. He would be twenty-five years old now. This is something I must resolve, Joe. By myself. And as my love for you only deepens, I realize how much I want you to be able to raise the child you long for. You have wanted to be a father for as long as I have known you. And you will be a great one. It breaks my heart that I can't give you that. But I can't."

He had protested that there had to be a way to figure this out, that he loved Sylvia more than his need for children. But the more they talked about it, the more the gravity of that decision weighed on them. Wouldn't he resent her? Would it be his dying regret? As it would be hers if she didn't find Terrell. Nothing was more important to her now. He had finally admitted how much he wanted a child. They had held each other and wept, still so in love but at an irreconcilable crossroads. They talked about taking a break so Joe could think about it all. On the slow walk home, they held hands, silent in their shared grief, the sun setting behind them. They both knew that once the break began it would be hard to find their way back to the life they had shared.

MISSISSIPPI 1999

Sylvia fished the safe deposit key from her pocket while she waited in line for the bank teller. She stared at it, running her thumb over the smooth round head. The upswell of grief swept over her again, but there was no resistance now.

"Good morning and welcome to First Charter Bank," chirped the young woman behind the counter, "How may I help you?"

Looking at the tight smile, the blank gaze of the teller, Sylvia felt compassion rather than irritation. At least Sylvia had work that nourished her.

"I need to collect the contents of my aunt's safety deposit box, her name is.... was, Faith Wiggins. It's number 256. I am the executor of her will. Here is a copy of her will, power of attorney and death certificate." She still found the transactional aspects of death jarring.

"I'm so sorry for your loss," replied the young woman, her eyes softening, "Do you have the key?"

"Oh, yes, of course," Sylvia said, sliding the key onto the counter.

"Just one minute," the teller replied.

She disappeared into an adjoining room and returned with the bank's copy of the key, then escorted Sylvia into the vault, flanked by rows of locked boxes on three walls. After retrieving box 256 she motioned Sylvia to an alcove at the back of the vault and left her to review the contents in private.

"Again, I am truly sorry for your loss," she said, lightly touching Sylvia's arm.

"Thank you."

Sylvia slumped into her chair and closed her eyes for a moment. Barely middle of the day and she was ready for a nap. She took a deep breath, reviving some energy and opened the box. Inside was the original copy of the will, power of attorney and Faith's birth certificate. There was a gold caduceus pendant in a small box and a gold cross on a matching chain. No other jewelry. At the bottom of the box was a card in an envelope with Sylvia's name written in Faith's distinct script. The card was clipped to two open-date first class airline tickets to Rome and five thousand dollars in cash. Sylvia opened the card. The message was simple.

'Last I knew, God was living in Florence......Italy. Love, always, Faith.'

Sylvia closed her eyes. The card slipped from her hand onto the table. She knew that Faith had intended the tickets for her and Joe. The sting of his absence hit her, a phantom pain that was always present. She reached for the box of tissues that sat on the corner of the table. It was several minutes before Sylvia felt composed enough to leave the bank. She opened her briefcase and found her sunglasses. After transferring the contents of the safe deposit box into the briefcase, she closed it and walked out of the bank.

It was a warm fall day. She crossed the parking lot and slipped into the front seat of the Miata. The engine hummed when she turned the key. She enjoyed the fifteen-mile drive to Faith's house, taking her time to behold the purple aster and goldenrod thriving in the fallow fields along the way. The probate hearing, rescheduled for October 25th, was still a week away. Sylvia had come to Mississippi early because she needed time alone to rest in a place that had been a sanctuary. But it was different this time. Faith's absence was everywhere. In the dust gathered on the kitchen counter, the faded newspaper on the drive, the unharvested tomatoes in the garden weighing the plants to the ground.

Sylvia hadn't seen Joe since the middle of August when they hiked the Barton Springs Greenbelt. There were lonely nights but there was also relief that she was no longer hiding the truth. She turned off the highway onto Faith's driveway, pulling under the porte cochere minutes later. The comforting scent of lemon oil and old books greeted her as she entered the kitchen door. She still expected to hear Faith's voice calling to her from the bedroom. Sylvia had a couple of hours before she needed to leave for Clarksdale. She and McLeod had agreed to meet for dinner that night and she had no idea what she would do if he refused the inheritance Faith had left him. She packed a small suitcase, then settled into the chair next to the bed. On the nightstand was a bible and a copy of *The Miracle of Mindfulness* by Thich Nhat Hanh.

Sylvia longed to talk to Faith about her spiritual journey one more time. Her aunt was so at ease reconciling such diverse religions. Sylvia recalled Faith's instruction during those last days in hospice. 'Just prioritize your spiritual life above all else and don't let any dogma thwart you. Best to pick one path, one discipline, and pursue it deeply but I believe they all lead to the same Source.' It seemed too simple, too easy in a way. Indeed, Sylvia was learning that meditation practice, while fruitful, was anything but easy.

She closed her eyes and let her attention rest on the rise and fall of her abdomen as she breathed in and out. For a minute she was just there, breathing, hearing the passing trill of a wren outside the open window, coming back to her breath, a slight breeze caressing her face then vanishing. Before she knew it, she was in an imaginary conversation with McLeod, anticipating his rejection of the estate. She caught her mind wandering and returned her focus to the breath but was lost in thought again within minutes, this time wondering what Joe was doing. She continued this meditation practice for thirty minutes, returning to the present moment and getting lost a dozen times. When she opened her eyes, she could feel her body was more relaxed.

She pushed up from the chair and walked through the kitchen and out the front door. The oaks to her left shimmered brilliant reds and golds, a light wind rustling the leaves. She picked up the harvesting basket that Faith kept on the front porch. The smell of fresh cut hay from the neighboring pasture greeted her as she made her way to the garden. Sylvia put the basket on the ground and took her time gathering the last of the tomatoes, peas and squash that hadn't withered or dropped to the ground. She pulled up a few of the spent lettuce and spinach plants, long since gone to seed, but decided she would wait until after the probate hearing to put the garden to bed.

Sylvia picked up the basket and started back to the house when the splintered old peach tree caught her eye. She walked over to it and smiled at the sight of the new tree at its center which had grown a foot since last year.

"How can you not believe in God when there is resurrection all around?" she heard Faith whisper.

Sylvia smiled and replied out loud, as though her aunt was by her side.

"I'm working on it."

~

She pulled into Clarksdale just as the sun set, splashing the sky with rich apricot hues. She turned left off Highway 49 onto Third street and found her way to Ray's Ribs, parking on the street out front and hesitating a moment before opening the car door. No briefcase, she thought, just my pocketbook. Tonight was not a night for business, it was a night for listening. Despite the balmy evening she felt a little shiver as she walked up the sidewalk to Ray's. A bell jingled as she opened the door.

"Welcome to Ray's and seat yourself," called the owner from behind the tall counter that separated the dining area from the kitchen, "Put your order on the line when you're ready."

The whole place seemed made of yellow pine – floors, walls, tables. Only the counter offered a contrast – corrugated tin on a wooden frame topped with red Formica. A clothesline ran from one end of the counter to the other with slips of paper attached by clothes pins. Sylvia took it all in, then saw McLeod wave to her from a corner table.

"Great place," she said, approaching the table, "Don't know about you but my mouth was watering before I opened the door."

"Usually hits me from a block away," McLeod said, rising to greet her.

She reached across the table to shake his hand, searching for some sense of comfort.

"I hope you are well," she said.

"Today's a good day, meaning aches are at a minimum and I have energy to spare. Could be because I spent the better part of the day practicing for the King Biscuit Festival tomorrow instead of practicing law."

"Well, that'll do it," she replied. She stood there wrestling with the impulse to bolt.

"Is there a restroom?" she asked.

"Around back," McLeod said, nodding toward the side door to his left.

"Thanks," she said.

The jitters had subsided a little by the time she returned to the table. She eased onto the bench opposite McLeod. In the center of the table rested a lazy Susan, holding napkins, forks, and a few condiments.

"Is there a menu?" she asked.

"Nope," he replied, "There's ribs, potatoes salad, coleslaw, baked beans and biscuits. Just write down how many ribs you want and which sides on a napkin, sign your name, then clip it to the line."

He chuckled at her furrowed brow.

"Here, let me order for us. Beer or sweet tea?"

"Your choice,' Sylvia replied.

McLeod clipped the napkin with an order for a dozen ribs, potato salad, and coleslaw to the clothesline. He grabbed a couple of mugs, plucked two beers from the tub filled with ice and returned to the table. Sylvia shifted on the bench as he sat down.

"Sylvia, I won't keep you in suspense. I have decided to accept the inheritance that Faith left to me, but we need to have that conversation we never finished when you visited in August."

Sylvia sighed audibly. She could finally let that worry go.

"Oh, thank God, McLeod, because I had no idea what to do with it otherwise. I am grateful that we can talk about this. At least I hope we can because I know that money is not reparations. I mean, well in fact, it can be the opposite. Like blood money?"

She was talking way too fast. She took a deep breath.

"What's the right way to do this?" she asked.

McLeod thought for a moment before replying. "I'm not sure there's a right way but I'll start by saying that I'm not keeping the money for myself. I want to use it to make reparations, not just for my father, but for the broader legacy of slavery that is woven into the fabric of this country."

Now to listen, Sylvia thought, to listen with every cell of her body. This wasn't just about McLeod or the Walkers. This was also about her son and millions of others.

"So what does reparations mean to you?" she asked.

"Real reparations?" He cocked his head slightly, raising his eyebrows, "True reparations? Not some kind of 'What can I pay you so we can get this over with' kind of thing?"

"Yes, real reparations," Sylvia replied, looking McLeod in the eye.

"Real reparation is to make whole again that which was damaged; to put together that which was torn asunder in such a way that it can start anew."

Sylvia nodded silently, then looked down at her beer.

"And you know, better than most, how seldom that is possible."

"Yes, I do," McLeod replied, "as do you from your time in the courts."

"But it wasn't personal for me like it was for you. No one in my family suffered permanent injury in an act of violence."

"Or from centuries of slavery, enforced by unspeakable cruelty. It's personal for me in more ways than one," McLeod said, his voice hardened, "My dad is only a piece of this. The worst is the unrelenting dehumanization that gets internalized. It chokes the soul. Surely you can see the direct line from the violence of slavery to the violence of the inner city."

Sylvia wanted to tell him that it was personal for her, too. But she was too ashamed to admit that racism played a part in her decision to give up Terrell. She pushed the feeling down.

"I've seen the consequences of violence on an individual level, when kids I represented in CPS custody later became my clients as a public defender. But I imagine you have a much bigger perspective."

"Try to imagine all your ancestors, all of your friends, portrayed as beasts – beasts of burden, creatures to be feared. A whole class of people rendered into animals so their masters can rationalize selectively killing anyone who asserts his humanity. The lynchings, the bombings, the shootings by police mean that the possibility of death is an immediate experience for most Black people, especially young men. If you must dance with death every day, why wouldn't you pick up a gun, try to gain a purchase on the grim reaper before he reaps you? It is not an excuse for the violence of the gang. But violence breeds violence."

Sylvia took a couple of deep breaths.

"Jesus, McLeod," she said, "how do we even begin to make reparations? Can we even stop it, the beast mentality? Prisons filling up with young Black men for nonviolent drug offenses?"

"Oh, Sylvia, it's so much more pervasive than the criminal justice system,' he sighed, "Seems like every step forward creates a backlash. Like that brief period during Reconstruction, after the passage of the Civil War Amendments promised freedom and equal protection. The Freedman's Bureau did so much. Didn't last ten years until the violence shut it down."

"You mean the Klan?" Sylvia asked.

"The Klan was just the ugly face of something much more insidious. They wore masks to do their lynching so you wouldn't recognize their faces when they were legislating. It took almost no time to snatch back voting rights and most legal protections from former slaves in the South. And the federal government let it happen, dissolving the Freedman's Bureau and refusing to enforce the new Civil Rights amendments. Racism may have been more blatant down here, but it certainly wasn't restricted to the South. Even the New Deal institutionalized it, excluding domestic workers and farm laborers from social security benefits. Redlining Black neighborhoods. The economic disparity got locked in."

McLeod took a drink from his beer and stared into his glass. Sylvia didn't try to fill the silence.

"The despair must be unbearable," she finally said, "Can I ask how your dad managed to go on, after his injury?"

McLeod nodded. "Mostly through the strength he found in my mother's love. She saw him as a whole man. He also had the help and guidance of Philip Randolph. The power of a mentor is inestimable. My dad found his dignity again in the civil rights movement. And he finally made it back to law school. If he could not repair his body, at least he could restore his soul. He passed that on to me."

"So is that how you live with it?" Sylvia asked, "Your work as a civil rights attorney?"

"That and playing the blues. I think I would lose my mind if I couldn't close my eyes and transport body and soul to that place that only music can take you."

"I'm glad you have that," Sylvia said.

A friend of McLeod's clapped him on the back as he passed on the way to the counter.

"You goin' over tonight?" he asked.

"First thing tomorrow," McLeod answered, "I'll see you there."

McLeod turned back to Sylvia. "Morgan Turner, another blues man. Plays a mean bass. You know your Aunt Faith is partially responsible for me finding my music. She did give me my first guitar. But my folks gave me the blues."

"Order for Walker," barked Ray from behind the counter.

They had almost forgotten about dinner.

"I can get it," Sylvia said.

"That's OK, I'm up," McLeod said, rising from the bench.

He returned with the bowls of potato salad and coleslaw balanced on the edge of the platter of ribs. Sylvia had taken napkins and forks from the lazy Susan and set a place for each of them. McLeod put the food down on the table between them. Sylvia snatched a rib from the platter and bit into it, suddenly realizing how ravenous she was.

"Ummm, my God," she moaned, "falls off the bone. Umm."

They paused to dig in, savoring the flavors of sweet ribs and sour slaw, mingled with the hint of yellow mustard in the potato salad.

McLeod took a drink of his beer and continued. "So your turn. What do you think about your Aunt Faith's decision to leave her estate to me?"

Sylvia considered his question, her eyes resting on the wall behind him, adorned with posters of past blues festivals.

"I think she was well intentioned. I know this about Faith; she loved your mother Delsey as though she was family. Said Delsey treated her like a daughter. I think she hoped her estate would benefit you. But I also see she was trying to unburden herself of guilt for not speaking up about what she saw as a teenager, for letting my grandfather and his neighbor get away with a crime. And like you said, it doesn't change what happened. I think she did her best. I am more interested in hearing how you and your parents were able to bear that."

McLeod wiped a speck of barbeque sauce from his cheek.

"I can tell you more about my folks while we are at the festival. You realize sharing that story is the idea behind the Truth and Reconciliation Commission of South Africa; that healing injustice requires hearing the stories of those who have been injured."

"Absolutely. Accountability is crucial but without a real understanding of the experience of Black people in this country, will anything change?"

"And the truth is that this country was built on a system of slavery. That racial discrimination persists in a very personal way. It's fear for your body, the ache for the freedom to pursue your dream, wondering if basic fairness applies to you," McLeod said.

"And restitution without empathy?" Sylvia replied,

seeing the weariness in his eyes.

"Yes. Without empathy, money is just a bribe to forego real accountability."

"McLeod, it's what Last Chance House is all about," Sylvia said, suddenly energized. "The Capital Offenders program at Giddings is clearly the best chance these kids have at not reoffending. When these kids experience empathy for their own abuse, but more importantly, when they finally experience empathy for their victims through therapeutic role play, they reconnect to some essential humanity that wakes them up. Chance House is a way to reintroduce them to the outside community."

"Same basis of my mentorship program at the Delta Center but in a proactive way," McLeod said, "If I can reach these kids before they lose heart, I can offer them some chance at self-determination."

"So reparations begins with empathy for the injured," Sylvia said.

"Then the appropriate monetary compensations can be determined," McLeod replied.

They both sat up a little, more animated than before.

"But my God, how do you apply that on a bigger scale?"

"Well, we could create a foundation...." McLeod said.

"To....?" she asked.

"To tell the truth of the legacy of slavery and to offer those who wish to listen a forum to hear the stories of its impact. To hear what might help turn the tide of that legacy."

"And create a fund for people to contribute to if they want to offer monetary reparations," she added.

"Yes, I've thought a lot about this," McLeod said, looking at his watch. "Sylvia, I promised Nora I'd be home by eight.

Let's talk more about this tomorrow at the King Biscuit festival. You're coming, aren't you?"

"Of course!"

The jingle of the front doorbell punctuated the shift in their conversation as a couple made their way out of the rib joint.

"You staying with Louise tonight?" McLeod asked.

"Oh, no, I was going to try to get a room at the Hellbound."

"I'm sure it's booked for the weekend. Favorite place for fans of the festival. But I thought Louise said you were staying with her. I told her you would be here for King Biscuit."

"I didn't presume to ask her. Figured I'd just connect up tomorrow in Helena."

"Nah, that's crazy. I'm calling her," McLeod said, flipping his cell phone open.

He dialed the number.

"No, I don't want to impose...." Sylvia protested.

"Louise, it's McLeod. How ya doin'?.... How do you have the energy for all that cooking?.... Of course we'll vote for your gumbo tomorrow night. Nora's bringing jambalaya.... Great! Hey, Sylvia Barbarino is in town tonight and I told her.... That's what I told her but she seems to think she can find a hotel room in town tonight.... OK, here, you talk to her."

McLeod handed the phone to Sylvia and went to pay the bill.

"Hello," Sylvia said.

"Sylvia!" Louise bellowed, "You get over to my house right now. I can't wait to hear your latest."

"But Louise, I didn't call, and I just thought...."

"No need to call. McLeod gave me the message. Come on

over and help me finish the gumbo and fry up the chicken legs I just bought."

"Well," Sylvia paused, "I'm not much of a cook."

"Well you will be after tonight," Louise laughed, "See you soon."

She hung up before Sylvia could reply.

Sylvia stared at the phone, then looked up to see McLeod's soft grin.

"I don't even know where she lives," Sylvia said.

"That's OK, you can follow me. It's on my way home."

They gathered their dishes with leftover rib bones and took them to the bussing trays along the back wall. McLeod wrapped one of the bones in a napkin and tucked it in his pocket."

"For Jazz, my yellow lab," he said.

They exited the side door and walked to the street. McLeod waited as Sylvia unlocked the Miata and got in.

"OK, I'll keep an eye on the rearview mirror for you," he said.

"McLeod, it was really good to talk tonight. And I can't wait to meet Nora. You'll have to tell me more about the two of you."

"I will and I enjoyed talking to you, too. We definitely have more to discuss."

He hopped into his car and pulled out slowly, making sure Sylvia was behind him, the red of his taillights guiding her.

~

Sylvia awoke to the smell of coffee drifting from the kitchen onto the screened porch where she lay. She could hear Louise moan along with Rory Block's version of 'Walkin' Blues', an old Robert Johnson favorite.

"Got up this mornin', said I
Feel round for my shoes.
Know by that, I got
My old walkin' blues,
Woke up this mornin'..."

"Wa ooo," Louise sang from the other room.

"Feel round for my shoes," Sylvia crooned as she swung her legs over the side of the bed. The old twin frame creaked as she stretched against the ache in her back and shoulders. She threw on a robe and two-stepped her way into the living room where Louise was packing for their trip.

"Coffee on the counter, honey's on the table and biscuits in the oven," Louise smiled.

"Is that some kind of recipe for relationship?" Sylvia asked as she made her way to the kitchen, a little shimmy accompanying her two-step.

"Not in my cookbook," Louise replied.

Sylvia returned to the living room with a mug of coffee and slumped down into an easy chair. Louise stopped packing and turned down the music. She sat in the one empty spot on the sofa, piled with blankets and bags of groceries for their weekend.

"Thank you for letting me go on last night," Sylvia said, "I know I talked your ear off."

"Not at all," Louise replied, "I wanted to hear everything, although I had an inkling from your last letter. I was just sorry to hear about you and Joe splitting."

"I love him, Louise, but I couldn't see how to reconcile the kid issue."

"Well, I can understand both sides but.... how old are you?" Louise asked, "Forty-five? Might give one pause."

"It wasn't just that. Joe had been asking since we got together six years ago."

Sylvia looked down at her coffee, swirling it in her cup.

Louise could sense that Sylvia wanted to say more but was unsure.

"You know, most folks assume if you are a woman that you want to have a child, that you're not complete unless you are a mother," Louise said.

"Yeah," Sylvia nodded, still lost in her thoughts and the swirl of coffee and cream.

"I came close to having a child," Louise went on, "I hadn't planned it, but I got pregnant with my first love. He was so excited that I thought I was too, despite the morning sickness and backache. I figured the cramping was normal until I started spotting around three months. I was already miscarrying by the time we got to the doctor."

"Oh, I'm sorry Louise. That must have been so hard, being that far along," Sylvia said.

"Well, Sylvia, the truth is I was more relieved than heart sick. It shocked me, because I didn't know until that moment that I didn't want to be a mother. I felt terribly guilty about it, like maybe I caused the miscarriage. I came to realize that I hadn't and I became meticulous about contraception. Started taking the pill as soon as it was available."

"Faith decided not to have children, but I really didn't talk to her about it much."

"Contrary to popular belief, not all women find fulfillment in motherhood," Louise said in a quiet forgiving way.

"Part of me still feels like I didn't do right by Joe, though."

"Were you honest with him?" Louise asked.

"Yeah, from the start."

"Then you didn't fail him. In fact, seems to me, you are truly loving him by encouraging him to become who he wants to be. Just the father of someone else's child."

Sylvia sighed. "Maybe you're right."

"Sounds like time for a little forgiveness, for both of you," Louise said. She relaxed into the sofa and was quiet. A raucous jay squawked outside.

"I actually am a mother," Sylvia said abruptly, "but I don't know my own child."

"Tell me," Louise said, without missing a beat.

"When do we need to leave for Helena?" Sylvia asked, searching Louise's face.

"Not for a couple of hours. I filled the propane tanks on the Airstream yesterday. She's all packed and ready to go. Just these bags and the cooler left to load." Louise waited.

"What about a camping spot? Do we need to leave earlier to get a good spot?"

"Got it covered. Some friends already reserved our spots in Tent City, down by the river. We are in no rush."

"OK," Sylvia said, resting back in the chair.

Louise went to the kitchen and returned with the coffeepot and a plate of biscuits with a small jar of honey.

"I'm sorry I assumed you didn't want to be a mother," Louise said as she set the coffeepot and plate on the coffee table and eased onto the sofa, "Projection probably. Always gets in the way of listening."

"Oh, no, you assume correctly," Sylvia replied, "or, at least, have every reason to assume based on what I said about Joe and me. It's just that it's more complicated."

"Usually is," Louise said, spreading some honey on a biscuit.

"Truth is, I don't know if I wanted to be a mom, but I am

and I can't deny or turn away from it anymore."

Louise nodded, sipping her coffee.

"I never told anyone about this, until I started seeing a therapist last spring. My best friend in college knew because she let me live with her until I gave up Terrell. I finally told Joe, but no one else."

"Well, I'll hold it in confidence if you feel like telling the story."

Sylvia looked at Louise for a long moment, then began.

"I was eighteen years old, fresh out of high school and I felt liberated in Austin. Even now I feel a thrill when I walk the UT campus. Everything was new and possible. I was still a virgin, old fashioned enough to wait for love before I gave myself to someone. And I found it – that love, that someone – in a freshman theater class. His name was Antwan Chatman. It wasn't just his looks. He possessed a depth, a soulfulness, unlike anyone I had ever met."

Sylvia stopped, savoring the memory as she poured herself another cup of coffee. "Are you sure you want to hear this?"

"I'm honored to have your confidence," Louise replied.

Sylvia continued.

"The first real connection was during an improv exercise where we took turns being a panhandler and a passerby, on the main boulevard next to the U. I was polite but avoidant as the passing stranger. Kind, but detached. He was just the opposite when it was his turn. He was curious, warm, respectful. I think that is when I first fell in love with him."

"It can happen in a moment, can't it?" Louise said.

"And I did mention that he was stunningly handsome, didn't I?"

"You alluded to that."

"We just started hanging out after class and the attraction proved mutual. Didn't take long for that to turn physical. It was such a tender introduction to lovemaking. One night we just didn't bother with protection. That's all it took, and I was pregnant."

The morning sun streamed through the window, warming the room.

"How did you feel when you found out?" Louise asked.

"Terrified...and excited," Sylvia replied.

"So you wanted to have his child?"

"Maybe, but I didn't see how it was possible."

"Because you were eighteen?"

"No, because Antwan is Black, and I couldn't face telling my family. God, I feel so ashamed saying it out loud. But when I do say it, it sounds like the truth."

"And if it is true?" Louise asked, leaning forward from her perch on the sofa.

"Then what does that say about me? Am I not racist?" Sylvia stood up and turned to look out the window. She didn't want Louise to see her shame.

"The seeds of racism have been planted in all of us, Sylvia. It's in the DNA of our country, there since its birth. White entitlement constantly lives in our unconscious."

Sylvia finally turned around to face Louise.

"To deny it only drives it deeper, makes us less aware," Louise said. She cleared a spot on the sofa next to her and patted it, inviting Sylvia to sit. "The question is what do we do with that?"

Sylvia nodded as she sat down next to Louise. She recalled something she read in one of the books she had found at Faith's house. "I remember this question by Thich Nhat Hanh. 'Do we water the seeds of ignorance and hatred, or do we cultivate those of empathy and curiosity instead?"

"And how do we awaken to our deeper intentions?" Louise added. "Can I ask you a question?"

"Sure," Sylvia replied.

"How did you decide to have Antwan's son? To give birth to Terrell?"

"It was never even a question, really."

"Because?"

"Because I loved him. I loved them both," Sylvia said.

"And what does that say about you?" Louise asked.

"Maybe it wasn't so black and white after all, so to speak," Sylvia said, "but I wish I had been braver. We could have gotten married."

"Is that what Antwan wanted?"

"He said so, but I don't know if it was what he really wanted." Sylvia squinted as though trying to get a clearer picture.

"But?"

"But I couldn't face telling my parents. I was the one who called it off. Antwan and I agreed not to see each other after I gave up Terrell. It would have been too painful."

She started to get up, but Louise patted her knee, coaxing her to stay.

"A little self-forgiveness here, too," Louise said.

"I know. Just wish I knew how."

"How often do you think of them?"

"I think about Terrell a lot. Antwan too, but especially Terrell. Sometimes I think that's why I ended up in juvenile justice. Was I looking for him in the faces of my clients? Like that isn't an incredibly racist assumption," Sylvia said.

A male cardinal, in all his crimson glory, perched on the feeder outside the window. He cocked his head as if listening.

"It's just as likely that he is starting his medical residency somewhere or clerking for a justice. How would I know?" Sylvia continued.

"Have you thought about trying to find him?" Louise asked.

"I wrote a letter to the Home of the Holy Infancy last month requesting that they pass my contact information along to him. It seems so selfish. Will I just hurt him again?"

Louise nodded thoughtfully, then smiled.

"Sounds like the concerns of a loving mother. McLeod might be able to give you a perspective that neither of us possess."

"Oh, I could never…," Sylvia said with a slight gasp.

"You could," Louise replied, "He won't judge you and he's wise."

Louise stood up to clear the cups and plates from the coffee table as a car pulled up into the grass drive, tooting its horn.

"Speaking of McLeod," Louise said as she waved to him through the front window.

"No, I can't…," Sylvia said, jumping up from the couch.

"Don't worry," Louise said, "He's just here to help me hitch the Airstream to the Silverado. You'll have time to talk to him at the festival. Come say a quick hello then you can wash the dishes and pack up the food while we hook up the trailer."

"So you two are friends," Sylvia said.

"Blues buddies, really. Amazing how music, especially

the blues, brings people together, no matter their backgrounds. It's the human thing we all share, love and loneliness, our nobility, and our failings. I feel indebted to the blues. It saved my life when I thought my losses would drown me. And when you think of where the blues came from, the sorrow songs of the slaves.... You begin to understand to whom we are indebted."

Sylvia went outside with Louise. McLeod met them at the porch.

"Good morning, ladies," McLeod said, "Ready for some blues?"

"Always," Louise replied.

Sylvia nodded in agreement. "I can't wait to hear you play," she said, "and to meet Nora."

"I'm looking forward to having some time to talk during the festival. Afraid I'm in a bit of a hurry now though. Nora's waiting for me at the house, so I better help Louise..."

"Yeah, I need to clean up and finish packing, so see y'all soon." Sylvia gave a little wave as she turned and reentered the house. She could hear the laughter as McLeod and Louise headed around the back where the Airstream waited.

~

Sylvia rode shotgun as Louise steered the Silverado north on Highway 49, the twenty-two-foot Airstream gliding behind them. Their friendship deepening with shared stories of the past. Louise took her time driving, meandering slowly while ignoring the shouts and honking, as cars buzzed past on her left.

Sylvia had decided to ride with Louise instead of taking her own car after Louise assured her they didn't need the extra car. The campground was only a half mile from town and McLeod and Nora would bring their car. The afternoon sun was still a couple of hours above the horizon, disappearing at times behind the billowing clouds rolling up from the Gulf. The flat expanse of farmland stretched before them in all directions. Forty-five minutes into the drive Louise took the left turn toward Lula. The smell of the mighty muddy river greeted them after a few minutes, signaling their arrival in Helena, Arkansas.

It wasn't until they ascended the Helena bridge that Sylvia got a sense of the scale of the King Biscuit Blues Festival. A line of cars crept across the bridge, over a half mile long. It snaked another three miles into the small town with a population of less than eight thousand. More than ten times that number would descend on the festival over the next three days. It took almost as long to get from the bridge to their campground as it had taken to get from Clarksdale to Lula. They continued to chat as Louise drove through Helena, pointing out the four music stages along Cherry Street. She explained that there were multiple smaller venues around town; bars and clubs, that filled up after the stage performances ended. And that didn't include the buskers playing for donations on the street. The music would play on until the wee hours of the morning. They passed through the north end of town and looped back on Cunningham Road to the festival campground. Tent city, perched on the east edge of town, teemed with RVs, tents and cars. Music drifted from the stages in town, along with gatherings of musicians in the camp. Blues and gospel, mixed with the strains of Zydeco and Rock-a-billy. A body could hardly stay still.

Louise pulled the trailer under a bank of trees along the side of the campground opposite the river. A maroon sedan, which Sylvia recognized as McLeod's, sat in the middle of a large parking spot next to another, larger Airstream. Louise tooted the horn and the door to the Airstream opened. McLeod popped his head out and waved to them.

"Give me a second," he said, disappearing into the trailer and returning with keys in hand. He headed to the sedan.

"McLeod's friends, Emmett and Maya, are patron saints. They renovated an old Victorian in Helena some time back and for the past five years they are the first in line when the gates open to Tent City. They pay for two spots and park their Airstream for McLeod's use."

"Colleagues of his?" Sylvia asked.

"Fans. You'll find he has quite a few folks here who know him only for his music."

McLeod parked the sedan in front of his trailer. Louise eased the truck forward until the trailers were alongside each other, then cut the engine.

"You beat us here," Sylvia said, smiling to McLeod as she dismounted the cab of the Silverado.

"Well, half of Clarksdale passes Louise hauling the old Silver Chalet up to the festival. Personally, I'm glad she takes her time. No need to rush."

"Isn't it the truth," Sylvia replied.

Louise got out of the driver's seat and disappeared into the Airstream. She emerged carrying a small plate holding a half dozen deviled eggs. She walked over to McLeod and handed it to him.

"You spoil me Mary Louise," he grinned, popping one of the eggs into his mouth.

"Mary?" Sylvia said.

"Forget it," Louise replied, with a wave of her hand, "He likes to pester me."

"And hey, M.T. Walker, those are for Nora, too.

"Hey Boo," McLeod hollered to Nora, "Louise brought her deviled eggs."

Nora appeared at the door of the trailer, stepping down carefully to join them. She was tall with a stately beauty, her close-cropped hair sprinkled with silver. She plucked an egg from the plate and delicately took a bite.

"Thank you, Louise, for both of us," she said, playfully shoving McLeod with her shoulder.

"Making me a better man," McLeod said, his smile almost boyish as he looked at Nora.

"Where are you playing tonight?" Sylvia asked.

"King Biscuit Lounge," he replied.

"OK, I have to ask," Sylvia said, "Who is King Biscuit?"

"None such," Louise replied, touching Sylvia's arm.

"Name comes from the KFFA radio show 'King Biscuit Time' started back in 1941 by Sonny Boy Williamson," McLeod explained. "May be the best blues harpist ever. The radio station got the local business, King Biscuit Flour, to sponsor the show. It's still going but the live band broadcasts are long gone. A couple of the original band members will be on the main stage tonight, Robert Junior Lockwood and Pinetop Perkins."

"Can we go?" Sylvia asked eagerly.

"Sure. I don't start my gig until nine o'clock so we can catch them on the way."

Louise looked west toward Helena.

"Don't know about you but I'm ready to mosey into town after securing the Airstream. Sun's gonna dip behind Crowley's Ridge in another thirty minutes."

"I'm with you, Louise," Nora said.

"Me, too," said McLeod, "Besides, those deviled eggs

won't keep my hunger at bay much longer. The gumbo contest is tonight, right?"

"Sure is," Louise answered, "You gonna carry the pot for me?"

"Of course," McLeod said.

"Creole or filé?" Sylvia asked.

"There will be both, I'm sure, but Louise's specialty is Creole," McLeod answered.

"Who knows? My entry might just win this year," she said.

"Are they saving the barbeque contest for Saturday?" Nora asked.

"Last I heard," McLeod replied.

"Louise, do you need help with the trailer?" Nora asked, nudging McLeod forward.

"OK, OK," he said, wrapping an arm around Nora's waist and drawing her closer. He kissed her lightly on the cheek.

"I'll secure the trailer while you gals freshen up. Shouldn't take me but fifteen or twenty minutes."

"Nice to finally meet you, Nora," Sylvia said. The women disappeared into the larger Airstream while McLeod went to lower the tongue jack on the trailer.

The sun was just setting as they took the levee walk into town. The musty smell of fallen leaves was stirred by a cool breeze that had come with evening.

"Smells like rain," Nora commented.

The plaintive wail of a slide guitar grew louder as they headed down Cherry Street toward Elm. They made their way through town, pausing to listen to Sugar Blue play his blues harp. The gumbo contest was inside the Delta Cultural Center, housed in the renovated 1912 Union Pacific train depot. McLeod placed the large pot of gumbo at one end of a long table. Louise talked to the organizers of the contest who had servers available for the cooks who preferred to attend the rest of the festival. She left a card with her name and phone number next to the pot and returned to the others. They each filled a bowl with a different Creole gumbo, having no taste for the filé variety.

They caught Pinetop Perkins and Robert Junior Lockwood on the main stage before heading to the King Biscuit Lounge. By the time they arrived, the place was packed. People began to settle as McLeod mounted the stage and began a sound check. Two microphones were set up, one for his guitar and one for his voice. Nora, Sylvia, and Louise found the small couch near the stage that had been reserved for McLeod. The venue was an intimate setting with a couch, some wingback chairs and a dozen small tables.

"Check, check," he said, adjusting the small amplifier next to his stool. The crowd grew quieter, a hushed anticipation building.

"Welcome back, Walker," said a voice in the dimly lit room.

"Thank you," McLeod said softly, leaning into the microphone, "Good to be back at the Biscuit."

"Where's Jazz?" shouted another fan, used to seeing McLeod's dog curled up next to him on the stage.

He tuned his Gibson L-00 reissue as he continued.

"She's fine, staying with a friend back home. Just getting a little old to travel."

He continued hand tuning, matching the tone of the strings at the fifth fret, his ear pitch perfect.

"I'm gonna start with some old familiars. A little Son House, some Lottie Kimbrough Beaman and Mr. Robert

Johnson, of course. I've got a couple of my own songs that I will save for the second set. I'll close out this first set with a run of songs off Keb Mo's new album "Slow Down"."

He did one last check, listening to the crystalline ping of harmonics, before slipping the steel slide onto his left ring finger. He closed his eyes and began the first licks of "Pearline." The slide skated down the strings, smooth as silk on glass. He appeared to shed ten years as his body transformed with the rhythm. The audience joined him in that other realm, transported by his masterful renditions of the slightly syncopated "Terraplane Blues", the sultry "Come on in My Kitchen". It was impossible not to bob and sway when he broke into the happy canter of "Rolling Log" by Lottie Beaman.

Waitresses were bringing a second round of drinks to most tables when McLeod paused before the Keb Mo' medley. He took a long drink of water and cleared his voice.

"I've never known a man who could make the blues feel so happy, but that's what these songs from "Slow Down" do to me. So enjoy."

He sauntered through "Muddy Water", "Everything I Need" and "A Better Man", a smile on his face, as he rocked to the music. He spoke again during the transitional chords to the next song.

"This one's for Nora," he said, looking right at her, head tilted, eyes a little downcast.

"I should have said it sooner."

He played "I'm Telling You Now" with a reverence that hushed the crowd.

After he finished they burst into applause. Nora wiped the corner of her eye. Louise reached over and squeezed her hand, then excused herself to go to the bathroom.

Sylvia sat mesmerized, a mix of joy and tenderness evoked by his performance reverberating through her body. She was speechless, mouth agape.

Nora chuckled when she saw Sylvia's expression.

"I know," she said, "This is the man I could never leave."

"I had no idea he was such a talented musician. I mean I could tell he was very skilled as a lawyer, but..."

"If only I had had more time with this man, we may never have separated, but lawyering consumed him," Nora said.

"You're separated?" Sylvia said. "But you seem..."

"Together?" Nora smiled.

"Yes," Sylvia said.

"It's complicated," Nora said, without further elaboration.

"Usually is, as Louise said to me just this morning."

"I can tell you this. I think music was the only way he could deal with his work. Unrelenting, systemic hatred and ignorance. He fought it every day and the blues were his only chance to wail."

"Like the sorrow songs?" Sylvia asked.

"Do you know about the sorrow songs?" Nora asked.

"Not really, just what I know about them being the songs of slaves. How gospel and blues were born there. I should read more."

"Well, start with *The Souls of Black Folk* by W.E.B. Du Bois. Good place to start."

"Thanks," Sylvia said.

Louise returned from the bathroom and sat back down on the couch.

"I could listen to him all night long," she said, looking at Nora.

"Me, too," Nora said.

It was half past eleven by the time McLeod finished his second set and two encores. He packed up his guitar and stowed the amplifier and microphones to the side of the stage. They walked back through Helena to Tent City, the night turning cool under a blanket of moist air. No one had the need to fill the quiet with conversation, letting the residual feelings of McLeod's music carry them home. A few buskers were still playing as they turned up Cherry Street toward the levee.

When they reached their campsite McLeod and Nora bid Sylvia and Louise a warm but quick goodnight, then disappeared into their trailer. Louise had made up the beds in the Airstream that morning before leaving Clarksdale, knowing they would probably need to fall into them after a long day. Within ten minutes they were both sound asleep.

Sylvia woke to the soft patter of rain on the aluminum shell of the Airstream. She tried to slip out of her twin berth without waking Louise, which was impossible given the close quarters. Louise rolled over in bed, propping herself up on one elbow.

"Want me to make you a cup of coffee?" she yawned.

"No thanks. I was going to head into Helena for breakfast," Sylvia whispered, "Do you want a coffee?"

Louise smiled and shook her head, rolling back over in bed.

"Nah, that sound is too cozy," she said, pointing to the top of the trailer, "I'm going to sleep in. Umbrella's under the sink."

"Catch you later," Sylvia said.

She dressed in the same clothes she had draped over the counter the night before. The rain came down in little more than a mist as she retraced the route along the levee walk back through town to the Delta Cultural Center. A small 'Open" sign hung in the window. The young man behind the counter looked up when she opened the door. He appeared in need of a second cup of coffee or some other antidote to a late night of music and drinking.

"Do you sell books here?" Sylvia asked.

"Some," he replied, nodding his head toward the shelves on the opposite wall.

"W.E.B. Du Bois by any chance?"

"Just *The Souls of Black Folk.*"

"That's the one!" she said.

He walked over and retrieved the slim volume from the shelf. He returned and placed it on the counter.

"Ten bucks," he said, ringing up the purchase on a vintage cash register.

Sylvia handed him a ten-dollar bill.

"Can you recommend a place nearby where I can get some coffee?"

"Sure, Muddy Water, back up Cherry Street three blocks, then take a right on Rightor."

"Thank you so much," Sylvia said.

"Enjoy your book."

The rain came down harder as she headed up Cherry Street. She ducked into the coffeeshop just as a thunderclap broke overhead. She found a corner booth in the half empty café. It was still too early for most festival folks. She ordered a large coffee and scrambled eggs with an English muffin. She opened the book and began reading while waiting for her food.

It took a few pages for her to adjust to Du Bois's literary style. But the poetic expression of his view, the depth of his perception had a profound effect on her. Sylvia had gone looking for the story of the Sorrow Songs and the last of the fourteen essays promised to reward her search. But it was the first essay, "Of Our Spiritual Strivings", that left her gut punched. It challenged her to imagine what it would be like for her mere existence to be a problem in the country in which she lived. She sipped her coffee, her eggs growing cold as she read his description of the split life that Black people faced as Americans.

"It is a peculiar sensation, this double-consciousness, this sense of always looking at oneself through the eyes of others, of measuring one's soul by the tape of a world that looks on in amused contempt and pity," he wrote.

What must that be like, she wondered. To be conscious of one's true soul but compelled to envision oneself through the eyes of a White world? To not do so would be lethal. To sacrifice your soul to ensure the survival of your body? What hell is that? One she had never faced.

She picked at her eggs, trying to digest what she had just read. She wondered if McLeod felt this way. She hoped to find time to talk to him about Terrell before the weekend was over. She finished her breakfast as the café slowly filled with patrons.

"Anything else, Hon?" the waitress asked, pouring her a refill.

The rain had let up while she was in the café. Sylvia wasn't really in the mood for music this morning and the weather seemed iffy. She wanted to cozy down in a chair somewhere quiet, taking time to read her book.

"Does Helena have a public library?"

"Yep. Well, part library, part museum."

"Sounds perfect."

"Not far from here," the waitress continued, "Couple of blocks up Rightor toward town you hit Pecan. Take a right and it's another couple of blocks. On the left. Can't miss it. Big pink building."

"Thanks," Sylvia said, "Just the check, then."

Stepping outside the café she opened the umbrella and tucked it close. She stayed mostly dry on the walk to the library. She could smell the history when she walked through the front door of the library. The moldering scent of archival texts blended with the nutty aroma of floor wax layered over the wood planks. She found a leather chair sequestered among the stacks in the back room and sat down. Reading slowly, she paused after a few pages to reflect on Du Bois's thoughts. The rain began to pour again, lulling her into a dreamlike state. She let herself doze off for a few minutes between chapters.

By late-afternoon she was halfway through the book. The rumblings in her stomach reminded her that it had been hours since she ate her skimpy breakfast. Waiting out the storm was no longer an option if she wanted to make it back to Tent City by dark. As she thought about the way back, she remembered a short cut that Louise had pointed out the evening before. If you had enough light, you could continue east when Elm Street petered out, crossing the railroad tracks, and walking through the woods to the camp. She trusted her sense of direction enough to chance it. Sylvia slipped the book under her shirt and pushed it down into her jeans. She kept the umbrella in front of her for the half mile jog back to Elm and Cherry. The trees offered shelter from the rain for the last short walk to the campground but she was soaked, except for the front of her shirt, by the time she reached the Airstream.

The sedan was gone, and Louise was not in the trailer. Sylvia spied a note taped to the wall next to the stove. Before reading it, she carefully removed the book, still dry, from the front of her jeans and placed it on the counter. She stepped into the narrow shower tucked between the kitchen and sleeping area and peeled off her wet clothes, heaping them on the small toilet. A minute later a warm stream of water quelled her shivering. After a few minutes she toweled off and put on a new pair of jeans and a light sweater. She read the note while brushing her hair.

Sylvia,

Looks like the main Friday night music events are canceled due to rain. McLeod and Nora are having dinner at Emmett and Maya's. They gave me a lift into town so I could visit with some friends from New Orleans. We will likely be back late as the clubs are still having performers. There's fried chicken, greens, and potato salad in the fridge. Made sure the gas was hooked up and stove working before I left. Make yourself at home and will see you in the morning.

Hugs, Louise

A momentary twinge of regret at missing them gave way to a quiet thrill that she had all night to read and think. She had so much she wanted to discuss with McLeod tomorrow. She turned to the task of heating up supper. The smell of fried chicken and collards filled the trailer. After eating she washed the dishes and snuggled into her bed. She read long after the light faded outside. Around ten o'clock she turned off the bedside lamp and fell into a deep sleep.

~

Saturday morning brought the sun. Tent City was alive with music again. Birds singing in the trees, conversations bouncing across the campground as people emerged from their tents and trailers. A few musicians warmed up their instruments. Sylvia heard Louise and Nora laughing outside as they approached the Airstream, then a knock at the door.

"I'm decent. Come on in," Sylvia said.

It was Nora who stepped inside, bowing slightly to get through the door. She handed Sylvia a cup of coffee.

"We missed you yesterday."

"And me, you," Sylvia replied, "Kept waiting for the rain to let up but at least I got what I was after." She held up a copy of *The Souls of Black Folk*.

"Well, you're quick off the mark, aren't you?" Nora said, a twinkle in her eye, "Hey, McLeod's making breakfast. French toast and bacon. Care to join us?"

"Sure, give me a minute to make the bed."

"Don't bother," Louise said, sticking her head in the door behind Nora, "Time for that later."

The conversation over breakfast was easy, sharing their escapades from the day before. After cleaning up they made their way to town via the shortcut Sylvia had taken the day before. McLeod had the ten o'clock spot on the main stage on Cherry Street across from the Delta Cultural Center, a sign of his growing reputation at the festival. They took the long route back to Tent City after his set, Nora and Louise walking ahead. Sylvia realized Louise was making space for her to talk to McLeod.

"You could do music professionally," Sylvia said.

"Thanks," he replied, "I do love it but the only touring I want to do right now is with Nora."

"You know, I wanted to talk to you..." Sylvia began.

"About the foundation?"

"That and..."

"Like I said yesterday, I've been thinking a lot about it," McLeod said," I think we can do it; we should do it. Endowing a reparations fund, giving people a way to contribute is the easy part. Criteria for distribution will be trickier."

"You *have* given it a lot of thought. Tell me more."

"We will need public input about distribution. It can't simply be decided by a board of directors. It will take a while to get consensus but we can start building the fund in the meantime. What I find more exciting is the idea of creating a network of community forums to facilitate a truth and reconciliation process. The TRC model in South Africa could be a starting point."

"That's exciting, McLeod! Have you thought about bylaws? Or who might be on the board? Please say Nora!" Sylvia said.

McLeod laughed. "Sure, I'll ask her. Let me get some thoughts down on paper about organizational structure."

"What can I do to help right now?" Sylvia asked.

"You could start the paperwork for articles of incorporation."

"Sure. I can start researching the Mississippi law next week while I'm waiting for Faith's probate hearing. I should list you as the registered agent since you live in Mississippi," she replied.

"Unless you want to move here. The foundation is going to need an Executive Director, you know," he said, smiling.

"But wouldn't you want to …?"

"No, I have promised Nora that I will retire after the first of the year. I think you should consider it."

"Well,…."

"Willing to work for a quarter of what you're making now?" he laughed.

"I'm not really worried about the money. And now that Chance House is up and running and Joe and I …"

"Think about it?"

"OK," she replied, "But McLeod, you are the one with the vision."

"Oh, don't worry. I'll keep the vision. I just need someone to administer the foundation."

"I am a workhorse," she said.

"You know, Sylvia, I have also been thinking about Faith's house. I don't want to sell it and there's enough money in her investments to get the foundation up and running. I could file a quit claim and pass the house on to you…. if you want it."

"What?" she exclaimed.

"It would make me feel a lot better about the meager salary you would earn at the foundation," he said.

She laughed and shook her head. "Well, you certainly have my head spinning. In a good way. Now I'm the one who needs time to think about things."

They walked along in silence for a few minutes.

"Would it be intrusive if I asked a personal question?" Sylvia asked.

"No, it's OK. Guess we have to get to know each other if we are going to work together, don't we?" he replied.

"Well, I was surprised to hear you and Nora are separated. Never would have guessed it."

"It's a long story but I'll give you the short version. I adore Nora. She is the love of my life. No woman could ever come close to her beauty, her intellect and wisdom. But I was wedded to my work first and foremost. Wanted to change the world. She basically raised Darius, our son, herself. I am trying to make amends for that, to them both. Trying to make reparations myself, for the injury I caused. Seems that, in the end, all reparations are personal."

"So are you going 'touring' with Nora?"

"We'll see," he smiled.

They arrived back at the campsite still absorbed in conversation, the late morning sun warming everything.

"Looks like you two are talking shop," Nora smiled.

"Some," Sylvia replied, "and getting to know each other. I'm sure McLeod told you about my Aunt Faith."

"Yes, he did," she said, reaching over and squeezing his hand, "It is a significant gift. He has some great ideas so y'all keep at it. Louise and I will be in her trailer."

McLeod retrieved two lawn chairs from inside and unfolded them in a grassy area next to the trailer.

"How about you?" he asked, as Sylvia relaxed into her chair, "You mentioned a Joe?"

"My boyfriend," she hesitated, "Ex-boyfriend, I guess."

"What happened?"

"Kind of a long story but I think Faith's attempt at reparations helped me come to a reckoning of my own. You see, Joe wants to have a family and I .... I already have a child, which he didn't know."

She went on to recount the story she had told Louise before their drive to Helena, her love for Antwan, their son Terrell, giving him up for adoption.

"I so badly want to know how he is. There is this longing

to meet him, but it feels totally selfish. I don't want to hurt him, again. I contacted the adoption agency but I'm not sure if it was the right thing to do. Louise suggested your perspective might be helpful."

"But I wasn't adopted. My parents were a constant in my life, gave me everything they had."

"I'm sorry," Sylvia said, "I shouldn't have presumed..."

"Wait a minute, hold on. If you are asking me to tell you his experience as a young Black man, I can't do that. I can tell you mine. I can tell you to read James Baldwin or Ralph Ellison, Richard Wright, or Toni Morrison. But Terrell's story is his own."

"You don't think it matters that his mother is White, and his father is Black?"

"Of course it matters, but is that what is most important? If I am hearing you right, you're saying you are open to a connection if he wants one."

"That's right."

"So let him choose. Give the adoption agency your contact information and let him choose."

"That's what I did but I haven't had the guts to read their reply. A letter arrived just before I left Austin to come here. I'm afraid it will say he doesn't want contact."

"That has to be OK, as painful as it would be. It must be his choice," McLeod said, pausing. "I appreciate you trusting me with your story, Sylvia."

"Thank you, McLeod."

"You're welcome," he replied.

They grew quiet and listened to the music drifting through the campground.

"I'm going to take a little walk. You've given me a lot to think about. Maybe running the foundation? And I need to open that letter."

"OK. I am going to steal Nora away from Louise. See you for lunch later?"

"Definitely."

Sylvia walked back through the woods and this time headed south along the levee until she came to the path leading to the banks of the Mississippi river. When she got there she gazed out at the roiling water; the silt below churned into a muddy soup. She thought about Faith, whose ashes lay downstream somewhere, slowly making their way to the sea. She thought about Joe, their years together receding. She wondered if she would ever meet her son. And now her life's work seemed to be turning in a new direction.

She saw the power of the current that swept the river along, then felt herself inside the current; the river never worrying about where it was going, changing course according to the conditions at hand, its destination never in question. Something in her let go and the feeling was exhilarating, this not knowing. Like Huck on the river, trusting the currents and his own heart. She walked home more briskly than she had set out.

When she got back to Tent City she waved to Louise, who was talking to the folks at the neighboring campsite. She had an idea on the walk back from the river, something she wanted to do before reading the letter. Sylvia slipped into the Airstream and found her briefcase. Reaching inside, she pulled out the airline tickets to Rome that Faith had left her. Taking an envelope from the front of the briefcase, she wrote "For Nora's Tour" on it. She tucked the tickets inside and decided she would slip the envelope into their trailer when they were gone later this afternoon.

Then she took the letter from the Home of the Holy Infancy from her briefcase and opened it. She unfolded the single sheet of paper and read:

Dear Ms. Barbarino,

I am writing to inform you that the adoptive parents of your son have agreed to forward your contact information to him. They made it clear that it was his decision as to whether to reply to you and they would not influence him either way. They want you to know that he is well, achieving great success in his chosen career. And that he has been the greatest blessing of their lives.

Sincerely,
Francis McPhail, Director, Home of the Holy Infancy

ACKNOWLEDGMENTS

Historical fiction is equal parts imagination and research. I am indebted to these authors who combine meticulous investigation with a storyteller's voice, making their books as evocative as the best novel: Larry Tye, *Rising from the Rails*, Owl Books, 2004 was the primary source for the history of the Pullman Porters; David M. Kennedy, *Freedom from Fear*, Oxford University Press, 2004 for the history of the Depression, Roosevelt administration and WWII; John Hubner, *Last Chance in Texas*, Random House, 2005 for the history of the Texas Giddings School.

Additional resources of historical fact included: Adam Fairclough, *A Class of Their Own*, Belknap Press, 2007; Henry Hampton, Steve Fayer, with Sarah Flynn, *Voices of Freedom*, Bantam Books, 1990 companion book to *Eyes on the Prize*, Blackside Productions; and Robin D.G. Kelley and Earl Lewis, editors, *To Make Our World Anew*, Oxford University Press, 2000.

Books that helped me develop a deeper understanding of the personal experience of racism, along with a recognition that as a white woman, there are inherent limitations in my understanding included: W.E.B DuBois, *The Souls of Black Folk*, A.C. McClurg and Co., 1903; Ta-Nehisi Coates, *Between the World and Me*, Penguin Random House, 2015; and Robin DiAngelo, *White Fragility*, Beacon Press, 2018.

There are so many people to thank personally. I am especially grateful to Lucinda Herring for her thoughtful and beautifully written review of my book. And to Russ Lockhart, PhD and Tad Crawford for their considered comments about the novel. Thank you to Gary Kelley for his exquisite and soulful illustration for the book cover. My author's platform www.babsmallpublications.com and the book's beautiful design would have been impossible without the extraordinary graphic and web design skills of Jeanne M. Juneau. I am deeply touched by Jerry Wennstorm's generosity in sharing his artwork for my blog and for introducing me to his agent Joe Kulin. I cannot express what a privilege it was to work with Joe during 2022. He guided me through the landscape of traditional publishing and elicited comments from acquisition editors that brought needed revisions to the manuscript. And he always believed in the quality of the book.

I want to thank my writing partner, Betsy MacGregor; and readers of the initial version of my book, Chris Holder, Justin Bailey, Heather Ogilvy and Dee Bailey. I am most grateful to A.T. Birmingham-Young for her professional editing of the original draft, which vastly improved the book. Thanks to Leslie Cotter, who joined me for that initial writing exercise that hatched the first words of this story, to Sue Keblusek who helped find the title and to Lynn and Bev and so many others for your friendship and support on this journey.

But above all, I want to thank Susan Scott, soul partner, creative midwife, editor extraordinaire, and fellow keeper of the story. Thank you for seeing the writer in me.

About the Author

Photo by Susan S. Scott

Babs Small is a retired pediatric hematologist/oncologist who has been published academically. This is her first novel. She lives on Whidbey Island, Washington with her partner, Susan, and dog/friend, Jasmine (Jazz). Jazz was named for her fictional counterpart in *Faith's Reckoning*.

Contact: www.Babsmallpublications.com/contact